THE ROSE GARDEN

Also by Maeve Brennan

The Springs of Affection
Stories of Dublin

The Long-Winded Lady
Notes from The New Yorker

MAEVE BRENNAN

THE ROSE GARDEN

short stories

COUNTERPOINT

WASHINGTON, D.C.

Library of Congress Cataloging-in-Publication Data
Brennan, Maeve.
The rose garden : short stories / Maeve Brennan.—1st ed.
p. cm.
ISBN 1-582-43050-0 (hc. : alk. paper)
1. United States—Social life and customs—20th century—Fiction. 2. Ireland—Social life and customs—20th century—Fiction. 3. Country life—Ireland—Fiction. I. Title
PS3552.R38 R6 2000
813'.54 21—dc21   99-045921

First Edition
Book design by David Bullen

Printed in the United States of America on acid-free paper that meets the American National Standards Institute Z39–48 Standard

COUNTERPOINT
P.O. Box 65793
Washington, D.C. 20035-5793

Counterpoint is a member of the Perseus Books Group.

Contents

100

Preface

This is a daydream. I am lying in the sand just below the dunes on the beach in East Hampton, where I lived for several years. It is a warm, sunless day, with a cool breeze blowing in from the ocean. My eyes are closed. I like the beach, and the sand. There is a big Turkish towel between me and the sand, and I am quite alone. The cats and my dog, Bluebell, walked over here with me, but two of the cats dropped out at the walled rose garden a short distance back, and the four others are hiding in the long dune grass just above me. Bluebell is down by the water. She is a black Labrador retriever, and she swims and rolls in the water and watches for a sea gull to play with, but the gulls fly off shrieking with outrage at the sight of her. I won't stay here much longer. In a few minutes, I'll get up and start for home—a five-minute walk through dune and grass and between trees and across the wide, sloping lawn that leads to the big house where the walled rose garden is. I live at the foot of that lawn. I'll just lie here a few more minutes and then I'll go back.

But I opened my eyes too suddenly, for no reason at all, and the beach at East Hampton has vanished, along with Bluebell and the cats, all of them dead for years now. The Turkish towel is in reality the nubbly white counterpane of the bed I am lying on, and the cool ocean breeze is being provided by the blessed air conditioner. It is ninety-three degrees outside—a terrible day in New York City. So much for my daydream of sand and sea and roses. The daydream was, after all, only a mild attack of homesickness. The reason it was a mild attack instead of a fierce one is that there are a number of places I am homesick for. East Hampton is only one of them.   *Maeve Brennan, 1976*

The View from the Kitchen

$\mathcal{H}$erbert's Retreat is a snug community of forty or so houses that cluster together on the east bank of the Hudson thirty miles above New York City. Some of the houses are small and some are middle-sized. No two are alike, and because they are separated by trees, hedges, wooden fences, or untidy vestiges of ancient woods, and because of the vagaries of the terrain, they all seem to be on different levels. Some of the houses certainly reach much higher into the air than others, because a few roofs can be glimpsed from the highway, and in wintertime, when the trees are bare, an occasional stretch of wall is disclosed to passing motorists, but otherwise the community is secluded. One characteristic all the houses have in common: They all eye the river. This does not mean that they all face the river. Some of them face vaguely toward the highway, as though they were not sure exactly where it was. Some face the private roadway, hardly more than a path, that strings them all together. Some face each other, while keeping their distance, and a few seem to stand sideways to everything. But in every house the residents have contrived and plotted and schemed and paid to bring the river as intimately as possible into their lives. The people with houses directly on the river are in luck, of course. The most any of them had to do was to knock out a side wall, widen a window, or build a porch. Those fortunate enough to have houses facing directly on the river had no problem, since the view was theirs for the taking. It is among the people with houses set back from the river that the competition for its favors is keenest. The tallest of these houses have had square wooden balconies balanced on their roofs, where the host and hostess and their guests may perch and drink and admire the view. Occupants of the smaller houses have been very ingenious in devising ways to trap and hold their own particular glimpse of the water. Some have centipede-like porches creeping sideways from their houses to the nearest break in the wall of trees and buildings that cuts them off from the river, so that the vantage point gained, while not exactly natural to the house, is still part of the establishment. It is of no advantage to repair to a neighbor's house in order to see the water and show it off to visitors; each householder feels he must have a view of his own to offer. Several tree houses have been built. One man went so far as to erect a slender round tower of brick in his garden. Only one person can squeeze up the steep spiral staircase of the tower, and only one can stand in the tiny room that tops it, but sooner or later each guest, glass in hand, makes the solitary, claustrophobic ascent and returns to report on the merits of the view from the tower, and to compare it favorably with all other points of survey around.

All the people who live at Herbert's Retreat own their own houses. Newcomers can seldom get a foot in, except in the summertime, when a few residents let their places for two or three months. The tone and welfare of the community are guarded by a board of trustees. There are almost no restrictions on the behavior of children and animals belonging to the community, but there are iron restrictions against strange children and strange animals. The general atmosphere of the place is one of benevolent freedom. The life there is casual and informal, but gracious. A good deal of quiet entertaining is done. All the residents know each other very well or fairly well. There are no strangers. Living there is rather like living in a club.

Late one November afternoon, a splendid dinner for three was in the first stages of preparation in the kitchen of one of the houses at the Retreat. This house was long, low, and white. It was not large, but it was charming. It was the property of Mrs. George Harkey, who was generally said to be a very romantic-looking young woman, although her face was not pretty. In her kitchen, Bridie and Agnes, the maids, were taking their time about getting the dinner. They knew that the guest of the evening had only just arrived, that drinks had only started, and that they had plenty of time before they need bother with the dining room, where the table was already set with silver and glass and linen, and with candles ready for lighting.

Bridie belonged to the house. She lived in. Agnes worked and lived at the Gieglers', up the road, and had come to help out for the evening. Bridie, who liked heat, had planted her broad self on a chair beside the stove. Agnes, hovering inquisitively around the strange kitchen, was at a double disadvantage. Not only was she relegated, for the time being, to the position of helper but she was new to the community, having come out from New York City only the week before. She longed to stand at the kitchen window, to watch the antics of Mr. and Mrs. Harkey and their guest, whose voices she could hear outside, but the balance of amiability was still uncertain between her and Bridie, and she feared to put herself in a position that might prove embarrassing if Bridie chose to make it so. However, Bridie's unwavering, ironic stare finally drove her to drift with a show of unconcern to the window, where she saw enough to give her courage to make a remark.

"They're at the statue!" she cried.

Bridie rose from the chair as though it had burnt her, and made for the window.

"Don't let them see you looking," she said, and the two of them crowded together at the side of the window, behind the curtain, and stared out.

They could see the river, separated from them by a long, descending sweep of lawn as wide as the house and guarded on either side by a dense barricade of trees and hedges. The grass on the lawn had only recently been planted. It was still thin and tender, but the earth had been rigorously plowed, raked, dug, and rolled to receive it, and there was no doubt that eventually it would present a carpet of emerald-green velvet leading precisely to the edge of the river. A naked woman in white marble, her limbs modestly disposed, stood to the right of the lawn, not far from the house. Farther from the house, and on the left, a gray stone clown, dwarf-sized, bowed his head dejectedly. The clown wore baggy pants, a flowing tie, and a jacket too small for him. His gray stone wig hung dead from one of his hands, and his face, with its despairing grin, had just been freshly powdered, and painted with purple lipstick. It was the guest of the evening, Mr. Charles Runyon, who had decorated the clown, using tools from the handbag of his hostess, Leona Harkey. Now Charles stood with his arm around Leona, and they laughed together at his handiwork. A little apart from them, George Harkey stood alone, joining uncertainly in their amusement, which was exaggerated and intimate and hard to live up to. It was evident he could think of nothing to say. At the start of the jest, Charles had handed him the handbag, asking him to hold it open for him. The handbag still dangled from his hand, and he glanced awkwardly down at it from time to time, and sipped uneasily from the glass he had carried out with him.

"That's the new husband?" Agnes whispered.

"That's him, all right," said Bridie. "Mr. Harkey. George, his name is."

"He's not bad-looking."

"Oh, he *looks* all right. How old would you say he was?"

"About thirty, I'd say, looking at him from here."

"That's what I thought. The same age as herself, then."

"The other fellow is older. Mr. Runyon."

"Mr. God Runyon," said Bridie emphatically. "Yes, he's a good bit older. He must be past fifty, that fellow."

"Why do you call him Mr. God?"

"Ah, the airs he puts on him, lording it around. And the way she kowtows to him. She'll make the new husband kowtow to him, too."

"How long are they married?"

"A month, it is."

"And how long was she a widow?"

"Four months," said Bridie, smiling grimly at Agnes's astonished face. "Finch, her name used to be."

"And he was killed in a car?"

"He was dead drunk and ran himself into a young tree. Destroyed the tree and killed himself. She had to get a new car. He was all over the windshield when they found him, and the front seat, and bits of him on the hood—blood, hair, everything. Ugh. I often wonder did they get both his eyes to bury him. His face was just pulp, that's all—all mashed. The police were mystified, that he could do himself so much damage against such a small tree. He must have been going awful fast. She never turned a hair. I was here when she got the call. Not a feather out of her."

"She's hard."

"That rip hasn't got a nerve in her body. And there she is now, laughing away the same as ever with Mr. God, and Mr. Harkey standing there in place of Mr. Finch. You'd hardly know the difference, except that Mr. Finch was fair-headed and this fellow is black."

"Where does Mr. God come in?"

"He's her *admirer*. He admires her, and she admires him. They *admire* each other. Oh, they talk a lot about their admiring, but you should have seen the way he hotfooted it out of the picture when Mr. Finch was killed. She was all up and ready to marry him, of course. She thought sure she was going to be *Mrs.* God. But Mr. God was a match for her. All of a sudden didn't he discover there were people all over the country he had to visit, Arizona and everywhere, and he ended up going to Italy. This is his first night back. This is the first time she's seen him since the summer. That's what all the fuss is about, getting you in to help with the dinner, and all. This is the first Mr. Harkey has seen of him, either. You can imagine what's going on in *his* mind. He never laid eyes on him before tonight."

"He has a great look of a greyhound. Mr. God, I mean."

"Oh, he's a very *elegant* gentleman. Did you notice the pointy shoes he's wearing. And the waistcoat with the little buttons on it. And the way he shapes around, imagining everybody is looking at him. He'd make you sick."

"They're coming in now. They'll be looking for more drinks, I suppose?"

"That crowd takes care of their own drinks. Out of shame, if nothing else, so we won't see how much they put down. As if I didn't have to carry the empty bottles out. It's a scandal. *He* makes the drinks. He stands up in front of the bar in there like a priest saying Mass, God forgive me, and mixes a martini for himself, and one for her, and maybe an odd one for the husband. Mr. Finch used to like to make his own. He had a special big glass he used to drink out of. He had a little song he used to sing when he'd had a few. He used to go off by himself in a corner of the living room, and he'd sing, very low—it wouldn't bother you, except that he kept it up—he'd sing

> "You're too nice, you're too nice,
> You're too nice for me."

"Is that all the words there was to it?"

"That's all. Then he'd get up and make himself another drink in his big glass, and he'd stand and look at the two of them, and sing it all over again, and laugh and laugh."

"And wouldn't they say anything?"

"No, because if they paid any attention to him, he'd point his finger at Mr. God and sing the same thing, over and over, except he'd say '*He's* too nice, *he's* too nice.' It used to get on their nerves."

"Look at them now."

"What did I tell you. That's the way it always is."

Leona and Charles were strolling arm in arm toward the house, carrying their almost finished martinis in their free hands. George, with the handbag, brought up the rear. George liked sweet Manhattans, and his glass was empty. Charles glanced over his shoulder at the river, and George stopped dead and looked over his shoulder, too.

"Leona, darling, it's exactly what I dreamed of for you," Charles said. "And of course you've done exactly what I would have done. Do you remember how we used to talk and *talk* about it? Who would ever have thought it would all come true?"

"Charles, darling, I hope it won't ever rain again," Leona cried in her dark, husky voice. "I want that poor dismal face to stay just as you painted it, to remind me that you are back at last, and to commemorate our first evening all three together."

Charles's reply was unheard in the kitchen, because the three celebrants had disappeared around the side of the house, and would by now be arranging themselves before the living-room fire.

Bridie turned away from the window. "I don't know where she thinks she's going to get the lawn from," she said, "if she's not going to let it rain. Would you ever think that only a month ago you couldn't see hardly an inch beyond that kitchen window there? The kitchen here was as dark as a cellar, even in the middle of the day. There was a hedge out there almost as high as the house."

"They cut the hedge?" Agnes said politely.

"Cut the *hedge*. God almighty, she couldn't get it down soon enough. I thought she was going to go after it with her nail scissors, the way she was carrying on. I tell you, Agnes, the poor fellow was hardly out of bed the first morning after they got back from the honeymoon when she started screaming about the hedge. 'The hedge must go!' she kept yelling. 'Down with the accursed hedge! I must have my view. Where is my wonderful, my promised view!' Did you ever hear the like of that?"

"Them and their view. You'd think it was a diamond necklace, the way they carry on about their *view*. Mrs. Giegler is just the same. The minute a person walks into the house, it's me view this and me view that, and come and look at me view, and dragging them over to the window and out on to the porch in every sort of weather. Damp, that's all I have to say about it. Damp."

"Oh, this one is a terror on the view. She's had her eye on that view ever since I've been here. She was bound and determined to get that view."

"Well, and now she has it."

"Two people had to die before she could get it. First the poor old daisy who owned the cottage that used to be down there died in her sleep one night, and then, not two weeks later, doesn't poor Mr. Finch go and smash himself up."

"And then she bought the cottage?"

"Not at all," said Bridie, rudely. "She couldn't afford to buy the cottage. There were dozens of them around here after it, but she

got herself on the inside first. Mr. Harkey inherited the cottage
from his aunt. That was the old one who died. Miss Harkey. An
old maid. They were all after that cottage. That's why she married
him in such a hurry, apart from the fact that she knew Mr. God
would never show his face in the house till she had a new husband."

"Mr. Harkey got the cottage from his aunt, and then this one
married him and made him pull it down."

"Pulled it down and carted it away as fast as I'm saying the
words. Oh, she was in a terrible hurry about it. She had them out
there marking the place for the lawn and planting the grass and
putting up the statues before you could turn around. He never
said a word, but I think he was sorry to see the cottage go. He said
to her that it was the only thing he'd ever owned in his life."

"I would've thought he had money, from the looks of him."

"Not that fellow. Oh, he likes to look as if he was somebody, but
he hasn't a penny except what he gets from his job. The old aunt
didn't leave him any money, only the cottage. I don't think she had
much else to leave. She kept very much to herself. She hadn't
much patience with the crowd around here. Well, Mr. Harkey
was all pleased. He came down here, just weekends, and began
settling in, cooking little meals for himself and all, and the next
thing you knew, there *she* was, charging down the road with little
housewarming presents for him—little pots of patty de fwa, and
raspberry jam *I'd* made, and a tin of green-turtle soup she paid a
fortune for. She thought he might like the unusual flavor of it, she
said. Oh, she'd never have looked at him, only for his view. It
would have matched him better to have sold up the place and
taken his money and run. She just took it out from under him. He
never had a chance, once *she* took after him."

"The poor fellow."

"Oh, I'd waste no sympathy on that fellow, Agnes. Do you

know what his job is? Well, now, I'll let you guess. The lowest thing, about the lowest thing you can think of. Go on, guess. I'll give you three guesses."

"An undertaker?"

"No."

"A pawnbroker?"

"No, but you're close."

"A summons server?"

"No. He's a credit manager."

Agnes emitted a low, prolonged shriek and sat down on Bridie's chair by the stove. Bridie smiled her satisfaction.

"A credit manager!" cried Agnes. "A credit manager. Oh, my God, the lowest of the low. A credit manager. And to think I'm going to have to put his dinner in front of him. Oh, the dirty thing."

"At Clancyhanger's," Bridie said.

"Clancyhanger's. The worst bunch of thieves and knaves in the country. The persecutors of the poor. Oh, the way they hop off you when you haven't got the money. Bridie, I've heard enough. I hope she cuts him up and eats him."

"Of course, *she* doesn't say he's a credit manager. That's not good enough for *her*. She makes out he's a junior vice president, if you don't mind. But I heard him talking to her the first time he came in here for a drink, and that's what he told her. He's a credit manager, and that's all he is."

"One of the ones that does the dirty work. When our Blessed Lord was crucified, he was standing there holding the box of nails."

"That's the sort he is. No real good in him. Although to look at him you'd think butter wouldn't melt in his mouth. Oh, he was all full of himself that first day he came in here. He had a girl he brought with him."

"A girl?"

"She was staying with him in the cottage. And there was only the one bed in the place, because I saw the furniture when it was carted out. She was *staying* with him all right, in the full sense of the word."

"Imagine doing the like of that, and probably not engaged or married or anything. Isn't it disgusting?" Agnes said enviously.

"This one may not have been married, Agnes, but she had the *experience* of being married, I'll guarantee you that much. Oh, I think she thought he was going to marry her. She was all busy, making curtains and cushion covers and all, and cleaning up the weeds in the garden down there where the old one had let it go. She was a nice enough girl, too, I'll say that much for her. All excited about the cottage. But she didn't last long after the Madam got to work."

"Tell us, Bridie, what did she do to her?"

"She didn't have to *do* anything. Not that one. She was all nice to the girl. All advice on how this should go in the cottage, and how that should go, all over her, she was, sweet and nice as you please. But then one night he came up by himself, and the first thing you know, she was on the phone asking him over for a drink. 'I love your girl,' she says to him, 'a dear girl. What does she do?' she says—as if she didn't know, I heard her questioning the girl myself. 'She works in the advertising department in the store,' he says. 'Isn't that interesting,' she says. 'But isn't it a pity she's not more at ease here,' she says. 'We're such a select little group, you know. A lot of artists and writers, *creative* people. We see each other all the time,' she says. 'It's so important to fit in, as you do,' she says. 'I want to give a little party for you, and introduce you to everybody. And there's my friend Charles Runyon, the critic— you know his name, of course.' That's Mr. God. 'You must meet him the minute he gets back from Europe. He's so charming,' she says. 'I know you'll adore him, as we all do.' And then she invited him to a dinner party she was giving, not mentioning the girl, and he didn't mention the girl, either, and he never brought her near the place again. Of course, he didn't know what he was getting in for, with this one. He thought she was all interested in his cottage. And all she was thinking about was how fast she could get it out of the way so she could have her precious view."

"And now I suppose all she's thinking about is how fast she can get *him* out of the way."

"Ah, no, she doesn't mind him, as long as he behaves himself and doesn't cause her any trouble. He's not a bad-looking young fellow, you know. And now she has Mr. God coming around again, paying her compliments and inviting her in to New York to see the new plays, and all. You'll see—he'll be out here every week-end, just the way he used to be. He has his own room here, even. He told her the way he wanted it, and she had it all done up for him. He hasn't even got his own car, but they fall over themselves around here to see which one of them will give him a lift out from the city. They think it's an honor, having him around. He's supposed to be very witty. A wit, he is. He never opens that narrow little mouth of his but they all collapse laughing."

"The way they carry on, it's not decent."

"Oh, the things I could tell you about their carrying-on," Bridie said ominously. "It would curl your hair."

"You mean her and Mr. God."

"No, no, nothing like that there. He's the sort that just pays compliments. I heard him telling her she has a face on her that belongs to the ages. What do you make of that?"

"Is that a compliment? What sort of a compliment is that? Isn't that a queer thing to say to a woman!"

"She liked it. She says she's in love with his mind."

"In love with Mr. God's mind?"

"She's in love with Mr. God's mind."

"In love with his mind. Well, that's a new one. I never heard that one before."

"Neither did Mr. Harkey, by the look of him."

"There he is now," said Agnes, who had resumed her stand by the window. Bridie came to look over her shoulder.

Flashlight in hand, George was making his way timorously over the darkened lawn. He passed the naked woman, at whom he did not glance. Passing the clown, he turned the light briefly on the painted face, and proceeded on. He walked slowly over the place where his cottage had raised its walls, and reached at last the edge of the river, where he stood stabbing convulsively with the flashlight out into the blackness. The path he lighted across and around and over and above the water was ragged and wavering. His hand seemed to be shaking.

"What's he up to now, I wonder," said Bridie.

"Maybe he's looking for his view," Agnes said, and grimaced nervously at her own smartness.

"Well, he's not going to find much down there," Bridie said, and gave her a companionable nudge in the ribs.

Emboldened, Agnes thumbed her nose at the window, and immediately collapsed on the table in a heap of shuddering, feeble giggles, with her hands covering her face. After a second, she moved one finger aside and peered up to see how Bridie was taking this demonstration.

Bridie winked at her.

The Anachronism

$\mathcal{T}$om and Liza Frye had an eighteenth-century brick house, painted white and filled with severely modern furniture, and two Jaguar cars, a white one for Liza and a black one for Tom. Both cars had governors on them so they could not do more than fifty-five miles an hour, for Tom and Liza did not believe in speed. They each had a flat gold cigarette case and a short gold holder, and their cigarettes were made specially for them. At night they slept in matching white silk pajamas. Their bed, wide and low, was as big as a small field. Actually, it wasn't a double bed at all but twin beds locked together by the legs and made up with separate sets of sheets. The sheets, like the pajamas, were fresh every night. One of Liza's favorite words was "immaculate." The word she liked least in the language was "appetite." Still, it was a word she often used. "I have no appetite for anything," she would say, or sometimes, "I don't believe in appetites. They're so common."

Liza was tall and excessively thin, with long, beautiful legs. She was proud of her figure, and preserved it by eating almost nothing. During the day, she fasted, and at night she dined, with Tom, on cottage cheese and shredded carrot. Their dinner was served on a tray in their bedroom, which was immense and possessed of, and by, a tremendous picture window that allowed a magnificent view of the Hudson River. Their house was built on the edge of the river, and their living room, directly under the bedroom, also had a gigantic picture window and a handsome view. Liza disliked having the living room disturbed, and Tom didn't mind dining in the bedroom. His real life was spent away from home anyway, and by evening he was usually too tired to want anything except sleep. Liza had pale-gold hair that she wore in a neat, caplike arrangement. Tom, a little shorter than she, was stout, and had a fat, glum face and large, suspicious blue eyes. He was suspicious because of his money, of which he had a great deal. Although it was safely stowed away in a trust fund, he lived in constant fear that someone would take it from him. Liza had had no money at all until she married Tom. She was thirty-nine, two years older than he. They had been married almost seven years.

They lived at Herbert's Retreat, an exclusive community of about forty houses on the east bank of the Hudson, thirty miles above New York City. It had been Liza's decision to move to the Retreat. Tom had been inclined to stay on in his comfortable, velvet-hung apartment on Beekman Place, but Liza insisted on having her own way. Liza felt, and often said, that the only way to impress one's personality on people is to deprive them of something they want. Shake them up. Make them see that what they have isn't much. It was hard to do this in New York, where people had so many distractions, but at Herbert's Retreat, that tightly locked, closely guarded little community, Liza made a strong impression. Right off, her modern furniture outraged all the other women, who had been concentrating on Early American. Liza called the furniture at the Retreat "country." "Country furniture is *sweet,*" she said, "but it's so sheeplike." In the same way, she refused to share the other women's enthusiasm for gardening. The narrow strip of ground that surrounded her house on three sides—the fourth side being almost one with the river—was given over to fine white gravel, which was raked and rolled every week by the Retreat gardener. When her neighbors chattered about their bulbs and seeds, Liza enjoyed saying, "I don't approve of flowers, except in their proper place. They certainly don't belong in the ground." Her own cut flowers, always white, were delivered twice a week from a nearby greenhouse by a girl who arranged the new flowers and took the old ones away with her.

Liza was a rigid housekeeper. Her furniture had all been designed for her, and she hated to see anything out of its appointed place. Her mother, Mrs. Conroy, who lived with her, had been begging for years for an old-fashioned cozy armchair, but Liza was adamant. Liza and Mrs. Conroy detested each other, but it suited them to live together—Liza because she enjoyed showing her power, and Mrs. Conroy because she was waiting for her day of vengeance. They were alike in their admiration for Tom's money, but Mrs. Conroy felt she should have more say in the spending of it. The old lady's only treasured possession was a set of nineteen shabby account books, records painstakingly kept by her dead husband, who had run a small stationery shop in Brooklyn. The account books read like a diary to Mrs. Conroy, who liked to pore over them when she was tired of counting up her grievances. Liza allowed her mother to keep the books so that she could threaten to deprive her of them. She had a special set of shelves built for them in her mother's bedroom, with sliding panels that concealed their ragged backs from view and that were kept locked, the key being retained by Mrs. Conroy, who never let it out of her reach. When her mother became obstreperous, Liza would threaten to have the books destroyed, and the old woman always knuckled under.

"I'm just a poor, forsaken old woman," she would wail in a tone of false anguish that hid rage.

"You're an invalid," Liza would say firmly, and if her mother was not already in her bedroom, she would be taken by the arm and conducted there.

Liza preferred to believe that her mother was an invalid. The fact was that the old lady was as strong as a horse, but Liza maintained that her mother had a delicate stomach and could eat only bland foods. Liza had discovered a preparation, quite expensive, that contained all the vitamins necessary to keep an old woman alive and healthy without putting any weight on her. This food, stirred into a bowl of skim milk, was what Mrs. Conroy got three times a day. It was delicious, with a vague flavor of vichyssoise. Sometimes Liza even took a dish of it herself. But Mrs. Conroy was tired of it. She continued to wolf it down, though, because she was by nature greedy. Liza, with memories of vegetable marrow, turnip, and porridge being squashed into her own rebellious mouth, enjoyed seeing her mother swallow this pap. My turn has come, she thought, congratulating herself on her life in general, because she had been sick with lack of money when she married Tom, having gone all her life without the things she felt were her due. It was not the things she enjoyed, however; it was the position they gave her. She loved the Retreat. She never left it, even for a night.

Once, years before, when she was only a poor, lovely-looking girl in a flower shop, she had come to the Retreat for a weekend. The assured, amused attitude of the women there, and their indifference to her, infuriated her. She went away hating them. After her marriage to Tom, she had come back determined to make them sit up and take notice of her. She didn't want to become one of them, she told herself. What she wanted was to keep them from being too pleased with themselves.

Tom, on the other hand, found the center of his existence in New York. His days were spent sitting in a window in his club there. This club, a massive, majestic building on upper Fifth Avenue, had been in Tom's heart since the day in his eighth year when his grandfather had brusquely interrupted a peaceful afternoon at home to rush him there in a taxicab. Tom, at eight, was already accustomed to being taken into splendid establishments, and he waited confidently for his grandfather to conduct him up the broad stone steps and through the great iron door, where respectful servants would bow and take their hats and coats. But his grandfather, instead of going forward, grabbed him by the hand and proceeded around to the side of the building, which overlooked a narrow, luxurious street. There on the sidewalk, the old man stood beside his grandson and glared up at the second-floor windows, three of them, each framing a seated, apparently lifeless man. Heavy curtains hung about the windows, and the room within was lighted, but not brightly. It was a towering room. Tom could glimpse the dark, carved, curving ceiling and part of a glimmering chandelier. The men in the windows appeared very old to him, but perhaps they were only elderly. Two of them seemed to be drowsing. The third, a thin-faced, upright man with silver hair, stared icily into the street. Tom's grandfather raised his stick and pointed upward in choler. "There he is," he growled. "There's the rascal who did me out of my rights. This is the only club in New York I'm not admitted to, thanks to him. He's responsible. He got them to turn me down." Turning his gaze on Tom, he shouted, "And you'll never get in there, either, you little rat." Tom loathed his grandfather, a self-made man who loved his grandson because he was his grandson but despised him because he was a rich little boy. When the old man was in a good humor, he liked to take Tom on his knobby knees and grin balefully into his plump, gloomy little face. "And what are you thinking *now,* dirty little boy?" he would whisper, and then, with a bellow of glee, he would part his knees and tumble his dejected burden rudely to the floor.

Years later, Tom's father became a member of the club his grandfather had been kept out of, and at twenty-one Tom, too, was admitted. The thin-faced old man Tom's grandfather had pointed out to him no longer sat in the second-story window. Tom quickly appropriated his chair. He felt timid about doing this, but to his astonishment no one else seemed to want it. The elderly men and the middle-aged men had been seduced away, first by the club movie room and then by the new television room, and the younger men darted in and out, having no patience for anything. Tom felt with disappointment that club life had lost its grandeur. There was a rowdiness, unheard but felt, that Tom was sure was not consistent with gentlemanliness. He struck up no friendships with his fellow-members.

Tom arrived at the club every day at ten o'clock. In the mornings, he sat in the chair by the window, reading the papers. At twelve-thirty, he made his way to the dining room and enjoyed a two-hour lunch, always eating alone, always at the same table. All the imagination and appreciation he was capable of were spent at the luncheon table. In the afternoons, he simply sat and watched the street. At five o'clock, he sent for his car, quartered at a nearby garage, and drove home to Liza.

Early one October, Liza received a telephone call that disturbed her very much. The call was from Clara Longacre, who invited her to drop over for bridge the same afternoon. Clara, at thirty, was the recognized social leader at the Retreat—merely because, Liza often thought viciously, of having grown up there. Clara's natural sense of superiority made it impossible for her to doubt herself. She *knew* she was better than anybody else. She was untouchable. Liza longed more than anything in the world to impress Clara, to deprive her, even if it was only for a minute, of her eternal self-satisfaction. Sometimes she lay awake in bed and gritted her teeth in the struggle to bring forth some scheme that would crack that natural armor. Now she was not disturbed at the invitation to bridge; she had often been to bridge at Clara's house. It was the tone of the invitation that had unsettled her. Always before, in speaking to her, Clara's manner and her amused tone of voice had implied an awareness that Liza was a *person*—a possible adversary, even. This time, she was merely casual, as if she had forgotten that Liza was in any way different from the others. Liza wondered distractedly if perhaps they were all beginning to take her for granted. After all, she had done nothing extraordinary for a year—not since she had torn out the whole riverside wall of her house to install those two outsize picture windows. At night, from the opposite bank of the river, her house appeared to be a glittering sheet of white light—the most spectacular establishment in the community, whether you admired it or not. Even that, which had outraged all the rest of them (they said that, like her furniture, it was alien to the spirit of Herbert's Retreat), had drawn only an amused smile from Clara. Liza had always felt that Clara's amusement might mask a *touch* of chagrin, enough to make a small victory for herself. This time Clara's voice had been casual and friendly, but that was all. I will not be patronized by her, Liza thought wildly. I must *show* her.

She went to the bridge party in a scattered, anxious frame of mind. Clara had also asked Arabelle Burton and Margaret Slade. They all come running when Clara rings the bell, Liza thought.

As they were adding up their scores at the end of the afternoon, Clara asked, "Aren't you and Tom having an anniversary soon, Liza?"

"Not till February," Liza said.

"I know it's February," Clara said. "How could any of us forget the month of your arrival, Liza? We had all just settled down after

Christmas when you charged in to rouse us out of our lethargy. How many years is it?"

"Seven," Liza said, and wondered if Clara was laughing at her secretly. They don't dare laugh at me to my face, she thought. I'm too quick for them.

"Seven is a very special anniversary in most marriages, isn't it?" Margaret Slade said indistinctly. As usual, she had a cold in her head. "I mean isn't it the most crucial year after the first, or something?"

"Is it?" Clara said. "Look, Liza, I'd like to give a party for you on your anniversary. Seven years is a long time. We should have a celebration. Will you let me?" She sounded perfectly sincere, and friendly, and Liza stared at her, baffled, not knowing what to say. Surely Clara was being patronizing?

"That's a wonderful idea—a seventh-anniversary party for Liza!" Margaret Slade cried. "We'll all bring appropriate presents. What *is* the seventh anniversary, anyway? Arabelle, you always know about things like that. What's the seventh anniversary— leather? paper?"

"Brass and copper," Arabelle said.

"Well, then, that's settled," Clara said. "It's a brass-and-copper party. That should be easy enough, but I'm afraid you're going to find yourself with a lot of ashtrays and hand bells."

"You'll have to tell us what you'd really like, Liza," Arabelle said. "Your house is so special I'm afraid anything I'd pick out would be an anachronism."

"Don't worry about that, Arabelle," Margaret said, blowing her nose heartily. "We're all in the same boat there. It would be hard not to bring an anachronism into Liza's house. We'll probably end up settling for the least anachronistic thing we can find, and hope for the best."

"Why not bring the *most* anachronistic thing we can find?" Clara said. "An anachronism party would be much more fun than just sticking to brass or copper. Liza, I think I'll give you a cobbler's bench."

"Oh, that's marvelous!" Margaret cried. "I'll bring a kerosene lamp."

"I'll bring a mustache cup," Arabelle said.

Liza smiled stiffly. They were baiting her. They had never dared make fun of her before. Trembling, she decided to meet their challenge.

"You must have read my mind, Clara," she said quickly. "As a matter of fact, Tom and I were laughing about anachronisms only the other night. As Tom said, a seventh anniversary is something of an anachronism anyway. The anachronistic lucky seven, and so on. So we decided to celebrate the occasion with our first anachronism. I won't tell you what I thought of. It's something quite extraordinary, I promise you."

Clara stared at her in astonishment. "You mustn't take us seriously, Liza. It's only a joke. We wouldn't think of defacing your house." To the maid, who had stalked in bearing the tea tray, she said, "Mattie, you'll have to take that back. You know I won't tolerate tea bags in the house. Please go back and make the tea properly, just as I showed you."

"They didn't have nothing but tea bags at the store, Mrs. Longacre," Mattie replied. "Afraid it's tea bags or nothing, Ma'am."

"Oh, all *right!*" Clara said, and glanced in exasperation at her friends.

This maid was new to the community, and probably would not stay long, because she was already complaining about the lack of entertainment around. It was seldom that one of the houses at Herbert's Retreat was not in an uproar with a maid just gone or about to go, a dinner planned and the hostess frantically phoning her neighbors to discover which of the remaining maids would be available to help out for the evening. All this gave the maids a great sense of power, of course. For some of them, the power was satisfaction enough. Those were the ones who stayed on year after year. The others flew in and out of Herbert's Retreat like birds, carrying their baggage with them, entering service there with misgiving and leaving with rancor.

"I forgot to pick up my tea at Vendôme on Thursday," Clara said when Mattie had left the room, "and I just had to tell that fool to get what she could in the village. Oh, just once, to have a good maid!"

Liza sat ready to deal with them one by one or all together when they took up the attack where they had left off. But if they *were* baiting her, as she thought, they seemed to have had enough of it. "Speaking of maids, as we do all the time," Arabelle said, "Clara, I loved your cute little story in this week's *Flyaway* about that maid in White's Hotel."

The *Flyaway* was the weekly publication circulated at the Retreat. Liza had not yet taken her new copy from its wrapper.

"The most extraordinary, wonderful caricature of an English maid I've ever seen," Clara said, pleased. "And of course White's Hotel is the perfect background for her."

Travel, hotels in Switzerland, hotels in Cannes, matching embroidery wools in that little shop on the Left Bank, driving through Cornwall on the wrong side of the road, White's Hotel in London—it was one way of dealing Liza out, and they didn't even have to do it on purpose. They couldn't avoid doing it. At such times, Liza sat, silent, with no stories to match with theirs, no recommendations, no frantic experiences. To travel, she and Tom would have to leave the Retreat, and she didn't dare. And anyway, even if they had picked up and gone to Europe the summer before, like Clara, she still held the trump cards. Liza could stay at White's Hotel if she chose to, but Clara's grandparents had stayed there.

"Even the men hang around in the hall trying to get a look at her," Clara said. "I simply had to write about her. I'm sending her the article, of course."

"Does she really wear high-buttoned boots, Clara?" Margaret Slade asked delightedly.

"High-buttoned boots, black lisle stockings, long black dress— alpaca, I suppose—apron like an English nanny's, for God's sake, not a maid's apron at all, but it's just right for Betty Trim, she's so outrageous anyway, and, to top it all off, a parlormaid's cap, but worn *backwards,* and behind it an enormous bun of the most wiggy-looking, coarse gray hair you've ever seen, except that it's not a wig. Oh, and of course she curtsies, and calls everyone 'm'lady.' It's simply killing. I swear she has the coldest, fishiest eyes I've ever seen in a human head. She never smiles, and the porter told me she thinks of nothing but money. Nothing. She could tell you the amount she made in tips any day in the last fifteen years, but she won't talk, of course. She's very closemouthed. She reads nothing but her savings book. She just simply loves and adores money. I can't understand why she's not a cashier, or something. Maybe it would break her heart to have to handle money she couldn't put away in her bank. I couldn't say all that in the *Flyaway,* of course. I want to stay in her good graces."

"Oh, Lord, and to think of what we have to put up with in our kitchens," Margaret said enviously. "Imagine having a pearl like that in the house."

"Oh, you can't imagine, Margaret," Clara said enthusiastically. "She never makes a mistake. She knows her place to the last millimeter, and your place, too. She used to be a parlormaid, but she's in the ladies' room now. She's a little queen there, of course. And

then tips. And she's independent. You should see the ladies trying
to charm her, but she never bats an eye. Isn't it killing the way we
all go down on our knees to curry favor with someone who's really
indifferent to us?"

"I know," Arabelle said. "Do you remember that ghastly Miss
Vesper at school? Why, we positively crawled."

Liza let her mind wander, as she often did when they spoke of
their snobbish school days. She was suffocating with a joyful idea,
and fearful that Clara might spot her excitement and divine its
cause.

That evening, Liza wrote to Betty Trim, the maid in the ladies'
room of White's Hotel in London, offering her five times her present salary, describing the lightness of the work she would be
expected to do, enjoining secrecy, and enclosing a check for the
fare over. Betty replied, demanding ten times her present salary
and an additional sum every month to equal the tips she had
received during the corresponding month in her best year, which
was 1947, and asking for a signed contract guaranteeing her job
for three years. She returned the check, saying she would require
a ticket on the *Queen Mary*, complete and paid for, when the date of
her departure was set, and she requested a bank draft to cover the
amount of her return fare. She also asked for traveling expenses.
Liza sent a ticket for the earliest date she could get, which was
December 19. For good measure, she made it a first-class ticket,
and added a generous check for expenses and a surprise Christmas
bonus. She also sent a signed contract, binding on herself and on
Betty, with a copy for Betty to sign and return. Betty replied, not
enclosing her own signed copy, because, she explained, it was too
much to expect a person to sign away her life in a strange land. She
did, however, return the ticket, saying that she could not leave her
job until after her Christmas and New Year's tips were in, and

suggesting January 2 as the earliest date on which she could be expected to start her journey. She added that a second-class ticket would be more suitable, considering her station in life. Liza sent her the ticket she asked for, and enclosed an additional bank draft for emergencies. She begged Betty to reply by cable. Betty replied by ordinary mail, confirming the arrangement and explaining that to her mind a cable that was not for an emergency was a wasteful extravagance.

Liza, groveling, was nevertheless triumphant.

"She needn't lift a finger unless she wants to, except to serve tea," Liza said to Tom. "And there'll be a cleaning woman in every day. What's more, you'll meet her at the pier in a taxi, and drive her out here. If the boat docks on schedule, you should have her out here by one, at the very latest."

"I *lunch* at twelve-thirty," Tom said. "You're losing your sense of proportion, Liza. Why can't you send this woman a bus schedule. Or rent a car for her. Or tell her to take a taxi out. Or tell her to sit in Schrafft's or someplace, and I'll pick her up at five. You can't expect me to interrupt my day like this! I'm always at lunch at one o'clock!" Tears of chagrin filled his eyes.

Liza turned back to her desk, on which two tall piles of square white envelopes stood neatly stacked. "Now, that's settled," she said. "I want you to take these out and post them at once. If Clara still has any idea of trying to give a benevolent little party for me, this should fix her. I wish I could see her face when she opens this in the morning. 'To celebrate our first anachronism, Miss Betty Trim, of White's Hotel.' She'll be the one they'll laugh at now, not me. She'll never dare make fun of me again."

The day of Betty's arrival turned out cold and desolate, with a raw wind. Tom drove in to town, rushed into his club, rustled busily through the morning papers, and stood for a minute at his window, his arm embracing the back of his chair. Then, sighing profoundly, he dashed outside into the taxi the doorman was holding for him. The shop windows, brilliantly lighted against the gray day, looked cheerless and efficient without their recent Christmas decorations. The wind swept mercilessly along the pavements, carrying shuddering, cowering human beings before it. Traffic across town was locked, and drivers of trucks, taxis, and private cars glared satanically into one another's eyes and breathed plumes of vapor with the invective that issued from their lips. Tom's driver, cursing, inched his way to the pier. Tom contemptuously ignored this hurly-burly. Slumped in the corner of his seat, warm in his gloves and muffler and his fur-lined coat, with enormous galoshes on his feet, he let his mind roam sulkily ahead through his spoiled day.

He recognized Betty with no difficulty. She was all in black, and very small—not more than five feet tall. About forty-five, Tom thought morosely, and she's no beauty. He could hardly bear to look at her, he hated her so much, but at his garage he motioned politely toward the front seat of his car, only to find her already fitted into the middle of the back seat between her two bulging pieces of luggage, neither one of which was a suitcase. She acknowledged his gesture with a flickering, uninterested glance, and then she fixed her eyes on the street ahead and waited, without impatience, to be driven into her new life.

The city streets seemed to interest Betty as little as they did Tom, and as the car left the city, she cast no glance at the wintry Hudson. The countryside, forlorn, cracked and bitten with frost, got no sign from her. She stared stonily ahead. She might have been a member of royalty, forced to ride in the state funeral procession of some detested relative. The truth is that inside Betty's head there was only a small blackboard, on which she added and subtracted diligently, using a piece of chalk, as she had been taught to do in school. The problems she solved were not large, for her brain was tiny, but she was thorough, and she went over each exercise at least ten times, proceeding slowly, using cunning, persistence, and inhuman concentration. She never put a figure down on paper. Only a fool would do that—someone willing to broadcast his private affairs to the world. She trusted no one. She knew that poor people's savings were often stolen. She had never taken a risk in her life, nor had she ever loaned a penny. Or borrowed one. In the car, she added the dollars she had in her purse now, shielding herself against the sudden misery that had come on her at the thought of her little hoard of money far away in London. Tom's voice interrupted her. He had turned off the highway onto a narrow country road, hardly more than a pathway, that appeared to have been cut at random through a wild wood. "Welcome to Herbert's Retreat," he said stiffly.

Betty turned her head to the right, and then to the left. Her eyes belittled all they saw. Beyond the irregular wall of trees and hedge, leafless now, that lined the road, houses, standing solitary, glimmered white in the dull winter air. Between the houses, a wilderness flourished—trees, bushes, remnants of old hedge, dry yellow weeds, and tangled undergrowth. Coming to his own fine house, Tom stopped the car with a jerk and scrambled out. He opened the rear door and lifted out the two pieces of luggage. Then he turned to give Betty a hand, but again she was before him, with both feet firmly on the ground. The front door opened and Liza stood there. Tom brushed rudely past her, dumped the luggage in the hall, and went into the living room, where he sat down and sulked.

"I hope you will he happy here, Betty," Liza said when her treasure was safely inside the front door.

"Thank you, m'lady," Betty replied, and bobbed up and down.

She really curtsies, Liza thought deliriously.

Betty's mean little eyes surveyed Liza. I could buy you and sell you, m'lady, she thought. She was satisfied that she knew all that was to be known of human nature. "I can sum them up in one glance, no matter who they are," she would say to herself—and the sum was always the same. Liza, not knowing she had been judged and dismissed, proceeded to show Betty through the house. The walls of all the rooms were clay-colored. The furniture was constructed of silvery piping. The chairs had white tweed sling seats. The tabletops were of thick plate glass. Upstairs, Liza paused with an air of extra importance before a closed door and smiled at Betty before she opened it. Then they were looking into Betty's own room, which was furnished like the rest of the house and contained a narrow bed. The window looked out on the nearest houses, and on the withered jungle that separated them.

"No river view here, I'm afraid," Liza said in a tone of bright apology.

Betty walked to the window and looked out. "I'm not much for looking at the water, m'lady," she said.

"My mother's room is just down the hall," Liza said. "She's resting now, so we won't disturb her. Your bathroom is downstairs next to the kitchen, as you saw. There's only one on this floor, and my mother shares it with us. These old houses—all fireplaces and no bathrooms, you know." She waved her hand in a gesture that was friendly but not, she felt, familiar.

"Thank you, m'lady," Betty said.

Alone, Betty moved first her arms, to lift her hat from her head, then her legs, to walk to the closet, which she opened, displaying no curiosity about it. She hung her hat by its elastic from a hook on the closet door. She then hung her coat on a hanger, sat down in her sling chair, tested it a minute, and, satisfied, bent over to unbutton her boots. Her house slippers were downstairs, locked up in one of her bundles, so, with the boots open and flapping, she clumped down the back stairs to the kitchen and set about making tea. When the kettle was on, she built a fire in the huge open fireplace, using paper towels and three logs from a beautifully geometrical pile that lay in a white basket against the wall. She was sitting in front of the fire having her cup of tea when the door opened and Mrs. Conroy shuffled in. Mrs. Conroy's face was immensely lined, but whether the lines had been put there by a life of goodness or by a life of badness it would have been hard to say. She simply looked very old. Her manner would have been called obsequious in a younger person, and her hands were gathered nervously around a large white handkerchief, which from time to time she pressed against her mouth, perhaps to hide a tremor—of age, or of amusement, or of malice.

Betty regarded the intruder bleakly. I could buy you and sell you, she thought as she got up.

"I'm Mrs. Conroy," the old woman said beseechingly, "Mrs. Frye's mother you know. I see you have the fire going. I dearly love a fire, but Mrs. Frye won't permit them in the house, although she won't object to you having one, I'm sure. She doesn't approve of open fires. She tries to keep me in my room. I dislike my room. I hate the furniture. I expect you do, too, coming from England. My room is exactly like yours, except that I have that unwholesome view of the river. I like to watch a street and see what the people are up to. I thought, being English, you might be having a cup of tea, and I thought perhaps you might permit me to join you here. Mrs. Frye won't permit me to have tea."

"I'm sorry, m'lady, but I don't permit ladies in my kitchen," Betty said.

"Only for a minute, to get the heat of the fire on my legs."

"It's out of the question, m'lady. I must ask you to leave my kitchen at once."

"I'm not let have tea, and I'm not let have a fire," Mrs. Conroy said. "I notice you give yourself tea and a fire, though. I notice you have a fire and a nice cup of tea there beside you."

"What I do for myself and what I do for other people are two entirely different things, m'lady," Betty said.

"I only wanted to get the heat of the fire on my legs a minute," Mrs. Conroy beseeched. "Radiators aren't the same thing at all. Don't you think I'm right? Radiators are no good, are they? . . . Well, you might at least answer me." In the doorway, she paused and said, without looking back, "You're just the same sort she is! Just the same!"

When the door closed, Betty sat down by the fire to finish her tea. As she brought the cup to her lips, she raised her eyes and saw Mrs. Conroy's handkerchief lying crumpled on the floor. She rose, picked up the handkerchief, and, boots still loose and flapping, went up the stairs and knocked on the door next to her own. A voice answered faintly. When Betty opened the door, Mrs. Conroy was sitting in her wing chair, which she had turned so that her back was to the window. One of her account books lay open on her lap. "Oh," she said. "I was hoping it was my daughter. She hates me to turn this chair around, but I'd rather look at a dry door than at that wet view any day of the week. She hates to have anything in the house changed, you know. You'd better remember that. She's very set in her ways."

"I'm returning your handkerchief, m'lady," Betty said rudely, and dropped it on the bed.

She was about to leave when she saw the shabby books on their shelves. The word "Accounts," inked on the back of each volume, sprang out at her. "Excuse me, m'lady," she said. "May I ask you a question?"

"Of course you may ask me a question, Betty."

"What sort of books are they you have, m'lady?"

"They belonged to my poor husband, Mr. Conroy. That's all he left me in the world, what you see there. He kept them himself; every stroke is in his own handwriting. He ran a little stationery shop in Brooklyn the last nineteen years of his life. We lived behind the shop. We didn't make a fortune out of it, but we got along. He had no head for business, but he enjoyed keeping his books. I look into them when I'm in the dumps. They remind me of so much; it's like as if I was reading his diary. He put down everything pertaining to the shop. Ah, it brings it all back, reading these old books."

"Might I see one of them, m'lady? I enjoy sums."

"Indeed you may, *indeed* you may!" Mrs. Conroy cried. Betty made a step toward the case, but the old lady was there before her, and lifted out a volume, dated Nov. 1899–May 1900, and handed it to her.

"The first year we were in the shop," she said. "Liza wasn't born then. She appeared in 1913, the only one we had."

Betty turned the pages of the book. "I always had a fancy for a little shop of my own somewhere," she said. "If I ever got enough money saved. Ah, I suppose I'll never have it, but it does no harm to think of it. I'd like to look at these, Mrs. Conroy. It's not hard, he has it all down nice and easy."

"Oh, it wasn't mathematics that interested my poor Alfred," Mrs. Conroy said. "Only, he liked to feel he was being business-like. He loved marking things down. 'My simple arithmetic,' he used to call it. 'I'm doing my simple arithmetic,' he'd say when I asked him what he was up to."

"I do like working sums, m'lady," Betty said. "I was always a great hand at addition and subtraction. I often thought I'd have been good in a bank, only I never got the chance. Would you let me borrow this for a day or two? I'll bring you up a cup of tea, if you like."

Mrs. Conroy regarded her for a moment. "Of course I'll let you borrow it," she said at last. "But I'll come down for the tea, if you don't mind."

Betty touched the bookcase. "Maybe I'd better take the first two or three, m'lady," she said. "That way I wouldn't have to be disturbing you so often."

A strong old arm came up and knocked her hand away. "One at a time, Betty. This room isn't going to feel the same with even that one missing. Mr. Conroy spent six months of his life on every one of these books. There's two to a year. It's going to take you a month anyway to get through that one. Now we'll go down and have our tea, nice and cozy by the fire. I won't bother you. I'll just enjoy the tea and you can enjoy your book, but mind you make no marks on it. And maybe you'd better make a fresh pot of tea. It'll have got cold, standing there all this time."

They had been sitting in the kitchen for some time when Betty looked up from her book. "You opened the shop November 15th, m'lady. That's the day Mr. Conroy starts here. And on December 22nd, m'lady, you went into the shop, went through all the Christmas numbers of the magazines, and left blue marks all over them."

"Indeed, I remember the day," Mrs. Conroy said cheerfully. "I had just finished making a blueberry pie for his dinner, and I didn't take the time to wash my hands. Oh, he was angry when he came to sell one of those magazines and had to mark down the price!"

"With good reason he was angry, m'lady," Betty said grimly. "And the place just started and not making money yet. Do you know how much money he lost with your blueberries?"

"Oh, I know, I know," Mrs. Conroy said, laughing. "Don't reproach me about it, Betty. He never let me forget about it. Turn over the page and never mind about it."

Betty bent to the book. A few minutes later she raised her head again. "Who was Miss Rorke, m'lady?" she asked.

"A poor old retired schoolteacher, Miss Rorke was. She lived up the street from us. Never had a penny, but she loved to read. Mr. Conroy let her take what she liked. He had a soft spot for her. She died then, and we never got a cent of it back. She ended owing us thirty-two dollars and seventeen cents."

"So far, she owes us two dollars and three cents," Betty said.

"Poor old Miss Rorke," Mrs. Conroy said contentedly. "Betty, I've been thinking. I'd like a cup of tea in my room first thing in the morning. As soon as you make your own. Say eight-thirty. That's fair, isn't it?"

Betty sat up straight. "Now then, m'lady, that's out of the question, so it is—morning tea in your room!"

Mrs. Conroy continued to watch the fire. "It was you who reminded me," she said. "Miss Rorke was a great strain on the regular book, the one you have there. There was too much of her, she was always in and out, so Mr. Conroy had an extra little book, for her and one or two others like her. I'm not saying you need it, but it would be a great help to you."

"All right," Betty said without rancor. "Half past eight you'll get your tea. Sugar and cream, the way you have it now."

"No cream in the morning," Mrs. Conroy said. "Cream makes me queasy in the morning. Just sugar, thanks, Betty."

They exchanged a glance. Betty's eyes were wary and calculating.

Liza burst into the kitchen. "I looked everywhere for you, Mother!" she cried. "You've turned your chair around again. And why aren't you up in your own room? What are you doing here in the kitchen?"

"I'm having my tea," the old woman said calmly.

"You know the doctor says it isn't good for you, Mother. Now please go on upstairs, and I'll get Betty to bring you a glass of hot milk. I see you've lighted the fire, Betty. I don't approve of open fires, but I suppose you're accustomed to having one. Go on, Mother."

"I don't want hot milk, Liza," Mrs. Conroy said, pressing her handkerchief to her lips. "Tea never did me any harm before, and I don't trust that country doctor of yours anyway. Of course, if you insist, I'll go upstairs. I'm dependent on your charity now, I know that. But first I'll take my book, please, Betty."

Betty snatched the book from the table. "No harm in Mrs. Conroy having a cup of tea, m'lady," she said.

"I'm the best judge of that!" Liza cried. "And what is that stupid old book doing down here? It doesn't belong down here."

"It does now," Mrs. Conroy said. "And another thing. I'd like you to put a nice, old-fashioned stuffed armchair in here by the fire for me. These pipe things of yours are hard on my back."

"We've had that all out before. I absolutely refuse to allow one of those atrocities in my— Is this a joke, Mother? Is this some terrible kind of joke? A kitchen is not the place for an armchair, and there's no room anyway, and people at Herbert's Retreat don't sit around having tea in the kitchen with the servants. And I would like to point out, Betty, that you are here to work, not to entertain guests at tea."

"I have my contract, m'lady," Betty said.

"And you can't very well afford to let her go anyway, can you, Liza?" Mrs. Conroy whispered. "Think how they'd love to laugh at you around here. And think how you'd feel if one of them got her instead. There are plenty of your friends who'd love to have a woman like Betty working for them. And you'd still have to pay her for the full term."

Liza stared incredulously at Betty for a minute, and then at her mother. "Very well," she said with difficulty. "Finish your tea. Perhaps it will make you sick. I hope not."

The derision in their eyes frightened her, and she started for the door.

"And one more thing," her mother said good-humoredly. "From now on, I'm going to leave my teeth in the bathroom at night."

"Oh, my God," Liza said, and left the kitchen.

"I cannot abide the sight of those things in the room with me," Mrs. Conroy went on. "This way, nobody will have to look at them."

They were silent for a while, Betty absorbed in her book, Mrs. Conroy peacefully watching the rise and fall of the flames. "I think I'll get a cat," she said suddenly. "Liza hates cats."

In the living room, sitting in sepulchral silence, Tom and Liza were first startled, then appalled, by the sudden screeches that came at them from the kitchen—screeches of laughter that was rude and unrestrained, and that renewed itself even as it struck and shattered against the walls of the kitchen.

The Gentleman in the
Pink-and-White Striped Shirt

$\mathcal{A}$t one minute before nine on a May morning, Charles Runyon opened drowsy eyes to the high-walled, sunless reaches of the Murray Hill hotel room that had been his home for nearly thirty years. Always, awakening in that room, Charles thought with satisfaction of the legend that had grown up around it. Charles's room was a mystery to the world. None of his friends— his present friends or those of former years—had ever entered it. There had been a period when columnists had conjectured almost weekly about its shape (it was long and narrow) and about its color (its walls, once pearl gray, had hardened to stone gray and chipped during Charles's tenancy, but he refused to allow it to be repainted) and its furnishings. The furniture, massive and shabby, contrasted curiously with the almost dainty elegance of Charles's personal appointments—his silver-backed brushes and hand mirror, his gold-topped bottle of sandalwood cologne, his leopard-skin slippers. His desk held a large pad of thick white paper, a crystal inkwell, and a feathered pen. It also held the porcelain tumbler from which he drank his morning coffee. His bookcase contained twelve copies of each of his own six books, the latest of which was ten years old, and on the lowest, deepest shelf he kept issues of magazines and newspapers in which articles by him had appeared.

Charles was a critic of the theater and of literature. He confined his efforts, these days, to a weekly column for a string of Midwestern newspapers. He said that this was the only regular writing he wanted to do, since the so-called novelists and so-called playwrights working today had made serious criticism impossible. Let the so-called critics have their little day, Charles said contemptuously. But he read the theater and book-review pages of the daily papers with fierce attention and held secret weekly sessions with *Variety* at the Quill and Brush Club, of which he was a member.

Charles's room had one tall, deep window, shrouded in ancient red brocade, which looked out on an air shaft. In his youth, Charles had been too much ashamed of his room to allow his friends to visit him there. In those years, it angered him that he had to be content with a cheap room hidden away in the back of the hotel, instead of being able to afford one of the splendid apartments in front. But his friends' curiosity, which at first made him uneasy, with time became flattering, and he grew fond of the room, and increased its mysteriousness by his reticence about it, and then by his arch evasiveness, and finally just by continuing to live there.

The years passed, and the old hotel changed hands and lost heart and dignity. The big front apartments were cut up into cubicles, the fine, long marble entrance hall grew dingy and was cluttered with soft-drink dispensers and a water cooler. The noble oak desk, discreetly placed at the rear of the lobby, was handed over to a cigarette vendor, who also dealt in razor blades and penny candy, and its functions were transferred to a sort of bathing box of varnished pine, built almost at the mouth of the elevator, in a position that flaunted the new managers' distrust of their guests. Rundown and shabby though the hotel was, it nevertheless suited Charles very well. And it was very cheap. He never thought of moving.

Besides, during the past few years Charles had spent nearly as much time away from New York as he had spent in it. He had formed a habit of going every weekend to Leona Harkey's charming house at Herbert's Retreat, thirty miles above the city, on the east bank of the Hudson. Charles occupied a unique and privileged position at the Retreat. Leona and her friends regarded him as their infallible authority on the rules of gracious living and on the shadowy and constantly changing dimensions of good taste. They were all a little in awe of him. Leona admitted, laughing, that she was afraid of him—but she adored him, too, she always added quickly, and she did not know how she had ever existed before she met him.

Lying in bed, waiting for Leona to telephone, Charles smiled. She really was a dear child, although he sometimes wished she could have been a little less wholehearted and a tiny bit more intelligent. Today was the eighth anniversary of their meeting, and they had a delightful celebration planned, for just the two of them.

At nine o'clock exactly, the phone rang. Charles laughed softly into the mouthpiece.

"Is this the gentleman in the pink-and-white striped shirt?" Leona sang. "Oh, is this the—"

"Not quite yet, my dear," Charles said. "The pink-and-white striped shirt is still nestling in its birthday tissue in a box on my dressing table, with its five little brother shirts."

"He *did* deliver them, then!" Leona cried. "Oh, Charles, I am so glad. I was so afraid that man would disappoint you. Oh, what a relief."

"My shirtmaker has never failed me yet, Leona," Charles said coldly.

Really, it was a task keeping Leona in check.

"Of course he hasn't, Charles. He wouldn't dare, would he, darling? But Charles, I want to tell you about my suit. It's divine, and almost exactly like yours. It was so sweet of you to let your tailor make it for me. And from your special cloth, too. We're going to look quite alike today, aren't we? Almost like twins."

"Almost like twins," Charles echoed generously, because it did promise to be a very pleasant day. "You know, Leona, this is quite an event in my life. I've grown very fond of you in the last eight years, my dear." He giggled gently. "How is the good George, by the way?"

"Oh, Charles, you know George. He trundled off an hour ago, just like a good little businessman. He's probably sitting behind his desk already, telling some wretched creature to bring back the dinette set or be sued, or something. What a job for a man to have."

George Harkey, Leona's husband, was credit manager of one of New York's larger and less fashionable department stores.

"Well, we all must work," Charles said briskly, sitting up in bed. "And I should have been at my scribbling an hour ago. We meet at the Plaza, then. At twelve-fifteen. That will leave us ample time to lunch and still get to the theater by curtain time. All right, my dear?"

"Twelve-fifteen," Leona said. "And Charles, I have a most amusing surprise for you."

"Splendid, Leona. I adore surprises. Now I really must go, Leona. Goodbye."

He replaced the phone, slid out of bed, wrapped himself in a dressing gown of thin gold wool—a gift from Leona—and plugged in his electric kettle, after assuring himself that it held enough water to make two cups of coffee. Leona and her friends would have been astonished at the absence of grace and charm in

Charles's domestic arrangements. They might even have been outraged, considering the stringent demands he made on their establishments. He puttered about, fetching a bottle of cream from his windowsill, measuring powdered instant coffee into his porcelain tumbler, and unwrapping a large, sticky delicatessen bun. Then he looked around for his morning newspapers. They were nowhere to be seen. He searched the room carefully, and at last, growing peevish, he even peered under his armchair, shook the window curtains, and pawed through his bed coverings. No sign of the papers. He was in the habit of buying the *Times* and the *Tribune* on his way home every night, and leaving them unopened, to read while he breakfasted.

Mike, the undersized, bespectacled elevator boy, who doubled as bellboy and porter, delivered the morning editions of the newspapers to the doors of other tenants in the hotel, but Charles was frugal, and refused to pay the small fee that this extra service cost. Now he was paperless, and his coffee was cooling. He gazed gloomily at the bun that had caused this disorder in his life—for there was no doubt in his mind that he had left the papers on the delicatessen counter the night before. His breakfast was ruined. Well, he wouldn't *let* it be ruined.

Knotting the sash of his robe firmly around his small middle, he unlocked his door, opened it, and looked out into the hall. There, in front of the opposite door, were the *Times* and the *Tribune.*

Charles paused, looked, listened, dived across the hall, grabbed the papers, and bounded backward to his own door, which resisted him. Gently and treacherously, his door had locked itself. No use to wring the handle, no use to push, no use to peer in the keyhole. The door was locked. A faint sound issued from inside the room whose tenant he had just robbed. He sprinted for the elevator and rang. Mike would have a passkey. Mike would let him into his room, and he would be safe again. With horror, he realized that he was still clutching the newspapers in his arms, and that the elevator, shuddering with age and unwillingness, was climbing up to his floor. He rammed both papers down the front of his robe, wrapped his arms about himself as though he were cold, and, when Mike threw back the elevator door, said, "I seem to have locked myself out of my room, Mike—of all foolish things. Would you bring your passkey?"

"How come you got locked out?" Mike inquired loudly as he sauntered along behind Charles, swinging the keys on their large brass ring.

"I was looking for the maid. She forgot to leave me any soap. The inefficiency of that woman is quite monstrous."

"You could of called the desk for your soap," Mike said.

Oh, yes, Charles thought. I could have called the desk for my soap. And you could have brought my soap up. And I could have given you a tip. None of that, my lad. "Will you hurry with that door, please?" he said sharply. "I could catch my death of cold standing out here."

Mike unlocked the door and pushed it open. Charles slipped past him, and turned to shoulder the door shut, but Mike, with one foot over the threshold, stood holding it open. He removed his spectacles, hawed breathily on them, and began to polish them on the section of his jacket that lay between his breast pocket and his dingy brass buttons. "You want I should bring you some soap?" he asked, and squinted into his spectacles before replacing them on his nose.

"Later," Charles cried, seeing the door across the way begin to open.

Across the hall, a flannel-clad arm appeared and began to feel confidently around on the floor. Hypnotized, Charles watched the disembodied hand pluck blindly at the worn edge of the carpet.

Above the arm, a tousled black head appeared, turned downward to the floor at first, and then turned up to reveal a pinched face full of sleep and bad temper.

"Why, good morning, Miss Carmichael!" Mike cried.

"Where the hell are my papers, Mike?" Miss Carmichael demanded, and, standing up, showed a tiny, spare figure enveloped in maroon flannel.

"Why, aren't they there, Miss Carmichael? I left them there," Mike said.

"Really," Charles said, "you must excuse me."

There was a second's silence.

"Would you mind removing your body from my door?" he said, and saw the suspicion in Mike's face turn to certainty.

"Why, certainly, Mr. Runyon," Mike said. "I'll do that little thing."

Charles kicked the door shut, locked it, hurled the papers onto his bed, dashed into the bathroom, and turned the shower on full, to save his ears from the altercation that he knew must be taking place outside.

When he emerged from the bathroom, he was calmer. He wasted no time in regrets. What had been done had been done. The question was how to survive the morning's absurd disaster with dignity.

He stepped into his shorts, which were of the same pink-and-white silk broadcloth as his new shirts. Then he lifted the papers from his bed to his desk and set about erasing Miss Carmichael's name. No use. Mike evidently wrote with an iron nail dipped in ink. The name had soaked through to the second page, and partly to the third. Charles sat down, lit a cigarette, and thought. He couldn't leave the papers here in the room, obviously. Mechanically, he put the bottle of cream out on the windowsill. Then, suddenly inspired, he returned to the desk and picked up the papers.

Of course. What could be simpler than to drop the wretched things down into the limbo of broken beer bottles, rusty hairpins, and odd shoes that lay eight floors below his window? In that mess, they would never be noticed, if anyone ever looked out there.

He raised the window an inch or two, and then, just as he was preparing to slide the papers out, there was a flurry and a thump on the fire escape across from him, and he stared straight into the dark and warlike countenance of Diamond, the floor maid, who was beating a tattoo on the rail of the fire escape with her dust mop, setting free a disgusting gray cloud that struggled a moment on the air before beginning to drift back into the rooms from which it had been taken.

The papers were still out of sight, and Charles let them drop to the floor. Raising the window a few inches higher, he gestured gracefully through the aperture, as though he were testing the quality of the air. His nonchalance undid him, for he upset the bottle of cream, which dropped from view with a soundless inexorability that was more alarming to Charles than anything that had yet happened that morning. A long, ascending skirl of wicked glee issued from the throat of Diamond, and her mop beats accelerated. From far below came the noise of a small crash, followed by swearing.

Charles plunged his head out the window and stared down. The square floor of the shaft was wet, and in the middle of it, brandishing a sputtering hose, stood a man whose upturned face looked, even at this distance, unpleasantly contorted. As Charles stared (should he throw down some money? or try to say something calming?), the man threw down the hose and vanished through a doorway.

Charles glanced up at Diamond, who was now resting herself comfortably against the rail.

"Gone to tell Mr. Dowd," she said. Mr. Dowd was the current manager.

Charles banged down the window and scurried to the middle of the room, where he stood chattering to himself with dismay. Deny it, of course, he said. Deny the whole thing. Knew nothing about it. Never saw a cream bottle. Heard nothing. Window was shut tight all morning . . .

He wrenched one of his new shirts out of its wrappings, dragged his new suit of slate-gray English flannel from its hanger, and began to dress himself. As, with trembling fingers, he tied his bow tie, which was also of the pink-and-white striped silk broadcloth, there was a knocking on his door. He stood still and waited.

"Got your soap here, Mr. Runyon!" Mike cried.

"Knock again," said Diamond's voice. "Knock good this time."

Mike dealt the door a mighty wallop. "I know he's in there," he said to Diamond.

"Maybe he's reading the paper," Diamond whispered, and the two tormentors moved off down the hall. Charles waited till he heard the elevator door close before he finished tying his tie. Then he dropped his hands to his dressing table and stared listlessly at himself in the mirror.

The phone rang. He picked it up and heard the intimate, confidential voice of Miss Knight, the telephone operator, who was very sensitive, and always smiled conspiratorially at Charles, because she knew that he was sensitive, too.

"Mr. Runyon," she whispered. "I wish you had confided in me about keeping food on your windowsill. The management is very strict about cooking in the rooms, Mr. Runyon, but some of the tenants have their little ways, so that they won't be found out. Oh, I know how it is. I like my cup of coffee in the morning, and maybe an egg, but—"

"Your feeding habits are even less interesting than I would have imagined them to be, Miss Knight," Charles said, and hung up.

Miss Knight was probably the only friend he had in the hotel, but he didn't care. He wanted to get out, to see Leona, to sit at luncheon in the Plaza, to be treated with the deference he expected and deserved. But there were still the papers to deal with. His topcoat went poorly with his new suit, but he would just have to wear it, and carry the papers out underneath . . . But no. In a burst of optimism brought on by yesterday afternoon's brilliant sunshine, he had sent the topcoat to the cleaner's, and his winter coat was already in storage. Grimly, he began to unbutton his new jacket.

A little later, Charles stood at the elevator, ringing the bell, for the second time that morning. His form no longer expressed the slender and fluid, yet snug, line that had given his tailor so much trouble and pleasure. From his neck to below his waist, he showed a solid, curving, birdlike bulge. He stood stiffly, and breasted his way warily into the elevator, turning an aloof and thoughtful profile to Mike's glances.

As Charles stepped from the elevator, the manager pounced from his place of concealment behind the desk. His round white face shone with the brimming contentment of the hotel man about to deal successfully with a tricky situation involving a guest. Miss Knight swiveled around to watch, ignoring frenzied appeals from her switchboard, and Mike let the elevator buzz.

"Mr. Runyon," the manager said. "That regrettable incident this morning—I'm terribly sorry, but we can't permit light housekeeping in the rooms. Sanitary regulations, you know. I'm sure you understand, Mr. Runyon."

"Really, Mr. Dowd, I haven't the faintest idea what you're talking about," Charles cried.

"Then that's understood, Mr. Runyon," the manager said, and

vanished behind the key slots. Miss Knight placed consoling hands on her switchboard. Her voice was soft and amused. Whistling, Mike entered his elevator and crashed the door to with the air of one who wields cymbals. Like a ghost, Charles passed through the lobby, through the entrance doors, and down the stone steps to the street. Only the hateful paper padding that was suffocating him seemed alive. He stood transfixed in the clean, clear spring sunshine and thought, I must not think, I must not remember . . . A taxi loitered near him, and he plunged into it and found he had to recline sidewise on the seat, because he could not sit. He directed the driver to the Altamont, a large commercial hotel on Eighth Avenue, where he could be fairly certain of not running into anyone he knew.

As he was getting into the taxi, a button popped from his jacket and dropped into the gutter. He felt it pop and saw it fall, but he let it go. Even had he wanted to leave the shelter of the taxi, he could not have bent to retrieve the button. A pity; the buttons for his suit had been specially ordered from Italy. Leona had the same buttons on her suit. Now he would have to go through the whole afternoon watching Leona preen herself in a complete set of his buttons, in a gigantic travesty of his suit—for she was taller than he, and her arms were very long. What a complete fool he had been to allow her to go to his tailor.

The men's room at the Altamont was at the foot of a curving flight of stairs immediately to the left of the main entrance. It was a dank, white-tiled vault, occupied, when Charles walked in, only by the attendant, who was sorting the brushes and rags in his shoeshine kit. Charles took off his coat and unbuttoned his shirt, and pulled the papers out and threw them into the wastebasket. Turning his back on them and on his memories of the morning, he sprinkled a few drops of cold water on his chest and rubbed himself dry with his palms, averting his eyes from the paper towels over the washbasin. The attendant, a lanky man whose eyes were so blinded by boredom that he no longer troubled to focus them, raised his head at the sound of the running water and then lowered it again.

Refreshed, Charles stepped back from the washbasin and slipped his arms into his shirt. He buttoned the middle buttons first and moved swiftly up to the top. Really, he looked remarkably *soigné,* considering what he'd been through. The habit of poise, he thought contentedly. He had fastened the top button and was reaching for his tie when he saw that his fingers were smudged with newsprint and had left a track all the way up his front. He snatched a paper towel, dampened it, and rubbed at the smudges, making them worse. Leaning closer to the mirror, he saw that the damage was complete. Now his shirt looked like a used rag. He turned incredulously from the mirror to find the attendant standing behind him.

"Them marks'll never come out," he said.

Charles tore the shirt off and flung it into the wastebasket, on top of the papers. "Here is ten dollars," he said. "Go upstairs and get me a plain white shirt, size 14½. You can get it at that shop in the lobby. And hurry."

The sleeves of the new shirt were much too long, and the collar would have been more appropriate on a secondhand-car salesman, Charles thought. He let the cuffs slip down around his knuckles, just to see how awful they looked, and then pushed them back to his wrists. His pink-and-white striped tie looked like a little ribbon against the sturdy cloth of the new shirt.

Out in the street again, he hailed a taxi. It was not yet noon. He had just time to get to the Plaza ahead of Leona. He would catch her before she entered the hotel, and tell her of his new plan, which was to drive out into the country and have lunch at some secluded inn. Leona would have no audience to perform for today, he thought with satisfaction.

As he entered the lobby of the Plaza, he glanced furtively around, putting his hand to his throat as though to adjust his tie. Leona had not yet arrived. He took up his stand by a window and waited to see her come down the street.

Leona had arrived at the Plaza a few seconds before Charles, and had gone straight through the lobby and down the hall to the flower shop, where she bought two of the glowing black-red carnations that he loved. One of these she pinned on her lapel, smiling at her own reflection as she did so. Perhaps it was a little naughty of her to have copied his shirt without asking his permission. But after all she had the suit; why not the shirt, too? Charles liked women to look absolutely perfect. How amused and pleased he would be when he saw her. Perhaps even a little flattered. She touched the narrow bow tie lightly, then took the second carnation and walked back to the lobby. There he was, waiting by the window. She called a bellboy and handed him the carnation and a dollar bill, and pointed to Charles, and whispered for a minute.

Crossing the busy lobby, the bellboy, who was very serious about his work, repeated to himself what he had been instructed to do and say. "First I say, 'Is this the gentleman in the pink-and-white striped shirt?' Then I give him the flower. Then I say, 'The lady in the pink-and-white striped shirt awaits your pleasure, sir.'" He held the carnation very carefully, fearful that the stem would snap.

Watching the boy approach Charles, Leona laughed excitedly. Dear Charles, she thought. I just can't wait to see his face when he turns around.

The Joker

$\mathcal{W}$aifs, Isobel Bailey called her Christmas Day guests. This year she had three coming, three waifs—a woman, an elderly man, and a young man—respectable people, well brought up, gentle-looking, neatly dressed, to all appearances the same as everybody else, but lost just the same. She had a private list of such people, not written down, and she drew on it every year as the holiday season descended. Her list of waifs did not grow shorter. Indeed, it seemed to lengthen as the years went by, and she was still young, only thirty-one. What makes a waif, she thought (most often as winter came on, always at Christmas); what begins it? When do people get that fatal separate look? Are waifs born?

Once she had thought that it was their lack of poise that marked them—because who ever saw a poised waif? You see them defiant, stiff, rude, silent, but aren't they always bewildered? Still, bewilderment was not a state reserved for waifs only. Neither was it, she decided, a matter of having no money, though money seemed to have a great deal to do with it. Sometimes you could actually see people change into waifs, right before your eyes. Girls suddenly became old maids, or at least they developed an incurably *single* look. Cheerful, bustling women became dazed widows. Men lost their grip and became unsure-looking. It wasn't any one thing that made a waif. Isobel was sure of that. It wasn't being crippled, or being in disgrace, or even not being married. It was a shameful thing to be a waif, but it was also mysterious. There was no accounting for it or defining it, and over and over again she was drawn back to her original idea—that waifs were simply people who had been squeezed off the train because there was no room for them. They had lost their tickets. Some of them never had owned a ticket. Perhaps their parents had failed to equip them with a ticket. Poor things, they were stranded. During ordinary days of the year, they could hide their plight. But at Christmas, when the train drew up for that hour of recollection and revelation, how the waifs stood out, burning in their solitude. Every Christmas Day (said Isobel to herself, smiling whimsically) was a station on the journey of life. There on the windy platform the waifs gathered in shame, to look in at the fortunate ones in the warm, lighted train. Not all of them stared in, she knew; some looked away. She, Isobel, looked them all over and decided which ones to invite into her own lighted carriage. She liked to think that she occupied a first-class carriage—their red brick house in Herbert's Retreat, solid, charming, waxed and polished, well heated, filled with flowers, stocked with glass and silver and clean towels.

Isobel believed implicitly in law, order, and organization. She believed strongly in organized charity. She gave regular donations to charity, and she served willingly and conscientiously on several committees. She felt it was only fair that she should help those less fortunate than herself, though there was a point where she drew the line. She never gave money casually on the street, and her maids had strict orders to shut the door to beggars. "There are places where these people can apply for help," she said.

It was different with the Christmas waifs. For one thing, they were not only outside society, they were outside organized charity. They were included in no one's plans. And it was in the spirit of Christmas that she invited them to her table. They were part of the tradition and ceremony of Christmas, which she loved. She enjoyed decking out the tree, and eating the turkey and plum pudding, and making quick, gay calls at the houses of friends, and going to big parties, and giving and receiving presents. She and Edwin usually accepted an invitation for Christmas night, and sometimes they sent out cards for a late, small supper, but the afternoon belonged to the waifs. She and Edwin had so much, she felt it was only right. She felt that it was beautifully appropriate that she should open her house to the homeless on Christmas Day, the most complete day of the year, when everything stopped swirling and the pattern became plain.

Isobel's friends were vaguely conscious of her custom of inviting waifs to spend Christmas afternoon. When they heard that she had entertained "poor Miss T." or "poor discouraged Mr. F." at her table, they shook their heads and reflected that Isobel's kindness was real. It wasn't assumed, they said wonderingly. She really was kind.

The first of this year's waifs to arrive was Miss Amy Ellis, who made blouses for Isobel and little silk smocks for Susan, Isobel's five-year-old daughter. Isobel had never seen Miss Ellis except in her workroom, where she wore, summer and winter, an airy, arty smock of natural-color pongee. Today, she wore a black silk dress that was draped into a cowl around her shoulders, leaving her arms bare. And Miss Ellis's arms, Isobel saw at once, with a lightning flash of intuition, were the key to Miss Ellis's character, and to her life. Thin, stringy, cold, and white, stretched stiff with emptiness—they were what made her look like a waif. Could it be that Miss Ellis was a waif *because* of her arms? It was a thought. Miss Ellis's legs matched her arms, certainly, and it was easy to see, through the thin stuff of her dress, that her shoulders were too high and pointed. Her neck crept disconsolately down into a hollow and discolored throat. Her greeny-gold hair was combed into a limp short cap, betraying the same arty spirit that inspired her to wear the pongee smock. Her earrings, which dangled, had been hammered out of some coal-like substance. Her deep, lashless eyes showed that she was all pride and no spirit. She was hopeless. But it had all started with her arms, surely. They gave her away.

Miss Ellis had brought violets for Isobel, a new detective story for Edwin, and a doll's smock for Susan. She sat down in a corner of the sofa, crossed her ankles, expressed pleasure at the sight of the fire, and accepted a martini from Edwin. Edwin Bailey was thirty-seven and a successful corporation lawyer. His handshake was warm and firm, and his glance was alert. His blond hair was fine and straight, and his stomach looked as flat and hard as though he had a board thrust down inside his trousers. He was tall and temperate. The darkest feeling he acknowledged was contempt. Habitually he viewed the world—his own world and the world reflected in the newspapers—with tolerance. He was unaware of his wife's theories about Christmas waifs, but he would have accepted them unquestioningly, as he accepted everything about Isobel. "My wife is the most mature human being I have ever met," he said sometimes. Then, too, Isobel was never jealous, because jealousy was childish. And she was never angry. "But if you understand, really understand, you simply cannot be angry with people," she would say, laughing.

Now she set about charming Miss Ellis, and Edwin had settled back lazily to watch them when the second waif, Vincent Lace, appeared in the doorway. He sprinted impetuously across the carpet and, without glancing to the right or to the left, fell on both knees before Susan, who was curled on the hearth rug, undressing her new doll.

"Ah, the grand little girl!" cried Vincent. "Sure she's the living image of her lovely mother! And what name have they put on you, love?"

"Susan," said the child coldly, and she got up and went to perch under the spreading branches of the splendid tree that blazed gorgeously from ceiling to floor between two tall windows. Beyond the windows, the narrow street lay chill and gray, except when the wind, blowing down the hill, swept before it a ragged leaf of Christmas tissue paper, red or green, or a streamer of colored ribbon.

Undisturbed by the child's desertion, Vincent rocked back on his plump behind, and wrapped his arms around his knees, and favored his host, then Miss Ellis, and, finally, Isobel with a dazzling view of his small, decaying teeth.

"Well, Isobel," he murmured, "little Isobel of the peat-brown eyes. You still have the lovely eyes, Isobel. But what am I thinking of at all!" he shouted, bounding to his feet. "Sure your husband will think me a terrible fellow entirely. Forgive me, Isobel, but the little girl took my breath away. She's yourself all over again."

"Edwin, this is our Irish poet," Isobel said. "Vincent Lace, a dear friend of Father's. I see you still wear the red bow tie, Vincent, your old trademark. I noticed it first thing when I ran into you the other day. As a matter of fact, it was the tie that caught my attention. You were never without it, were you?"

"Ah, we all have our little conceits, Isobel," Vincent said, smiling disarmingly at Edwin.

Vincent's face appeared to have been vigorously stretched, either by too much pain or by too much laughter, and when he was not smiling his expression was one of dignified truculence. He was more obviously combed and scrubbed than a sixty-three-year-old man should be, and his bright-blue eyes were anxious. Twenty years ago, he had come from Ireland to do a series of lectures on

Irish literature at colleges and universities all over the United States. In his suitcase, he carried several copies of the two thin volumes of poetry that had won him his contract.

"My poems drive the fellows at home stark mad," Vincent had confided to Isobel's father, the first time he visited their house. "I pay no attention to the modern rubbish at all. All that crowd thinks of is making pretty-sounding imitations of Yeats and his bunch. Yeats, Yeats, Yeats, that's all they know. But my masters are long since dead. I go back in spirit to those grand eighteenth-century souls who wandered the bogs and hills of our unfortunate country, and who broke bread with the people, and who wrote out of the heart of the people."

At this point (for it was a speech Isobel and the others were often to hear), he would leap to his feet and intone in his native Irish tongue the names of the men he admired, and with every syllable his voice would grow more laden, until at the last it seemed that he would have to release a sob, but he never did, although his small blue eyes would be wet and angry. With his wild black hair, his red tie, and his sharp tongue, he quickly became a general favorite, and when his tour was over, he accepted an offer from one of the New York universities and settled down among his new and hospitable friends. Isobel's father, who had had an Irish grandmother, took to Vincent at once, and there had been a period, Isobel remembered, when her mother couldn't plan a dinner without being forced to include Vincent. At the age of fifty, he had lost his university post. Everyone knew it was because he drank too much, but Vincent blamed it on some intrigue in the department. He was stunned. He had never thought such a thing could happen to him. Isobel remembered him shouting at her father across the dinner table, "They'll get down on their knees to me! I'll go back on my own terms!" Then he had put his head in his hands and cried, and her mother had got up and left the room

in disgust. Isobel remembered that he had borrowed from everyone. After her father died, her family dropped Vincent. Everyone
dropped him. He made too much of a nuisance of himself. Occasionally, someone would report having seen him in a bar. He was
always shouting about his wrongs. He was no good, that was the
sum of it. He never really had been any good, although his quick
tongue and irreverent air had given him the appearance of brilliance.

A month before, Isobel had run into him on the street, their
first meeting for many years. Vincent is a waif, she had thought,
looking at him in astonishment. Vincent, the eloquent, romantic
poet of her childhood, an unmistakable waif. It was written all
over him. It was in every line of his seedy, imploring face. Two
days before Christmas, she had invited him to dinner. He was
delighted. He had arrived in what he imagined to be his best
form—roguish, teasing, sly, and melancholy.

Edwin offered him a martini, and he said fussily that he was on
the wagon. "I will take a cigarette, though," he said, and selected
one from the box on the table beside him. Isobel found with disagreeable surprise that she remembered his hands, which were
small and stumpy, with long pared nails. Dreadful hands. She
wondered what wretchedness they had brought him through in
the years since she had known him. And the famous bow tie, she
thought with amusement—how poorly it goes under that fat, disappointed face. Clinging to that distinctive tie, as though anyone
connected him with the tie, or with anything any more.

The minute Jonathan Quin walked into the room, Isobel saw that
she could expect nothing from him in the way of conversation. He
will be no help at all, she thought, but this did not matter to her,
because she never expected much from her Christmas guests. At a
dinner party a few days before, she had been seated next to a news-

paper editor and had asked him if there were any young people on his staff who might be at a loose end for Christmas. The next day, he had telephoned and given her Jonathan's name, explaining that he was a reporter who had come to New York from a little town in North Carolina and knew no one.

At first, entering the soft, enormous, firelit room, Jonathan took Miss Ellis to be his hostess, because of her black dress, and then, confused over his mistake, he stumbled around, looking for a chair to hide in. His feet were large. He wore loose, battered black shoes that had been polished until every break and scratch showed. He had put new laces in the shoes. Edwin asked him a few encouraging questions about his work on the newspaper, and he nodded and stammered and joggled his drink and finally told them that he was finding the newspaper a very interesting place.

Vincent said, "That's a magnificent scarlet in your dress, Isobel. It suits you. A triumphant, regal color it is."

Isobel, who was sitting in a yellow chair, with her back to the glittering tree, glanced down at her slim wool dress.

"Christmas red, Vincent. I think it is the exact red for Christmas, don't you? I wore it decorating the tree last night."

"And my pet Susan dressed up in the selfsame color, like a little red berry she is!" cried Vincent, throwing his intense glance upon the silent child, who ignored him. He was making a great effort to be the witty, rakish professor of her father's day, and at the same time deferring slyly to Edwin. He did not know that this was to be his only visit, no matter how polite he proved himself to be.

It was a frightful thing about Vincent, Isobel thought. But there was no use getting involved with him. He was too hard to put up with, and she knew what a deadly fixture he could become in a household. "Some of those ornaments used to be on the tree at home, Vincent," she said suddenly. "You might remember one or two of them. They must be almost as old as I am."

Vincent looked at the tree and then said amiably, "I can't re-member what I did last year. Or perhaps I should say I prefer not to remember. But it was very kind of you to think of me, Isobel. Very kind." He covertly watched the drinks getting lower in the glasses.

Isobel began to think it had been a mistake to invite him. Old friends should never become waifs. It was easier to think about Miss Ellis, who was, after all, a stranger. Pitiful people, she thought. How they drag their wretched lives along with them. She allowed time for Jonathan to drink one martini—one would be more than enough for that confused head—before she stood up to shepherd them all in to dinner.

The warm pink dining room smelled of spice, of roasting turkey, and of roses. The tablecloth was of stiff, icy white damask, and the centerpiece—of holly and ivy and full-blown blood-red roses—bloomed and flamed and cast a hundred small shadows trembling among the crystal and the silver. In the fireplace a great log, not so exuberant as the one in the living room, glowed a pow-erful dark red.

Vincent startled them all with a loud cry of pleasure. "Isobel, Isobel, you remembered!" He grasped the back of the chair on which he was to sit and stared in exaggerated delight at the table.

"I knew you'd notice," Isobel said, pleased. "It's the center-piece," she explained to the others. "My mother always had red roses and holly arranged just like that in the middle of our table at home at Christmas time. And Vincent always came to Christmas dinner, didn't you, Vincent?"

"Christmas dinner and many other dinners," Vincent said, when they were seated. "Those were the happiest evenings of my life. I often think of them."

"Even though my mother used to storm down in a rage at four in the morning and throw you out, so my father could get some sleep before going to court in the morning," Isobel said slyly.

"We had some splendid discussions, your father and I. And I wasn't always thrown out. Many a night I spent on your big red sofa. Poor old Matty used to find me there, surrounded by glasses and ashtrays and the books your father would drag down to prove me in the wrong, and the struggle *she* used to have getting me out before your mother discovered me! Poor Matty, she lived in fear that I'd fall asleep with a lighted cigarette going, and burn the house down around your ears. But I remember every thread in that sofa, every knot, I should say. Who has it now, Isobel? I hope you have it hidden away somewhere. In the attic, of course. That's where you smart young things would put a comfortable old piece of furniture like that. The most comfortable bed I ever lay on."

Delia, the bony Irish maid, was serving them so discreetly that every movement she made was an insertion. She fitted the dishes and plates onto the table as though they were going into narrow slots. Her thin hair was pressed into stiff waves under her white cap, and she appeared to hear nothing, but she already had given Alice, the cook, who was her aunt, a description of Vincent Lace that had her doubled up in evil mirth beside her hot stove. Sometimes Isobel, hearing the raucous, jeering laughter of these two out in the kitchen, would find time to wonder about all the reports she had ever heard about the soft voices of the Irish.

"Isobel tells me you've started a bookshop near the university, Mr. Lace," Edwin said cordially. "That must be interesting work."

"Well, now, I wouldn't exactly say I started it, Mr. Bailey," Vincent said. "It's only that they needed someone to advise them on certain phases of Irish writing, and I'm helping to build up that department in the store, although of course I help out wherever they need me. I like talking to the customers, and then I have plenty of time for my own writing, because I'm only obliged to be there half the day. Like all decent-minded gentlemen of leisure, I dabble in writing, Mr. Bailey. And speaking of that, I had a note the other day from an old student of mine who had through some highly unlikely chance come across my name in the *Modern Ency-clopedia*. An article on the history of house painting, Isobel. What do you think of that? Mr. Quin and Miss Ellis, Isobel and her father knew me as an accomplished and, if I may say so, a reason-ably witty exponent of Irish letters. Students fought with tooth and with nail to hear my lecture on Irish writers . . . 'Envy Is the Spur,' I called it. But to get back to my ink-stained ex-student, whose name escapes me. He wanted to know if I remembered a certain May morning when I led the entire student body, or as many as I could lure from the library and from the steps of the building, down to riot outside Quanley's—a low and splendid drinking establishment of that time, Mr. Quin—to riot, I repeat, for one hour, in protest against their failure to serve me, in the middle hours of the same morning, the final glass that I felt to be my due."

"Well, that must have been quite an occasion, Mr. Lace, I should imagine," Miss Ellis said.

Vincent turned his excited stare on Isobel. "You wouldn't remember that morning, Isobel."

"I couldn't honestly say if I remember it or not, Vincent. You had so many escapades. There seemed to be no end to your inge-nuity."

"Oh, I was a low rascal. Miss Ellis, I was a scoundrelly fellow in those days. But when I lectured, they listened. They listened to me. Isobel, you attended one or two of my lectures. I flatter myself now that I captivated even you with my masterly command of the language. Isobel, tell your splendid husband, and this gracious lady, and this gracious youth, that I was not always the clown they see before them now. Justify your old friend, Isobel."

"Vincent, you haven't changed at all, have you?"

"Ah, that's where you're wrong, Isobel. For I have changed a great deal. Your father would see it. You were too young. You don't remember. You're all too young," he finished discontentedly.

Miss Ellis moved nervously and seemed about to speak, but she said nothing. Edwin asked her if she thought the vogue for mystery stories was as strong as ever, and Vincent looked as if he were about to laugh contemptuously—Isobel remembered him always laughing at everything anyone said—but he kept silent and allowed the discussion to go on.

Isobel reflected that she had always known Vincent to be talky but surely he couldn't have always been the windbag he was now. Again she wished she hadn't invited him to dinner, but then she noticed how eagerly he was enjoying the food, and she relented. She was glad that he should see what a pleasant house she had, and that he should have a good meal.

Isobel was listening dreamily to Vincent's story about a book thief who stole only on Tuesdays, and only books with yellow covers, and she was trying to imagine what color Miss Ellis's lank hair must originally have been, when she became aware of Delia, standing close at her side and rasping urgently into her ear about a man begging at the kitchen door.

"Edwin," Isobel interrupted gently, "there's a man begging at the back door, and I think, since it's Christmas, we should give him his dinner, don't you?"

"What did he ask you for, Delia?" Edwin asked.

"He asked us would we give him a dollar, sir, and then he said that for a dollar and a half he'd sing us our favorite hymn," Delia said, and began to giggle unbecomingly.

"Ask him if he knows 'The boy stood on the burning deck,' " Vincent said.

"Poor man, wandering around homeless on Christmas Day!" Miss Ellis said.

"Get an extra plate, so that Mr. Bailey can give the poor fellow some turkey, Delia!" Isobel cried excitedly. "I'm glad he came here! I'm glad we have the chance to see that he has a real Christmas dinner! Edwin, you're glad, too, although you're pretending to disapprove!"

"All right, Isobel, have it your own way," Edwin said, smiling.

He filled the stranger's plate, with Delia standing judiciously by his elbow. "Give him more dressing, Edwin," Isobel said. "And Delia, see that he has plenty of hot rolls. I want him to have everything we have."

"Nothing to drink, Isobel," Edwin said. "If he hasn't been drinking already today, I'm not going to be responsible for starting him off. I hope you people don't think I'm a mean man," he added, smiling around the table.

"Not at all, Mr. Bailey," Miss Ellis said stoutly. "We all have our views on these matters. That's what makes us different. What would the world be like if we were all the same?"

"My mother says," said Jonathan hoarsely, putting one hand into his trouser pocket, "that if a person is bad off enough to ask her for something, he's worse off than she is."

"Your mother must be a very nice lady, Mr. Quin," Miss Ellis said.

"It's a curious remark, of Mr. Quin's mother," Vincent said moodily.

"Oh, of course you'd have him in at the table here and give him the house, Vincent!" Isobel cried in great amusement. "I remember your reputation for standing treat and giving, Vincent."

"Mr. Lace has the look of a generous man," Miss Ellis said, with her thin, childlike smile. The heavy earrings hung like black weights against her thin jaw.

Vincent stared at her. "Isobel remarks that I would bid the man in and give him the house," he said bitterly. "But at the moment, dear lady, I am not in the position to give him the leg of a chair, so the question hardly arises. Do you know what I would do if I was in Mr. Bailey's position, Miss Ellis? Now this is no reflection on you, Mr. Bailey. When I think of him, and what is going on in his mind at this moment, as he gazes into the heaped platter that you have so generously provided—"

"Vincent, get back to the point. What would you do in Edwin's place?" asked Isobel good-naturedly.

Vincent closed his mouth and gazed at her. "You're quite right, my dear," he said. "I tend to sermonize. It's the strangled professor in me, still writhing for an audience. Well, to put it briefly, if I were in your husband's excellent black leather shoes, I would go out to the kitchen, and I would empty my wallet, which I trust for your sake is well filled, and I would tell that man to go in peace."

"And he would laugh at you for a fool," Edwin said sharply.

"And he would laugh at me for a fool," Vincent said, "and I would know it, and I would curse him, but I would have done the only thing I could do."

"I don't get it," Jonathan said, with more self-assurance than before.

"Oh, Mr. Quin, Vincent is an actor at heart," Isobel said. "You should have come to our home when my father was alive. It was a one-man performance every time, Vincent's performance."

"I used to make you laugh, Isobel."

"Of course you did," Isobel said soothingly.

She sat and watched them all eat their salad, wondering at the same time how the man in the kitchen must feel, to come from the cold and deserted winter street into her warm house. He must be speechless at his good fortune, she thought, and she had a wild impulse to go out into the kitchen and see him for herself. She stood up and said, "I want to see if our unexpected guest has enough of everything."

She hurried through the pantry and into the white glare of the kitchen, where it was very hot. She rigidly avoided looking at the table, but she was conscious of the strange man's dark bulk against her white muslin window curtains, and of the harsh smell of his cigar. She wanted him to see her, in her red dress, with her flushed face and her sweet, expensive perfume. She owned the house. He had the right to feast his eyes on her. This was the stranger, the classical figure of the season, who had come unbidden to her feast.

Fat-armed Alice was petting the round brown pudding where a part of it had broken away as she tumbled it out of its cloth into its silver dish. Delia stood watching intently, holding away to her side—as though it were a matador's cape—the stained and steaming cloth.

"Take your time, Alice," Isobel said in her clear, nicely tempered voice. "Everything is going splendidly. It couldn't be a more successful party."

"That's very considerate of you, Ma'am," Alice said, letting her eyes roll meaningfully in the direction of the stranger, as though she were tipping Isobel off.

As she turned to leave the kitchen, Isobel saw the man at the table. She did not mean to see him. She had no intention of looking at him, but she did look. She saw that he had hair and hands, and she knew that he had sight, because she felt his eyes on her, but she could not have given a description of him, because in that rapid, silent glance all she really saw was the thick, filthy stub in his smiling mouth.

His cigar, she thought, sitting down again in the dining room. She leaned forward and took a sip of wine. Miss Ellis's arms, Vincent's bow tie, this boy's broken shoes, and now the beggar's cigar.

"How is our other guest getting along out there, Delia?" Isobel asked when the salad plates were being cleared away.

"Ah, he's all right, Ma'am. He's sitting there and smiling to himself. He's very quiet, so he is."

"Has he said nothing at all, Delia?"

"Only when he took an old cigar butt he has out of his pocket. He said to Alice that he strained his back picking it up. He said he made a promise to his mother never to step down off the sidewalk to pick up a butt of a cigar or a cigarette, and he says this one was halfway out in the middle of the street."

"He must have hung on to a lamppost!" Jonathan cried, delighted.

"Edwin, send a cigar to that poor fellow when Delia comes in again, will you?" Isobel said. "I'd like to feel he had something decent to smoke for once."

Delia came in, proudly bearing the flaming pudding, and Edwin told her to take a cigar for the man in the kitchen.

"And don't forget an extra plate for his pudding, Delia," Isobel said happily.

"Oh, your mother was a mighty woman, Isobel," Vincent said, "even though we didn't always see eye to eye."

"Well, I'm sure you agreed on the important things, Mr. Lace," Miss Ellis said warmly.

"I don't like to disappoint or disillusion you, Miss Ellis, but it was on the important things we disagreed. She thought they were unimportant."

A screech of surprise and rage was heard from the kitchen, which up to that time had sent to their ears only the subdued and pleasant tinkling of glasses and dishes and silver. They were therefore prepared for—indeed, they compelled, by their paralyzed silence—the immediate appearance of Delia, who materialized without her cap, and with her eyes aglow, looking as though she had been taken by the hair and dropped from a great height.

"That fellow out there in the kitchen!" she cried. "He's gone!"

"Did he take something?" asked Edwin keenly.

"No, sir. At least, now, I don't think he took anything. I'll look and see this minute."

"Delia, calm yourself," Isobel said. "What was all the noise about?"

"He flew off when I was in here with the pudding, Ma'am. I went out to give him the cigar Mr. Bailey gave me for him, and he was gone, clean out of sight. I ran over to the window, thinking to call him back for his cigar, as long as I had it in my hand, and there wasn't a sign of him anywhere. Alice didn't even know he was out of the chair till she heard the outside door bang after him."

"Now, Delia. It was rude of him to run off like that when you and Alice and all of us have been at such pains to be nice to him, but I'm sure there's no need for all this silly fuss," Isobel said, with an exasperated grimace at Edwin.

"But Mrs. Bailey, he didn't just go!" Delia said wildly.

"Well, what did he do, then?" Edwin asked.

"Oh, sir, didn't he go and leave his dirty old cigar butt stuck down in the hard sauce, sir!" Delia cried. She put her hands over her mouth and began to make rough noises of merriment and outrage while her eyes swooped incredulously around the table.

Edwin started to rise, but Isobel stopped him with a look. "Delia," she said, "tell Alice to whip up some kind of sauce for the pudding and bring it in at once."

"Oh dear, how could he do such a thing?" Miss Ellis whispered as the door swung to on Delia. "And after you'd been so kind to him." She leaned forward impulsively to pat Isobel's hand.

"A shocking thing!" Vincent exclaimed. "Shocking! It's a rotten class of fellow would do a thing like that."

"You mustn't let him spoil your lovely dinner, Mrs. Bailey," Miss Ellis said. Then she added, to Edwin, "Mrs. Bailey is such a *person!*"

"I never cared much for hard sauce anyway," Jonathan said.

"I don't know what you're all talking about!" Isobel cried.

"We wouldn't blame you if you were upset," Vincent said. "But just because some stupid clod insults you is no reason for you to *feel* insulted."

"I think that nasty man meant to spoil our nice day," Miss Ellis said contentedly. "And he hasn't at all, has he?"

"Let's all just forget about it," Edwin said. "Isn't that right, Miss Ellis?"

"Are you people sympathizing with me?" Isobel said. "Because if you are, please stop it. I am not in the least upset, I assure you." With hands that shook violently, she began to serve the pudding.

When they had all been served, she pushed her chair back and said, "Edwin, I have to run upstairs a minute to check on the heat in Susan's room before she goes for her nap. Delia will bring the coffee inside, and I'll be down in a second."

Upstairs, in the bedroom, she cooled her beleaguered forehead with eau de cologne. She heard the chairs moving in the dining room, and then the happy voices chorusing across the hall. A moment later, she imagined she could hear the chink of their coffee cups. She wished bitterly that it was time to send them all home. She was tired of them. They talked too much. It seemed twenty years since Edwin had carved the turkey.

The Stone
Hot-Water Bottle

Over the years, Leona Harkey had made many gifts to her friend and idol, Charles Runyon, the noted literary man and theater critic, but of all the things she had given him, he liked best an old-fashioned stone hot-water bottle she had found one day, quite by accident, in a junk shop. Leona had wandered into the shop on the chance of finding something odd and funny that might please Charles, whose tastes were so unpredictable and yet so rigidly formed, and there, on a rickety table heaped with unmatched bits of china, the hot-water bottle lay, looking as though it had been waiting for her to come and find it. The minute her eyes fell on it, Leona remembered the story Charles had told her of one particularly terrible year during his lonely childhood, when a hot-water bottle just like this one was his dearest possession and his only consolation, because it was his only link with a dearly loved grandmother who had died, leaving him to the mercies of a crowd of cruder, less understanding relatives. Triumphant and excited, Leona knew she had made a find.

Charles was enraptured by his new possession, which before being presented to him had been purified and polished by Bridie,

Leona's massive Irish maid, and encased, by Leona's dressmaker, in a tight, zippered jacket of olive-green quilted velvet. Furthermore—and this was another proof of Leona's imaginativeness—attached to one end of the velvet case was a lengthy loop of twisted velvet ribbon, so that when the bottle was not in use, it could hang decoratively from a brass hook near the head of Charles's bed. Charles had two beds. One belonged to the Murray Hill hotel where he had lived for over thirty years. The other belonged in Leona's beautiful house at Herbert's Retreat, thirty miles outside New York on the right bank of the Hudson River, where Charles spent his weekends. It was understood, of course, that the stone hot-water bottle was intended for his room at Leona's.

Another happy thing about the hot-water bottle was that it was found in early October, just as the nights were getting cold; Charles was able to start using it immediately. Every night thereafter during his weekend visits, Bridie took the hot-water bottle to the kitchen, where she stripped it naked and filled it with boiling water. Then, covered again, it was returned to Charles's room and placed in his bed. Charles often claimed that the most blissful moment of his week came on Friday night, when his toes first touched the delicious velvety warmth of his hot-water bottle. After closing his book, but before turning out his bedside lamp, he hung his treasure back on its hook, where he could see it in the morning without being made aware of the chill that had come over it in the night. He couldn't bear to face the fact that the hot-water bottle grew cold in the night.

"One of the worst things about that terrible year when I was seven," he told Leona one Friday evening in November, "was waking up in the morning to find that my darling grandmother's hot-water bottle had died in the night. Because that is how it felt, you know—dead, cold and dead. Every morning, it was as though she had died again and left me. I used to cry myself to sleep with my arms wrapped around it—you know the way a child does. And then one of my aunts, Aunt Jane, the grimmest-faced one, decided I was making a fetish out of it (imagine, she used that word; where do you suppose she ever heard it?) and she took it away. She took it, Leona. Can you consider such cruelty? I never saw it again. Leona, darling, you know, this one looks exactly like it. Do you suppose it's the same one? Could it be?"

"Of course it could be. Of course it's the same one, Charles. Why, Charles, if you could see the little hole in the wall where I found it! The sort of place that ordinarily I'd never dream of entering. But I felt drawn in, and there was your hot-water bottle, in plain view. It must be the same, Charles. And don't you adore the little velvet coatee I had made for it?"

"I do adore it, Leona," Charles said, "and I adore you, my dear, sweet, romantic Leona. What ever would I do without you?"

Leona's eyes filled with tears, and she searched for an answer that would be pretty and responsive and yet light in its expression, because Charles detested any display of mawkishness, and Leona had suffered too many verbal trouncings to trust herself to speak impulsively.

"Dear Charles," she said cautiously, but for once she need not have feared. Charles was far away in memories she could not share except as a listener, and even then, although she did not know it, Charles edited himself carefully, because the truth of his background was too crowded and hearty to suit the slender, witty, cynical being he had become. They were in Leona's living room, and Charles, in narrow black slacks and saffron velvet jacket, was sitting in his favorite armchair, which was covered in a pale-blue linen. His silky gray head was inclined toward the firelight, and his sharp gray eyes glinted with thought.

Leona watched him respectfully from a chintz sofa. Charles must never be disturbed when he was musing, although he did not dislike having a witness to his silence, which was impressive, if studied. Leona, whose mind was uncomplicated, although her appearance was not, never ceased to be grateful that he allowed her the privilege of his friendship. Leona's fear of Charles, which was real, went in two directions. She was afraid of offending or disappointing him, having many times been obliterated by his scathing and horribly accurate tongue. She was also afraid of losing his favor, because his presence in the house every weekend gave her an unquestioned position among the women who lived at the Retreat, and their admiration, or envy, was the foundation on which Leona built up her importance. From the homage of her friends, Leona drew all the pleasure she got from her pretty, well-ordered house, her gracious life, and her distinguished wardrobe. Charles chose all her clothes, and she knew that without him she would never have attained her present perfection of chic and assurance. She was a tall, slender, shapeless girl with a pale face, vague features, and a head of thick, dark hair that she had always worn in a chignon low on her neck, just as she had habitually worn tweed skirts with sweaters in the daytime, and surplice dresses of dark wool at night. Always before she knew Charles, that is. Charles had changed her. He had started by taking her, on his first weekend at Herbert's Retreat, to the hairdresser, where under his intense supervision her present coiffure—a dark and cloudy halo that framed her face and shadowed it—came into being. Then he had insisted on a pale-mauve lipstick that defined her tiny mouth without emphasizing it, and, finally, he had taught her the several tricks that now gave her eyes their startled, yet languorous and enormously mysterious, gaze.

"Marie Laurencin!" he shouted gleefully that day when the miracle was accomplished and Leona sat transformed in her Early American living room. "But a sly, malicious Marie Laurencin. What fun, darling."

And they had both shrieked with laughter, Charles because he knew that Leona's near stupidity had no slyness in it and that her malice would always be, at its sharpest, a vapid reflection of his own, and Leona because she was pleased and excited.

"But your clothes, darling," he said severely when the little paroxysm of mirth had evaporated. "Your clothes are frightful. Now, let me see. No velvet, Leona—not even in a skirt. You are definitely not a velvet girl. I, on the other hand, am absolutely velvet—in moderation, of course. Velvet is immoderate stuff, Leona, and must be strictly disciplined. Always remember that, my dear. No, don't remember it. Forget it. Forget velvet altogether. Tweed, yes, but only in its thinnest, most gossamer interpretations. That thing you're wearing looks like tree-trunk bark. Thin, soft tweeds in divine colors: mauve, of course; periwinkle, of course; olive, apricot, cerise, maybe. And do bear in mind, my love, that a suit or a dress—anything you wear—is meant to illuminate you. You look positively surrounded in that thing you have on. That suit has conquered you, Leona. See the brazen independence of those grisly tweed shoulders. Why, they must be several inches above your own dear little shoulders. Clothes may be impertinent, Leona, and delightfully so, but they must never be domineering. Do run upstairs and take that thing off at once, Leona. It affronts me."

When Leona returned, in a dress that Charles also disapproved of, although not so violently, he smiled at her and said, "What an exciting day we've spent, Leona. We've turned you into a beauty. We'll spend this weekend deep in plans, and by next Friday you'll have at least two or three really splendid things. To begin with, a tremendous fireside skirt with a hem that measures at least a mile around. Now, let's see. For the skirt? Let me think."

"Taffeta?" Leona said timidly, for in those early days she was still unguarded enough to express her uninvited opinion.

Charles covered his face with his hands for a moment, and

when he spoke, it was with mighty patience. "Taffeta," he whispered. "Taffeta. Taffeta? The first refuge of the fat young wallflower, who hopes vainly that the crisp rustle of the electric-blue skirt—it's always electric blue at that age, Leona—will drive the bepimpled stag line mad with desire. And the last refuge of the thin and fading wallflower, who depends on the vulgar shimmer of this execrable fabric—baby blue in the later stages, Leona—to avert the attention of prospective partners from her worried and disappointed countenance and to encourage them to perambulate her at least once around the badly waxed surface of the country-club floor. Tafetta? Leona, how *could* you?"

"I'm very sorry, Charles," Leona said breathlessly. "I just didn't know. You see, I just don't know anything. I won't make a single other suggestion. You'll see."

"Leona," Charles said seriously, "I'm beginning to think I came into your life just in time to save it. Do you realize the sort of woman you were about to turn into? Taffeta! And that sinister tweed. Two years—no, a year—from now, it would have been too late. I could have done nothing for you. I'll unswaddle your personality, Leona, and I'll dress you as it deserves to be dressed. Oh, you may not always like what I do, my dear, but I can promise you one thing. We'll have an awful lot of fun."

"Oh, I'll love it, Charles. I'll love it!" Leona said fervently.

"You are a creature of flame and smoke, Leona. I see it all now. I won't have to think anymore. Flame red, flame yellow, flame orange, and all the magical blues and grays you see in smoke. Oh, Leona, my mind is brimming with ideas. Do fetch some paper, lots of paper, and boxes and boxes of pencils. We must start our list, beginning with the fireside skirt, which will, I think, be made of awning canvas, striped in mauve and the very clearest yellow, and quilted, and lined with thin black cotton. You're going to look divine, darling. Do you know that?"

Two weeks later, when Leona, wearing the fireside skirt for the first time, confronted Charles as he arrived from the city, he was already an indispensable part of her life.

So long ago all that was, Leona thought affectionately now, gazing at Charles's bent, musing head. Eight whole years ago. Poor Tommy—how furious it used to make him, having to drive Charles out every Friday. And George gets just as furious now, although he's not as quick to show it as poor Tommy was. George is such a fool.

Tommy Finch, Leona's first husband, who had brought her as a bride into his family's pleasant old home at Herbert's Retreat, was dead, having run his car into a tree one night. George Harkey, to whom Leona was now married, was a stolid young man who spent his days at Clancyhanger's, one of the less celebrated New York department stores, where he was credit manager. Leona had married George chiefly for the sake of the tiny riverside cottage he owned, which cut her house off from the view, so highly prized by all Retreat dwellers, of the broad waters of the Hudson. Now Leona had her view, the cottage having been demolished without delay after her marriage to George. Unfortunately, she also had George. But a husband—even a dull, embarrassing husband like George—was better for Leona's purposes than no husband at all. She ignored George as completely as possible, and, so powerful was her pride in her house and in her position at Herbert's Retreat, she had almost forgotten that George's cottage ever existed. Her living room was no longer Early American. Charles had seen to that. Now it was a witty, sophisticated, and dashing mélange of bright linens and chintzes, and reflected, as Charles said, the marriage of an informed eye with a wayward and original fancy. A wonderful room for a party, people always said when they saw it for the first time.

Leona loved to entertain, and her parties, which were always expertly planned and very successful, owed a good deal not only to Charles's advice but also to his presence. He was the only celebrated representative of the world of arts and letters who was familiar to the residents of the Retreat, and since most of them commuted daily to the comparatively unexciting circles of business and finance, they respected him immediately for his reputation, and learned to respect even more keenly his talent for withering with a look or drawing blood with a word. Charles treasured Leona's house for its comfort and for the verve with which he had endowed it. He treasured Leona for her subservience and for her appearance. "I invented you, my darling," he liked to say.

"I know, Charles. I know you did. Oh, I remember," Leona always answered, and at such times she would gaze anxiously into his eyes, as though she feared that by closing them he would dismiss her back into the nothingness from which he had rescued her.

Tired of musing, Charles suddenly sat straight up in the pale-blue armchair and laughed impishly at Leona's startled face. Leona, whose expression was not entirely spontaneous, was glad to be able to talk again.

"Charles," she said, "I have wonderful news. I just can't keep it to myself any longer. The most wonderful surprise. You'll never guess what it is. All right, Charles, I know you hate to guess. I'll tell you." She drew a deep breath and smiled tremulously. This was really too good. "Aunt Amelia is coming next weekend," she said. "Lady Ailesbury-Rhode, Charles. Can you believe it?"

"*Tommy's* aunt, wasn't she?"

"And my aunt by marriage. I always call her Aunt Amelia."

"Always? You only met her once, didn't you, when you dragged Tommy to visit her in Ottawa during your honeymoon?"

"Oh, Charles, you sound so cross. I can't help showing off just a little. She's going back to London to live, and she'll be in New

York for two weeks, staying with friends. She called me this morning and said she'd like to come here next weekend. Well, I feel quite deflated. I thought you'd be pleased. I'm planning a marvelous party, Charles. Don't you want to hear about it?"

"Of course I want to hear about it. I'm always interested in your little do's, Leona. I simply wanted to say that titles are not so uncommon as you seem to imagine, my dear. I don't think you should permit yourself to be quite so fluttery about this Lady Ailesbury-Rhode. You're being quite girlish, my love. You're flapping. It isn't altogether becoming, Leona."

"Oh, Charles, I'm sorry. Don't scold me. I'm afraid I got carried away. I'm such a fool. But do let's talk about the party. Imagine how jealous Dolly and Laura—and, oh, all of them—are going to be. Why, if you think *I'm* bad, you should hear *them*. I mean they're simply slavish about titles. Of course, I don't care a bit, one way or another, but it is fun to have the only titled relative at the Retreat. Don't you see, Charles?"

"Of course I see, Leona. Rather, I understand your excitement, although I deplore it. I rather hoped you had matured beyond that kind of behavior. But the other girls will indeed be green with envy. Pea green. You say the old lady—she is *quite* old, isn't she?—telephoned you this morning. Had she written you from Ottawa?"

"Well, no, Charles. Why should she?"

Charles smiled disagreeably. "I hope you won't find her difficult. Bridie is a very precious servant, you know. You don't want Bridie flouncing out in a rage because some titled Englishwoman steps on her toes. You'd better be on guard, my dear. House guests are a very touchy proposition, especially when they happen to be people you don't know awfully well."

"Oh, Charles," Leona said reproachfully.

There was a nervous silence.

"After all, this was Tommy's house," Leona went on, "and it's only right that his aunt should come out here for a visit, probably the only visit she'll ever have a chance to make here. And think how she'll enjoy you, Charles! She's no doubt expecting to meet a lot of dull little husbands and wives. You'll be a revelation to her."

"All right. But don't say you weren't warned. Let's talk about the party. Whom did you think of asking?"

"Everyone!" Leona cried. "Just everyone in the Retreat, Charles, darling. Cocktails, a buffet supper, the works. We'll probably go on all night. It's going to be *the* best party. It'll be the last really big party before Christmas."

Aloof, even frigid, frowning a little to show he still harbored misgivings, Charles began to plan the party for Lady Ailesbury-Rhode.

The gratitude Leona felt toward Charles blinded her to the possibility that he might be jealous, and ordinarily she would have taken his disparaging remarks about her relative as an indication that he was in a bad mood; that is to say, annoyed with her. For Leona, a consistent worshiper, could imagine and could perceive only two moods in her god. Either Charles was mercifully disposed to her or he was not. Out of favor with him, she felt painfully bewildered and could hardly endure herself while she waited for him to approve of her again, and then, when the change came and he smiled on her and called her darling caressingly instead of with sarcasm, the pain went out of her bewilderment, and she found its absence pleasant and called herself happy. Charles's pronouncements on Lady Ailesbury-Rhode shocked her, but only for a moment. Her anticipation of her coming social triumph had already swelled into an airy, lightheaded satisfaction that could be punctured by no one—not even Charles.

On the following Friday afternoon at three o'clock, Lady Ailesbury-Rhode had not yet arrived, and Leona ran upstairs to take

another last look at her guest's bedroom. There was nothing there
that she could improve, and she descended nervously into her
large, square center hall just as the doorbell rang. It seemed to
Leona later that the uniformed chauffeur was already in the hall,
and had deposited Lady Ailesbury-Rhode's suitcase there, before
Bridie answered the door, but that, she knew, was only because
she had become so confused. Lady Ailesbury-Rhode advanced on
Leona, shook her hand briskly, and demanded, in clear, high-
pitched tones, to be taken to her room. She was a short, round
woman with a complacent, bad-tempered face and discolored blue
eyes, and at the sight of her Leona felt so great an awe that she
almost curtsied. Instead, she led the way upstairs. Bridie followed
with the suitcase.

"I'm going to take a nap," Lady Ailesbury-Rhode announced.
Then, to Bridie, "I'll have my tea in here. You can bring it up at
four-thirty—and, mind you, I'll know instantly if the water is not
boiling. You don't use those disgusting tea bags, I presume."

Before Bridie could answer, Leona spoke for her: "Of course
not, Aunt Amelia. Why, Bridie would no more consider using a
tea bag than—than I would. Would you like some toast with your
tea?"

"One slice of very thin bread, lightly buttered, please. Nothing
else. Well, this all looks very nice, Leona. Charming house—I was
out here once or twice when poor Tommy's mother was alive. We
must have a long chat after I've had my nap. Now, there's just one
thing, my dear. I see you've put no hot-water bottle in my bed.
Perhaps you forgot. But I really would like it. Would you have
your maid bring it here as soon as possible? I shudder to think of
those icy sheets."

There were several hot-water bottles in Leona's house, but her
thoughts flew naturally in the direction of only one.

"Bridie will fill it at once, Aunt Amelia," she said penitently.
"How thoughtless of me. Bridie, fill the olive-green velvet bottle.

Aunt Amelia, Bridie will have it here in just a minute. How careless of me to forget it."

"An olive-green velvet bottle? My dear girl, haven't you anything else? It sounds unsafe."

"It's a rather special hot-water bottle, Aunt Amelia. I'm sure you'll approve of it when you see it."

The old lady's words of pleased surprise when she saw and felt the pretty object sent Leona into a daze of pleasure that still possessed her when Charles arrived at the house at five-thirty. Leona met him at the door. George was putting the car away.

"A drink and news before you go up to change or afterward, Charles?" she asked.

"Afterward, if you don't mind," Charles said crisply. "Did Lady Ailesbury-Rhode arrive?"

"She's in her room, taking a nap. She had tea at four-thirty, so she should be down quite soon now. Do hurry, Charles, darling, so that we can have a little moment together before she comes. I've so much to tell you, darling."

Half an hour later, Charles came downstairs and joined Leona, who was sitting in front of the living-room fire, waiting to pour the first martinis of the evening. The martinis were in a tall crystal shaker, and on the tray beside them stood two tiny glasses, frosted from their sojourn in the refrigerator. Leona's air of anxiety as she poured the martinis was genuine. Charles had been known to make an ugly scene over an inferior martini. He sat down and sipped his drink before he spoke.

"Leona," he said suddenly, setting his glass on the table beside him, "where is my hot-water bottle?"

The shock, the violent realization of what she had done, cleared Leona's brain miraculously, and in one instant she saw her dreadful mistake and began, almost calmly, to think of a way to recover herself.

"Why, it's in the kitchen, Charles," she said. "Bridie noticed a loose thread in the quilting yesterday, and she actually offered to repair it herself. Now, there's proof that she really adores you. She never offered to mend anything for me. Quite the opposite."

Charles sighed, smiled, lay back in his chair, and took his glass in his hand. "Wonderful Bridie," he said. "And wonderful Leona. This martini is perfection, darling."

"The Maitlands are coming for dinner," Leona said. "And Tom and Liza. I didn't ask anyone to come in afterward. I thought we'd better have an early night tonight. I don't want to wear Aunt Amelia out. After all, she's not so terribly young."

"Stop worrying about this evening. I'll shoo them all home myself, if I have to. Now, tell me about your aunt. What was she wearing? I want to hear all about her."

Leona wondered how she could go on talking so calmly. She was horrified at what she had done, and more horrified because of the stupid, useless lie. Why could she not have said honestly that she had lent the hot-water bottle, knowing he would understand? But he would never understand. And now I'm going to have to tell him before he goes to bed tonight, she said to herself, and how am I going to do that? Watching Charles's familiar gestures, seeing his mocking moves, his narrow, malicious smile, and his sharp eyes, which she knew could turn in an instant from tolerance to a destructive rage, she was terrified. How am I going to tell him, she wondered. How in God's name am I going to tell him?

But it never occurred to her not to give the velvet-covered hot-water bottle to Lady Ailesbury-Rhode again at bedtime.

Leona had been working as a secretary in a bank when she met Tommy Finch, and she had never really recovered from the incredulous elation she felt when he married her. Secretly, she was still as impressed by Herbert's Retreat now as she had been the day he brought her out to show her the house, just before their wedding. She had never forgotten her first sight of the Retreat, when Tommy turned in to the narrow private road that meandered from the highway in toward the river. The thirty-nine beautiful houses it connected had been built here and there at random, two hundred years ago, in a fine, thickly wooded glade that remained wild and green except for the smooth grass lawns and rims of grass that the householders claimed for themselves. Leona had never even heard of Herbert's Retreat until she met Tommy, but from the first she became fiercely attached to it. She loved the fact that it was a restricted, protected, rigidly exclusive community. During her first days there, she was timorously happy that Tommy's neighbors so easily accepted her. As she settled down, her pride stiffened. She began to take her own presence in the Retreat for granted and to feel she belonged naturally, not just by acceptance. Still, at the bottom of her heart, deeper even than her dependence on Charles, lay an irresponsible, unreasonable fear, carefully smothered most of the time, that someday some distant relative of Tommy's would turn up and take the house from her. It couldn't happen, she knew; she had her rights. But the rights, as she held and counted them, seemed slippery in her hands. She was not really very sure of herself, and Lady Ailesbury-Rhode's title only intensified her desire to get down on both knees and say to the old lady, "See? I'm the same sort of person, really, that you are. I belong here. See how naturally I fit in? See what a good job I do? Isn't the house charming? And beautifully appointed? No one else could do things so well. There can't possibly be any question that I belong here. Please say that you approve of me."

All during the familiar, laughing flurry of the Maitlands' and the Fryes' arrival, and during the decorous, excited interval that marked Lady Ailesbury-Rhode's descent into the company, and while poor George, who came downstairs very late, was fumbling at the bar for one of the warm, sweet Manhattans he loved, Leona's thoughts were with her titled guest. Even while her head seethed with distress over her predicament with Charles, she was judging the effect on the old lady of the room, the service, and the other guests. Charles was doing splendidly. Suave, humorous, attentive, he was showing quite plainly that he and Lady Ailesbury-Rhode belonged to the same world and that they were at home together. Lewis Maitland, tall, blond, and with a heavy, conventional handsomeness, spoke very little. Dolly, his thirty-year-old baby-girl wife, bubbled mutely, holding her cocktail glass carefully and casting inquisitive, delighted glances in all directions. Willowy Liza Frye was silent, too, her graceful, high-held head immobile in a halo of conscious poise. Tom Frye's plump face swelled with diffidence as he recounted some affectionate anecdotes of days spent in London as a schoolboy and as a young man. Lady Ailesbury-Rhode's clear, clipped voice dominated the cocktail hour and the dinner table, and after dinner she invited Charles to sit next to her on the sofa, where they engaged in a companionable, witty exchange of views on the deterioration of polite society since the beginning of the First World War.

Before meeting Leona, Charles had been the prey of any woman with a guest room for an extra man who would pay for his weekend in smiles and talk. Now he told a few reminiscences of those days, transfiguring the women, the houses, and the occasions until Leona was sick with the thought that she might lose him. Lady Ailesbury-Rhode's descriptions of the old, leisurely days in England entranced her hearers, and they all murmured protestingly when, at ten-thirty sharp, she stood up to go to bed. Leona offered to see her to her room, but the offer was refused, and after walking with her pleased, flushed guest to the foot of the stairs she slipped out to the kitchen, where Bridie, bathed in a blinding white light from the ceiling, was sitting on a chair that was all but invisible under her great, starched bulk. A cup of tea steamed on the table beside her. At her back, the window was uncurtained against the night. She was holding her spectacles against her eyes with one hard red hand, and reading the morning obituaries. Seeing Leona, she lowered the spectacles.

"The dinner was perfect, Bridie," Leona said. "The other maids went home, I suppose. You must be very tired."

"Ah, I'm used to that, Mrs. Harkey. You have to get used to being tired when you're in service. I was wanting to ask you—I put Her Ladyship's hot-water bottle in her bed at a quarter past ten, just like she said. Now, which hot-water bottle do you want me to leave up for Mr. Runyon? Or maybe he won't want one at all now, since the one he likes is in use."

Bridie had been waiting for this interview since the afternoon. You're on the spot now, Ma'am, she thought, watching Leona's distress. Let's see you wriggle out of this.

Leona said nothing, and Bridie continued, "He never had one before, Ma'am. Before you got him the stone one, I mean. Maybe he won't miss it."

Leona looked at her helplessly. "Frankly, Bridie," she said, laughing in the way she knew a maid would understand—not being too friendly but showing that she understood perfectly well that Bridie was human, too, and that this domestic emergency must involve them both—"Frankly, I don't know what to do. Lady Ailesbury-Rhode would have thought it odd if we'd given her an ordinary hot-water bottle tonight. You heard what she said about the velvet one this afternoon."

Bridie emitted a short, barking laugh. "If you'll excuse me for saying so, Ma'am, I think we'd all have heard about it if she hadn't found that same bottle in her bed when she went up tonight. All over it, she was, when I took the tea up in the afternoon. She had it hanging on the bedpost right beside her head. 'Where did Mrs. Harkey find it?' she asked me when I was fixing the bed tray.

Well, I told her about how you had the little cover made for it and all, but sure she knew all that. You told her yourself this afternoon. She just wanted to talk about it. It's the sort of thing an old lady would fancy, you know, Mrs. Harkey. She took a fancy to it, right enough."

"She hung it on the bedpost, Bridie?"

"Yes, Ma'am. Where she could see it. Now, about Mr. Runyon—"

"Wait a minute, Bridie. Let me think."

Trembling, Leona sat down and patted her face nervously until her glance caught her own dim, ghostly reflection in the dark glass of the window. Then she put her hands in her lap and turned to Bridie and said, "I want you to help me. No, wait a minute, this is going to be difficult. You're going to have to be very, very careful."

This is the best yet, Bridie thought as she listened to Leona's instructions. Wait till I tell the girls about this. Oh, Lord above, this is the best yet!

When Leona returned to her living room, she was greeted with a flurry of excited cries from Dolly, who was evidently determined to make up for her evening of silence. Charles was back in his own chair by the fire, and a glass of brandy stood at his elbow. He winked at Leona. Oh, how wonderful he is, Leona thought. I must not let this terrible thing come between us. In spite of their pleasure in Lady Ailesbury-Rhode, her presence had been a strain on all of them, and now they subsided easily into the comfortable, companionable idle chat that was familiar to them. Even Charles seemed less guarded than usual. Leona's mouth was dry, and she sipped her brandy, waiting till Bridie should judge the time had come to go upstairs. After half an hour, Leona heard her slow, heavy tread, and the pause as she reached the landing. Then there was no sound from upstairs. Bridie must be waiting for the chance to get into Lady Ailesbury-Rhode's room. Leona threw Charles a glance of tremulous appeal, which he misinterpreted.

He stood up and clapped his hands gaily. "All right, boys and girls. Leona is much too polite and much too fond of you all to tell you so, but she has a big day tomorrow. And I want to go to bed."

A minute later, she stood in the doorway with him, waving goodbye and nodding with frantic enthusiasm at Dolly's repeated promises to see her tomorrow, to call her up first thing, to run right around if she needed anything at all.

Charles closed the door and leaned against it, making a comical face. "My God," he said, "I thought they'd never go. You don't think I was too abrupt with them? I don't think so."

"Of course you weren't abrupt, Charles, darling."

"Dear child, you're positively tottering," Charles said. "Come and sit down, and we'll have one little nightcap before we go up. I'll get it, darling; you look all in."

Leona wondered what in the name of heaven was keeping Bridie upstairs so long. Surely the old lady was asleep by now. All Bridie had to do was walk to the bedpost, take the hot-water bottle, take it to the kitchen, refill it, and have it in Charles's bed by the time he got upstairs. I'd better keep him here a few minutes longer, she thought.

George said good night and went upstairs to bed. Charles stood on the hearthrug, gazing into the mirror that hung over Leona's mantelpiece. He swirled his brandy gently in his glass and stared at his reflection.

"Your Aunt Amelia was quite taken with me," he said. "In fact, we flirted a little, there toward the end of the evening. She must have been quite a belle in her day. What is it you women see in me, Leona?" He turned his head and glanced sidewise at her, teasing her. "Tell me, Leona, darling, what do you see in me? Let's talk about it. . . . Oh, well, if you won't talk— No, you've had your chance. I'll puzzle it out myself. Mirror, mirror— No, that's too boring. But they do say the eyes are the windows of the soul." He leaned forward, smiling into his own eyes.

A dreadful squawk reached them from upstairs.

Charles leaped back from the mirror. "What was that?" he cried.

But Leona was already halfway up the stairs. She switched the landing light on as she reached the top, and saw Bridie, hair in disarray, eyes glittering, come out of Lady Ailesbury-Rhode's bedroom with the velvet hot-water bottle hugged to her bosom. Then Lady Ailesbury-Rhode appeared, wearing a camel's hair dressing gown, slippers of maroon leather, and a hair net.

"Leona, what is the meaning of this?" she asked. "I awoke from a sound sleep to find this woman clutching my foot."

"She had it in the bed with her, Ma'am," Bridie said.

"I'm dreadfully sorry, Aunt Amelia," Leona said, and started to cry.

Lady Ailesbury-Rhode blinked with embarrassment. "Oh, don't take on so, child. I appreciate your thoughtfulness, although I don't usually need the hot-water bottle refilled in the night. Oh, Mr. Runyon, there you are. What a pickle you find us in."

Leona realized that Charles had run upstairs after her, and was standing behind her. She moved to lean against the wall.

George's bedroom door opened, and he came out, knotting his dressing gown and blinking. "Anything wrong?" he asked. "I thought I heard voices."

"A little misunderstanding, George," Lady Ailesbury-Rhode said. "Leona, dear, if your maid will take the hot-water bottle to the kitchen and refill it now, I shall be delighted. So kind of you. Good night, my dear."

She withdrew into her room and closed the door. George disappeared into his room. Bridie rustled past Leona and Charles, and went downstairs. She tried to catch Leona's eye as she went past, but Leona no longer cared for plots or signals. She felt Charles standing near her, and longed for him to speak to her, but he walked down the hall to his own room and went in, shutting the door. Leona ran after him, and, receiving no response to her knock, she opened the door and stepped into the room. Charles was sitting in his great easy chair by the window, smoking. He looked coolly at her.

"Well?" he said.

"Oh, Charles," Leona sobbed, "what can I say? How can you ever forgive me? But I was so confused when she arrived, and I wanted everything to be just right. And then I was frightened and I didn't know what to do. Please try to understand, Charles! Here we're going to have this lovely party tomorrow night, and don't let's spoil everything. I'll make it up to you, Charles, I promise I will. I promise, Charles!"

"Sorry, my dear. I won't be at your party tomorrow," Charles said.

Leona stopped crying and stared at him. "Not be at the party, Charles?"

"I shall be leaving first thing in the morning, Leona. I can call a taxi from the village to take me to the station, I presume."

Leona watched him take a puff of his cigarette. She thought of Lady Ailesbury-Rhode's domineering voice, and of Bridie's imperfectly hidden derision, and of Dolly's inane laughter, and of the olive-green velvet hot-water bottle, and of the eternity she had spent this evening, alone and frightened, trying to make everything go right for everybody.

"All right, Charles," she said wretchedly. "Bridie will call your taxi whenever you want it."

She closed the door and walked, weeping, down the hall to her own room, where she threw her clothes on the nearest chair and fell into bed, and, strangely enough, dropped off at once into a deep sleep.

When she awoke, it was ten o'clock. She had meant to be up at eight, because of the party. There was so much still to be done. And then she remembered that although Lady Ailesbury-Rhode was still under her roof, Charles had gone. Forever, Leona thought. Tears rolled down her face. I can't go through with this day, she thought. Not without him.

There was a tap at the door, and Bridie came in, bearing a tray of coffee and toast.

"When you didn't come down for breakfast, Ma'am, I thought I'd let you sleep. You looked that tired last night." She gazed avidly at Leona, who sat up and reached for her robe, which was not in its accustomed place beside her bed. "I'll get it, Ma'am," Bridie said, and took it from the closet.

Leona ignored her glance at the untidy heap of clothes on the chair. She had no more favors to ask of Bridie, and she wasn't going to stand any nonsense from her.

"Has Lady Ailesbury-Rhode had her breakfast, Bridie?" she asked, lighting a cigarette.

"She had tea in her room at eight, Mrs. Harkey. And she came down to breakfast at nine. And now she's out walking with Mr. Runyon. He's showing her around the place."

"Mr. Runyon?"

"Yes, Ma'am. He gave me a note to give you. He was all worried for fear I'd wake you up with it. Here it is. He gave it to me when I brought him up his coffee, but I promised him I wouldn't give it to you till I thought you were ready to get up."

"All right, Bridie," Leona said. "Never mind those clothes. You can pick them up later. I'll be down in an hour."

Bridie left reluctantly. As soon as the door closed, Leona tore the note open. "Dear Leona," it said, "I was joking, of course. I was punishing you a little. You have been a bad girl, you know. What a delicious day for our party. My big oak turned quite gold in the night, and threw two of his leaves right through my window and onto my table, where they are still resting, the darlings. See you at lunch. Or sooner?"

Oh, Charles, Leona thought. Oh, thank you, Charles!

Light with joy and anxious for a complete reconciliation, she dressed quickly. As she came from her bedroom into the hall, she saw that his door, at the far end, stood open. She peered in. The room was empty, and it had not yet been tidied. She walked to the writing desk and touched the oak leaves gently. Dear Charles . . . She looked at the chair in which he had sat last night, so hurt, so cruel, and so unforgiving. Dear Charles, she thought gratefully, I'll make amends somehow. She glanced at his pier glass and saw herself wearing a dress of thin red wool, artfully fitted to her long figure. The clear, bright color made her skin glow and deepened the dark haze of her hair. A flame, she thought. Dear, dear Charles. She rested her elbow on his white mantelpiece and thought of him. Then, in surprise, she saw that his fireplace was scattered with ashes, although the logs had not been charred and the kindling under them was whole. She reached down. Charles had been burning paper, but not enough to start a blaze. A letter or something, she thought idly, and would have turned away, but her eye was caught by a tiny white ball that had rolled away from the grate and was caught by the floor boards. She picked it up and smoothed it out. "Dearest Leona," she read. "Of course you have realized by now that I was jesting. I was, you know. I was hurt and I tried to hurt you. I'll be here for the party. And I'll be here next weekend and next weekend and next weekend. What times we are going to have together. And do you know, that splendid oak outside my window (the one I call *my* oak, darling) blazed" . . .

The note was unfinished. Leona put it in her pocket and looked at the ashes in the grate. There must have been several notes. She grew thoughtful. Why, Charles was *anxious* to stay. He was just as anxious to stay as she was to have him here.

Before leaving the room, she cast one last glance around it. It was, after all, a very nice room. It was an enchanting room. Any man would be glad to have such a room.

That night, Leona gave the best party she had ever given. Everyone said so. Lady Ailesbury-Rhode was charming, and Charles Runyon was in top form. Leona looked radiant, in a clinging dress of woodsmoke-blue silk that left her sloping white shoulders bare. She was really a marvelous hostess. She seemed to be everywhere at once, and yet she never seemed worried or abstracted. Her confidence was superb, and as she wandered, smiling, from group to group, and from room to room, the eyes of her friends followed her with admiration and envy. Curiously enough, no one noticed that she did not exchange one word with Charles all evening. Only Charles noticed.

This was a new game for Leona, and she loved it. She could feel Charles's tension as she moved lightly through the rooms. She knew that he was watching her, however entertained and entertaining he might seem to the others. She knew it by the turn of his head as she came near his chair, which she passed quickly, laughing to someone at the far side of the room. She knew it by the set of his back as he stood talking near the buffet table and heard her voice calling to someone at his side. She had first felt her power as they met in the living room before lunch, and she challenged his amused, ironical gaze with an amused, ironical gaze of her own, and saw his puzzled frown. How long, Leona thought, pushing open a window to let the cold night air into the loud, warm rooms—how long will I punish him? Will I forgive him tonight, when they've all gone home and he wants that last little nightcap by the fire? Or will I go straight to bed and let him spend the night wondering? I might forgive him before lunch tomorrow. Or wait until Aunt Amelia leaves. That might be best—to wait till she leaves. He'll really be worried by then. But I would like to talk over the party tonight. Oh, well, I have hours yet before they go. And she closed the window (a little of that air was enough) and wandered idly toward the spot where Charles stood, the center of a delighted group, fascinating everyone, as always. Everyone but me, Leona thought, and ignored his hopeful eyes and passed casually by to watch for another opportunity to ignore him. Leona thought she had never had such fun in her life as she was having ignoring Charles.

The Divine Fireplace

*T*hirty miles above New York, on the east bank of the Hudson River, there is a green, shadowy, densely wooded glade known as Herbert's Retreat. In the glade, still standing in it, many of them after two hundred years, are thirty-nine elegant white houses. A single narrow road, capricious, twisting, and unpredictable, meanders through the dark labyrinth of trees to make the only visible link between the houses, which are isolated and almost hidden, each one from the next. The road is strictly private, in keeping with the spirit of the Retreat, which is solemn, exclusive, and shaped by restrictions that are as steely as they are vague. The most important fact, not vague at all, about Herbert's Retreat is that only the right people live there.

One rainy Sunday morning early in April, an olive-green bus, very smart, with "Herbert's Retreat" printed in small capitals on its door, made its way slowly through the Retreat, stopping at every house, and from each doorway, in turn, a female figure, wearing a flowered hat and sheltered under a large umbrella, flew forward and climbed aboard. The Irish maids were going to Mass in town, eleven miles away. The maids looked forward to these Sunday-morning rides, which gave them the chance of a great gossip. And the ride gave them a chance to escape from the monotony of their uniforms. Their positive, coaxing voices rose and fell, but rose, mostly, in an orgy of sympathy, astonishment, indignation, furious satisfaction, and derision. Not one of them was calm, or thinking about saying her prayers, and every time the bus stopped they all peered eagerly through the streaming windows to see who was getting in next, as if they didn't know.

The Tillbrights—wild Harry Tillbright and his pretty second wife—owned the last house the bus stopped at before it swung out onto the public highway, so Stasia, the Tillbrights' maid, was the last to be picked up. This Sunday, as Stasia, dressed and ready, with her gloves on and her prayer book in her hand, waited in the Tillbrights' hall, she was in a painful state of mind, half wishing the bus would hurry and half wishing it wouldn't come at all. She wanted to be in her seat telling the girls about all that had gone on in her house last night, and at the same time she hated to leave, for fear something further would happen while she was away. She didn't want to miss one minute of this day, which was going to be about the worst the Tillbrights had ever known. It was terrible to Stasia to think she might miss the fearful, glorious moment when their two lady guests started to wake up and realize the condition they were in. Not to speak of the condition the house, the adored, cherished house, was in. And all their own fault. There will be murder here today, Stasia thought happily. No, no, I'm wrong, she thought—not murder today; the murder was last night. Today is when they pay the price. She could have danced with excitement, except that she was suffocating with it. She wanted to howl with laughter, but she dared not make a sound, for fear of rousing them too soon. What pleasure it would have been to run upstairs and gallop in and out of their bedrooms, shouting "Haw haw haw," giving them worse headaches than they already had. To charge into Mr. and Mrs. Tillbright's room and bend right down over the pillows they shared and roar into their defenseless ears, "Come on down and see what you did to your grand kitchen! And your living room! Wait till you see the carpet in the living room!" To keep after them, tormenting them till they howled for mercy. Except that they won't have the strength to howl this morning, Stasia thought. It was too good a story to believe, almost; too rich. The girls would be carried away. If I get any more carried away than I am, thought Stasia, I won't be able to talk at all.

To calm herself, she admired her reflection in the mirror on the wall. The beige gabardine suit was a nice fit. The copper-colored straw hat was nearly a match for her bushy hair, and the crimson poppies she had tacked around the crown did away with any danger of sameness. Her slippery nylon gloves were about the same green as the stems of the poppies, and she had a shiny green plastic bag hanging from her arm, and matching green sandals with delicate straps that wound twice around her bony ankles.

Stasia was forty-seven, with a pointed white face and very large ears. Somebody had once complimented her on her merry Irish eyes, and she had endeavored to live up to the remark ever since, rolling her eyes enthusiastically until it became a habit, and showing that she, at any rate, knew what was going on in the room and behind the scenes, even when there was nothing going on at all. Stasia's merry, knowing looks frightened some of her employers and irritated others. Stasia didn't care. "Some people have no sense of humor," she would say when she lost a job. She always got very good references, and then, too, as she said herself, she had the real Irish sense of humor, and there were very few could stand up against it. Stasia was famous for her sense of humor, which she brandished like a tomahawk. And she was a great storyteller. All the maids were agreed on that. Nobody could tell a story like Stasia. And the funny faces she made. Stasia was a scream.

Stasia didn't exactly tire of admiring herself in the mirror, but the silence in the house began to get on her nerves. Still no sound from upstairs, but they might start stirring around at any minute. Stasia tiptoed across the hall and, for the eighth time that morning, she opened the living-room door a crack and peered in. There on the sofa, stretched out flat with her shoes still on her feet, lay Miss Phoebe Carter, in sleep so deep that it might have been coma. Poor, pretty, high-voiced Miss Carter, so snippy and sure of herself when she first waltzed into the house last night on Mr. Tillbright's arm, so to speak. Stasia's smile as she regarded Miss Carter was not entirely without sympathy. Uninvited guests must expect what they get, of course, but this was a hard lesson. That rustly cocktail dress isn't going to be worth much when you get up off that sofa, Stasia thought, and removed her gaze to the steak that lay on the carpet, some distance from the fireplace. It was a huge steak, and thick, and it had been juicy. The carpet showed darkly how full of juice the steak had been before being rudely tumbled from its platter, which lay, right side up, well within the island of grease, which seemed to Stasia to have spread since the last time she looked. And how could I have gone in there to start cleaning up, with the young lady asleep on the sofa there, she thought, rehearsing for Mrs. Tillbright. Pretty, sweet, fluffy Mrs. Tillbright, she wouldn't be feeling so pleased with herself this morning. Stasia closed the door carefully, shutting Miss Carter in, saving her, with any luck, until the rest of them roused themselves to come downstairs and find her.

The bus should be here now, even allowing for a minute or so's delay on account of the rain. Stasia opened the front door and peered out. No sign of the bus, and the rain was coming down heavier. A pity about the rain. The old umbrella would be a nuisance. She turned back into the hall and saw Mr. Tillbright on the stairs. The shock of seeing him suddenly like that made Stasia think she was perhaps imagining things. But it was Mr. Tillbright, all right, dressed in the same pin-stripe suit he had worn to town yesterday, but without a tie. He was carrying his shoes in his hand, and bringing himself downstairs very tenderly, one step at a time. He hadn't seen Stasia.

"Good morning, Mr. Tillbright," Stasia said cheerily. "Isn't it a terrible day?"

Mr. Tillbright did not speak until he was safely on the hall floor.

"I have to get back to town," he said then. "Very urgent. Call just came through. Tell Mrs. Tillbright, will you? I'll stay in town overnight. Tell her I'll call her from the hotel."

"And what hotel will I say?" Stasia asked.

"I said *I'll* call *her*," Mr. Tillbright snarled.

Trying to run away, eh, Stasia thought, and she watched him fumble with the quaint little wall cupboard in which the car keys were kept. She said nothing, and after a minute or so he spoke, without turning around to look at her. No manners, none of them have any manners, Stasia thought good-humoredly.

"Have you any idea where the keys of my car might be?" he asked.

"Well, don't you remember, Mr. Tillbright? Mrs. Tillbright collected up all the car keys last night and said she was going to put them in a safe place. Your car's keys and her car's keys, and I believe she got hold of Mrs. Lamb's car's keys. While she was at it, you know. She thought all the keys ought to be together, she said. She said as long as none of you were going out last night, the keys ought to be out of harm's way. Of course she didn't know then that you'd be having to go to the office so early on a Sunday morning."

Mr. Tillbright said, "Since you know so much, perhaps you know where Mrs. Tillbright put the keys."

"I don't know where she put them," Stasia responded, with dignity, "but I think they should be someplace in the bedroom.

She was going to the bedroom when I saw her with them in her hand."

Mr. Tillbright sat down suddenly on the bottom step of the stairs. "I've simply got to get out of this house today," he said, into his long, well-kept hands. "I've got to get in to town."

He stood up as suddenly as he had sat down, and turned around and started back up the stairs. He was still in his stocking feet. Well, you're in a bad way, all right, Stasia said to herself, and heard the bus pull up outside.

She clambered into the bus backward and bent, because she was trying to shut her umbrella and save her hat and get her heels on solid board all at the same time. She plumped herself down beside Delia Murphy, who smiled and nodded, under a platter of blue cornflowers.

"Delia, Delia," said Stasia, "do you know what happened?"

"What happened, Stasia?" Delia asked, and the other maids stopped talking for the moment and began to listen, on the chance that Stasia had something worth hearing.

"Oh, you'll never in your life guess what that crowd did last night!" Stasia said, all of a sudden unwilling to part with her precious story. But she had to go on. Thirty-eight Irish noses were pointed at her in implacable demand. There was no stopping now. With a shrill crow of joy, Stasia plunged.

"They uncovered a fireplace in the kitchen!" she cried. "A bricked-up fireplace. Behind the stove. Behind the *stove*. They tore out the stove, and there's a hole as big as a coffin in the wall, with bricks falling out of it, and wires hanging out of it, miles of wires—you never saw the like of it. And the floor all covered with dirt and dust and bits of plaster and lumps of mortar. If a bomb had hit it, it couldn't look worse."

The maids exchanged glances of incredulous pleasure. They never ceased to marvel at the interest their employers took in their old houses and their old windows and walls and floorboards and doors and cupboards, and in their old fireplaces, of which there could never be too many, apparently, dirty and troublesome as they were, and unnecessary, too, with the central heating.

"Are they out of their minds, or what," Delia asked, "destroying the kitchen like that?"

Stasia looked mischievous. "Didn't Mrs. Tillbright find out that his first wife, the first Mrs. Tillbright, had the fireplace in the kitchen blocked up, and he never said a word to *her* about it when *she* came to move in, and when she found out about it last night she flew into a rage and insisted that he tear out the side of the kitchen. 'Me fireplace!' she kept screeching. 'I want me fireplace in me kitchen and I want it now, do you hear me, *now.*'"

"Of course they were—having something to drink?" said Alice Flaherty, leaning forward in her seat, which was behind Stasia's.

"Drinking like horses," Stasia said. "They'd been at it all day, too. Well, I know Mrs. Tillbright and that Mrs. Lamb had been at it from five o'clock on, because I was there in the house with them. Mr. Tillbright and this Miss Carter didn't turn up till seven, and a child could see they'd had a few—more than a few—by the look of them."

"You're driving us mad, Stasia," Delia said. "Will you go back and begin at the beginning? How did Mrs. Tillbright find out about the fireplace being in the kitchen? *He* didn't tell her, did he?"

"Not *he,*" Stasia said. "It all started when Mr. Tillbright brought this Miss Carter home for dinner—walked into the house with her, bold as brass, and not after telephoning to say could she come or anything. Well, Mrs. Tillbright was as mad as a hatter. She had invited this Mrs. Lamb out to spend the night, Saturday night, last night, and Mr. Tillbright knew that. Mrs. Tillbright would have been provoked enough if she'd been there by herself when he landed in with the girl, but to have this Mrs. Lamb see it, Mrs. Tillbright was fit to be tied. She doesn't really *like* Mrs. Lamb. It seems, or so I gather, Mrs. Lamb used to be a great *friend* of Mr. Tillbright. I don't know when. Since this one married him, for all I know. Anyway, Mrs. Lamb knew Mr. Tillbright's first wife. And Mrs. Tillbright only invited her out for the weekend to show her all the changes she'd made in the house, and what a fine place it is now, and all, and how happy herself and Mr. Tillbright are together. Oh, Lord—" Stasia was overcome with amusement. "How happy they are, and all!" she cried, and the maids nodded and laughed along with her.

"This Mrs. Lamb just got a divorce, you see," Stasia went on, in a lower voice, "and Mrs. Tillbright said to him, 'Oh, we must have poor dear Norma out for the weekend and cheer her up.' Cheer her up, is it, I thought to meself. Of course, what she was thinking was, Kill two birds with the one stone, have her out here and show off in front of her, and at the same time discourage him from any notion he might have of cheering Mrs. Lamb up on his own. Well, Mrs. Lamb arrived out yesterday evening around five, in this little bright-blue convertible, the sort of car a kid would have, but certainly not at all suitable for a woman her age. 'A parting gift from Leo, darling,' she says, patting the car, and she and Mrs. Tillbright give each other a kiss.

" 'Darling Norma,' says Mrs. Tillbright, 'how does it feel to be free?' 'Divine, simply heaven, so it is,' says Mrs. Lamb. 'You must try it sometime, Debbie. But then you and Harry are so comfy together, aren't you, dear? So—well, domesticated. I do hope you don't find it dull.' 'Oh no, we don't find it dull at all,' Mrs. Tillbright says, very soft, with one of them little secret smiles. Mrs. Lamb gave her a *look,* and I gave a little secret smile meself, thinking about the racket they kicked up the other night—Wednesday night it was—over Mr. Tillbright leaving his clothes strewn all over the bedroom and the bathroom, awful untidy habits he has, I can't blame her.

"Well, the next thing, Mrs. Lamb flounces into the house as if she owns it. You can see that every stitch she has on her is brand-new, just bought for the weekend—a little pointed yellow hat and pointed yellow bootees, and she's no spring chicken, you know.

"Well, she stood stock-still in the hall. 'Where's Harry?' she says. Mrs. Tillbright gives a nasty little laugh. 'Don't sound so disappointed, darling,' she says. 'Harry'll be here, don't worry. He had to run into town to see a client.' 'On a Saturday?' says Mrs. Lamb. 'That's not the Harry I knew. Or is it? Dear Harry. He's such a darling. But so unreliable, isn't he? You must be careful not to hold him on too tight a rein, Debbie darling. Just be patient. He'll grow up. It just takes some men longer than others, that's all.' 'Let's go upstairs, shall we?' says Mrs. Tillbright. 'I want to show you your room,' she says.

"Up the stairs we go, me bringing up the rear and carrying the bag Mrs. Lamb had brought along, heavy as lead it was. 'Oh, our bedroom door is open,' says Mrs. Tillbright when she got to the top of the stairs, and she goes across the landing and stands looking into her own bedroom as if she'd never set eyes on it before. And how else would it be but open, I thought, and you breaking your neck upstairs to open it when you heard the car coming.

" 'Wouldn't you like to see our little nest, darling?' she says, all quaint like. 'Harry adores this view,' she says, running into the room and across to the window. 'Come see,' she says, dragging Mrs. Lamb after her by main force. 'We had the bed made special,' she says. 'And this is Harry's very own armchair,' she says, 'for, you know, I'm dreadfully lazy. I'm ashamed to say it, but I am. And best of anything in the world I like to lie in bed on Sunday morning,' she says, shy, you know. 'And Harry must keep me company at breakfast, he won't have it any other way. I just have a cup of black coffee without sugar,' she says, 'and Stasia brings his big breakfast up, kippers or bacon and eggs, finnan haddie, lamb chops, whatever he fancies—Stasia and I like to pamper him a little, he always had such a barren sort of life, poor baby—and he sits there in his chair by the window and glances at the paper and reads me little bits out of it. And we chat—oh, you know,' she says. 'Sometimes we don't even get downstairs till lunchtime,' she says. 'It's scandalous, really.' And she gives a great laugh.

"Indeed so, I thought. That's the first I ever heard of any of that, and the last, I hope. Breakfast in bed, indeed! And I went off down the hall and left the bag, and then I went downstairs, and I filled the ice bucket and put it in the living room, and then *she* came down, all smiles.

" 'Will you be wanting tea, Mrs. Tillbright?' I asked her. 'Ooh, I don't know, Stasia,' she says. 'I'll let you know. You left ice, didn't you? That's all right, then. Mr. Tillbright will be home at six sharp, and when you hear him come in, bring up more ice, will you?' I said I would, and I went off down to the kitchen, and I heard Mrs. Lamb coming down the stairs and going into the living room, and then I heard no more out of them, and it got to be six, and it got to be seven, and at half past seven didn't I hear His Lordship's voice in the hall. So I got out the fresh ice and I hurried along to see what was what. No sign of him, he'd gone upstairs, but his girlfriend was there, large as life, making herself at home. Miss Carter, she is, and a bold-looking piece of work if I ever saw one. Not more than twenty-two or so, I'd say, and all done up in a tight cocktail dress that showed her chest.

"Over she goes and stands in front of the fire. 'Mmm,' she says. 'Delicious! Harry and I nearly froze in that open car. I'm afraid I'm not dressed for the *country*,' she says, and she looks at what the other two have on, and you can see she's right satisfied with herself. Mrs. Lamb has blossomed out in a pair of light-gray velveteen slacks and a yellow pullover like a boy's pullover, and Mrs. Till-bright is wearing the same as she was wearing before—that great big skirt she has, her fireside skirt, she calls it, and a little white baby blouse. That Miss Carter doesn't know when to shut up, or she doesn't want to shut up, I don't know which. 'I'd let myself go terribly if I lived in the country,' she says, looking at the other two. 'I don't wonder that people go to pieces out here. I mean the whole thing is to keep warm, isn't it? It must be so demoralizing—for women, especially.' 'I don't live in the country,' Mrs. Lamb says, very sharp altogether. 'Oh, I know that,' says Miss Carter. 'Even if Harry hadn't told me all about you on the way up here, I'd know by your clothes. They have that wonderfully *considered* look, as though you'd really thought about what would look best on you. I bet I know why you chose that particular pullover,' she says, with a big nod. 'Why did I choose it, pray tell?' says Mrs. Lamb, getting all red.

"Mrs. Tillbright speaks up, trying to be a hostess. 'I hope you have a ride back to the city tonight,' she says to Miss Carter. 'I hope Mr. Tillbright—Harry—explained to you that Mrs. Lamb is stay-ing with us, and we have only one guest room.' Miss Carter gives a great squawk, as if she had a pain. 'Heavens, Mrs. Tillbright!' she says. 'It's too sweet of you, but you know, I wouldn't spend a night in the country to save my life. I can't *stand* the country! I simply can't imagine how you live out here, although I think your house is just as sweet as can be. I mean I can see you've worked over it. Goodness, no, I'm not staying. I have to be at a party at eleven, for one thing. Harry and I were having a drink, and he suggested that I run out here for dinner and see the house, and all. And of course I jumped at the chance to meet you and see where Harry lives. He's told me so much about it I feel as though I knew every room. What did you decide about the new furniture for the patio? Harry says you want rough, woodsy stuff, but I think wrought iron has so much more chic, don't you?'

" 'Where the hell *is* Harry?' says Mrs. Lamb, and just at that exact moment Mr. Tillbright comes running down the stairs, two at a time, with a big white woolen shirt on him and a red scarf tucked in at the neck. Miss Carter lets out another squawk. 'Harry,' she shouts, 'you look scrumptious!' And she looks at Mrs. Tillbright. 'If you don't get that outfit copied,' she says, 'I will. Harry darling, you look so chic. Honestly, men have *the* most wonderful clothes. If all the men out here dress like that, I think I'll take your sweet wife up on her weekend invitation.' 'Oh, that would be fine, fine,' says Harry, and you can see he's beginning to wonder what he's got himself into. 'Not this weekend, darling,' Mrs. Tillbright says to him. 'We're full up this weekend. And in any case, Miss Carter says she has to get back to town to some party. I hope you've arranged a ride for her.' 'Somebody's bound to be driving in,' Harry says, and makes himself a drink and one for Miss Carter. 'Who?' says Mrs. Tillbright. 'I don't know of anyone who's driving in. The weekend people won't be leaving till tomorrow or Monday. I don't know of anyone who's driving in tonight who would be willing to take Miss Carter.' 'Oh, hell,' says Mr. Tillbright, 'I'll drive her in myself, get her to her party, and be back before you can count to a hundred. Nothing to it.' 'Oh, grand,' says Miss Carter. 'That's settled then.' 'It's not settled at all,' says Mrs. Tillbright. 'Stasia, what on earth do you want?'

" 'I wanted to know what time you wanted the dinner, Ma'am,' I said, all quiet and polite—which she was *not* being. 'It's all ready, Ma'am, only to put on the steak.' 'Steak!' says Miss Carter. 'Oh, goody, I'm starved!'

" 'Oh, we're not in a hurry,' says Mrs. Tillbright. 'Take your time, Stasia.' 'Harry, aren't you going to take me down to see your

kitchen?' says Miss Carter. 'I hear you have the most divine old-
fashioned kitchen,' she says then, to Mrs. Tillbright. 'Take the little
girl to see the kitchen, Harry,' says Mrs. Tillbright, 'But see that
she doesn't burn her little fingers,' says Mrs. Lamb. 'You should
know about burnt fingers, Norma dear,' says Mrs. Tillbright, very
nasty. 'Oh, poor sweet!' says Mrs. Lamb. 'It's just the same old
dreary story, isn't it? And you put up such a brave front all evening,
positively gallant. I do admire you so, dear.' 'Oh, cut it out, you
two,' says Mr. Tillbright. 'Mind your own business,' says Mrs. Tillbright. 'Your pants are too tight, Norma,' she says. 'You look perfectly awful, and the reason is you are awful. Not interesting
awful,' she says, 'just dreary, sad, pathetic awful. Do you know
what? I feel sorry for you.' And she gives a great giggle.

"Mr. Tillbright is getting to look very sorry for himself. 'Debbie,' he says, 'why don't you go upstairs and lie down a while? Get
a little rest, why don't you?' 'Some women just cannot drink,' says
Mrs. Lamb, and tosses off her own martini, trying to hold in her
stomach at the same time.

"'I'll let you know when to put the steak on, Stasia,' says Mrs.
Tillbright, and I march off to the kitchen, wondering what'll happen next, since it's plain they're all well over the edge. Well, they
all come after me, Mr. Tillbright and Miss Carter and the other
two. Miss Carter is singing a little song, whispering like, and Mrs.
Lamb said, 'Your kitchen used to be divine, Harry. We had such
happy times here in the old days, you and Berenice and I. I hope
you haven't changed it much.'

"'Well, it looks just like any other kitchen,' says Miss Carter,
when they're inside the door. 'I mean it's bigger, and there are the
beams in the ceiling and all, but it's not really so terribly unusual, is
it?' 'What did you expect—a wishing well?' says Mrs. Lamb.
'Well, a fireplace, anyway,' said Miss Carter. 'I mean the whole
point of having a kitchen in the country is that you have a fire-

place, isn't it? I mean why live in the country at all when you can live in the city.' 'But, Harry, where is the fireplace?' says Mrs. Lamb, all astonished. 'Let's get back to the drinks and leave Stasia in peace,' says Mr. Tillbright, very sudden and nervous. 'But, Harry, tell me,' says Mrs. Lamb, 'what *happened* to the fireplace? There used to be a divine fireplace right there,' she says to Mrs. Tillbright. 'Didn't Harry even tell you it was there? Harry, you *are* naughty.' 'You're out of your mind, Norma,' says Harry. 'You're thinking of some of the other kitchens around here. Some of them have fireplaces. Come on, let's go have a drink. What are we standing here for?' 'Oh, I suppose you and Berenice had it bricked up, Harry,' Mrs. Lamb said, 'but I do think it was mean of you not to tell Debbie about it. You know how she adores fireplaces.'

" 'Harry,' says Mrs. Tillbright, 'if there's a fireplace there, I want it.' 'Damn it all,' says Mr. Tillbright, 'I had it bricked up—Berenice and I had to have it bricked up, because we needed that wall for space when we were breaking that door through to the patio. Stop being a silly little fool, Debbie.' 'But it used to be so cozy, Harry,' says Mrs. Lamb. 'Silly to have a kitchen without a fireplace,' says Miss Carter.

" 'Harry,' says Mrs. Tillbright, 'I want that fireplace, and I want it now.' 'Oh, come on, now, Debbie,' he says. 'Come on yourself,' she says. 'Get moving. Where is it?' 'Now, honey,' he says, 'let's all go get a nice fresh martini and talk it over.' 'I'm not moving out of this spot,' she says. 'All right,' he says, 'I'll bring the drinks down here.' And he goes off, and when he comes back with the martini shaker, she's got the hammer and she's tapping all along the wall, above the stove and the sink and all.

" 'Oh, for God's sake, Debbie,' he says, 'will you stop it. It's behind the stove, if you want to know.' 'That's what I thought,' says Mrs. Lamb. Miss Carter sat down by the kitchen table and started to cry. 'Oh,' she says, 'men are so awful! Imagine hiding the fireplace. Harry, how could you be so mean to your dear sweet little wife?' 'Move the stove, Harry,' says Mrs. Tillbright. 'I'll do nothing of the sort,' he says. 'All right, then, I'll move it,' she says. 'I'd better turn the oven off, so,' I said, and I went over and turned it off and took off the kettle I always keep hot there. Mrs. Tillbright goes over and starts pushing and pulling, trying to move the stove.

"Miss Carter gave another of her screeches. 'Harry,' she says, 'she'll strain herself trying to move that thing. You do it for her.' 'Oh, don't you do it, Harry,' says Mrs. Lamb. 'You know what might happen. Harry isn't as strong as he looks,' she says to Miss Carter. Well, Mr. Tillbright gave Mrs. Lamb a look, I can tell you.

"'I'm going to have another drink,' he says, and they all have a drink—Miss Carter and Mrs. Lamb all excited, and Mrs. Tillbright just boiling with temper.

"'I hope you're not going to regret this, Debbie,' says Mr. Tillbright when he's finished his drink, but by that time he doesn't care much about anything. He goes over and gives the stove a wrench, and it comes away and stands lopsided and rocking—you know those old crooked floors, one leg of the stove had been made short to fit against the wall. And there's a terrible clatter from inside the oven.

"'Aw, Mr. Tillbright,' I said, 'I wish you'd told me you were going to do that, and I could have taken the dinner out.' He grabbed open the door, and the eggplant casserole and the cherry pie and all that I was keeping hot all come tumbling out, and the good dinner plates and the little bit of chicken I was keeping for meself—I was mortified that they saw it. All that good food.

"'Well, there goes your dinner,' says Mr. Tillbright to Mrs. Tillbright. 'Oh, damn the dinner,' she says. 'Let's get the wall opened up.'

"Well, girls, they got every sharp thing in the house—chisels and screwdrivers and shears, all the carpentry stuff out of the basement, even the good poker out of the living room—and they began to loosen the bricks. Well, that's all, except a bit of the ceiling came down—not very much. And every bit of electricity in the house is dead, of course, and who can put it back together again I don't know, or what will be done. When the hole was big enough to suit them, they took the steak and carried it up to the living room, holding it up over their heads as if it was a football player. They said they were going to cook it in the fireplace—"

"All the electricity gone," said big Bridie, the bully, sprawled in her usual seat, which ran all the way across the back of the bus.

"Oh, they don't know that yet," Stasia said.

"Wait till he starts to shave himself," Delia said.

"He won't even be able to take a bath," Stasia said. "None of them will. The pump works by electricity."

"The radio!" Molly Ronan said, with horror.

"And the dishwasher," said Josie, the youngest maid.

"And the toaster and the rotisserie and the—everything," Delia said. "And with no water at all in the house."

"Not to mention the deep freeze," Bridie said.

The deep freeze. They had all forgotten the deep freeze.

"Trust you to think of that, Bridie," Stasia said, awed.

"All that reindeer meat," Bridie said. "All the reindeer meat, all gone, unless they finish it up today."

"And the pheasants, and all," Lily Rooney said. "Remember how pleased they all were, coming back with their pheasants and their trout and their salmon, and all."

"But the deer meat," Stasia said pleasurably. "Mr. Tillbright was so set up with that little red hunting hat of his."

"Oh, they're all great hunters," Delia said. "A rabbit would put the fear of God into any one of them, if they weren't carrying their gun."

"Aw, Lord, I forgot to tell you about the steak on the rug!" Stasia cried, seeing that the bus was stopping in front of the church. "And Mrs. Tillbright hiding the car keys, and Mr. Tillbright trying to sneak out this morning."

"We're late," Delia said. "The bell has stopped ringing. We'll hear it all on the way back, Stasia."

"And Miss Carter on the sofa," Stasia wailed. "I forgot all the best parts."

She would never get their attention all the way back again. They'd be crowding around and chattering and interrupting her, getting the story all wrong.

The Servants' Dance

*O*n Saturday morning, Charles Runyon awoke in a mood of rapturous gaiety. This day, this evening, this weekend, promised—no, guaranteed—a triumph so complete, both in secret and in public, that it must surely, Charles felt, become one of the succession of platforms that marked his progress through life, each platform raising him higher, the better to survey the world and the men and women in it. My stage and my actors, he said to himself; my arena. Charles was a literary gentleman whose main interest was the theater. He lived alone in a single room in an old and famous hotel in the Murray Hill district. He never entertained, having, as he laughingly explained, no facilities for doing so, but he went out a great deal, and had a reputation, undefined but definite, as a wit and an epigrammatist. His weekends were spent at Herbert's Retreat, thirty miles from New York on the east side of the Hudson, and always at Leona Harkey's, where one bedroom was sacred to him.

Now, lying in his narrow, canopied four-poster there, he stretched his stringy little arms and his long stringy neck, and yawned. Then he got out of bed, pattered over to his writing table, and snatched up a large notebook, in which, the night before, as every night, he had recorded his impressions of the evening. The notes had been very enjoyable to write. They were copious and would be memorable. Edward Tarnac, Charles's old enemy, the one member of this river community who had ever been able to get under his skin, had returned to the Retreat after five years' absence, and he had returned a ruined man. Ruined at thirty-eight, Charles thought, with a tender side glance for his own unmarred years, which numbered fifty-four.

He pulled open the curtains. Leona's lawn, starting immediately beneath this window, slanted smoothly down to the river's edge, two hundred yards away. It was a lovely view, a sunny day, a glorious prospect, and still only ten o'clock in the morning. Charles rang for his café au lait and sat down in the great chintz-covered armchair that Leona had thoughtfully placed near the window but not so near that Charles, thinking or reading, could be seen from the garden. He still had his notebook in his hand, and he glanced at a passage here and there.

Bridie (Charles liked to refer to her as "that splendid Irishwoman of Leona's") clumped in with the tray. The glare of pure hatred that was her characteristic expression descended in full force on Charles's silky gray head, but he was indifferent and she was silent, respectfully handing him his orange juice, pouring his coffee and his hot milk (Sye-mull-tane-eusssly, Bridie, she said to herself, the coffee and the milk sye-mull-tane-eusssly), and departing.

Sipping his coffee, he began to read over his notes, but very soon he set both coffee and notes aside and lay back in his chair, to savor—not the sweetness of this present triumph, because, after all, he had that now, but the bitterness of the long grudge he had cherished against Edward Tarnac. The grudge was partly inexplicable to him, and this intensified it. Edward had been well-to-do, free, charming, happy, handsome, attractive, and athletic, but still, when one came right down to it, how many did not have those qualities? It was the literate, cultured, aloof fellows like himself, the true gentlemen, who were the exception. Indeed, it was curious that Edward had always succeeded so in irritating him, at times beyond endurance.

And then Tarnac had always been so self-confident, so sure that everybody liked him. Why, quite often he had even spoken to Charles as a friend, chatted with him as a friend, completely forgetting the times he had slighted Charles, the gibes, the smart little mockeries that rankled in Charles's mind and glowed there, polished daily until they had the brilliance of jewels. No more, though. This weekend would wipe all that out. Last night was almost enough. Oh, Charles thought, the satisfaction of seeing someone brought down who has been riding high! Well, Tarnac had been thoroughly humiliated, somewhere, somehow, since leaving the Retreat. That much was obvious. The apologetic air of him now, where once he had been so—cocky was the only word for what he had been. He no longer took it for granted that people liked him. Quite the other way around now. Odd, to see him and Lewis Maitland together now. They were bosom friends in the old days, and so much alike that they might have been brothers, with Edward always shining just a little the brighter. Edward had always patronized Lewis—unconsciously, perhaps, but Lewis had felt it. Charles had seen to that. Now the shoe was on the other foot.

Oh, I'm not the only one enjoying this weekend, Charles thought. Whether Lewis knew it or not, he must have been waiting for the opportunity for years. And then to run into Edward on the street like that was sheer good luck. And apparently Edward was delighted to come up for the weekend. Thinking we'd all be glad to see him. The appalling nerve some people have.

I would never have done that, Charles thought, smiling a grim, happy little smile. I would never have come back. As long as he stayed away, we couldn't be sure what had become of him, no matter what reports we heard. But now! It's an object lesson, he thought, and, suddenly anxious for talk, for the delicious rehashing of last night's scene, he bounded to his feet, dashed into his shower, and emerged, clean and shiny, to select from his wardrobe a pair of brown Bermuda shorts, beautifully cut, and a beige wool shirt. He buttoned the cuffs of the shirt, knotted a beige-and-brown silk scarf carefully around his neck, put on a pair of knee-length beige socks and brown sandals, and, opening a door in the side wall of his room, stepped onto an outdoor staircase that curved to bring him, as he hopped lightly from the bottom step onto the grass, in face with the river.

There was Leona, coming out of the kitchen door and talking animatedly to Bridie. Her Bermuda shorts were of red linen, and her navy-blue wool shirt was open at the throat and rolled to her elbows. She paused to strap on her wristwatch, and then, seeing Charles, she smiled brilliantly and hurried to take his arm.

Leona's lawn was as wide as her house, and its green velvet expanse was unbroken except for two statues—one of a white marble woman, which stood far to the right and about a third of the way down, and another, much nearer the river and on the left, of a gray stone clown who raised his sad grin to the heavens. On each side, the lawn was bounded by a high, dense wall of old trees, old hedge, old thicket, all sorts of old greenery—uncared-for now and growing wild but still putting forth fresh leaves and new shoots—that shielded Leona's domain from the view of the neighboring houses, although their white stone walls, glittering in the sunlight like her own, sometimes showed a flash of brightness through a break in the foliage. The house on the right belonged to Lewis and

Dolly Maitland, Leona's closest friends—except, of course, for Charles, who, in addition to being her dearest companion, was her lion, her literary light, and also, although she did not say this, her claim to distinction in the community.

Leona was tall and slim, with a halo of cloudy black hair that swept becomingly around a face crowded with unformed features. Surely, one thought, the nose would grow larger, or the mouth would settle, or a bone would show itself on one cheek, at least. Even the eyes seemed to have been left unfinished. Brown, they should have been a shade lighter or a shade darker. "My mysterious Leona," Charles called her. "Mysterious, dreaming, romantic Leona."

Walking arm in arm to the river, they did not speak, Leona because she was always careful to discover Charles's mood before conversation, and Charles because he didn't want to get to the subject closest to his heart before he was comfortably settled in a chair.

From the house, two pairs of eyes watched them. Through the kitchen window, the beady Irish eyes of Bridie followed their movements with malevolent attention, and from the window of the second-floor bedroom he shared with Leona, George Harkey, who had just got out of bed, watched his wife and Charles Runyon with a muffled brown gaze in which curiosity and resentment struggled for supremacy with a very bad hangover.

Charles walked rather stiffly, perhaps because he missed the comforting concealment of a jacket, and from the back his small, shapely figure wagged more than a little. Leona's shorts gave to her slow and sinuous prance a very curious effect, as though with every step she was on the verge of sitting down hard, but she continued fairly upright, flirting her cigarette, until they reached the lawn's edge. There, where the ground fell steeply to the river, Leona's latest improvement was now, after months of talk and effort, ready to be enjoyed. Just below the level of the lawn but well above water level she had built a wooden deck, six feet wide and running the whole width of the lawn, with a low railing around it. This was not a jetty, for Leona disliked sailing. This was purely a deck. It was painted a very pale blue, and furnished for lounging, with red canvas sling chairs and tables of black wrought iron. It was a delightful spot, private, uncluttered, Leona's realization of the perfect boat, on which she could ride the restless waters of the river while remaining safely anchored not merely to the land but to her own lawn.

"The deck is really charming," Charles said, lowering himself into a chair, but his tone was perfunctory.

"Wasn't it clever of me to have it built so low, so that it doesn't interfere with the view from the house at all. Even from the up-stairs windows you simply can't see it, unless you know it's here."

She would have gone on, for the house—the frame and expres-sion of her personality—interested her endlessly, but Charles, with a brisk nod, stopped her. He lit a cigarette, threw away the match, snuggled back in his chair, and looked her straight in the eye. "Well, Leona," he said, "and what do you think of our friend Tarnac now? Quite a revealing evening we had last night, eh?"

They had already discussed the evening at length, and at dou-ble length, before they went to bed, but realizing that Charles wanted every detail of it recalled, and herself eager to savor it all again, Leona said, "Oh, Charles, isn't it appalling to see a man so shattered? And in such a short space of time. Why, you know, Charles, I walked into Dolly's living room last night and I simply didn't know him. I actually didn't recognize him. He was stand-ing over by the fireplace with Lewis, and I looked at him, and I looked at Lewis, and I said, 'Where's Edward?'"

"I know, darling, we all heard you."

"And then, of course, I was so overcome when I saw who it was that I simply lost my head."

"I'm afraid you were very cruel, Leona."

"I didn't mean to be cruel. You know I'm never intentionally cruel. Besides, what you said was much, much worse, and you didn't even have my excuse of being flustered. No, you were perfectly cold-blooded. You waited till we were all settled with our drinks, and everything was all smooth and lovely, and then—Oh, Charles, it was perfectly killing. I'll never forget how funny you looked, peering around the room until Dolly was driven to ask you what was wrong, and you said, 'I'm looking for Edward's pretty girl. Isn't she coming down?' "

She paused to laugh at the recollection, and Charles neighed softly.

"And then Edward said, 'What pretty girl?' and you said, 'Why, surely you're not up here alone, Edward. Why, Edward Tarnac without a pretty girl is only half the picture.' "

"That stung," Charles said with satisfaction.

"You know, Charles, I was quite worried for you. If you'd said that to him five years ago he'd have thrown his drink at you."

"But that was five years ago, wasn't it? And instead of throwing his drink he swallowed it, didn't he? Oh, he's learned what's what, these last few years. He's learned his lesson, all right. And then, of course, your poor George had to put his foot in it."

"Oh, poor George is such a fool, Charles. Not a glimmer of social sense. Instead of letting it drop then, he had to pipe up, 'And why shouldn't he come up alone if he wants to?' And naturally that set you off again."

"Well, really, what could I do? George has such a sagging effect on conversation, don't you think? And of course, being a newcomer, he couldn't be expected to know how things were. Obviously I had to tell him what we all know—that Edward's appearance in solitary, as it were, showed how greatly he had changed."

"And Lewis enjoying it all hugely. Edward always made Lewis

look rather dim. Not now, though. Edward's face is so ruined-looking, somehow."

"Positively raddled. Of course, Edward always looked much younger than his age. You know that, Leona. He kept those boyish looks of his a very long time."

"Oh, that was another thing, Charles. Did you have to keep on calling him Boy? Really, I was squirming."

"Don't be a hypocrite, Leona. You know you loved it all. And he had it coming to him. Of course, when you consider how he was brought up, the youngest son, an adoring mother, a trust fund from that uncle of his—"

"Do you know, Charles, I don't believe he has a penny of that money left."

"Well, what would you expect? You remember how he threw money around. That boat, and those silly little racing cars, and that procession of vacant-faced girls, and that endless, exhausting masculinity, constantly being paraded before us—just a show, of course. The psychiatrists know about that. But so wearisome. And terribly bad manners, if you remember."

"Yes, Charles, you have a few scores to settle with him, haven't you, dear?" She stopped, afraid that she had gone too far. Charles would not tolerate familiarity. But he answered her calmly.

"Certainly not. His kind of schoolboy humor never affected me, except to bore me. I do know it used to be impossible to have any good conversation when he was around. Those insufferable interruptions, and—Do you remember his abominable habit of saying 'Now the question direct'?"

" 'Cutting through the grease,' he used to call it."

"Exactly. Exactly. A thoroughly uncivilized mind, if you call it a mind. A man who will express himself in such terms is capable of any gaucherie. No sensitivity, no character, no breeding, and of course, now that all that juvenile charm has been drowned in liquor, you can see what he is. It's pitiful, of course." He sat up and glanced, with impatience, toward the green wall of foliage that concealed the Maitlands' house. "Aren't Lewis and Dolly coming over," he asked, "and our beaming friend Edward, for lunch? Aren't they late? It must be after noon."

Leona laughed melodiously. "Charles, Charles," she said in affectionate reproval. "Are you so eager to sharpen your teeth on poor Edward again? They'll be here soon. Lewis is probably mixing his famous whiskey sours. He said he'd bring a jug over. He and Edward will probably need them."

"Dolly, too," Charles said, settling himself comfortably again. "I fancy she got quite a shock when she saw our returned hero last night. She used to have quite a thing about him, you remember."

"She's trying to forget it now," Leona said.

"Trying to forget what?" Dolly cried, jumping gaily down onto the deck. She was a short, bouncy girl with brown hair, which she had braided into pigtails. "This thing is divine, Leona. I'm going to lie down flat." She lay down flat on her back, sighing luxuriously in the sun's heat. "The others will be right along," she said. "Lewis is bringing the whiskey sours, or will bring them, after he's had a few himself."

"Where is Edward staying in town? He wouldn't tell me last night," Charles asked.

"That's just it," Dolly said. "He won't say where he's staying. He says he's looking for an apartment." She stopped a moment, then turned to them with a conspiratorial grimace. "Listen," she said. "Don't tell Lewis I told you, but he tried to borrow money last night. A hundred dollars."

"Did Lewis give it to him?" Charles asked sharply.

"Not he. You know Lewis. Lewis never lends money, to anyone."

"Well, Tarnac is down and out, then," Charles said.

"Oh dear. I hope he's not going to start borrowing all around," Leona said. "But I was quite cool with him last night. I doubt if he'd have the nerve to ask me."

"I hope he asks me," Charles said. "I'll give him short shrift. But then I was cool, too, to say the least."

"That's another strange thing," Dolly said. "You know, ordinarily he'd have struck out at you last night. You know how belligerent he used to be. But I got the feeling that everything you and Leona said to him just passed over his head. He didn't seem to care. It was Lewis he was looking to. I suppose he always knew you two disliked him, but apparently he thought of Lewis as a friend."

Charles nodded. "Everyone saw how Lewis felt about Edward—except Edward himself, of course. That blessed obtuseness of his saved him from a lot in those days."

"He tried to settle down to a heart-to-heart talk after you people left," Dolly said, "but he got to the borrowing part too soon, and Lewis cut him off short."

"Oh, why doesn't he get on the bus and go back to New York!" Leona cried impatiently. "He's ruining the whole weekend."

"Nonsense, my dear," Charles said. "Far from ruining the weekend, he's adding a certain excitement to it. Besides, he'll undoubtedly stick around now in the hope of retrieving himself. Not that he has a chance. He must see that he made a mistake in coming here. He should never have come, that's all."

"Oh, don't think he doesn't know that now!" Dolly cried. "You know how he was last night—almost apologetic. Today he's just morose. I don't think he's said two words all morning. Don't worry, though, Leona. I don't think he'll make any scenes. He's hardly in a position to, after all. And of course he doesn't want Lewis to tell about his attempt to borrow money."

"It's what we were talking about earlier, Leona," Charles said.

"What used to pass as—uh, conversational dexterity in our friend would now be sheer bravado. He can no longer meet us on our own ground. He has to pretend not to notice. He's no longer an equal, after all."

"Really, Charles!" Dolly cried. "Aren't you carrying this a little too far? He's broke, of course, and obviously he's been on a long bender, but I think it's nonsense to talk about him not being an equal, and so on. I mean, I think that's silly."

Leona sat up straight. "Dolly," she said, with a nervous glance at Charles, "please remember to whom you are speaking."

Charles, whose face had grown small, dark, and closed, was silent for a moment, while Dolly, confused, cast about for words of apology.

"Don't apologize, Dolly," he said at last. "I may seem silly to you, and of course, you must say what you think. We won't discuss it."

"Yes, of course, Charles," Dolly said, on the verge of tears. "I only thought—"

"Don't think, dear," Charles said. "It does not become you."

"I can't tell you," Dolly said desperately, directing herself at Leona, who was still stiff with outrage, "how glad I was to get away from the house this morning. Susie woke up at six sharp, and screamed continuously from six-thirty until after eight. I nearly lost my mind."

"Oh, yes, Susie. How old is she now?" Leona asked coldly.

"Four," Dolly said disconsolately. "That was her fourth birthday the other day, Leona. When I had the party."

"I detest children," Charles said. "They're so short."

"Here come Lewis and Edward with the whiskey sours!" Leona cried. "And not a minute too soon, either. We have the glasses all ready here, Lewis. Edward, what do you think of my new sun deck?"

"Great," Edward said with no enthusiasm. "Just great, Leona."

He pulled a chair from the group around the table, turned it to face the river, and sat down apart from the company.

"Come now, Edward!" Leona cried, with a smile for the others. "I have to almost twist my neck off if I want to see you. Why don't you come in with the rest of us?"

"I'm all right, thanks," Edward said. He was wearing gray slacks and last night's shirt without a tie.

Edward and Lewis were both tall, both blond, and both strongly built. They both had the same kind of regular, clean-cut, blue-eyed good looks. Lewis's face, bland in his youth, had grown blander. The restlessness that had always characterized Edward had worn his face, and the self-confidence had gone, taking the shine with it. Also, he was suffering from a bad hangover, and looked, generally, perhaps more unhappy than he felt. Lewis at once started to pour the whiskey sours.

"I hear you're looking for an apartment, Edward," Charles said smoothly. "Perhaps I could help you. I hear of things—friends in the theater going to Hollywood and Rome and such places. What have you in mind? I mean, what price have you in mind?"

Edward gulped the first drink and handed his glass back to Lewis for a refill. "I'm not going to hurry about the apartment," he said. "I want to look around a bit, find what I really want. I'm all right for the time being. And since I know what your next question is going to be, I'll save you the trouble of asking. I'm staying at the Tenley, on Washington Square. Now you know."

"The Tenley!" Dolly cried. "Oh, poor Edward, but that's a terrible old fleabag. Oh, I'm sorry, Edward, I didn't mean anything."

"It's all right, Dolly," Edward said. "It's a fleabag. You're absolutely right."

"I thought they'd torn the Tenley down years ago," Charles murmured. "It was one of the hangouts of my rather rowdy youth."

Lewis kicked impatiently at the table leg. "Not to change the subject, but isn't Bridie bringing the lunch down here? Edward and I were a little ahead on those whiskey sours."

"Which reminds me that I need a drink," Edward said, passing his glass over his shoulder.

"Oh, she's bringing a basket down any minute now," Leona said. "She's rattled, as all the maids are today. They can think of nothing but the ball."

"The ball!" Charles shrieked. "Great heavens, Leona, do you know that I completely forgot the ball. And I thought of nothing else all week. I even brought my embroidered French waistcoat along. I should look superb in the waltzes. I'm going to cut quite a figure, Leona."

"I'm sure you are, darling," Leona said, "and the girls will go wild over you, as usual. They adore waltzing with you, Charles." She turned to Edward. "I suppose you know the maids are having their ball this weekend?" she inquired, smiling. "Tonight's the big night. Or did you remember?"

"I remember the ball," Edward said. "I thought it was always on Saint Patrick's Day."

"It used to be," Dolly said, "but they had too much competition from New York, so they changed it."

"Charles puts us all in the shade," Lewis said, and gazed at them with the air of fascinated and respectful amusement that Charles always inspired in him.

"You did rather well yourself, Lewis," Charles said, pleased. "Last year, some of the policemen were quite jealous."

"Oh, I'll admit I have my little following," Lewis said, grinning.

"Well, of course some of the maids must cherish secret passions," Dolly said. "Poor things. How they must look forward to tonight."

"There's no secret about their collective passion for Charles,"

Leona said. "Charles maintains that only servants can dance the waltz really well, Edward. Female servants, that is. He says their souls are clad in caps and streamers. They hold their heads up to keep the caps on, whirl to make the streamers flutter, and so they achieve the perfect posture for the waltz. You see, Charles, how well I remember what you say?"

"Your memory is phenomenal, darling," Charles said, "and quite accurate, too. That is just how I imagine them when I dance. I keep my eyes shut tight, of course, and the hall seems filled with black and white dresses, the full black skirts, the frilly white aprons, and streamers—oh, it's a charming picture. My waistcoat provides the significant, necessary note of color. Can you see it all, as I do now?"

"You should have been a painter, Charles," Dolly said shyly.

"Dolly banal," Charles said, but kindly. "We can always count on you, can't we, dear."

"What are you wearing, Leona?" Dolly asked hastily. "I bought a pair of black net stockings with rhinestones on the insteps. After all, it is sort of a fancy-dress thing for us. And why not give those nice cops something to look at, I thought."

"Very generous of you, darling," Leona said. "I'm wearing the white crêpe, you know. That should get them."

"They were eager enough last year," Lewis said. "I was afraid they'd eat you girls up. The atmosphere got almost primitive."

Leona laughed throatily. "Well, I do think they like us to come," she said.

"I think it's a nice thing for us to do," Dolly said. "I think it's something we ought to do," she added virtuously.

"Well, of course, they're honored that we come to their little party," Charles said. "Why, it's positively feudal. And whether they know it or not, that's why they enjoy it."

"Feudal my foot," Edward said. He stood up suddenly, staggered, and was obliged to grab the handrail. "Feudal my foot," he repeated. "You're all itching to go. You wouldn't miss going for the world."

"Well, that's our old Edward," Lewis said unpleasantly.

"I always thought you were a friend of mine, Lewis. Did you know that?" Edward said.

Lewis looked first at Dolly and then into his glass. "Of course I'm your friend, Edward," he said.

"That's just it!" Edward shouted, ludicrous in rage, "You're not my friend! None of you are. You all hate me. I should never have come. I thought there was something here. I thought we were all friends here. Old friends." He seemed about to weep.

"Edward," Leona said. "Edward, darling, you've had quite a lot to drink, and you're sitting in the sun. Please go and lie down. Please, Edward. Do go into the house."

"That's right," Lewis said. "What you need is sleep. You can lie out on Leona's side porch. There's shade there. Can't he, Leona?"

"Of course he can!" Leona cried. "Do you want any of us to go with you, darling? Oh, poor Edward, you've been through such a lot, and—"

"Never mind about all that now, Leona. Never mind what I've been through. I know what you'd like. You've had your spectacle, and you want me to go away quietly, don't you? You'd like that, wouldn't you? You'd like me to get on the bus and go back to New York. But I'm not going back to New York, see? I'm going to stay here till I'm good and ready to go, and I'm going to make this weekend so miserable that you'll remember it for the rest of your days. I'm not leaving. I've no shame. I'll make everything you say about me true—you see if I don't. But don't get your hopes up. I'm not leaving." From the lawn, where he was standing now, he waved his arm at them. "I'll be back," he said, and started his unsteady progress toward the house.

Charles made a disgusted gesture. "I always knew it," he said. "The fellow is a peasant."

Lewis said, "I don't envy him his head when he wakes up about four o'clock this afternoon and remembers all this. Did you know he took a bottle up with him last night, Dolly? He must have been drinking all night."

"Really," Leona said, "I do wish he'd go. I've seen enough of him to last me a very long time."

Charles smiled. "Oh, we may as well see the finish," he said. "Mr. Tarnac seems to have gone through so many metamorphoses since his arrival. First, an almost touching friendliness. Then this morning, morose silence. Now, a futile aggressiveness that is more pathetic than anything. And tonight, I expect, painful penitence. We'll just have to be nice to him, my dears, but don't get so soft-hearted that you invite him down again, Lewis—for all our sakes."

They were distracted by a shout. Edward had retraced his steps and was standing only a short distance away from them, balancing himself against the stone clown. "Do you know what you people are?" he shouted. "I just thought—do you know what you are?"

"Oh, God, what now?" Leona whispered. "Charles, what will I do? The servants will hear him!"

Charles stared grimly at the floor of the deck, hoping that by avoiding Edward's eye he would also avoid his attention. The others, too, looked down, praying for silence.

"You're the people who never make mistakes, that's what you are!" Edward bellowed. "Do you hear me? You're the people who never make mistakes! Not a single mistake does a single one of you ever make in your whole lives! That's what I think of you." He turned back up the lawn, and disappeared in the direction of the Maitlands' house.

They all took exaggerated attitudes of relief.

"Goodness," Dolly said. "I couldn't imagine what he was going to say. I was petrified! Is that bad, never to make a mistake? Really, I think Edward must be losing his mind."

Charles smiled benignly at her, and then his gaze continued past her and across the wide river to the opposite side, where the green bank rose solid to the tranquil blue sky. "I must congratulate you again on your deck, Leona," he said. "An excellent idea. Such an educated view, my dear."

"And here at last is Bridie with the food," Lewis said. "I'm hungry enough to eat a horse."

"And poor George, bringing up the rear," Leona said. "As usual."

"I still cannot believe that you're actually married to a credit manager," Charles said. "Not that George isn't a dear, but it seems such an unlikely occupation. Almost exotic."

Leona, who always referred to George as a vice president of the store where he was employed, turned almost purple with shame, but she understood that she was being punished for her earlier boldness, and didn't try to defend herself.

At five o'clock that afternoon, jaded with talking about the dance, anxious now only to get on with it, willing even to have it past, so that they could start enjoying the discussion of it, most of the maids at Herbert's Retreat lay down on their beds for an unaccustomed ceremonial nap before getting dressed for the evening. The fine white stone houses, those beside the river and those scattered a little distance from it, were silent—the families departed for cocktails and dinner, the maids, supine, for once acknowledged mistresses of the kingdom they regarded, in any case, as their own.

The kitchens were deserted, but from every kitchen ceiling a freshly pressed dress, a long dress, hung and shivered gently in the mild breeze that stole up at intervals from the river. The maids' dresses were of bright colors—pink, yellow, blue, violet, red, and green—because the girls liked to escape as thoroughly as they could from the grays and black-and-white of their daily uniforms.

Only in Bridie's kitchen was there a black dress to be seen, a matronly taffeta that hung with uncompromising stiffness from the center beam. Not far from the dress, Bridie herself, scorning sleep, sat at her table by the window, stirring one of her eternal cups of strong tea. She had commanded her friend Agnes, who worked for the Gieglers, to join her, and at this moment Agnes sat drooping, with her pale eyes fixed on Leona's lawn and her ears half attentive to Bridie's conversation, which consisted, as usual, of a series of declamatory, denunciatory, and entirely final remarks.

"Naps in the afternoon," she said fiercely, slamming her wet teaspoon on the table. "If they were in their beds at a decent hour at night, when they ought to be sleeping, they wouldn't be looking to lie down at this time of day. What do they want with naps, big strong lassies like them? Cocktails they'll be after next, I suppose. Cocktails with the family, I suppose."

She drew up with a jerk, intrigued by the last picture she had conjured up. Suppose now, she thought, Mr. Harkey, or Mrs. Harkey herself, were to come out here and invite me to sit down for a cocktail with them. She glanced covertly at Agnes, who was still contemplating the grass.

Bridie went on with her meditations. Well, then, I would sit down with them, she thought—not on one of the comfortable chairs but on an ordinary chair, just to show them that I know as much about good manners as they do, and I'd take a drink, whatever they were having themselves, and I wouldn't be pushy, but neither would I be backward. "Mrs. Harkey," I'd say, "as one woman to another—" "Oh, go on, Bridie," she'd say, smiling a little bit. "Won't you call me Leona? It's ridiculous for us, living along here in the same house year after year, and not being real friends."

This pleasant scene was interrupted by Agnes, who spoke up suddenly in her thin, incurious voice. "Here's Josie. I would've thought she'd be lying down along with the rest of them. I wonder what she's after."

Bridie peered out the window. Josie, the newest maid at the Retreat, and one of the youngest, was crossing the lawn on quick fat legs, coming from the Maitlands' house, where she worked. She was a short, stocky girl, with a pretty face.

"She should have come round by the house," Bridie said. "Mrs. Harkey hates to see anybody using up that lawn of hers . . . Well, and what brings you here this time of the day, Josie? I thought you'd be asleep like the rest of them."

"I couldn't sleep," Josie said. "I'm too nervous. And I'm all alone there, except for that Mr. Tarnac, and he's up in his room sleeping it off."

Bridie nodded heavily at Agnes. "What was I telling you?" she said. "And where are all the rest of them?" she asked Josie.

"They've all gone off driving somewhere. And then they're taking the child to her grandmother's, so they can go to the dance."

"And they didn't ask Mr. Tarnac to go with them?" Bridie asked.

"He wouldn't go. Sure, he's in no fit state to go anywhere. He's been falling-down drunk ever since they got in last night. And the rest of them all making fun of him and all. I don't know what sort of a fellow he is to put up with it. You should have heard them at dinner last night. You should have heard that little Mr. Runyon of yours. The things he said, I couldn't begin to remember the half of them."

"It's a pity Mr. Tarnac couldn't stay where he was, and not give them the satisfaction of laughing at him," Bridie declared. "The men around here were always envious of him, with his money and his big boat and his racing cars and all. And the women, that used to be throwing themselves at him, are congratulating themselves now that they stayed clear of him. The one here was forever inviting him over. And that Maitland lassie was very sweet on him. Oh, I believe to this day that there was more went on there than anybody'll ever know about. But that little Mr. God—I hate to see him so set up. I hate to see him getting any kind of satisfaction. I heard him last night, himself and Mrs. Harkey talking after they came home. Laughing and carrying on about Mr. Tarnac's clothes and the way he's all broken up, and each of them repeating to the other what they'd said. And then this morning they couldn't wait to start in on it again."

Josie, who had been listening respectfully, turned to Agnes. "Did you know Mr. Tarnac, Agnes?"

"No, he was before my time," Agnes said regretfully. "But Bridie's been telling me all about the big house he had and how he sold it and all. And lost all his money. It's a terrible thing, a man to throw away a fortune like that."

"But still and all," Bridie said, "he's a decent sort of a man, and I always liked him." She almost believed she was telling the truth, but the fact was that when Edward Tarnac lived at the Retreat, he was no more to her than one of a group she hated; it was only in his new role that she liked him. She took the cups and saucers off the table and carried them over to the sink.

Agnes sighed. "What are you wearing to the dance tonight, Josie?" she asked.

"Me ballerina," Josie said. "And me ballerina-type sandals. And I've dyed a pair of stockings to match. Pink. Do you think it'll be all right?"

"Lovely," Agnes said. "Pink is lovely on you, Josie—lovely with your skin."

"That's another thing!" Bridie shouted, splashing noisily among the dishes. "There'll be Josie in her pink stockings, and you in that green getup of yours, Agnes, and that crew from here'll be there laughing at you behind their hands and making little of you. That's all they come for, to have something to laugh about. They make me sick."

Josie was red with indignation. "What's Mrs. Maitland going out and buying special black net stockings for, then, if she's only coming to laugh? Special stockings that she paid twelve dollars for. She's dying to come to the dance, so she is. She went and spent twelve dollars for special stockings to wear to the dance. What would she do that for if she's only coming to laugh? You're only making it up, Bridie, to stop us from enjoying ourselves."

Bridie, who had abandoned the sink, stared at her in astonishment. "What's that about stockings? Now, Josie, don't start crying. I wasn't trying to stop you from enjoying yourself. I was only thinking *they'd* be trying to stop you enjoying yourself. Now sit down and tell me and Agnes about the stockings Mrs. Maitland bought. Black, did you say they were?"

"Black net," Josie said, subsiding, "with a whole lot of rhinestones here—" She indicated her own chubby instep. "And she went all the way in to some special actresses' shop in New York to get them. I heard her talking to Mrs. Ffrench about them yesterday afternoon when I was waxing the hall. 'Aren't they the sexiest things you ever saw in your life?' Mrs. Maitland says. 'Do you think our visiting policemen will like them?' she says. 'Why, I should think they'd go berserk,' Mrs. Ffrench says, and they both laughed and laughed. 'I don't know why you bother,' Mrs. Ffrench says. 'I think they're a dull collection, myself.' 'Oh, I think they're sweet,' Mrs. Maitland says, 'and very attractive, some of them. Lewis was quite jealous last year. And you know, they're wonderful dancers. I wouldn't miss this for anything.' Well, I was curious, wanting to know what they were talking about, so I went into the living room on the excuse of asking them did they want anything, and there was Mrs. Maitland with the long shorts on her, y'know? And the stockings up against her leg. She put them away quick, but I found them in her drawer this morning, and I looked at them. And the price was on them, twelve dollars. I'm telling you, wild horses wouldn't keep her from the dance. She's dying to go."

"Well, I declare to God," Bridie said. She sat down at the table again. "What else did they say, Josie?"

"Nothing, except Mrs. Ffrench asked Mrs. Maitland, 'What's Charles going to surprise us with this year?' she says. 'He had such an amusing outfit last year,' she says, 'and the girls made such a fuss over him,' she says. 'Oh, the girls adore Charles,' Mrs. Maitland says, 'and he's like a little child about the dance, he's so excited about it. He pretends not to be, of course,' she says, 'but you know it gets to be a bit of a bore, he can talk of nothing else all day afterward. You know, Charles is a tiny bit conceited,' she says, 'and he rather fancies himself in the waltz.' And then they went on talking about the party Mrs. Ffrench is giving next Friday. That was in the afternoon, before Mr. Maitland and Mr. Tarnac got here."

"'The girls adore Charles,'" Bridie repeated. "'The girls adore Charles.' Sure they were all laughing their heads off at him, the way he was shaping around on the dance floor with his eyes closed and all. You never saw such a sketch in your life. We were all breaking our hearts laughing at him. And he brought those special little flat patent-leather shoes of his, too. I saw them when I was doing the room this morning. Well, I declare to God. And that one upstairs, Mrs. Harkey—I wonder what she's going to doll herself up in. I declare to God, all the parties and all they have to go to, and they have to take over our little party, too. Wouldn't you know it of them."

"And every time one of the fellows asks one of them to dance, one of us is left sitting!" Josie cried. "Oh, I know there's extra men

and all, but still I don't think it's fair. And all the money they have
to spend on themselves and all, and us trying to struggle along on
what we make—How can we put up an appearance against them?
It's not fair, so it's not." She stood up. "Well," she said, "I'd better
be getting home. I have to get ready for the dance, although I
haven't much heart for it now."

Bridie folded her arms and leaned on the table. "Wait a minute
now, Josie," she said. "Maybe there's something we can do about
all this. What do you say, Agnes?"

"Sure what could we do?" Agnes asked nervously. "You don't
want to get into any trouble, now, Bridie."

"No need to get into any trouble," Bridie said. "We could just
pass the word around. They only come around to look. That's
what Mrs. Harkey said to me. 'We're only going to drop around
for a little visit,' she says to me, 'Just for a look. It's such fun to sit
and watch.' Well, then, let them look, if that's what they want.
We'll boycott them. Very polite, of course, as though we thought
they just came to look. As though we didn't think they wanted to
dance. Who can make any trouble out of that?"

"I don't want to risk my job," Agnes said.

"No fear of that," Bridie said. "How can you risk your job
when they won't know anything about it? They'll just think the
fellows are shy, or something."

Josie sniggered. "Oh, God," she said, "there she'll be sitting up
there with her black stockings on her, and nobody coming near
her!"

Agnes smiled meanly, stood up, and brushed bread crumbs
from the front of her skirt. "We'll have to make sure all the girls
know about it, Bridie," she said.

The dance began at nine o'clock. At eleven, George Harkey still
waited, surrounded by the empty chairs he was holding for Leona,
on a dais at one end of the long village hall. His solitary dinner at

the village bar-and-grill had been preceded by five very sweet Manhattans, and he was drowsy. He tried, with a monotonous lack of success but nonchalantly all the same, to count the eyelashes of his left eye with the fingers of his right hand and the eyelashes of his right eye with his other set of fingers. Head bent, eyes alternately glazing and wandering, he still could not entirely avoid seeing the feet of the dancers as they galloped past his perch. Underneath him, the dais, which had been built for some pageant, thudded industriously in time with the dancing, and around him the empty chairs rattled. Suddenly the hall darkened slightly. Someone had turned the lights down. To George, who had just then been gazing intently into the palms of his locked hands, the change seemed tremendous. The music, the laughter, the pounding of feet, and the voices, which formerly had come at him in one bright, enveloping blast of exhausting but familiar sound, now seemed to deepen and at the same time to grow more shrill. It was an ominous alteration. Was he in the same room? Had he, perhaps, slept?

He raised his eyes fearfully and gazed down the length of the hall. Dimly, far away across the sea of jiggling heads, he perceived the glitter of instruments. There was the stage, there were the musicians. In front of the stage stood a bank of the same thick, stiff green shrubbery that sprouted at intervals in tubs along the side walls, separating into chummy groups the empty chairs that had been set aside for tired dancers. Were there any tired dancers? George couldn't tell. The nausea that had been caressing him at intervals all day embraced him without warning, and roughly. He closed his eyes tight and gripped the seat of his chair with both hands, but still, in his horrified vision, the dance floor swung right, swung left, with sickening precision, as though some giant pendulum had control of it, and the dancers, oblivious, whirled giddily on, and he was increasingly aware of the Manhattans and of the two tough pork chops that since suppertime had lain, almost forgotten, inside him.

The wave passed, leaving its victim trembling but not seriously impaired. He opened his eyes, put his hand to his hip pocket, and took out a large silver flask. He unscrewed the top, poured some whiskey into one of the two sticky glasses that some earlier Retreat visitors had left on the chair beside him, and drank. That was better. He hoped no one had noticed him, but it was too late to worry now, and he poured another drink, finished it off, and set the glass on the floor, so carelessly that it turned on its side and rolled dismally under one of the chairs.

He recorked the flask, crossed his legs, and sat back to survey the festivities, with the suave, aloof smile he had often seen Charles Runyon wear. On George's square, earnest face the smile sat awkwardly, but he knew only that he felt tired, and tried to solve the problem by leering on one side of his face while he rested the muscles of the other side.

At this moment, through the wide entrance door at the side of the hall, he saw Leona enter, pause, and raise her arms in greeting to the merrymakers. She was wearing a sleeveless white crêpe dress that clung to her tall, slender figure, and there were diamonds in her ears. She raised herself on tiptoe, waved to the band, and pranced gracefully to the dais and to George. Behind her, Charles, Dolly, and Lewis followed confidently, their smiles radiating pleasure, camaraderie, and, above all, approval.

Leona tripped up the steps and stood beside George, regarding him with a humorous *moue* that he found peculiarly repellent.

"Well, George, all alone? Poor George has been sitting here all alone," she said to Charles, who had already taken a chair and arranged himself in an attitude.

"Never mind the poor-George stuff," George muttered, but no one heard him.

Dolly plumped herself down beside him. "Where is everybody?" she demanded. "Are we the only people here?"

"The Gieglers were here," George said, "but they left. The Ffrenches left, too, and the Pearsons. Some of the others were here. The Allens, I think. Anyway, they're all gone. But now you're here," he added with an effort.

"George, how do you like my fancy dress?" Dolly asked.

She was wearing her favorite cocktail skirt, of black satin cut in a wide circle, and with it a tight, sleeveless, modestly low jerkin blouse of black-and-white striped satin that laced at the back with red corset strings. There were towering red heels on her black satin sandals, and a small triangle of rhinestones glittered on each black net instep. Her hair was piled in curls on top of her head and decorated with a bright-red rose.

"You look fine, Dolly," George said. "What do you mean, fancy dress? It's just a dress, isn't it?"

"Well, it's a little costumey, don't you think? Lewis said I looked like a French doll."

"Dolly means it's not quite what one wears," Leona interrupted, leaning across George to twinkle brilliantly at Dolly. "You must excuse George, Dolly. I suspect he's not seeing quite clearly. Didn't you dance at all, George?"

"No one asked me to dance," George said. He stood up. "No one asked Nat Ffrench to dance, either," he said, "or Rita, or the Gieglers, or anybody. Nobody asked anybody to dance. So they left."

"Been to the bar, George?" Lewis asked boisterously. He was in great good humor, and looked large, solid, and secure in his well-cut dark-blue suit.

"I didn't go near the bar," George said. "It's in the room behind the stage. You have to walk right through the dance to get to it."

"That's where it always is," Leona said happily. "Go on, Lewis. You play waiter. I'll have a Scotch-and-water."

"I think I'll leave now," George said. "I'd like some fresh air. I'll go along home, I think."

"You'll do nothing of the sort, George," Leona said. "You're not going to march out the minute I come in. Did you see Bridie?"

"She has a chair down there near the stage, I think," George said. "I really think I'll go now, Leona."

"Sit down, George," Leona said.

"Oh, for heaven's sake, sit down and shut up, George," Charles said.

"All right," George said. "Didn't know I was so popular. But I'll sit at the back here. See, I'll sit here."

He tilted a chair back against the wall and sat down, sleepy but resigned to staying awake. He closed his eyes.

"Isn't this gay?" Leona said. "Well, for goodness' sake, will you look at Edward! I forgot all about him. He's dancing with the Ffrenches' maid, Eileen something. He didn't come in with us, did he? I thought he stayed in the car."

"He woke up when I was getting out," Dolly said. "I took it for granted he'd gone to the bar."

"Well, I never," Charles said, two or three minutes later. "Our Edward is getting quite a whirl. There he is again, with a different girl."

"The Bennetts' cook," Leona said absently.

"Never you mind, Charles!" Dolly cried gaily. "Wait till the waltzes start. You'll put poor Edward completely in the shade."

"Really, Dolly!" Charles snapped. "This brawl means nothing to me. Be serious, my dear, even if you can't be intelligent. I'm here to observe, not to dance."

"Haw-haw," George said from the back. They all turned to stare at him. He had the flask in the open again.

"George, what on earth! What are you doing with that ridiculous flask?" Leona cried.

"My own flask." George, unperturbed, took another swallow, keeping his eyes fixed on Leona.

"Well, here's a pretty how-de-do," Charles whispered angrily. "You should have let him go home, Leona."

"He'll go in a minute," Leona whispered back. "Let's just ignore him."

"It's bedlam in the bar," Lewis said, returning with their drinks, "but I must say they gave me quick service. They're a nice bunch of fellows, those cops, or whatever they are." He put the loaded tray on the floor of the dais and began to hand drinks around.

"What are they, anyway, Leona?" Charles asked. "It really interests me. It is in the nature of a social phenomenon, you know, this gathering. Who are these imported stalwarts?"

"Policemen, mostly. Firemen, I suppose, too," Leona said. "Who cares, as long as they can dance?"

"The Department of Sanitation is represented, too," Dolly whispered, gazing at a red-faced young man in a white linen jacket, who was dancing with the Gieglers' long-faced Agnes.

"Complete with carnation in lapel," Charles remarked. "My, aren't we chic!"

Leona giggled. "You're both perfectly terrible," she said. "That's a very respectable-looking coat. And a very nice-looking young man, too. I think you should be ashamed of yourselves."

Dolly choked suddenly, and hid her face behind Leona's shoulder. "Leona!" she spluttered. "Will you look at our Josie in the dyed pink stockings. Did you ever see anything like it in your life?"

"Macabre, my dear," Leona murmured. "Poor thing, she must have slaved to get that color. It matches her ears, though."

Charles threw an arm casually over the back of his chair, and his black flannel coat slipped open to show more than a glimpse of the gray-and-rose brocade waistcoat he was wearing.

"This dais was a charming thought," he said expansively. "What do they use it for? May queens and things? I adore sitting here, being at once a member of the audience and a player. And yet, not really of either group. The critic's lot is a lonely one, my dears. I feel remote from the rollicking servants, and just as remote, in a different way, from you delightful people. The cold, uncompromising eyes give me no peace. I say it ruefully, I assure you." He sipped his ginger ale and smiled at them complacently.

Lewis made an impatient movement, and Dolly glanced at him warningly. "Well, I wish we'd start dancing," she said. "I'm getting restless, sitting here like this. How do they make chairs this hard?"

"There is something strange about it," Lewis said. "How long have we been here? Twenty minutes? Half an hour?"

"I suppose they're shy," Leona said. "George said none of the Retreat people who came danced."

George, who had been dozing, came to at the sound of his name and sat up, looking around blearily.

"Well, where's the rush, girls?" he inquired. "I thought we were going to be stampeded. What happened to the stag line?"

Leona shot him a venomous glance. Turning to Lewis, she said in a low voice, "Did you notice anything in the bar? I mean, were they friendly and everything?"

"Sure," Lewis said. "They went out of their way to help me get the drinks. They were—well, you know, the same as they always are."

"I'm afraid you girls outsmarted yourselves," Charles said, chortling faintly. "The poor creatures are paralyzed by the splendor of your attire."

Leona turned impulsively to Lewis. "Lewis, why don't you and Dolly start things off by dancing together. Not that I care that much about dancing, but if they're shy—"

"Nothing doing," Lewis said.

"Oh, Leona, we can't do that," Dolly said. "They have to ask us. We can't just jump right into the middle of their dance. After all, we don't really come here to dance. We just come—well, to be nice."

"You're stuck," George said. "It's a boycott. They're on to you, girls."

"That's ridiculous, George!" Leona cried indignantly. "They're dancing with Edward."

George shrugged.

"If it were a boycott," Charles interposed, "we'd know it by their demeanor. They'd giggle or point their fingers or something. These people can't control their emotions. They have to show what they feel. But I can see no evidence of hostility in this assemblage."

"Neither can I!" Leona cried. "Why, they're smiling and friendly and all. There's Bridie waving at me now. They're just shy, incredible though it may seem. Well, who ever would have thought it? It's too bad. Not that it matters, of course."

"I didn't know Edward could even stand up," Dolly said suddenly, "and look at him now. The life of the party."

"The parlormaids' Don Juan," Charles said. "The scullery sheik."

George emitted a rude crow of mirth. "A rehearsal, by God!" he cried. "Is that what you're going to say to Tarnac tomorrow, Charles? I've always wanted to see you working on those witty sayings of yours. Try some more, Charles. We'll tell you the good ones."

Charles froze into a dark knot of rage. Leona turned pale.

"Shut up, you," Lewis said. "Do you hear me? Shut up. We know Tarnac; you don't."

George waggled a finger at him. "Now, now, Lewis. Just

because Tarnac is dancing and you're not. No one asked me to dance, but you don't see me getting all red and angry."

Lewis crouched like a beast on his straight wooden chair. "Come outside," he said. "I'll break your neck for that."

"Break it here," George said with enthusiasm. "Come on, break it. Hit me. Come on, hit me."

"Oh, God!" Leona moaned. "Will you two stop it! Stop this at once. The servants, Lewis! Have some sense! Oh, Charles, smile as though nothing had happened. Dolly, stop glaring at George that way. Lewis, pull yourself together, please."

Lewis squared around to face the dancers again. Behind him, George grinned.

"All right," Lewis said. "All right. But I won't forget this, Leona."

"How could you, dear?" Leona said soothingly. "And neither will George," she promised, in a different tone.

"Oh, let's go home. Let's get out of here, for heaven's sake!" Dolly said.

"You can't go home that fast," George said. "Maybe it *is* a boycott. Maybe they're not shy at all. Maybe they want to teach you a lesson. Us a lesson, I mean. Us a lesson."

"I couldn't care less!" Dolly cried. "It's all a great bore as far as I'm concerned. Let's you and me go anyway, Lewis."

"Little feelings hurt?" George inquired, and sniggered.

Lewis set his glass carefully on the floor, and then clenched his fist melodramatically. "Listen, little man," he said to George, "my wife's feelings are not hurt. My wife's feelings could never be hurt by a crew of drunken servants and street-sweepers and God knows what."

"Oh, Lewis, old man, *I* know that," George said, "but do *they* know that?"

"What do I care what they think!"

"Keep your voice down, Lewis," Leona said coldly. "For once, George is right. We have to stay a little while, I'm afraid, deadly though it is. We can't let them think they drove us out. We'll stay a reasonable time, and then go. I still don't think they're doing it on purpose. It would be too silly."

"We'll know tomorrow, anyway," Dolly said, sighing. "Edward will tell us."

"I must say he has a nerve," Leona said. "He hasn't come near us once. After all, Dolly, you are his hostess."

"Edward has reached his proper level, my dear," Charles said. "Look at the pathetic fellow, capering around."

"Utterly smug," Dolly said. "Oh, God," she added. "He heard us talking this morning on the deck, Leona. About the dance, I mean, and these damned stockings and all. Do you suppose he'll tell them? I really can't bear to think of them laughing at us."

"I don't think he'll say anything," Lewis said. "I don't think he'd go that far."

"I really think we've stayed long enough, don't you, Charles?" Leona said.

"We will not go home, children," Charles said. "I know you girls are disappointed you weren't asked to dance. Lewis and George, too, of course. But we mustn't let our little peeve show. This is much too interesting a scene to miss, and I intend to sit it out. Chins up, now. We're not leaving. Don't look so down, Dolly. There'll be other dances."

"What do you mean there'll be other dances?" Dolly cried furiously. "You're the one who's been making all the fuss about coming to this wretched thing. What about your special waistcoat and your waltzing slippers?"

Charles regarded her with cool amusement. "Leona knows all about that, Dolly," he said. "I have a severely infected foot, which obliges me to wear a pliable shoe. I never had the slightest intention of dancing tonight, but I didn't want to spoil your fun by refusing to come, and in any case the spectacle interests me, and you are making it even more interesting, my dear, with this childish display of temper because the little boys didn't notice your sexy new stockings. Isn't that so, my sweet? Leona, you remember my telling you about my wretched foot?"

"Of course, darling," Leona said. "You should apologize, Dolly."

"Haw, haw, HAW," George said. "He made that all up just now to save his face, such as it is."

"Leave the room at once, George," Leona said.

"Make me," George said. "Go ahead, make me. Make me."

"Make you what?" Charles asked in contempt.

Leona threw Charles a glance of anguish. "Oh, Charles, don't provoke him. Poor George is not himself this evening."

"Poor George," George said, apparently to himself. "Poor George," he said again. He stood up. "POOR GEORGE!" he roared. "POOR, POOR George!"

The nearest dancers hesitated and then went on. George smiled and sat down again.

"I'll kill you for this, George," Leona said.

"I'll do it again, and I'll do worse than that, Leona," George said, "unless you say after me now, 'Nice George.'"

Leona stared at him and then spoke quickly. "Nice George," she said.

"Keep smiling, children," Charles said brightly. "Remember, it's all just a little joke. Don't let them guess there's anything wrong."

"Now, Leona," George said, "say, 'Rich, handsome, good George.'"

"Rich, handsome, good George," Leona gabbled.

George looked pleased. "'Popular George'?" he suggested.

"Popular George."

"Good enough," George said. "Now Charlie—'Nice George,' please. If you don't say 'Nice George,' Charlie, I'm coming over there and twist your ears, one to the front, one to the back. 'Nice George.'"

"Nice George," Charles said, sneering. Leona, Lewis, and Dolly, all three turned their gaze uneasily from him.

"Stop making faces, Charlie," George said good-humoredly. "Now all together—'Rich, handsome, witty George, good George, nice George.'"

"Rich, handsome, witty George," they chorused feebly, "good George, nice George."

George took out his flask. "'Pleasant, popular, *able* George.'"

"Pleasant, popular, able George."

In the swollen peace that followed, Leona and Dolly smiled stiffly at each other. "I really never felt so much of a fool in my life," Dolly said.

"We can leave in about an hour, don't you think?" Charles said.

"An hour, Charles, yes, let's say an hour at the most," Leona agreed fervently.

They continued to sit, smiling. Behind them, having tasted heaven, George slept. Before them, the dance went on.

Next morning, Charles awoke as usual at nine-thirty, but he did not immediately open his eyes. He waited, lying very still, breathing calmly and deeply, until his first impression of uneasiness, of being on guard, had passed into a determined surge of good spirits, and then, to his delighted surprise, into a playful well-being that carried him out of bed and across to the table where his notebook lay. He lifted the book, admiring the neatness—that is, he thought, the dispassionateness—of last night's entries. He had stayed awake almost until dawn, sitting here in silence until his temper was cool enough to let him write as he knew he should write. Now it was all in hand. The day was full of promise. He was going into battle, and his adversaries, meager enough in their normal state, would all have horrifying hangovers.

"George," he murmured, and read. It was disagreeable stuff, but he absorbed it bravely. George was easy game. George would learn his lesson well. Thinking of the awakening George must at this moment be enduring with Leona, Charles could almost find it in his heart to be sorry for the poor wretch. Edward would squirm, too. That would all be perhaps too easy.

But then came the difficult part, because already, at the memory of the evening, Charles was beginning to rage again. He was churning with rage. He could burn the memory of his own ludicrous part in the whole business from the minds of the others, by turning their derision back on them, but could he forget it himself? Because if he did not forget it, or destroy it, its damage would show, and the others would know for certain that he had been as vulnerable as they to the general humiliation. "They must not know," he said aloud. "It must not show," he said. "Today will prove what I am—a man above all this petty frenzy. I am different from all these people," he told himself angrily. He stood up and strode barefoot around the room.

Suddenly he stopped in the center of the woolly white rug and, gazing down at his untidy bed, clutched his head with both hands. "I simply must remember that I am an observer," he said. The image that had come to him again and again last night as he sat on the dais returned once more: He saw himself before leaving for the dance, posturing in front of this very pier glass, taking the attitudes of the waltz, actually dancing backward with the hand mirror, watching the swing of his coat and the curve of his trouser legs. "I cannot bear this!" Charles said wildly, and started to catalogue the shame of the others. Dolly's net stockings, he thought, and that absurd rose. Leona's open chagrin. Lewis's deathly embarrassment. And George with his sad little flash of courage. And Tarnac—why, he had enough gibes prepared to keep Tarnac reeling for a year.

Gradually Charles's head grew quiet. He opened the curtains. Another perfect day. It might be yesterday—but he thrust that thought quickly out of sight. He sat in the chintz chair and permitted himself an unusual indulgence: he smoked a cigarette before breaking his fast. Then he rang for Bridie, and when she appeared, he stared at her in amazement, for even he could not ignore the extraordinary violence she brought with her into the room.

She handed him his orange juice and poured the hot milk and coffee. He eyed her curiously as he sipped the orange juice. Her face was actually twitching with some emotion. Something must have upset her last night. He felt he could not bear it if she left the room before he knew what it was.

"A very pleasant party last night, Bridie," he said smoothly. "Very pleasant indeed. The girls looked so pretty in their little best dresses."

"I suppose they did, sir." Bridie hurled herself at the window curtains, and snatched them apart with such force that the whole inside window frame was left naked, ruining Leona's lovely draped effect. Charles frowned in surprise. More here than meets the eye, he thought, and wondered how best to approach this maddened woman.

"Poor dear Mr. Tarnac," he said tentatively. "Pathetic fellow, I'm afraid he's had a bad time these last few years. A pity, really."

"Mr. Tarnac is all right," Bridie said. She stared at him, and it seemed to Charles that for the first time that morning she remembered who he really was. "Oh, Mr. Tarnac's a lovely man," she said spitefully. "The girls all think he's God's gift to the women. They're all head over heels in love with him." She had rehearsed this speech the night before, as she sat watching the dance and watching the watchers on the dais. She got little satisfaction from it now. She wondered if anything would ever happen in the world again that would be awful enough to satisfy her.

Jealousy, Charles thought, with disgust. This laughable monolith fancies herself in love. He picked up his notes, dismissing her. "The girls' opinion is always of immense interest to me. I must tell poor Mr. Tarnac what you said when I see him at lunch."

"You won't see him at lunch, nor at dinner either," Bridie cried, "for he went off back to town with the rest of that crew. They were all mad to get back to the city. The way they drove off, I wouldn't be surprised if the half of them were found dead, and I wouldn't be sorry, either."

"Who went back to the city? What do you mean?"

"Mr. Tarnac went back with all the fellows that were up here for the dance, and a few of the young ones that are working here, too. A lot of use they'll be around here today, if they ever come back here at all."

Charles laughed. Really, it was too good, that sodden fool Tarnac dashing around with a carful of drunken servants.

"And where on earth did these wild young things go, Bridie? To some dance hall, perhaps?"

Bridie took a deep and unsteady breath. "Oh, great God," she said, "when I heard of it! I could have dropped dead, so I could. I could have killed them."

"What did they do, Bridie?"

"Oh, Mr. Runyon, wait till I tell you. I had a nice chair that I sat on the whole evening, between the door where you come into the hall and the door where you go into the bar. Near the stage, I was. A couple of us sat there, and then from time to time other girls would come along and sit with us a minute or two. You know the way it is. And you know the way you talk. The boys would bring me a little drink now and then. Not that I took much, but you know, Mr. Runyon, I'm not accustomed to it. Oh, Mr. Runyon, the things I said. Things I wouldn't want repeated. I won't have a friend in the place when it gets out. I don't know where to go or what to do. I'm nearly mad, thinking about it all night long, and praying to God the records would be broke by the time they got back to town."

"What records, Bridie?"

"The records they made at the dance. Didn't one of the young fellows in the band—a radio mechanic he is, bad luck to him—rig up one of them wire-recording things right behind where I was sitting. Every word I said. If they'd only have given me a hint. But of course nobody knew, only the young fellow himself, the young blackguard, and a couple of his friends that helped him fix it up. Things I wouldn't have repeated for the world—I—"

"And that was why they were in such a hurry to get back to town, to play the records over?"

"Why else. All laughing they were—"

"And Mr. Tarnac was with them, and some of the girls from here?"

"Josie next door, for one. Lazy young lump, she—"

"Bridie, please pay attention. Tell me, did they put recorders anywhere except behind your chair?"

"In the bar, they had one. I wouldn't have minded that, I wasn't in there. And one in the vestibule as you come in, but I hardly stopped there at all. And another one under the platform you and Mrs. Harkey and Mr. Harkey were on. I wasn't near there."

She stopped suddenly, astounded, listening to what she had just heard her own voice say. And to think that I missed that, she thought, and realized how far she had drifted from her moorings in these last few hours.

"Yes," she said, "that's right. There was one under where you were sitting, too, Mr. Runyon."

Staring greedily into his eyes, she saw and recognized what she had never hoped to see again—a chagrin as hot and as bitter as her own.

The Bride

$\mathcal{A}$t seven o'clock on the evening before her wedding day, Margaret Casey finished her packing, locked her suitcase, and sat down on the edge of her bed to catch her breath. Her room was on the top floor of the house in Scarsdale where she had worked as a maid for ten years. She was alone in the house. The phone was shut off, the refrigerator was disconnected, the windows all were locked, and all the beds, except hers, stripped for the summer. The family had early that morning driven off to their cottage in the Berkshires, where they would remain until October. Margaret had dreaded the moment of their departure, fearing her own tears, which fell easily, but at the last minute she smiled brilliantly, and waved, and saw the car disappear out onto the road calmly enough, although for a moment there she felt she must cry after them to come back, come back, if only for an hour, and not leave her by herself at a time like this.

Of course, it was her own idea in the first place to get married the day after they left for the summer. Summer had seemed a comfortable, indefinite time away the night last February that she had given in to Carl's persistence and given him her promise. She liked Carl, but she wasn't much inclined to marry him. All that night, she lay awake in a panic, thinking of ways to break with him. It would be heartless to tell him straight out that she had no use for him. Crafty, she decided to do one thing at a time. First she would give Mrs. Smith her notice, and then she would just steal away to another town and find a new job and not let Carl know anything about it. But when she went in, when they were having breakfast, and gave her notice, the sight of Mrs. Smith's stricken face was too much for her, and to ease her guilt she blurted out that she was going to marry Carl, and settle down, and stop working, and have a home of her own. Mr. and Mrs. Smith were astonished and delighted at her good fortune, and their pleasure made her so generous that she embroidered the case a little, describing the house (not yet built) that Carl hoped to buy, and telling about his plan to go into business with his brother someday, not right away. Mrs. Smith said she hoped Margaret would let her give a little wedding breakfast here in the house after the ceremony, but Margaret quickly said no, that her plans were made to be married the day after they left for the summer. After some argument, Mrs. Smith gave in to her, and laughed, and said that after all Margaret was the bride and it was only right she should have things her way. Back in the kitchen, Margaret sat as astonished as though they had ordered her out of the house. All I wanted to do was give notice, she thought, and here I've gone and committed myself.

Still, July seemed a long time off. There would surely be some way to free herself. She could pick a fight with Carl, or she might confide in Mrs. Smith and ask her advice. But it grew harder and harder to speak up. Anyway, she found herself growing fond of Carl. It was the first time in her life she had ever had anyone of her own, and he was very considerate of her. He was coming along now in a few minutes to take her out to dinner.

She contrasted this evening with the evening, twelve years ago in Ireland, before her sister Madge was married. That evening, Madge never stopped posturing around in her wedding dress of blue silk, showing off before the neighbors while her mother sat in the middle of the room crying because she was losing her big girl and the family would soon be all scattered. "Next thing little Margaret will be leaving me," cried the mother, and Margaret had darted to her mother's side and protested that no, no, she would never leave, and the neighbors nodded approvingly and said that was a good daughter, that one. Still, good daughter and all, it was Madge who was the favorite, and when, after a year, Madge decided to economize by moving back into her old home, Margaret felt very out of place with the perpetual fuss over Madge's baby and Madge's husband and Madge's aches and pains. Margaret was already out working by then, and when her uncle in New York wrote offering to lend her the passage over, she accepted at once, believing up to the last minute before she left that the mother would come to her senses and forbid her to go. But the mother appeared delighted to see Margaret get her "chance," and there were fewer tears shed over Margaret's departure for a foreign land than over Madge's decision to marry a boy she had known all her life.

Margaret had found great satisfaction in the money orders she sent home weekly, knowing the power they gave her mother over the household. After the debt to her uncle was paid off, she sent more and more money home, stinting herself to send as much as she could. She always meant to start saving her fare home, but she really believed that when the time came for her to see her mother again, the money would turn up somehow. She wanted to go back there and best Madge, once and for all. She had a dream of saving up enough to go back and start a little business, enough to support her mother and herself, or to go back with a comfortable nest egg and find some good man to marry. None of her hopes had come true. All of her hopes had turned into regrets; only the hurt, strained feeling in her heart was the same. Everything had turned out wrong. The mother was five months dead now, and there no longer seemed any way to get back at Madge, sitting triumphant there in possession of all the old bits of ornaments and furniture and everything that remained of the old home. Not that Madge had offered to send her anything—not even a few of the old photographs—and it would be too bitter to reveal her jealousy and longing by asking for them. Madge had known what she was doing, all right.

If only God had given Margaret the strength to wait a while longer, something might have turned up. She might have won the Sweep, or some old lady might have turned up who wanted a companion to travel to Ireland with her, or somebody—her uncle, maybe—might have died and left her a legacy. There was no limit to the things that might have happened, if she'd only had patience. But the night she heard her mother was dead, Carl was so sympathetic that she committed herself further than she had ever meant to. It was the way he put his arm around her that undid her, the closeness of his body giving her a warmth she had forgotten since her mother's lap. How well he knew the time to take advantage of me, she thought angrily. His persistence had put her off the first time she met him. She should have been firm then, and got rid of him for good. That was the German in him, enabling him to hang on until he got what he was after. He would never fit in with the crowd at home. They would laugh at him behind his back and say he was thick. Madge's cruel eyes would cut clear through the smart American clothes to see the soft, good-natured, easily hurt fellow underneath. Madge would laugh to hear Mr. Smith say that Carl was a fine, steady fellow who would always be a credit to the community. Mr. and Mrs. Smith had been very nice about the whole thing. Mr. Smith had given Margaret three months' salary as a wedding present, and Mrs. Smith gave her her wedding outfit. Her dress, a jacket and skirt of navy-blue shantung, hung now in the closet, with the new shoes in a box on the floor underneath and the new hat in a box on the shelf above. Except for her rosary beads, she had nothing old and familiar from Ireland to bring with her into her new home. Madge had stolen everything, and without even lifting a finger.

One time, when Margaret was a little girl, before her father died, her mother and father had gone for a ride in a charabanc, out into the country. When they came back, they talked about the hotel where they'd had tea, and about the woods and rivers they had seen. They promised that Margaret would have a charabanc ride one Sunday, and she believed them and began to go every Sunday to watch the buses fill up with passengers. A lot of young people used to go, laughing and pushing and jostling each other to see who would get the best seat. Margaret had her seat all picked out—the one up in front near the driver—but she never had the chance to ride in it. There was always some excuse to keep her from going. Sometimes one of the charabancs went on a mystery tour. The driver of the charabanc knew where he was going, but the passengers had to guess, and never could be sure of their destination until they arrived there. The people going off on the mystery tours seemed even gayer than the usual charabanc crowds. Margaret longed to go with them, although she had a half fear that the mystery charabancs never came back at all. She might just as well have gone on one and not come back, for all the good she had made of her life.

A joyful shouting came from downstairs, and Margaret ran out onto the landing. It was Carl. He had let himself in by the back door. He was accustomed to back doors, being a plumber. When he reached the second-floor landing, he looked up and saw her.

"How's my girl?" he shouted, as though they were miles apart. His voice was hard in the emptiness of the house. He had been drinking, she could hear it in his voice, but she would say nothing about it this time. He threw his head back and stretched his arms wide, clowning in his unaccustomed happiness, but she was not touched by his emotion. She stared down at him in astonishment and fear.

"What's the matter?" he shouted, throwing himself down on his arms on the banisters. "Were you afraid I wasn't going to come? Were you afraid I might leave you at the church? You can get *that* idea out of your head. You're not getting away from me *that* easy."

She wanted to scream at him that he was beneath her, and that she despised him, and that she was not bound to him yet and never would be bound to him, but instead she spoke civilly, saying that she would be ready in a minute, and warning him not to come up into the room, because her wedding dress was hanging there and she didn't want him to see it ahead of time, for fear of bringing bad luck on the two of them.

The Holy Terror

She was the ladies'-room lady in the sedate Royal Hotel in Dublin. Mary Ramsay, rough-voiced, rough-handed, rough-mannered in every way. Her tongue would take the skin off you, they said in the hotel. They were all afraid of her.

In the ladies' room, if she happened to turn her back on you (maybe to get a towel, or the coat brush) you would see how that great swollen rump of hers rolled and heaved across the floor. She was tormented with arthritis—legs, arms, everywhere. It pained her to stand, and it pained her to sit down, and when she was still for any length of time the stiffness forced her to get up and move about. Her loose men's slippers, slit at the sides for further comfort, left her flat-footed; and then the great big legs began; all wrapped in black wool stockings, they pressed up under the skirts and out of sight into unimaginable depths and darkness of folded, petted flesh. She was well fed, that one.

It was a miracle, they all said later, how she lasted so long at the hotel, especially in that job, where you usually look to see someone neat and tidy, even if she isn't so young. But on the day the blow fell, everything in the ladies' room was as it had been for twenty years, which was the length of time Mary Ramsay had been queening it there. She had been with the hotel for thirty-seven years, doing one thing or another. There was no denying the fact that she had given her life to the place.

She had a shabby, low-seated bamboo chair set in beside a screen in the corner of the outer room, where the mirrors and dressing tables were. Sitting in that chair, with one cushion under her and one at her back, she had a full view of everything that went on, and yet she was screened from the door. There she sat the better part of the time, and there she took her meals, too, between the rush hours, from a tray on the table beside her.

She had collected privileges with her years of service. She still had her own little comfortable room on the top floor, although most of the hotel employees had to board out, with things as crowded as they were. That room of hers contained everything she owned, but she had money in the bank. She delighted in saving, and the tips mounted up.

In her bedroom she slept, and conferred there occasionally with her crony Mrs. Bailey, the oldest switchboard operator. The rest of the time, from ten in the morning until ten at night, she sat down among the mirrors and washbasins of the ladies' room. She seldom if ever took her day off. The ladies' room was her theater and her kingdom. She hated to miss a minute there. The power she had.

Her thick gray hair was done up in a bird's nest on her head, and underneath, those bland mean eyes of hers looked you through and through. As you faced the mirror, combing and powdering, she would come to stand near you, watching every move. She had the right to be there, in fact it was her duty. There was no getting away from her. There she stood, one hand on the back of a chair, perhaps, the other in her apron pocket, where it chewed the day's tips. Her conversation was personal and uncharitable. She was all eyes and ears. She enjoyed this daily vigil. She took a merciless pleasure in watching women as they passed before her in their most female and desperate and comical predicaments. She said often and often, "I can price anyone," and her heavy, derisive glance scoured you up and down.

To a woman like that who is pleasant you give a tip. Since Mary was so unpleasant, you gave her twice that amount, and left apologetically, with her sardonic gaze burning a spot on your neck. Of course she knew who to be nice to. The more important guests, and the Americans, rejoiced in her favor. With the passing of the years, she had acquired a sort of name for herself. She could hardly fail to. Her rudeness passed for independence, and even for wit. Women smiled ingratiatingly at her contemptuous face in the mirror and then turned to smile again and extend their hands gratefully for a towel. They inquired about her health and asked her advice about one thing and another. This was especially true of American visitors, who made her almost famous as an Irish *character*. She was even mentioned in some American lady's newspaper column as a "real Dublin character, possessed of dry Irish wit."

They courted her and quoted her and brought her lipsticks and nylons. She hoarded these gifts, which were of no use to her, and bribed the hotel maids to do little odd jobs for her. There is no telling what she might have done, if she had been possessed of more brain or of more ambition. But the ladies' room satisfied her and suited her. Her dislike of the women she served possessed her completely, and she watched their posturing with a hard, avid pleasure. Her curiosity about the secrets of their dress never ended, as her eye pondered up and down. Nothing escaped her. One of the bolder hotel maids, a malicious, observant thing herself, said one time that she thought there was a man under Mary Ramsay's skirts, she was that queer.

It was well said, and nothing escaped her, and she forgot

nothing. The things she heard (and the things she guessed at) washed about forever in her sour, secretive mind. She bore in her heart a long, directionless grudge, a ravenous grudge. The church, she knew, was on her side, for did it not forbid and condemn all vanity and the sins of the flesh?

Those tray meals were a great thing in her life. She fed herself with appetite and liked to feel her mouth full of food. The appetite she had had from a child, and had never had reason or necessity to stint it. Stout was her drink.

Her breakfast she used to have alone, after all the others had finished, since her duties started late in the morning. She had a snack—a glass of milk or a cup of cocoa—during the course of the morning. During the slowest hour of the afternoon she had a lunch tray. Tea came later, and supper last of all. Before going to bed she had a little something. What bit of good will she had, she spent on her food. She felt solicitous and kind and tender toward the heaped-up food, before she set on it, to devour it. She ate very quickly, and the tray was usually whisked in and out within twenty minutes or less. She hated to be disturbed with her tray.

The others at the hotel were afraid of her and of her petty, inescapable revenges. They thought she got away with a lot. She and her friend Mrs. Bailey at the switchboard had a corner on all the gossip in the place. Placed as they were at two strategic points for gathering information, they knew everything that went on. If you kept on the right side of them, you might be in the know too. Miss Ramsay also maintained a grim companionship with the chief doorman, who had come to work at the hotel the same year as herself.

The Royal was a gracious, comfortable, old-fashioned hotel that had started to go down and was now flourishing again with the big tourist trade. Near the newsstand, not far from the switchboard, at the back of a glass showcase filled with linen tablecloths and lace collars and poplin ties, the entrance to the ladies' room was hidden, and there Mary Ramsay lurked in the deeps of her bamboo chair, renewing her contempt for life both in and out of her kingdom. At the same time, or at a similar time, her arch-enemy, Miss Williams, the new assistant manager, was nerving herself to take a bold step.

Miss Williams, from Belfast, had an economical little body, a strong undaunted stomach, and a very thin nose, shaped like the blade of a scythe. She ate very little and slept only an hour or so at a time, but she walked a great deal. She had been at the Royal only six weeks—having been brought in to pull it together before the summer season—but they said that she had already walked around the hotel more often than any other living soul. When she walked she hurried, never without reason, but if she had anything to say she said it standing still.

Everything was of enormous importance to her. To her, the hotel was a large engine, and she inspected its workings tirelessly. She loved order. She liked the hotel best at night, when all the bed-room doors were closed tight, the lounge empty, the newsstand shuttered, and the dining-room tables laid for breakfast. It would have given her great satisfaction to go from room to room straight-ening the guests out in their beds, like knives and forks. She often played with this notion before dropping off to sleep, starting with the big suite on the second floor and working up bed by bed to the top of the building, where the image of Mary Ramsay's humped huddling and harsh snoring drove all order and patience from her mind. Then the ladies' room would rise up before her, with that creaky bamboo chair, those trays of food, the smeared mirrors, and above all that garrulous, greedy heap of a woman.

For six weeks she plotted. Mr. Sims, the manager, told her very plainly that he washed his hands of the whole thing. Miss Wil-liams smiled and primly said to leave it all to her. Suddenly one morning, on her way to the dining room, she wheeled around and walked in the opposite direction, in search of her prey. The prey was sitting in state, looking over the morning death notices and sucking sweet tepid cocoa out of a cup. She rolled a menacing eye toward the intruder, till she saw who it was.

"It's a lovely morning, Mary," said Miss Williams in her rapid whirring northern accent.

She stepped quickly over to the nearest window and threw it up as far as it would go. She had great strength in those thin little arms of hers. By the time she turned back, the cocoa cup was in its saucer among the wet biscuit crumbs and the newspaper had vanished behind a cushion. Mary lumbered over to the washbasins, where she snatched up two used hand towels, bundled them together, and began to wipe over the mirror.

"Take your eye off this place for a minute," she said, rubbing round and round, "and it gets to be a pigsty. Some of the ones that come in here, you'd think they'd never been in a decent place in their lives. D'you know that, Miss Williams? You feel like saying to them, 'Where have you been accustomed to living, I'd like to know?' And the airs they put on."

Miss Williams pressed her two little lips tightly together and stretched them slightly, producing a disagreeable smiling effect. She put her head a little to one side and her heels together and said nothing. She was a great believer in giving people enough rope to hang themselves, so she kept still now while Mary rambled along from one complaint to the next. Mary was relieved. She expanded as she talked. She had never seen Miss Williams in a chatty sort of mood until now. The soap cupboard was reflected in the mirror, and Miss Williams methodically counted the bars and boxes, while Mary talked herself out of a job.

Miss Williams finished counting. She exhaled and looked Mary in the eye.

"You have a lot of work here for one person, Mary," she observed. Mary's head was still swimming pleasantly with a wash of grievances. There was her health, the bad conduct of the public, and the negligence of the rest of the staff. Every time she paused for breath something new floated to the surface of her mind and kept her talking. She took Miss William's remarks to be merely a polite interpolation.

"Ah, sure I manage the best I can," she said with a deprecating fall to her voice. "I'd work till I'd drop. That's the sort I am. I know we're shorthanded and for the sake of the hotel's good name I'd keep going day and night, if I had to. No matter what—"

"We're not shorthanded at all, Mary," said Miss Williams, sweetly.

Mary gaped at her.

"Sure and we are, then, Miss Williams. They can't get the people. Sure we all know that."

"You've been misinformed, Mary. Any shortage that may have existed is gone, and there's no need for you to continue working yourself to death as you have been. It seems to me, and Mr. Sims is in full agreement with me, by the way, that there's work here, more than enough, for two pairs of hands."

Mary turned from the mirror with a face full of truculent suspicion. Miss Williams smiled at her, disclosing a perfect set of tiny false teeth, seed pearls, as alike and as dainty as peas in a pod. The pod was Miss Williams's smile, her suave, ready smile of annihilation.

She continued, "In the six weeks that I've been here, I've been very much aware of your long hours, and of all that you do, Mary. This morning I had a talk with Mr. Sims about it. As a matter of fact, Mr. Sims and I have discussed you many times."

Mary listened in fascinated silence.

"We've decided that you simply have to rest, Mary. That's all there is to it. It's absurd, all these long hours, every day of the week, week in, week out, year in, year out. So beginning on Monday, you'll divide your time with Mona Casey. And you'll take your full day off, Mary, and no ifs or buts."

"I don't want that young strap in here with me, getting under my feet, annoying the people," said Mary, with knots in her tongue. "Mr. Sims knows that, so he does."

"Mr. Sims is well aware of how you feel, Mary. He knows you don't want anybody in here with you, and I know you don't want anybody, but you're going to have somebody whether you like it or not. For your own sake, Mary. Now you've got to be reasonable about this. You aren't as young as you once were, Mary. None of us are."

That knocked the wind out of her, reflected Miss Williams, without regret. The direct approach, she thought, and this observation skimmed like a sweet bird across the sea of her composure.

"Mona, is it," said the stunned Mary. "That one."

And not even bothering to say pardon to Miss Williams, she made her way across the floor and dropped into her chair. When she began to come to herself a little, Miss Williams had gone. She was sitting alone in a rage. Her eyes wandered in disbelief, and she rocked slightly in agitation. In her cup, the cocoa had settled down into a dark puddle. It looked hard. Maybe the cold air from the window has frozen it, she thought, in a separate burst of pettishness, feeling the draft on her back. She dipped in a finger and it came away stained and sugary. She stuck the finger mechanically into her mouth, and just at that moment there was Miss Williams again, cool as a cucumber, nice as you please, butter wouldn't melt in her mouth.

"Another thing, Mary," she said smooth and fast, grasping the nettle again, "and this I sincerely regret, although I know that *you* will understand. It's the crowds, you know, the summer crowds from England and America, besides the regular people coming up for their holidays. Things are getting out of hand. Of course it means more money all round, more work and more money.

"To come to the point, I'm afraid you must give up your room. We'll have to start redecorating in a week at the latest, but I've a couple of very good addresses here, not too far away, very pleasant rooms, I'm told.

"I'm sorry about this, but now you've had your room longer than most, haven't you? Let me know what arrangements you make, and then we'll talk about hours and days off and get a timetable set up."

She had disappeared again.

"They grudge me my bed," said Mary aloud. "After all these years."

Her friend Mrs. Bailey barged in, with her hair still sticking up where the earphone had untidied it.

"What's this, what's this I hear? I hear she's taken your room away from you."

Mary nodded somberly, pursing her lips.

"Out of my room," she said, "and out of a job, you might say."

Mrs. Bailey leaned back against the washstand and gazed at the ceiling, treasuring this moment of astonishment. Then she bent expertly forward in an attitude of horrified disbelief.

"You don't mean it," she bleated greedily.

"After all these years," said Mary, rolling the calamity on her tongue. Mrs. Bailey's horror warmed her and brought her to herself. She looked her old friend straight in the eye.

"Mark you me, she didn't get off scot free," she said, nodding her head menacingly with each word. "I cut the ground from under that lassie's feet. I turned her inside out. Inside out."

Mrs. Bailey's surprise was over. A woman who had buried two husbands and several children, she was past being swept off her feet for very long, even by such an event as this. Now she sank into the rhythm of the interchange with a knowing smile. She crossed her arms and settled her plump behind against the washstand with a mirthful nod.

"I'll warrant you did. She came out of here as though all the hounds in hell were after her. Tell us, what did you say to her ladyship, Mary?"

The glance they exchanged was palpitant with understanding, but Mary, in her new sensitive role as defendant, felt with dismay that something was missing. The glance had been used too often. This was a larger occasion. She thrust her head forward.

"You know I have a tongue, Bessie."

She had that reputation.

"I told her what I thought of her, all right. She was a different lady going out of here than when she came in, I guarantee you that. I didn't spare her. I promise you. May God forgive me, the things I said. And Bessie, I told her what *you* said of her. I wish you could have seen the look on her ugly visage when I told her what you said. It would have done your heart good, Bessie."

Bessie was electrified. She leaned away from the washstand as though she had been stung.

"Mother of God," she gasped. "Are you trying to get me the sack, with your idle, malicious gab?"

Mary was not to be deflected from her path, and she proceeded with righteous tread. The scene was now charged with that high, hysterical emotion that she judged worthy of the occasion.

"That one'll rue the day she was born," she hissed. "She'll be sorry she ever crossed Mary Ramsay's path."

"What was it you told her about me, y' interfering old rip?" cried Bessie, and fled, unable to bear her anguish any longer.

Mary contemplated the retreat of her old friend without any invasion of soft emotion. She knew the world well enough to know what they would all be saying behind her back, and Mrs. Bessie Bailey was no exception. Sitting among the ruins of her kingdom, she pondered.

She contemplated the future with a curdled eye. The walks to and from the rooming house—she looked dourly at the list of addresses Miss Williams had given her—the long and lonely hours in her room, while Mona—that strap—collected the tips that were rightfully hers. No trays, probably, either. It was easy to see which way the wind was blowing. And all the laughing and talking and finger pointing that would go on behind her back. She got up finally and made her way thoughtfully to Mr. Sims's office. She captured him at the newsstand, and he was amazed at the lack of fire in her eye.

"Poor old thing, she looks quite done in," he thought.

Miss Williams, who might have been on guard, had flown on swift feet about her morning tour of inspection. Mary Ramsay followed Mr. Sims to his office, and the door closed respectfully behind them. It was an extraordinary occasion, although Mr. Sims did not realize it, because Mary was at last after all these years going to use her most cherished and deadliest weapon.

She felt calm with vengeance.

"Mr. Sims, I have no word of reproach for you. I have no complaint. I accept this cross that the Lord has seen fit to lay upon my shoulders, though it does seem a bit hard with my bad health and all. But before I go—Miss Williams as good as told me I'm not wanted here any longer—there are some things it's my duty to tell you. Things have been coming to a head around here for a long time now."

She talked for an hour. She began with Mrs. Bailey and worked painstakingly down to the kitchen maids. Some of the secrets she betrayed were thirty years old. She told about her friend the doorman and what had happened to the champagne—a gift of friends in London—that Mr. Sims was supposed to receive last Christmas. She told a few other things about the doorman too. She told about the young chap on the front lift and what he'd been up to in the storeroom on the top floor, and not with any of the maids, either. She told about the angelic little page boy, Mikey, little freckled Mikey, and his furtive pastimes. Mr. Sims listened, pinned to his chair by her cold wet voice.

"That Miss Williams is out to get your job too, Mr. Sims," she said with conviction. "She's been talking against you to everybody in the place. She says you're easygoing and other things I couldn't repeat to you."

Mr. Sims reflected bleakly that the remark had not been made Mary Ramsay wouldn't repeat. Every treasured bit of scandal, every scrap of information, every whisper that had ever been whispered in the Royal was trotted out and thrown down on his desk.

"And now, Mr. Sims, you have a better idea than you had an hour ago of who you can trust and who you can't, haven't you, now," said Mary, sitting back and looking approvingly at him, settling herself for a chat. She was triumphant. She saw herself being offered Miss Williams's job.

"You can speak your mind to me, Mr. Sims," she said with sly expectancy, but saw with surprise that he was on his feet, making for the door, so she collected herself out of the chair and followed him, smiling graciously.

"I may as well tell you, Miss Williams wants me to take my week off now, and I'll take it. I may as well be out of the way during the unpleasantness. It isn't as if I had to work, you know. I can be independent of the lot of you. I tell you that.

"And in a week or so you'll know where you stand, Mr. Sims. The air will be clear by that time. You'll be thankful I warned you in time. But all I ask for is my old place back, just as it used to be.

At my age you don't want changing about, Mr. Sims. Maybe you know about that yourself."

"Quite right, Mary," said Mr. Sims passionately.

He showed her out with ceremony. He was a dishonest man. He sent for Miss Williams, and she came in on the double, having left a trail of startled, delighted faces all the way down from the third floor.

"The woman's a lunatic, that's all there is to it," he said crossly after a few minutes' talk. He felt like a fool.

Miss Williams sniffed with pleasure. She was as excited as she was ever likely to get.

"I might have known," she said. "Indeed, I might have known."

"Of course there's no question of her coming back now," he said. He was nervous and very angry.

Having sowed her seeds, Mary took herself off. It wasn't until she received Miss Williams's letter, short and to the point, that she realized she had no way of going back, and then it was too late.

The Bohemians

$\mathscr{M}$r. Briscoe was an actor by profession. Mrs. Briscoe, who dyed her hair to keep it as near as possible to the rich dark red it used to be, taught music for a living. She was forty when she met him. He was forty-seven. They were a fine battered pair, marked for life by their ravenous hopes. They both had the glittering, exploring eyes of people who have never learned to control their dreams.

They met late one Saturday night, at an artistic sort of a party. Mr. Briscoe, a Londoner, had come from England the day before on the promise of a part with an English company playing a season at the Gaiety. The part had fallen through, and he was now stranded in Dublin, broke but unafraid. He came along to the party with an acquaintance he had run into in a pub. Mrs. Briscoe, then Miss Jane Rooney, had also come with an acquaintance, a Miss Finch, who played in the three-piece orchestra at the Dublin Art Theatre.

Jane was wearing a dress of dark-purple tweed, cut rather in the fashion of the Rossettis, and she had her thick, coarse red hair coiled low on her neck. She wore handmade silver jewelry of Irish design, set with amethysts. She was a tall, extremely thin woman, with a long slender nose and a very small mouth. Her tiny, dry lips, overcome as they were by her long nose, seemed to deny all the desirous demands of her eyes. She was very brave. When left alone at a party—as she often was, because she was extravagantly artistic, and often, after a glass of something, provoked foolish, heartfelt arguments—she would rear back her large head of hair, reveal her minute, contemptuous smile, and dart her heated glance in all directions, in search of a more receptive audience. She was unattractive to men, and usually had to find her way home alone. This did not drive her, as it drove less exalted souls, to the weak expedient of slipping away quietly in the middle of the evening. On the contrary, she always stayed to the end, and walked away from the pairs and groups without a sign of discomfort. *This* had been happening to her all her life.

Mr. Briscoe saw her standing alone, from his own solitary point of vantage next to the table with the glasses on it. He started moodily in her direction, holding a full glass in his right hand.

"Why are you so proud?" he asked masterfully.

She retrieved her gaze from a distant part of the room and fell in love with him, as she had often fallen in love before.

Greatly pleased with the impression he had made, he conducted her to a sofa. "I am a London actor, out of work and penniless. My name is George Briscoe. I was impelled to speak to you because you are the only beautiful woman in the room. I am not married," he said to her, drinking and staring at her.

He was a wide man, with a face and hands of dazzling whiteness, and a low forehead, from which he combed his hair straight back to conceal as well as possible the baldness of his crown. He wore a yellow checked waistcoat.

"I am a magnificent actor, but I cannot find work. They no longer want real actors on the stage. They want robots, automatons, expressionless vacuum heads. Above all, they want thin young men. An older man can only get a job if he has been rewarded with a title, or if he has made a name in films. Unless he wants to found his own company." He gave her a bland smile in which there was no resentment. "Tell me anything you would like to tell me," he added.

"I am Jane Rooney, teacher of music," said Jane with a harsh laugh of delight and embarrassment. "I dabble in all the arts. I am devoted to the theater in all its forms."

"My dear girl," he began, leaning toward her, "the theater has only one form." Jane began to listen.

"I would like to escort you home," he said much later. "If you do not live too far away."

When they arrived at her flat he suggested that he come in with her. "Otherwise," he said sensibly, "I shall spend the night on the streets."

Since there was only one bed in the flat, he settled himself on a chair in her little parlor, but after an hour he arose, sighing, and found his way into the bed alongside her. Jane lay rigid, staring at the ceiling with bulging eyes. She had never lain next to a man before.

"I hope you aren't a restless sleeper, my dear," he said, settling himself comfortably, and fell asleep.

Jane lay awake all night, and when the first breath of day came into the room she slipped out of bed and away to the kitchen, where she said her prayers and cried nervously. "God forgive me," she said, "but I couldn't very well send him out in the cold."

When eight o'clock came, she got off her knees and set a tray for his breakfast. She had to give a piano lesson at half past nine.

"Good girl," he said when he opened his eyes and saw the tray. "Oh, I can't sit up," he said roguishly, holding the blankets up under his chin, "till you give me something to cover my naked-ness. A big towel will do," he said, brushing aside her embarrass-ment.

She brought a large shawl, and turned aside while he arranged himself.

"You're all dressed and ready to go out," he said admiringly. "What a clever girl you are."

After the first lesson she had a second, but as soon as she was free she hurried home. He was sitting in the parlor, with a fine red glow in the grate and one of her collections of plays in his hands. He closed the book and held out his hand to her. "I hope I didn't disturb your sleep, Jane," he said.

She fell on her knees beside him and pressed her plain face against his hand. "I was so afraid I would never see you again," she said.

He stroked her thick springy hair. "What a wonderful color your hair is," he said. "Is it really this color?"

"Oh, yes. I wouldn't dye it," Jane said quickly.

George found the little flat very comfortable. He was not lazy. He did some housework while Jane was out and even helped in the kitchen. They went for a stroll every night, and once to the pictures, walking very casually past Jane's landlady's door.

At the end of a week, Jane's landlady stormed up the stairs and demanded to see Jane alone, and asked her what did she think she was up to. "I'm surprised at you," she said curiously. "I'd never have thought you were that sort."

"I'm as much that sort as anybody else," Jane said. "Anyway," she added, "it isn't the way it looks. He's been very gentlemanly, if you know what I mean."

Mrs. Dolan drew back with an imploring smile. "Have a heart, girl," she said. "I'm a married woman. You're not expecting me to believe a thing like that?"

"Believe it or not as you like, Mrs. Dolan. What can I do? Put him out on the street?"

"Well, you can't let him impose on you like this," said Mrs.

Dolan. She thought of the glimpse she had had of him as she came in. "He looks a helpless sort of poor fellow, the way he's settled down beside the fire. It seems a heartless thing to do, to tell him to get up and go."

"I know," Jane said. She was wearing the green tweed skirt and beige jersey, with a necklace of large amber beads, that she usually wore in the daytime.

"Why wouldn't you marry him?" Mrs. Dolan asked coaxingly.

"He hasn't asked me," Jane said in surprise, and began to dab at her eyes.

Mrs. Dolan gazed in indecision at the kitchen door. She opened it and looked in at George, where he sat with his book.

"Would you come out here a minute, sir?" she cried.

"Certainly, Mrs. Dolan," he said. "We'll leave the door open, if you don't mind. This is such a very small kitchen."

"Mr. Briscoe, if you don't mind my saying so, you've got this girl into terrible trouble," Mrs. Dolan said.

"Mrs. Dolan is afraid for my good name," Jane said, with an attempt at a smile.

"Why wouldn't you marry her, sir?" Mrs. Dolan said. "No hurry, of course, sir," she added, not wanting to spoil Jane's chances. "But later on, when you've made up your mind."

"I'm a poor man," George said. "An out-of-work actor. How can I ask any woman to marry me?"

George was not one to fight fate. After Jane discovered this about him, she marveled that no woman had run off with him before she found him.

In the second year of their marriage she became pregnant, and they had to move, because children were not allowed in the flats. Using Jane's savings, they bought a small red brick house on a terrace in the suburbs. Their house was covered with a Virginia creeper, the same rich red brown as Jane's hair. The big pointed leaves clustered thickly around the front door and around the windows, and made their house seem older and more opulent than its neighbors. They had a small front garden and a larger back garden, and Jane grew very enthusiastic about her flowers. There was a laburnum tree at the back, and little John's first recollection was of the laburnum in full bloom, brighter, yellower, gayer, and more splendid than anything he ever saw in his life again.

" 'John Briscoe' is a good-sounding name, no matter what he decides to do," George said.

George could hardly ever get a part, and it depressed him to be turned down. He learned Robert Emmet's "Speech from the Dock," and began to go around to all the schools declaiming it, with a sash over his right shoulder and a sword in his hand. Jane had many friends among the schoolteachers. That is how the thing got started. He was reciting the speech for them all at home one Sunday night, and one of the teachers asked him to give it for her students. Afterward he learned the "Lament for Owen Roe" (did they dare, did they dare, to slay Owen Roe O'Neill), which he recited in a ragged jacket, sitting down with his hands clasped on a walking stick, and his eyes half shut, because he was convinced that the man who wrote it was blind.

He was paid a little money for these performances. When John passed his seventh birthday he went with his father one day to help with the properties, and after that he always went, and always accepted the fee from a minor teacher while his father was talking and charming the head of the school. Once they got outside, he would slip the money into his father's pocket, not saying anything.

The Briscoes used to have very successful Sunday evenings. Other music teachers came, and amateur concert singers, and once in a while even an actor would come, and bring a friend — perhaps a fellow who wrote poetry. They used to sing and have long, delightful discussions. George was always the center of attention, and Jane guarded the hospitality of the house and rested herself, and sometimes led into the discussion with some foolish theory of hers, as she had in her single days.

George never grew impatient with her. He never grew impatient with anyone. She knew herself to be less intelligent and less well informed than he, and when she spoke up he would give her a jesting look and shake his head to prevent her getting too excited. He talked a great deal about his years on the fringes of the London theater, and though the guests by no means believed all he told them, they enjoyed listening to him, because he was different from themselves. In years gone by, Jane had always been a hanger-on at the parties she attended. She found it pleasant to be at the center of things. She hardly changed, except that her hair began to fade, and then she dyed it, so that really she didn't change at all. She still had her hopes, and they were still the same, and her dreams were still alive and complete, but she was so comfortable with them that they no longer glittered recklessly in her eyes, nor did she ever now smile contemptuously about her as she said in her own mind, "Look at me, what I am, what I shall be."

Her husband, however, while taking life calmly, watched the future with confidence in his own prophecy. "The old days are coming back," he would say. "They'll want my sort of acting again. All this dead man's walk is just a passing fad. We'll go to New York, when John is old enough, and I'll get a character part, perhaps go to Hollywood. Nowadays what they want in Hollywood is really good English character actors, with a solid training behind them." He took to wearing a black cape.

John was proud of his father, and of his mother, because they were different from the other parents on the terrace. His father went to work when he pleased, when there was a performance at one of the schools. Even his mother kept irregular hours. They were bohemians. They let John stay up as late as he liked, and every Sunday night he sat on the little piano stool and listened to the conversation. Often a teacher from his own school would come, and he could boast of her visit in class the next day. Sometimes his mother would give him permission to invite a teacher on his own. One of the teachers told him that his mother's house was a veritable salon, and that John should appreciate the privileges of his upbringing.

Another good thing—John used to be let off from school a half hour early on performance days. Those days, he would meet his father near the strange school, and they would walk into the strange classroom or, if there was a hall, onto the stage, and all the strange children would stare up at him and be envious. His father would be wearing the black cloak, and he would take if off and John would hand him the sword and sash or whatever he wanted. John felt very important.

When he was nine, John began to write poetry. One Sunday night, he stood up during a lull in the conversation and asked his mother for permission to speak. She smiled beamingly at him and nodded, and glanced around at the others, and his father turned away from his discussion with the girl who taught French to smile and clap his hands noiselessly, for encouragement.

"I would like to read a poem I have written," John said in a rather artificial voice that was modeled after his father's reciting voice. "It is called 'To My Mother.'

> "I love my mother, darling Jane,
>   Who brought me to this world of pain.
>   She is my dear, my hope, my joy.
>   I'll always be her loving boy.
>
> "She works that I may dine on cake.
>   I'd walk through fire for her sake.
>   If she should die I could not live.
>   To be with her my life I'd give.

> "At night upon my knees I pray
> That she'll be safe an extra day.
> I love her more than all the rest.
> I love my mother, Jane, the best."

When he had finished, John sat down on the piano stool and stared at the floor. His face was flushed. His mother rushed forward and took him in her arms. She pressed her face against his cheek. She was weeping. The rest of the audience murmured appreciatively. George came over to pat his son's head. "I am greatly moved," he said. "We must see that you have your chance."

"That young man will be heard of," said one of the men present, a government worker who acted in his spare time. He had a long gaunt face, and he took his pipe from his mouth and nodded at John. "Mark my words," he said, "a new young poet for Ireland."

"Will you read that for the class tomorrow, John?" his English teacher asked deferentially.

After that, John read a poem every Sunday, and on Mondays read it again before his composition class. The other children tried to make a joke of him, but he took comfort in the words of his elders, and realized that all people of talent suffered from the sneers of the ignorant. He tried to tell the other children this, and they laughed more than ever.

When John was fourteen, he had enough poems for several volumes, but it was hard to find a publisher. However, on two occasions his poems appeared in the Sunday newspaper.

About this time, his father began to write a book about theories of acting. "Those things sell well in the United States," he said.

He and John used the same typewriter—John to type his poems, George to type pages of manuscript. Jane was very happy with all this activity. She was very proud of them both. She still wore her tweed Rossetti dresses, her hand-wrought jewelry, and her amber beads. At Christmastime she painted little cards and sent them to her friends.

Their house had French windows, upstairs and downstairs. On summer evenings they used to sit near the open windows, and the people walking by would glance in at them and know who they were. John never went out to play with the other children. He enjoyed sitting between his distinguished parents—the musician, the young poet, and the actor. On winter evenings they lighted the fire and drew the blinds. Sometimes John played chess with his father. George often read out parts of his book, and explained them at length to his wife and son. Sometimes John retired upstairs to write a poem. It was understood between them that John needed solitude for his poems. He had a little room of his own at the back of the house, overlooking the pretty garden. Beyond the red wall of the garden was a tennis club, and the green lawns stretched away to a large grove of tall trees. He was able to lie on his back in bed and watch the clouds pass across the sky.

Every poet has to wait for recognition, and while waiting John decided to take a government examination. He passed without trouble and got an appointment. They were all very happy. Now all three were adults, John thought, working.

At last his father's manuscript was completed, and they put him on the boat for England and a publisher. He had considered an Irish publisher and rejected the idea, because he believed, he said, that English bookmen have a wider circulation, and more money. "When I come back with all the money," he said, "we'll move to the country somewhere, wherever Jane likes, and lead a proper life." He stood against the rail, waving to them.

"How fine he looks," Jane said.

"He's an actor to his fingertips," John said proudly. "Look at the way his scarf is slung over his shoulders."

George came back before they expected him, with no warning. He let himself in quietly with his key one night and sat down in front of the fire as though he had been out for a stroll. "They wanted me to leave the manuscript," he said. "I wouldn't hear of it. Thieves they are, every last one of them. As soon as we can scrape together the fare, we'll go to America, and I'll find a better publisher there. But I won't send it out. Whoever reads it, I'll be there in the room to see he takes no notes."

"You're right, Father," John said. He was a slim, nice-looking boy, with clear skin and a long slender nose like his mother's. "Better wait and have it done properly. Isn't that right, Mother?"

"Of course it is," she said. "And we'll all go together. I won't let you go off alone like that again, George. Do you hear me?"

A fortnight afterward, she caught pneumonia and died inside of a few hours. She came home one afternoon at her usual time, and instead of going down to the kitchen to start the tea, she stood in the parlor door and told George she thought she'd go up and lie down. By the time they thought of calling a doctor she was too far gone to be saved. After she was buried, John took the amber beads out of her drawer and put them with his own things.

"I hope you're not letting up on your writing, John," his father said one night. "Your mother put all her hopes in you."

"I'm going to dedicate my first volume to her, Father—to her memory," John said.

He wrote a great many poems about his mother's death. When spring came, he and George went out and trimmed the grass in the back garden, but left her flowers untended.

One morning in May, John went in to rouse George, who never awakened of his own accord, and found him dead in bed.

There was nothing to do but sell the house and move into a flat in the middle of town. He did quite well for a while, between the money he got for the house and his salary. However, after two years the money was all gone—not a penny left. He had only his salary and he had to move into lodgings. Now that he needed it so badly, the work grew enormously distasteful to him. It deadened his spirit. He found it hard to write in the evenings. Still, he occasionally put down a poem.

One day, strolling idly along the quays, reluctant to go back to his room at the boarding house, he passed a row of used-furniture shops. An old piano stool standing outside the door of one of them caught his eye, and he stopped for a closer look. It was the one they had had at home, the very same. Indeed it was. He stood staring at it, and thought his heart would break, remembering the pleasant evenings, and the loving eyes, and all the words of praise so freely given.

He wrote a poem about this encounter. In his poem, which was a sonnet, he said that it was winter, not only in the city of Dublin but in his heart; that he felt once again that art is long and life is fleeting; that things had not turned out as he expected; and that it is a hard thing for a person to be left in the world after his mother and father are gone.

The Rose Garden

$\mathcal{M}$ary Lambert, an Irish shopkeeper, was left a widow at the age of thirty-nine, after almost ten years of marriage. She was left with two children—Rose, seven, and Jimmy, two. As far as money was concerned, she was no worse off than she had been, since it was she who supported the family, out of the little general shop she kept.

Her husband, Dom, first showed his illness plainly in the month of October, but he lingered on, seeming to grow stronger at Christmastime, and died early in February, at about seven in the morning. Mary and a young priest of the parish, Father Mathews, were in the room with him when he died. Mary had Dom's comb in her hand, because he had asked her, one time during the night, to comb the hair back off his forehead. The comb was broken in half. She was accustomed to use the coarse-toothed half for her own hair, which was long and black. The fine-toothed half had been suitable for his lifeless invalid's hair. Even in health his hair had been fine and lifeless, but now it just looked dusty against the pillow. Father Mathews, who was anxious to get away, asked Mary if she would like him to send the woman next door up to see her, but

she shook her head violently, and said that she'd be forced to make
an exhibition of herself soon enough, at the wake and the funeral,
and that for the time being she'd just as soon be left alone.

She sat down beside the bed, on the chair she had carried up
from the parlor the morning she first had to send for the doctor. It
was a straight-backed mahogany chair with a black horsehair seat.
Ordinarily there would be no chair in the bedroom. She had
expected the doctor to sit on it, but instead he had put his black bag
down on it. She stared at the room. The room, its walls, its dull
color, its scarce furniture, its dust, its faded holy pictures, its bad,
sick aspect, disgusted her, and the body on the bed was a burden
she could not bear. The seat of the little parlor chair was hard under
her. There was no rest in the room. Her legs were tired. One leg
was shorter than the other, so that she had to walk crookedly, leaning forward and sideways. The exertion she had to make gave her
great power in her right leg. She wore long skirts, and tall black
boots laced tightly in but leaving her knees free. The laced boots
were very solid and hard-looking, as though the feet inside them
were made of wood. The feet inside were not made of wood. She
had a great feeling in them, and in all parts of her body.

She was big, with a narrow nose, and a narrow-lipped mouth
too small for the width of her face. She was well aware that she
was ugly and awkward, especially from the back. She said that the
crookedness in her legs came from climbing up and down the
twisted stairs of this house, in which she was born. The house was
really two corner houses that had been knocked into one. The
houses had been thrown together, and the staircase twisted deter-
minedly from one house up into the other, although it was impossible to tell whether it had been built from the first floor up or
from the second floor down, the construction of it was so ungainly
and uneasy. The stairs thrust its way, crooked and hard, up
through the house, and some of its steps were so narrow it was

difficult to find a foothold on them, and some started wide and narrowed to nothing at the other side, so that they could not be depended on going down as they could going up. It was a treacherous stairs, but no one had ever been known to slip on it, because it forced respect and attention, and people guarded themselves on it.

Mary knew it very well. She knew where the hollows were, and the worn places, and where it turned, and where it thinned off. It changed appearance as the hours of the day went by, and looked entirely different at night, in lamplight or candlelight. In the wintertime the bottom step was always slippery with wet feet in from the street. In the summertime the top step was warmed by sun from a stray window, and when Mary was a child she often sat there for hours, because her father spent all his time in the shop downstairs. Her mother had died at Mary's birth. Her father, a retired policeman, was sixty when she was born. In his shop, in what had once been the parlor of one of the houses, he sold bread, sugar, milk, tea, cigarettes, apples, penny sweets, and flour. The milk stood in a big tin can on the counter, with a dipper hanging from the side of it, to measure out the customers' pints. The same farmer who brought the milk brought eggs and butter. There was a sack of potatoes slumped open against the wall in one corner.

From the time she could walk, Mary hung around the shop. Because of her crippled leg, she often was allowed to miss school. Sometimes her father would sit her up at the window, which was filled with sweets, pencils, and cigarettes, and she would play with the sweets, and eat them, and look at the other children playing in the street or looking in at her. She grew fat, and by the time she was twenty she had settled into a wide, solid fatness. She developed a habit, in the street, of whirling around suddenly to discover who was looking at her ungainly back, and often she stood and stared angrily at people until they looked away, or turned away. Her rancor was all in her harsh, lurching walk, in her eyes, and in the pitch of her voice. She seldom upbraided anybody, but her voice was so ugly that she sounded rough no matter what she said.

She was silent from having no one to talk to, but she was very noisy in her ways. When she was left in charge of the shop, she would push restlessly around behind the counter, and move her hands and feet so carelessly that by the time her father got back, half the stock would be on the floor. There would be cigarettes, spilt sugar, toffees, splashes of milk, and even money down there by her boots. Her father would get down on his knees and scramble around, picking up what could be picked up, and cursing at her. She cared nothing for what he said. She had no fear of him, and he was not afraid of her, either. He had forgotten her mother, and she had no curiosity about her mother.

The counter in the shop was movable, and when she took charge, she made her father help her shove it forward from where she sat, to give her legs plenty of room. She always went to early Mass, when the streets were deserted, so that no one would have a chance to see her awful-looking back and perhaps laugh at her. During the whole year, there was only one occasion, apart from Mass time, when she willingly went outside the door, and that was in June, on the Feast of the Sacred Heart, when the nuns of the Holy Passion, who occupied a convent on a hill over the town, opened their famous rose garden to the public.

These nuns lived and had their boarding school in a stately stone building surrounded by smooth green lawns and spiky boxwood hedges, and hidden from the world by towering walls and massive iron gates. Except for the one day of the year when they threw open their garden, they had very little to do with the daily life of the town. Their rose garden was very old. An illustrious family had once owned these grounds, and it was they who had marked out the garden, and dug it, and planted it, and enjoyed it, long ago, years before the nuns came. Surrounded by its own

particular wall, and sealed by a narrow wooden door, the garden
lay and flourished some distance behind the convent, and it could
be reached only by a fenced-in path that led directly out of the back
door of the convent chapel. Only the nuns walked there. It was
their private place of meditation, and because of its remoteness,
and also because of the ancient, wild-armed trees that dominated
the old estate, it could not be viewed from any window of the
convent.

All during the year the nuns walked privately in their garden,
and opened it to ordinary people only the one day. It is a pity that
everyone in the world could not be admitted at one time or another
to walk in that garden, best of all to walk there alone, it was so
beautiful in the sun. The nuns walked there undisturbed, apparently, and still it was altogether a stirring place, warm red, even
burning red, the way it filled the nostrils and left a sweet red taste
in the lips, red with too many roses, red as all the passionate instruments of worship, red as the tongue, red as the heart, red and
dark, in the slow-gathering summertime, as the treacherous parting in the nuns' flesh, where they feared, and said they feared, the
Devil yet might enter in.

Even if there wasn't much of a summer, even if the sun was
thin, what heat there was somehow collected itself inside the high
stone walls of the garden. The walls should have been covered by
a creeper, a red leaf or a green leaf, but instead they were bare and
clean, warm under the hands. The tall walls of the garden were
uncovered and stony under the sun, except for one, the end wall,
which was covered by forsythia, yellow at its blooming time, on
or about Christmas Day. Then the forsythia wall would stand up
overnight in a brilliant tracery of true yellow, a spidery pattern of
yellow, more like a lace shawl than a blanket, but none the less
wonderful for that. Of course, the forsythia showed to great advantage then, with the rest of the garden a graveyard.

When word came of the yellow blooming, the nuns would come out together in twos and threes, with their black wool shawls around their shoulders, to witness the miracle. It was a great pleasure to them, confused in their minds with the other joys of Christmas, and they compared the delicate golden flowers to "baby stars in the canopy of heaven" and "tiny candles lighted to honor the coming of Our Lord." All of their images were gentle and diminutive, and they spoke in gentle excited voices, crying to each other across the frosty air, "Sister, Sister, did you hear what Sister just said?" "Sister, have you noticed how clear and silent the air is this morning?"

But with the coming of June the roses arrived in their hundreds and thousands, some so rich and red that they were called black, and some so pale that they might have been white, and all the depths between—carmine, crimson, blush, rose, scarlet, wine, purple, pink, and blood—and they opened themselves and spread themselves out, arching and dancing their long strong stems, and lay with lips loose and curling under the sun's heat, so that the perfume steamed up out of them, and the air thickened with it, and stopped moving under the weight of it.

Mary loved that burning garden. From one summer to the next, she never saw the nuns, nor did she think of them. She had no interest in them, and there was not one among them who as much as knew her name. It was their urgent garden she wanted. She craved for her sight of the roses. Every year she made her way up the hill, alone, and went into the garden, and sat down on a stone bench, covering the bench with her skirt so that no one would offer to share it with her. She would have liked to go in the early morning, when few people would be there and she would have a better look at the garden, but she was afraid she would be too much noticed in the emptiness, and so she went in the middle of the afternoon, when the crowd was thickest.

Once she had seen the garden in the rain. That was the year she remembered with most pleasure, because the loitering, strolling crowd that usually jammed the narrow paths between the rose beds was discouraged by the weather. She had the garden almost to herself, that time. Wet, the roses were more brilliant than they ever had been. Under the steady fine rain the clay in the beds turned black and rich, and the little green leaves shone, and the roses were washed into such brightness that it seemed as though a great heart had begun to beat under the earth, and was sending living blood up to darken the red roses, and make the pink roses purer.

Another year, the day turned out cold, and all the roses stood distinctly away from each other, and each one looked so delicate and confident in the sharp air that Mary thought she could never forget one of their faces as long as she lived. She had no desire to grow roses herself, or even to have a garden. It was this red garden, walled, secret, and lost to her, that she wanted. She loved the garden more than anyone had ever loved it, but she did not know about the forsythia that came in December to light up the end wall. No one had ever told her that the forsythia bloomed, or how it looked. She would have liked the forsythia very much, although it could not have enveloped her as the roses did. All during the year, she thought backward to her hour in the garden, and forward to it. It was terrible to her, to think that the garden was open to the nuns and closed to her. She spoke to no one about her longing. This was not her only secret, but it was her happiest one.

Mary's father used to take in lodgers—one lodger at a time because they had only one room to spare. The lodgers were men who visited the town from time to time, commercial travelers. Sometimes a man would take a job in the town, and stay with them for a few months or so. Once they had a commercial traveler who made a habit of staying with them every time he came to town, and then he got a job selling shoes in a local shop, and stayed almost a year. When he left for good, to take a better-paid job with a brother-in-law who had a business in Dublin, Dom Lambert came, and moved into the lodger's room.

Dom was a meek and mild little draper's assistant, with wide-open, anxious blue eyes and a wavering smile. He was accustomed to watch his customers vacillate between two or more rolls of cloth, and his smile vacillated from habit. He had small, stained teeth that were going bad. When they ached, he would sit very quietly with his hands clenched together and ask for hot milk. He told Mary that his skull was very thin. He said it was as thin as a new baby's, and that a good crack on it would be the finish of him. He was always stroking his skull, searching for fissures. He was afraid a roll of cloth might tumble down on him off a shelf and he would die with customers in the shop. Even a spool of thread, he said, might do considerable damage.

Dom dressed neatly, in dark draper's suits. He was most particular about the knot of his tie, and he wore a modest stickpin. He was proud of his small feet, and polished his shoes in the kitchen every morning, assuming various athletic positions according to whether he was wielding the polish brush, the polishing cloth, or the soft finishing brush. He brushed his suits, too, and did his nails with a finicky metal implement he carried in his pocket. He tidied his own room, and made his bed in the morning. Every morning he left the house at eight-thirty, and he returned at six-thirty. He liked to read the paper at night, or play a few games of patience, or go for a stroll. He went to bed early, and in the morning descended looking brisk and ready to do his day's work. Still, his color was bad, and he often had to hammer his chest to dislodge a cough that stuck there.

When Dom had been living nine years in the house, Mary's

father died very suddenly one night. Mary was lying awake in the dark, and she heard her father's voice calling loudly. She found him hanging half out of bed, holding the little white stone holy-water font, which he had dragged off its nail in the wall.

"The font is dry," he cried to her. "Get me the priest."

He waved his dry fingertips at her, which he had been feeling in the font with, and died. Dom helped her to raise him back against the bolster. She lifted the dry font from the floor and upended it over her father's forehead.

"There might be a drop left in it," she said, but there was nothing. The font was sticky and black on the inside, and when she put it to her nose it smelled like the room, but more strongly.

"He went very quick," Dom said. "Are you going to call the priest?"

"I don't know what I'm going to do," she said. "I meant to fill the font with holy water this coming Sunday."

"Are you going to shut his eyes?" Dom asked, pressing his hands painfully together, as though he already felt the cold man's lids resisting him.

"No," she said. "They'll be closed soon enough."

She took up her candle and walked back to her room, her white flannel nightdress curved and plunging around her large body. She got into bed and pulled the clothes up around her.

"Good night now," she said to Dom. "There's no more to be done till morning."

She raised herself on her elbow to blow out the candle.

Dom said, "Are you not afraid to be in here by yourself, with him dead in there like that?"

"He can't do anybody any harm now," she said. "What ails you, Dom? Are you trying to tell me you're afraid of a poor dead man?"

"I'm afraid of my life," Dom said. His shirt, which was all he had on, shivered in the leaping candlelight.

"Let me stay in here a minute," he said.

"Are you afraid he'll come after you, or what?"

"Let me kneel up here against the bed till it gets light!" he begged. "I'm not able to go back into that room by myself, and pass his door. Or put on your clothes, and we'll go together to call the priest."

"I'll do nothing of the sort," said Mary. "If you won't go back to bed, throw that skirt there around your shoulders, or you'll catch your death."

She dragged her great black skirt from where it hung over the end rail of the bed, and flung it to him. Then she blew out the candle and fell asleep, although she had intended to stay awake. As the room grew light, she woke up, to find Dom huddled against her in sleep. He was lying outside the covers, with his nose pressed against her shoulder, and her skirt almost concealing his head. As she watched him, he opened his eyes and gazed fearfully into her face. He started to close his eyes again, to pretend he was asleep, but thought better of it.

"I only wanted to get in out of the cold," he said.

"That's all very fine," said Mary, "but don't go trying to get on top of me."

"Oh, God, I wouldn't do the like of that!" Dom said.

"I don't know, now, there was a man lodged here before you came. He weighed a ton, it seemed like."

"A great big man!" said Dom, who was shocked.

"The same size as yourself. Maybe not even as big, but he was like lead. He came in here two nights running, just before he went off for good. The first night he came in, it was black dark. I thought for a minute it was my father getting in the bed with me, and then didn't I realize it was the commercial traveler. The next night, in he came again. I let on in the morning nothing had happened, and so did he."

"And did you not tell your father?"

"Why would I tell him?"

"Maybe it was your father all the time."

"It wasn't him. It was the commercial traveler, all right. If nothing else, I'd have known him by the feel of the shirt he had on him. Anyway, my father hadn't that much interest in me."

"Lord have mercy on him—your poor father, I mean," said Dom, who was growing uncomfortable and ashamed as the increasing light disclosed them to each other.

Mary had run out of small talk, but because she wanted him not to go, and because she had as much ordinary courage as any other human being, she spoke up. "I'll move over," she said, "and you lie in here beside me. As long as you're here, you may as well settle yourself."

The bed in which they lay, like all the beds in that house, was made with only one sheet, the undersheet. There was no top sheet—only the rough warm blanket, and then another blanket, a thinner one, and on top of all a heavy patchwork quilt. The beds were high up off the floor, and made of brass, and all the mattresses sagged. The floors sagged, too, some sliding off to the side, and some sinking gently in the middle, and all of the rooms were on different levels, because of the way in which the two houses had been flung together. There were no carpets on the floors, and no little mats or rugs. The bare old boards groaned disagreeably under the beds, and under Mary's feet, and under Dom's feet.

Mary and Dom got married as quickly as they could, because they were afraid the priest might come around and lecture them, or maybe even denounce them publicly from the pulpit. They settled down to live much as they had lived before Mary's father died. Most of their life was spent in the kitchen. This was a large, dark, crowded room set in the angle where the two houses joined, and irregular because it took part of itself from one house and part from the other. The only window in the kitchen was small and high up, and set deep in the thick old wall. It looked out on a tiny, dark yard, not more than a few feet square, in which there was an outhouse. In this window recess Dom kept his own possessions— his playing cards, a pencil, a bottle of blue-black ink, a straight pen, a jotter, a package of writing paper with matching envelopes, and the newspapers. After Rose got big enough to be with him, he began to keep a tin box of toffees there, and he liked to play a game of coaxing with her, with a toffee for a prize. The toffees were not of a kind sold in Mary's shop, which offered only cheap loose sweets, sold five for a penny, or even eight or ten for a penny. Rose liked those sweets, too, but she liked the tin-box toffees in the bright twists of paper best of all.

Rose was her father's girl. Everyone said so. Mary said so, more often than anyone else. She said it bitterly to Dom, and mockingly to Rose, but once she had said it she shut up, because it was not to start a quarrel that she said it but only to let them know that she knew.

Jimmy, the little baby, was Rose's pet. Dom liked him, but Rose clung to him, and when he fretted she would hang over the side of his cradle and talk to him, and dangle toys in front of him, and try to make him laugh.

Mary and Dom were not long married when Mary began to nag at him to give up his job at the draper's. Her reason for doing this, which she could not reveal to him, was that she could not bear to let people see him smile. She was unsmiling herself, as her father had been, and she believed that people only smiled in order to curry favor. People like herself, at any rate. "People like us," she was always saying, "people like us," but she did not know what she meant, unless it was that the rest of the people in the world were better off, or that they had some fortunate secret, or were engaged in a conspiracy in which she was not included.

Dom's smile did not disturb her until one afternoon she went over to the draper's to buy the makings of a dress for herself. She did not want him to wait on her, because she was ashamed to let him know how many yards it took to go around her, but she watched him with a customer, and it was then, against his own background of trying to sell and trying to please strangers, that she saw the history of his hopeful, uncertain smile, as he eagerly hauled down rolls of cloth and spread them out for inspection. After that day she gave him no peace till she got him out of his job. She told him that he could take over the running of her shop, and Dom liked that idea, because he had always wanted to be his own man, but he was just as anxious-faced behind her counter as he had ever been, and she gradually edged him back into the kitchen, out of sight.

She only wanted to take care of him, and protect him from people. She had known from a child that if she asked she would get, because of her deformity. She had always seen people getting ready to be nice to her because they pitied her and looked down on her. Everyone was inclined to pity her. How could they help themselves? She was an object for pity. The dead weight of her body, which she felt at every step, was visible to all the world. She almost had to kneel to walk. Even her hair was heavy, a dense black rug down her back. She was always afraid people might think she was asking for something. She always tried to get away from people as quickly as she could, before they got it into their heads that she was waiting for something. What smile could she give that would not be interpreted as a smile for help? In fact, that is what she thought herself—that if she smiled at them it would only be to ingratiate herself, because she had no other reason to smile, since she hated them all. If she had said out loud why she hated them, she would have said it was because they were too well off, and stuck up, and too full of themselves. But she never would give them an opening for their smiles and greetings, and she came to feel that she had defeated them, and shut them all out. To have rescued Dom's weakness from their sight, and from their scornful pity—that was a triumph, although she was unable to share it with him, since she did not know how to explain to him that while she thought he was good enough, other people would never think him good enough, and therefore she had to save him from them, and hide him behind herself.

To pass the time, Dom began to do odd jobs around the house. Once in a while he took a broom and swept the upstairs rooms. Sometimes he got a hammer and some nails and wandered around, trying to tighten the floor boards or the stair boards, but the rigid, overstrained joints and joinings of the house rejected the new nails and spat them back out again before the tinny glitter had even worn off their heads. He often spent the whole day at a game of patience, and when Mary came back out of the shop to see about their middle-of-the-day meal, he would be sitting hunched over the kitchen table, with the cards spread out in front of him and a full cup of cold tea, left over from his breakfast, at his elbow. When Rose got to be big enough, he liked to tell her about the days when he was a draper, and he collected a few reels of thread, and some needles and pins, and bound some pieces of scrap cloth into near rolls, and the two of them would play shop for hours.

Before Rose was born, Dom scrubbed out the old cradle in the kitchen, and polished it till it shone. The cradle had been there for Mary, and after she grew out of it it was used as a receptacle for old and useless things of the house. Before Dom scrubbed it, Mary cleared it out. It was a huge wooden cradle, dark brown and almost as big as a coffin, but seeming more roomy than a coffin, and it had a great curved wooden hood half covering it that made the interior very gloomy. It stood on clumsy wooden rockers. There was no handle to rock it by. Mary remembered her father's hand on the side of it, and the shape of his nails. She had slept in the cradle, in the kitchen, until she was four, or nearly five. Her father had looked after her himself, so the cradle was left within easy distance of the shop. She could well remember her father looking in at her. Sometimes a woman would look in at her, but her father did not encourage visitors. He had the idea that all women were trying to marry him, or to get him to marry again, and he kept them out.

If Mary made a sudden movement, or jumped around, the cradle would rock far to the left and far to the right on its thick, curved rockers, and she knew that no power on earth could stop it until in the course of time it stopped itself. If she tried to clamber out, the cradle would start its deliberate plunging, right, left, right, left, and she would cower down with her face hidden in the bottom until the cradle was still under her again. She was always afraid alone in the dark bottom of the house. Her father slept upstairs. At night she would see his face, darkened by the candle he held aloft, and then the very last thing she would see was his shadow falling against the shallow, twisting staircase.

In the cradle, when she set about emptying it, Mary found a dark-red rubber ball with pieces torn, or rotted, out of it, and some folded, wrinkled bills, and a new mousetrap, never used, and a pipe of her father's, and two empty medicine bottles with the color of the medicines still on the bottoms of them, and a lot of corks, big and little, and a man's cloth cap, and a stiff, dusty wreath of artificial white flowers from her own First Communion veil, and a child's prayer book, her own, with the covers torn off.

When they were first married, Dom used to walk to early Mass with Mary on Sunday, but after a while he began making excuses, and they got into the habit of attending different Masses. She continued to go to the early Mass, and he would go later. When Rose started to walk, he took her with him. He would wash her, and do her hair, and see that her shoes were polished, and then she would give Mary a kiss goodbye and run off down the street after him.

One weekday morning, about a year before he died, Dom gave Mary the shock of her life. Instead of lying on in bed, as he usually did, he got up at seven-thirty, and shaved himself, and did himself up the way he used to in the days when he was at the draper's. When she saw him go out, she said nothing, but after a few minutes she locked the shop door, and went back and sat down at the kitchen table. People came knocking, but Mary paid no attention, and when Rose came to stand beside her she pushed her gently away. At three in the afternoon, she told Rose to mind the baby, and she put on her hat, and her Sunday coat, and went out looking for Dom. There was no sign of him on any street. At the draper's she stood and looked in, but he was not there. The man who had taken his place was only a youngster, very polite and sure of himself, she could see that. It occurred to her that even if she met Dom, she'd hardly know what to say, so she turned around and went home.

"Oh, I thought I would never see you again!" Mary cried.

Dom did not look up, but Rose looked up from her bead box.

Dom asked, "What put that idea in your head?"

"I thought you'd gone off on me."

"Can't a man even go for a walk now, without the house being brought down around him?"

"I was full sure you were gone for good, when I saw you walking out of the door this morning. I didn't know what to do. I didn't know what I was going to do."

"Where would I go, will you tell me that?"

"Is that all you have to say to me, after the fright you've given me—that you have no place to go to? Is that the only reason you came back?"

"Rose," he said, turning from the stove. "Give us a look at the little necklace you're making there."

Mary got the tea ready. When they were all sitting at the table, she said loudly, "I suppose it was on Rose's account you came back. You were afraid I wouldn't take good enough care of her, I suppose?"

"That's a nice thing to say in front of the child," he said.

"You take her part against me."

"Somebody has to take her part."

"And who's to take my part?"

"Aren't you able to look after yourself?"

"I wish to God she'd been born crooked the way I was. There'd have been no pet child then."

"God forgive you for saying the like of that!" he shouted, and he jumped up out of his chair and made for the stairs.

"God has never forgiven me for anything!" she screamed after him, and she put her head down against the edge of the table.

Rose slipped around the table and put her arm around Mary's neck. "I'll mind you, Mammy," she said.

Mary looked at her. Rose had her father's uncertain smile, but on her face it was more eager. Mary saw the smile, and saw the champion spirit already shining out of Rose's eyes.

"Who asked you to mind me?" she said. "Go on and run after your father. You're the little pet. We all know that. Only get out of my sight and stay out."

Rose got very red and ran upstairs. Mary got to her feet and lumbered up after her. Dom was lying on the bed with Rose alongside him.

Mary said, "Nobody's asking you to stay here! Nobody's keeping you. What's stopping you from going off—and take her with you. Go on off, the two of you."

"I wish to God I could," Dom said. "I declare to God I wish I could, and I'd take her with me, never fear."

That night, as they lay in bed, Dom said, "Mary, I'm terrible sorry about what I said to you today. I don't know what got into me."

"Oh, Dom, never mind about it," she said. "I gave you good reason."

Encouraged by these words, she put her arms around him. With his body in her arms, she was comforted. That is what she wanted—to be allowed to hold him. She thought it was all she wanted—to be allowed to hold a person in her arms. Out of all the world, only he would allow her. No one else would allow her. No one else could bear to let her come near them. The children would allow her, but their meager bodies would not fill her arms, and she would be left empty anyway.

As Dom fell into sleep, his body grew larger and heavier against her. Holding him, she felt herself filled with strength. Now if she took her arms from him and stretched herself out, she would touch not the bed, and not even the floor or the walls of the room, but the roofs of the houses surrounding her, and other roofs beyond them, far out to the outer reaches of the town. She felt strong and able enough to encircle the whole town, a hundred men and women. She could feel their foreheads and their shoulders under her hands, and she could even imagine that she saw their hands reaching out for her, as though they wanted her.

In all her life, there was no one had ever wanted her. All the want was hers. She never knew, or wondered, if she loved or hoped or despaired. It was all the one thing to her, all want. She said every day, "I love God," because that is what she had been taught to say, but the want came up out of herself, and she knew what she meant by it. She said, "I want the rose garden. I want it," she said. "I want to see it, I want to touch it, I want it for my own." She could not have said if it was her hope or her despair that was contained in the garden, or about the difference between them, or if there was a difference between them. All she knew was what she felt. All she felt was dreadful longing.

When Father Mathews found that Mary wouldn't allow him to get one of the neighbors up to take his place at the bedside, he didn't know what to do. It seemed un-Christian and unfeeling to leave her alone, but he was dying to stretch his legs and get a breath of fresh air, and above all he wanted to get away out of the room. He decided that the most likely thing would be to talk his way out, and so he said again what he had said before—that Dom's fortitude was an example to the whole parish, and that he had left his children a priceless legacy of faith and humility, that the priest and the teachers at the school would have a special interest in the bereaved little ones, and that Dom's soul was perhaps even at this instant interceding for them all before the throne of the Almighty.

"What about me, Father?" Mary asked.

"What was that?" asked Father Mathews.

"What about me, Father? That's all I'm asking you."

"Oh, Mrs. Lambert, your heart is heavy now, but have no fear. God will comfort you in His own time and in His own way."

"I might have known you wouldn't give me a straight answer, Father."

"Mrs. Lambert, Our Blessed Lord enjoins us to have *faith*," Father Mathews said gently.

He was developing a headache out of the endless talk, in this airless room, with no sleep all night, and he was beginning to wonder if he hadn't already done more than his duty.

Mary stared indifferently at him, and he hesitated to speak for fear of provoking her into some further rigmarole. After a few seconds the rising silence in the room pushed him to his feet almost in spite of himself, but at the door he turned and whispered that he would speak to Father Dodd immediately about the arrangements for the funeral, which would probably be on Thursday. He then said that he would call back later in the day to see how she and the children were getting along, and he added that Father Dodd himself might even find time to come—just for a few minutes, of course, because he was greatly taken up at this time of the year, between Christmas and Easter.

As he felt his precarious way downstairs, he couldn't help rehearsing a question that he knew he would never ask, because it would seem uncharitable. The question was what sort of a woman is it could sit beside her husband's body, with her unfortunate children in the next room, and think only about herself?

The Beginning
of a Long Story

The front door should have been painted before this. Now it was too late. The mother had put off having the front door painted, and now the winter had settled in and the weather was very bad. It was much too late in the year to do any outside painting. It was the worst winter Dublin had seen in years. Everybody said so. There was nothing but rain, day after day. Everything got very damp, and every funeral marked the last chapter in a story that always began with somebody getting his feet wet. The mother mourned over her garden, which was being killed by the frost, and she worried over the colds and the flu and the pneumonia that were in the air, and she said that every time she went to the front door she was mortified because it was in such bad condition it made the house look like a tenement. The house did not look like a tenement. It looked like itself, a small plain house in a row, faced from the other side of the terrace by a row of other houses just like it, all made alike of undistinguished gray stone with slate roofs and tiny front gardens protected by iron railings. It was a very ordinary house, a regulation uniform for the lives of certain families, or for some families at a certain stage in their lives. It was better than a workingman's house but not good enough for a successful man and his family to live in. It was a clerk's house, and the man who lived in it was a government clerk with a wife and three small daughters.

Ellen was the eldest. She was eight. The mother had kept her at home for the day because of the flu that was going around. The flu had been going around all winter, and no more that day than usual. The flu was only an excuse. The fact was that the mother had woken up that morning filled with the passionate determination to keep all three of her children safe at home under her roof and with her all day long. It was her gesture against the cruelty of the winter, to deprive it of Ellen's warm body for one day. Johanna, the middle one, was already out of school with a cold, and Bridget was too young to be sent to school. Bridget was only four.

The mother had a fire going in the back bedroom for Johanna, who was in bed there, and the coal range was going all day in the kitchen, but the other rooms in the house were cold. The front sitting room was cold. The back sitting room, which they also called the dining room, was cold. The front bedroom, where the mother and father slept in their big brass bed, was cold. The bathroom, halfway up the stairs, was cold, and the little room they called the boxroom, next to the bathroom, was cold and felt damp. The narrow linoleum-covered hall that led from the kitchen to the front door was like a dungeon, it was so cold. The mother said it was just like a dungeon in the hall. All the cold air that forced its way in when the front door was opened died in the hall when the door was shut again, and died on the stairs that led up to the halfway landing.

There was dark-red carpet on the stairs, held in place by brass rods. The mother polished the brass rods every week, starting at the top and kneeling on every step on her way down. It was not a long way. One time she had taken all the rods out of the stairs and had taken them down to the kitchen to give them all a proper cleaning and Bridget had worked her way in under the carpet and had sat there on the bare stair, making a big lump in the middle under the carpet, and nobody could go up or come down. There was no one upstairs. They were all downstairs. The mother and Ellen and Johanna had stood at the foot of the stairs and implored Bridget to have sense and come out but Bridget only laughed and said she would come out when she liked. Ellen thought they might all take hold of the end of the carpet and pull it taut and tight so that Bridget would be squeezed out, but Johanna said that if the carpet got Bridget the wrong way—if it got her flat on her back—it might smother her and she might be dead by the time they got her out.

"Oh, don't say the like of that to me," the mother said sharply. "Don't ever say a thing like that again."

The stairs were very narrow, but the mother thought that if she made a quick rush up the stairs and got a good hold on Bridget she might drag her out by main force, but as soon as she set her foot on the bottom step Bridget began to wriggle around under the carpet and the mother got nervous and put her foot down into the hall again.

"She's so small," she said to Ellen and Johanna, "and her bones are not all formed. If I came down with my foot on some part of her I might damage her for life."

At the end of an hour Johanna began to cry because she wanted to go upstairs to the bathroom and the mother lost patience and shouted at Bridget that if she didn't come out from under the stair carpet this very minute she'd come up there and drag her out and whack her till her bottom was bright red. When Bridget heard the words "whack" and "bottom" she began to cry. When Bridget cried she bawled and her mouth got very large. When she cried her mouth got enormous. Ellen and Johanna rushed around to the end of the stairs to see if they could get a look at her and Bridget

edged toward them away from the wall and tilted the carpet up so
that they could see her and greeted them with a wild howl to show
them she was not just pretending to cry. Her mouth was stretched
wide, and around it her face was only a bright-red rim with her
little nose stone white in its center. Ellen knew that a stone-white
nose is a bad sign. It meant that the rage had carried the blood to
the top of Bridget's head.

"Oh, Mammy," Ellen cried, "she's working herself into a passion."

The mother ran around to the side of the stairs and took two of
the banisters into her hands and stared between them at Bridget.

"Oh, and she's got her mouth wide open and it's filling up with
dust," she cried. "Oh, Bridget," she entreated, "come on out and
don't be frightening your poor mother. I didn't mean it, Bridget.
Mammy was only pretending. You know I wouldn't whack my
little Bridget. It's only that I was afraid you'd be lonely in there by
yourself. Come on now, Bridget, come on."

Bridget stopped wailing and looked at them all, and Johanna
got up on her toes and waved at her little sister as though she had
not seen her for a long time.

"Come on, Bridget," Johanna said. "She's not going to whack
you."

Bridget began to smile, and she crawled out and went triumphantly into her mother's arms. The mother clutched her and
squeezed her and kissed her and murmured to her as though she
was a brave child who had come through some terrible danger.
Johanna and Ellen watched them.

"You'd think she'd done something great," Johanna said.

"It's awful the way she's always looking for notice," Ellen said.

Bridget had got so dirty from sitting under the stair carpet that
they had to take off all her clothes and wash her all over. When the
father heard the story, when he came home that evening, he

laughed and said it served the mother right for working too hard and trying to do too much.

"If it isn't the brass rods on the stairs," he said, "it's the brasses on the front door. And if it isn't the brasses on the front door, it's something else. You'll wear yourself out."

The mother replied that nothing made a house look as neglected as neglected brass. She added that it was very important to keep up the appearance of a place, especially here in Dublin, where the people were only looking for an excuse to look down on you.

The father threw his evening paper to the floor beside his chair and then he picked it up again and began looking at it. "That's enough of that," he said, and his face turned red with anger. The mother's face turned red, too. The father looked at his paper and the mother went on with her knitting and Ellen and Johanna looked at each other.

Everybody in the room was thinking about the same thing. They were all thinking about the terrible row the mother and father had had over the tennis club, and how the father had run out of the house and not come back for hours. The tennis courts lay beyond the long cement wall that was the common end wall for all the back gardens of all the houses in the row. The gardens were separated from one another by cement walls, and united by the common end wall. The tennis club was very up to date. It was all surrounded by trees, and in the summertime it was very smart with deck chairs and brightly painted wooden chairs placed around the edges of the courts and at tournament time there was a stand for the judges and a platform for the prize-giving. The afternoon of the row, the father had said that they could all go up and sit in the back-bedroom window. There was a grandstand view of the tournaments from the back-bedroom window, the father said. It was summertime and they were all in the garden and they could hear the cries and shouts and cheers coming over to

them from the courts at the other side of the wall, but they couldn't
see anything. But the mother said that she didn't want her children sitting up in the back-bedroom window staring at the people
who belonged to the club. If anyone on the courts looked up and
saw them, she said, and knew what house they were looking from
and who they were, they might think the children were hoping to
be asked over. Everyone knew, the mother said, that the people
who belonged to the club thought they were better than anybody
else, and she didn't want her children put in a position like that.
Her face was red and her voice was shaky, but she kept on talking
until she had finished.

"Put in a position like what?" the father had asked.

"Put in a position of looking as if they were asking for favors,"
the mother had said, and looked as if she might cry.

The father said, "Oh, dear God!" and jumped up from the
grass where he had been lying. Once he was up he looked as if he
might get down on the grass again, but instead he marched away
up the garden and in a minute they heard the front door bang.
The children all rushed into the house and along the hall to the
front sitting room and looked out through the windows and saw
him flying off down toward the main road. The children were
glad he was gone, as long as he was going to be cross. But when
they got back to the garden the mother looked at Ellen with a
frightened, afflicted smile, and Ellen knew that she was nearly
crying.

The mother came from the country. She was the eldest child of
a small farmer and she had five brothers. Of her life at home she
had two remarks to make—she had loved to attend a cow in calf,
and calving, and she had hated having to black her father's and
brothers' Sunday boots. But sometimes she talked to the children
about the place at home, and told them how her father white-
washed the house every year and painted the outside doors and

the window frames bright green and always kept the thatch in the best of condition. Her father was better at thatching than any man in the parish, she said, and their place was one of the best-kept places in the parish. But in Dublin, where no one knew her or her family, she felt she had to prove herself. She felt awkward in Dublin, although she liked being in the city. The women on the farms in Ireland had no life at all, she said. In the country, everything was for the boys, the sons. She felt that the people in Dublin looked down on her for her country accent, and she was afraid that her clothes would never look as smart as they should. She often wondered if people were laughing at her. She was very uncertain. She was always unsure of herself except when she was dealing with her children. Besides her children the only people among whom she had any force were the poor men and women who came begging at her door, and her force, for these, could be measured by the kind and quantity of what she gave them—a penny here, twopence there, a half a loaf of bread, a cup of tea at the door or at the kitchen table, a knitted shawl for an expected baby, a pair of old shoes, old gloves, a jam jar of kitchen fat, a child's vest that was old and small but still useful.

When she was with a poor person, standing inside her front door talking to them as they stood on her front step, or doing something in the kitchen while they sat and had tea at her table, she was ashamed of having as much as she had, but when she was with other people—the people her husband used to bring home occasionally the first year or two they had the house, or with her children's teachers at the school, or with people in shops—she was ashamed of her own appearance and of the shortcomings in her dress and in her children's dress. She used to become heartbroken over the shortcomings in her children's dress. One winter she sat down and cut up her own heavy coat to make coats for Johanna and Bridget, and then she made round caps to go with the coats from the material that was left over, but the little outfits were never a success. She turned the material when she cut it up and the children did not recognize what it was they were wearing. When the children asked their mother where her big coat had gone, she told them she had pushed it up the chimney for a joke and that it had turned into black smoke. After that, when the children saw smoke coming from the chimney they said it was their mother's coat up there.

Johanna was capricious at the best of times, but when she was in bed sick she was very hard to deal with. Today she had decided that she wanted the back bedroom and the fire that was in it all to herself. Ellen would have liked to sit by the fire there and read her book, and Bridget said she might like to stay there, too, because it was a novelty to have a fire in the bedroom, but Johanna wouldn't listen to them. She said she was too sick to have people talking in the room. She wasn't too sick to sit up in bed with a shawl around her, playing with her crayons and her books, but she was too sick to let Ellen and Bridget share her fire. Ellen said Johanna was selfish, but Johanna only smiled and said nothing. Johanna often said nothing.

The kitchen was small and square and it had a red tile floor. The fire in the coal range turned red with the heat and roared like a lion behind its little iron door. The three stray cats that had found lodging in the woodshed for the winter had been let in for the day and they had curled themselves up on the floor as close to the range as they could get, and as the day wore on and they got over their wariness at being inside the house they breathed more easily and their fur went up and down and their round curled bodies seemed to expand and grow softer, as though they had made themselves into sponges to soak up as much heat as they could while they had the chance. Bridget was wedged into the small child's chair that Ellen and Johanna had owned in their turn, and Ellen had made a table for her out of one of the kitchen chairs and put the old tin tray with the plasticine on it. The mother finished the washing early and pegged it across a line she had put up under the kitchen ceiling. The arms of the father's shirts hung down like streamers, stiff and dry, and brushed the mother's light-brown hair as she moved about the kitchen. At four o'clock she went up to the back sitting room to light the gas fire to warm up the room for the evening, and then they all moved up there, Ellen with her book, which was about the adventures of a fifteen-year-old Spanish princess in a strict girls' school in England, and Bridget, laboriously, with the plasticine on the old tin tray. The back sitting room had linoleum, and the grate was really a coal grate but a gas fire had been fitted into it. Folding doors divided it from the front sitting room, where there was a patterned carpet and an open grate and French windows that opened out like doors. The linoleum in the back sitting room was not the same as the linoleum in the hall. The linoleum in the hall had been there when they moved into the house, and they had paid extra for it. The only other decoration that had been left in the house by the people who had been there before was the shiny paper—red and green diamonds all over it—that was pasted over the inside of the glass panel in the door of the bathroom upstairs. Bridget could not be left alone in the bathroom because she would tear the paper off, reaching up and tearing off little bits that she would lick and paste to her face so that she could run around the house saying, "Look at me. Who am I? No, no, I am not Bridget. No, I am not a strange little woman. No, I am not the child next door. I am a bathroom window." Only her mother and her father and her sisters could understand anything Bridget said.

The dining room smelled fresh and cool after the hot stuffy kitchen, and the mother said it was nice to get out of the kitchen after having been there all day. She smiled at Bridget, who had already settled herself on the hearthrug. Then she pulled Bridget gently to her feet and kissed her, and she bent down low and lifted the plasticine tray from the floor and put it up high on the mantelpiece.

"Upstairs now, Bridget," the mother said, "and you're to lie down at once and shut your eyes up tight."

Bridget went off upstairs obediently, because she knew there was a fire in the room upstairs and that the room would be nice and warm. The mother opened the big lumpy cotton bag of mending and darning that sat on top of the sewing machine, but she tied it up again without taking anything out. She yawned and sat down on her low chair by the fire, and when the knock came at the door she told Ellen to run and see who it was.

The man who had knocked at the door was not standing up on the mat in the recess, out of the rain. He was standing below the step, with his cap in his hands. He was all wet, and his eyes were full of rain. Ellen thought he might be blind, but then she saw it was only that he was all wet, and the rain was so straight and heavy that even at this short distance it fell like a curtain between them. She had to hold the door with both hands to keep it from blowing wide in the wind.

"Would you ask your mother if she has a pair of old boots she wants to give away?" the man said.

"A pair of old boots," the mother said when Ellen went back with the message. "I've no boots. I'd better go out. He must be in a bad way, to go around in this weather."

Ellen wanted to go with her and look at the man again, but the mother closed the door into the hall so firmly that Ellen stayed where she was, listening. She heard the front door open and close, and then she heard her mother go along the hall on her way to the kitchen, and after her mother the man. She felt left out. She would have liked to go into the kitchen, too. She was standing in the middle of the room, trying to think of an excuse that would take her back to the kitchen, when her mother came in.

"Poor fellow," she said. "God help him, I gave him something to eat. I left him there by himself. I knew he wouldn't touch anything as long as I was in the room. Now, don't you go down there bothering him. I wish I had a pair of shoes to give him. He hasn't even a pair of socks on him. I gave him a pair of socks. I'm going to run up and see if I can get Johanna to lie down for a sleep. She's been sitting up in the bed all day. I'll be down in a minute. And don't you go near the kitchen."

Ellen was always very curious about the poor men and women who came to the door, especially when they had a boy or girl of her own age with them. She liked it when her mother gave her something to give to them. She was interested in the man in the kitchen, and when she went back by the fire to her book she continued to listen for the sound of the kitchen door opening, or for some sign that he was in the house. There was no sound, except the slapping of the rain outside and the rattle at the windows where the wind tugged the house. Then the door opened, and Bridget came in, smiling and hanging from the doorknob.

"I *sat* down the stairs," Bridget whispered. "I was good. I was quiet."

"Where's Mammy?" Ellen asked.

"Mammy's asleep. In Johanna's bed."

Johanna often refused to go to sleep unless her mother lay down beside her. Ellen lifted the old tin tray of plasticine off the mantelpiece and put it on the floor at a safe distance from the fire, and Bridget sat down beside it and began to pummel it.

Ellen went very quietly out of the room and down the three steps from the hall to the kitchen and opened the kitchen door and peered in. The man was asleep. He lay huddled over the table, and his arms were around his head, hiding his face. As she opened the door he spoke out suddenly in a loud voice, but did not move, and she stepped quickly back out of the kitchen and closed the door. When she heard him speak out loud again, she slipped back into the kitchen and closed herself in with him and stood watching him. She hoped he would not speak again. She wanted him to be quiet, as he had been, and she thought that if she stared at him he would be quiet, or wake up, but the words came out growling and roaring and bubbling in a voice that was much too fierce to belong to the poor little man who lay all wet across the table. She was as distressed as though a dog or a cat had implored her in words that she knew but could not understand because the voice was animal. The man didn't sound at all as he had sounded when he asked for the boots. He was wearing the socks her mother had given him, and his broken boots were drying on a chair by the range, together with his cap. She wished he would come out of his nightmare and raise his head. The warmth of the fire was lost on him. His voice stumbled on, and then he gave a great groan, or a sigh, or a cry, and gave up. She thought he was beginning to wake up; he stirred and his fingers opened, but he lay quiet. She hurried out of the kitchen and went upstairs to get her mother, but her mother lay on Johanna's bed, fast asleep. She was sleeping with her head thrown back and her mouth a little open. Ellen moved to waken her, with a little touch on her shoulder, but then she held back and did not waken her. It would be nice if her mother could just sleep on.

She went downstairs and into the back sitting room, where Bridget still played with her plasticine. The gas fire gave out great warmth. No one but Bridget could play with the plasticine, because she had mauled all the colors together and ruined it to suit herself. Ellen sat down on the floor beside Bridget.

"Bridget," she said, "everybody is asleep except you and me. Johanna's asleep. Mammy's asleep. Everybody's asleep."

"Everybody," Bridget said, and paused to look thoughtfully up into Ellen's face.

The clock on the mantelpiece—the glass clock that you could see the works of—said ten minutes to six. The father would be home soon. Ellen knew that she ought to do something, but she sat still. She sat up close to Bridget and watched Bridget's hands in the plasticine and smelled the plasticine. The room was much too dark. She ought to light the light. She ought to wake the man and then wake her mother. Or wake her mother and let her wake the man. There were a whole lot of things she ought to do. She didn't know which of them to do first. Then, too, her mother would want time to get the washing down off the line before she began to get the tea ready. The tea would be late now anyway, and there now, there was her father at the door, opening it with his key, coming into the hall. All the time she had been sitting doing nothing he had been waiting in the rain for the tram, getting into the tram, sitting in the tram, and walking from the tram stop up to their gate. She ran out into the hall to confront him. Any other night she would have raced to meet him, but tonight she edged toward him, waiting while he shook out his coat and spread it all over the hall stand to dry, and shook out his hat, and took his evening paper out of his pocket. He turned and saw her, and as he looked down at her she remembered the Saturday afternoon she had been sent to do a message at one of the shops up the main road, and on her way back through the shopping crowds she had seen him coming toward her and he had not seen her. She had waited for him to see her, and then she had run up to him and touched him and said "Da!" and he had said he was delighted to see Miss Ellen promenading on such a fine day and he had brought her into

Kennedy's and bought her a bag of glacier mints. When they parted, she to go along home and he to go wherever he was going, she stood and watched with tears in her eyes because they had said goodbye, till he was far away in the crowd, and then he disappeared from sight so suddenly that she ran across and put one foot off the path and down into the road, craning to see if she could get a last glimpse of him, and there he was standing down in the road looking for her, and he raised his arm up high and opened his hand and then shut it again, and opened it and shut it again, in the gesture of farewell that he always gave to all of them. And she turned and ran home so wildly that she collided with a woman who was wheeling a big baby in a pram, and the woman caught her by the shoulder and said, "You young bandit, mind where you're going! What's wrong with your mother that she can't teach you manners?" and Ellen pulled herself away and shouted, "Let go of me, y'oul bag," and then she was terrified that her mother would find out how she had spoken to the woman, and she walked properly the rest of the way home.

But tonight she whispered to her father, "Da, don't make a sound. Johanna's upstairs asleep and Mammy's in the kitchen making a surprise for the tea. And the back sitting room is lovely and warm, only Bridget is at her plasticine."

The father said, "Oh, the plasticine," and made an exaggerated show of tiptoeing down the hall and into the room, getting lower and lower toward the floor as he went and then, when he got near the fire, stepping on Bridget, who gave a cry of happiness and outrage and struck out at him.

"What's that?" he cried. "What's that? What's that I stepped on—a lump in the rug? Is that what it is?" Then he pretended that Bridget had caught fire and he smacked her all over until she hung limp as a rag doll from his hands. At last he sat down in his chair by the fire and tried to open his paper, which was all wet.

Ellen slipped out and up to the bedroom. The room was dark now, and she felt her way across to Johanna's bed, but before she could speak the mother woke up and sat straight up in bed.

"Oh, Ellen," she said, "you gave me a fright. What time is it? Put on the light. Why didn't you wake me? Is your father in?"

"He's in the dining room, Mammy," Ellen said. "He only just came in. He's reading the paper. And Mammy, the poor man fell asleep in the kitchen and he's still there."

"The poor man—the poor man that wanted the boots. Oh, Ellen, Ellen, why didn't you wake me? What possessed you to let me sleep on? Oh, what'll I do now?"

She got stiffly off the bed and put her hands up to her hair, which was straggling after her heavy sleep.

"Oh dear," she said. "Oh dear, dear, dear."

There was still a red glow in the fireplace, and she went across and poked it up and put on a shovel of coal.

"Don't you get out of bed," she said to Johanna, who watched her sleepily. "And Ellen, you go on downstairs and keep your father company. And keep the door to the hall shut."

When Ellen went back to the back sitting room, her father was spreading his paper over the table to dry it.

"The news is wet tonight, Ellen," he said. "It's a rotten old paper anyway. I wonder why I buy it. Now, where are the cards? We'll have a game of old maid before tea."

As her father was shuffling the cards, Ellen heard a sound in the hall. She knew what had happened. The man had stumbled against the top of the three steps up from the kitchen. The father heard him, too, and he got up.

"Don't tell me she's carrying the tea up here?" he said. "And me with the old paper all over the table."

He opened the door. The mother stood against the banisters, looking at them. The man stood beside her, caught in flight, and his face wore the artful, afflicted smile that Ellen recognized from seeing it on her mother's face. He was afraid. The father walked past the man and along the hall and opened the front door and the man followed him. As the man was going past him the father said, "Have you a place to go for the night?" and then he put his hand in his waistcoat pocket and gave the man something—sixpence or a shilling, maybe both. "Good night, good night, good luck," he said, and shut the door, and came back down the hall and into the dining room and sat down again in his chair by the gas fire. They all went in after him.

The mother said, "I'm sorry, John."

The father looked up at her.

"It isn't that I mind the cups of tea and all the rest of it," he said. "It isn't that I mind the way every man, woman, and child that comes near the place can get around you. What I mind is hiding down there in the kitchen and teaching the children to tell me lies. That's what I mind. And I won't have it. Do you hear me? I won't have it."

"I was only afraid you'd be angry," the mother said.

"You're always being afraid," the father said. "That's all I hear— that you're afraid. What's there to be afraid of? What's wrong with you? And you're making Ellen the same way."

"Oh, leave Ellen out of it," the mother whispered.

"How did he get here, that's what I'd like to know," the father said. "What brings them all to this house? Not content with opening the door and giving them money I can't spare, you have to invite them to come in and sit down and make themselves at home. What's the matter with you?"

"He only wanted to know if I had a pair of old boots," the mother said.

Bridget turned from watching her mother's face and looked at her father's shoes. Ellen also looked at them, and the father looked down at them.

"I'm wearing them out as fast as I can," he said, and he began to laugh. Then he stopped laughing and he put his elbows on his knees and buried his face in his hands. Bridget tried to do the same thing, although she was standing up.

"Would you like your tea on a tray by the fire here?" the mother asked.

"All right," he said.

The mother brought a tray to her husband, and Ellen carried a tray up to Johanna, who was sitting up in bed with her crayons and a picture book.

"There was an awful row," Ellen said. "And Mammy is crying in the kitchen and she won't have any tea."

"Oh, she's always crying," Johanna said.

The back bedroom held two narrow beds for Ellen and Johanna and a high-sided iron cot, painted white, that Bridget still slept in. They always left one side of the cot down so that Bridget would know she wasn't really a baby any longer. Halfway up the stairs, in the boxroom, the father had a gramophone and a set of French Linguaphone records, and a set of the *Encyclopaedia Britannica* that he was buying in installments from a man who came selling it at the door. There was a lumpy little bed in the room, a spare bed. Later in the evening, as she was going upstairs to bed, Ellen heard a French voice talking in there, a man's voice. That meant her father was sitting in there alone, sitting on the edge of the bed, listening to the gramophone, learning French. He often went in there to have an hour to himself after tea, or on a Sunday afternoon. Sometimes after tea he went to see a play in town, but the mother never went with him, because she had the children to mind. He said that when Ellen was bigger she could go with him. He liked to go for long walks in the Dublin hills on Saturdays and Sundays in the good weather, and in the summertime he often went to Wicklow and had a few days by himself. He said that when Ellen's legs were longer she could go on the walks with him, too. Sometimes in the summer holidays the father took them all to Killiney or Greystones for the day, but the strand was always crowded, and one or another of them generally lost something in the soft sand. Ellen had lost her First Communion medal and the chain that held it around her neck. The father liked to go swimming, and he used to dip the children in and out of the water and then carry them back on his wet sharp shoulders to the mother, who would dry them under a very big towel that would keep the other people from seeing them when she stripped their bathing dresses off.

The window of the little boxroom looked out over the roof of the shed where they kept the coal and the firewood and the empty boxes where the stray cats made their beds on nights like tonight. The roof of the shed was of corrugated tin, and Ellen thought that when her father had finished listening to the record he would hear the great drumming the rain made when it hit the tin, and she wished she could hear that sound from her own bed.

Ellen did not know how long she had been asleep that night when she woke to find her mother fitting herself into the bed beside her.

"Oh, Ellen, don't wake up," the mother said. "I'm perishing with the cold and you're as warm as a little bull always. I'll just get warm. I'll just lie here a minute."

Ellen moved quickly over and made room, and she and her mother lay squeezed together. The mother turned on her side and her long plait fell across Ellen's face. Ellen put her arm out into the night and lifted the plait gently and laid it across the top of the pillow. The mother made a little sound and settled more deeply into the warmth of the bed. Ellen put her arm out again, and put her hand timidly against her mother's face. She felt her mother's hard forehead, her eyelids, her cheek, her pointed nose, and at last her mouth.

"What is it, Ellen?" the mother asked.

"I was afraid you were crying," Ellen said.

The mother took Ellen's hand and put it back under the covers. She was very careful, as though it were not Ellen's hand at all but a small creature she had found lost and was putting back into its nest.

"Ellen," she said, "I was only cold."

"Now you won't be cold anymore," Ellen said.

"I'm getting lovely and warm now," the mother said. "Only my feet, and they'll soon warm up."

They slept. When Ellen woke again it was still dark, not yet time to get up. She felt comfortable and safe. Her mother had said she was as warm as a little bull. Other times her mother had said that Ellen was strong as a little horse, good as gold, bold as brass, growing too fast, growing out of her clothes, getting bigger every time you looked at her.

Around the house the rain fell contentedly without interruption. The rain had all the time in the world. Ellen thought that the poor man would surely come back, and she hoped that when he came back she would be by herself in the house. Her father would be off out somewhere and her mother would be out, too. And Bridget and Johanna would not be there. She would open the door to him and bring him down to the kitchen and give him something to eat. She would turn her back so that he would know she was not looking at him when he was eating or looking at his food. She wouldn't ask him any questions or bother him with talking to him, and she wouldn't tell him she had heard him talking in his sleep, and after a while he would get used to her and he would begin to talk of his own accord and he wouldn't be afraid anymore.

The Daughters

$\mathscr{A}$t eleven-thirty in the morning, a weekday morning, a nervous lady of about forty sat alone on a love seat in the lobby of a little hotel on lower Fifth Avenue and waited for her father to escort her to lunch. The lobby was square and paneled and furnished in chintz, and would have been really cozy if it had not been for the large, walled recess in which the upper half of a clerk was always visible, and the cashier's cage, with its hand-sized aperture for the placing of money, and the two elevators with their uniformed attendants, and the brilliantly lighted glass doors—a wide one leading to the restaurant, and a narrow, pursed one to the bar. The lady on the love seat, Miss Lister, was one of the hotel's permanent guests. As she watched the elevators she fidgeted, with her gloves, and with the collar of her navy-blue coat, and with the modest silver pin at her throat, and once or twice she put up her hand and touched the maroon sailor that sat like an offering on her neat brown hair.

The older of the elevator attendants stepped into his car and closed the doors, answering a summons from above. Miss Lister stopped fidgeting.

Two or three minutes later, the elevator doors opened. Miss

Lister sighed. The people emerging from the car were strangers to her. First came a blooming, buxom lady, dressed in a cashmere sweater, a sporty plaid skirt, and two ropes of pink pearls. By her side an old man tottered. She held his elbow as though it were a handle while his feeble shoes sought the door industriously. A magenta-haired lady in a mink stole followed them from the elevator and skipped to catch up with them. "Isn't he wonderful?" she exclaimed as they all three came toward Miss Lister. "Isn't he remarkable? My, oh, my! There's the chair, now. There's the chair. Easy does it, now. There!"

As the old man dropped into an easy chair beside the love seat, his knees shot up, his feet came together, and he appeared to be locked into position. At the same moment, the buxom lady, who was now flushed the same deep pink as her pearls, plumped violently onto the love seat, causing Miss Lister to bounce. The newcomer delivered, sidewise, a dazzling smile of apology, disclosing a full set of strong white teeth. She had a splendid complexion—the complexion of a physical-education teacher who has just walked off the hockey field after a brisk game in bracing winter weather. The large pale hand with which she patted her honey-colored permanent was festooned with three ornate, thickly clustered diamond rings.

"He's really ninety-three?" the magenta-haired lady said, bending graciously from her hips, which were sheathed in black silk bouclé. "Imagine! Ninety-three years old!"

"Ninety-three his last birthday," the buxom lady said, and crossed her legs and took a pack of cigarettes out of her large, handsome handbag—an opulent bag, a big, rich, capacious bag, with wide smiling jaws that snapped shut at a touch of its mistress's capable fingers. That bag had a confident air. That bag would be familiar and unafraid before safe-deposit boxes. A bank president's desk would be just a home away from home to that bag. Oh, the commanding serenity with which that bag would rest beside a cashier's cage! Miss Lister wistfully fingered her own narrow beadwork envelope, in which the change from even a two-dollar bill might feel cramped, and resumed her apprehensive survey of the two elevators.

"We're aiming for a hundred," the buxom lady said. "And when we reach a hundred, we're going to aim for a hundred and one to ten. Aren't we, Daddy? We're going to live for a lot more years. Aren't we?"

The old man, who was nicely dressed in a dark-gray suit, with a black wool cardigan buttoned across his meager chest, did not raise his eyes, which were fixed on his bony, upthrust knees. His lips were pressed together, his silky white hair was combed to one side, and he looked like a newly washed old saint.

"He can't hear much," the buxom lady said, "but I like to think he knows I'm trying to include him in the conversation."

"Is it all right to talk directly *to* him?" the magenta-haired lady inquired, in a whisper. The buxom lady nodded vigorously, smiled, blew out a cloud of smoke, and smiled again.

The magenta-haired lady drew a deep breath, smiled rather foolishly, and said, in a loud voice, "Aren't you the lucky one, Mr.—"

"Mr. Whitticombe," the buxom woman said. "I'm *Miss* Whitticombe."

"Oh, Mr. Whitticombe, aren't you lucky to have such a wonderful, wonderful daughter?" There was no response from the old man. "Oh, Mr. Whitticombe," the magenta-haired lady shouted, "aren't you the lucky one, going to Key West? *Key West!*" she screeched, in desperation, clutching at the back of his chair and smiling with all her strength. The old man's eyes, which had once been blue, swiveled upward. She bent over him, and her smile sweetened expectantly.

"Damned old fool," the ancient squeaked, and lowered his gaze to his knees.

The magenta head, the mink shoulders, the shiny black hips jerked backward in shock.

Miss Whitticombe laughed heartily. "Isn't he adorable?" she said. "He says that all the time."

"I suppose he doesn't know what it means anymore," the magenta-haired lady said doubtfully.

"I imagine not," Miss Whitticombe said, and tapped the ash from her cigarette. "His mind, you know," she added cheerfully.

"Oh, yes, of course. I suppose he's forgotten everything," the magenta-haired lady said sympathetically.

"Everything except food," Miss Whitticombe said. She leaned toward her father. "Milk, Daddy!" she cried suddenly. "Milk!"

The old man raised his head and looked at her, and then he turned and looked thoughtfully toward the entrance to the dining room.

Miss Whitticombe nodded triumphantly, and the magenta-haired lady gasped with admiration.

"Well!" she cried. "He really does understand, doesn't he? *Mn-hmn!* He's nobody's fool, is he? He understands when he wants to. He knows what he wants, all right. Isn't that just like a man?"

Miss Whitticombe beckoned to one of the elevator attendants.

"I'd like to order something from the dining room, William," she said to him when he came over. "Ask them to send in a small glass of warm milk—just barely warm—for my father. A fruit-juice glass—they know. Tell them it's for Miss Whitticombe."

When the boy had gone, she smiled at the magenta-haired lady.

"It's like a little cocktail for him," she said. "He has it before lunch and dinner when I have my martini. We could go into the bar, but he can't manage those three steps down."

Smiling, the magenta-haired lady adjusted her stole and jerked her bouclé blouse taut over her stiffly defined waistline. She put out her hand. "I must run," she said. "It's been so nice, Miss Whitticombe. Really, I've made more friends in the elevator here. I'm Mrs. Ryce, by the way. R-y-c-e. Perhaps we'll meet again during our stay in New York. I certainly hope so. Goodbye, Miss Whitticombe. And Mr. Whitticombe, of course. Bye. Bye now."

Miss Whitticombe turned to Miss Lister, who was still watching the elevators. "I'm sorry I bumped you like that," she said. "I'm afraid I wasn't looking."

"Oh, it doesn't matter at all," Miss Lister said, hardly looking at her. "I'll only be here a minute anyway. Oh, there he is now."

She lunged forward as an elderly man stepped out of the elevator, but then she sank back again, for this man—erect, white-haired, large-faced, and grim—advanced directly to the cashier's office, without a glance to the right or left. In one hand he carried a walking stick and a pair of gray suede gloves that matched his gray silk tie. In the other he held a sheet of paper. He thrust this paper at the cashier, and then he leaned lightly on his stick, placed his face sidewise to the grille, and spoke his mind.

"What do you mean by loading my bill with these extras? Do you take me for a fool? What the devil does this mean? Room service, a dollar-twenty. Laundry, five dollars and seventy-five cents. Is this how you make your profits, cheating your guests? Here, can't you see? Here. Explain that, if you can." He had a powerfully disagreeable voice. The door marked MANAGER opened, and the manager walked out, a small man, walking with graceful stealth. He took his angry guest by the elbow and guided him a few steps to the main desk, where he leaned against the broad counter and began to talk rapidly, in a low voice that was not audible to the attentive audience on the love seat.

"Oh dear," Miss Lister said. "Oh dear. It's the same every week."

But just today I was *hoping* he wouldn't. It's so dreadfully embarrassing."

"Your father?" Miss Whitticombe asked with interest.

"Yes."

"How extraordinary!" Miss Whitticombe said. "He reminds
me so much of my father at that age. My father had—yes—a little
less hair, and, of course, he was a much bigger man, and he wore a
mustache, a big mustache, but there is a very definite resemblance.
My father used to carry a stick, too." She laughed gently. "How
old is your father?"

"Seventy-seven, nearly seventy-eight," Miss Lister said.

"Ah, yes. Well, I wouldn't worry too much, my dear. I mean the
manager seems to be handling him very nicely. Mr. Tuttle is such a
diplomat—and a dear man, don't you think so?"

"No, I don't," Miss Lister snapped. "I think he's a horror. And
the elevator men, and the waiters—they're all horrors. The switchboard girl won't even answer my phone. I hate this place." She
subsided dismally.

"I know," Miss Whitticombe murmured. "I know just how you
feel. I remember the feeling very well. But I've always found this
little place very agreeable. We stop here twice a year, you know.
We were here in May, on our way to the Cape. And now we're
headed for Key West. I adore New York this time of year, don't
you? But how I used to dread the winters here. And summer in
New York—ugh."

Miss Lister was not paying any attention. Suffering deeply, she
watched the conversation at the desk. Miss Whitticombe watched
also.

"Just the same," she observed. "Even his gestures are the same.
My, he does have a temper, doesn't he? Are you having lunch in
the dining room?"

"Not today," Miss Lister said. "We do, usually. But—it's so

awkward—we had a little difficulty last night at dinner. My father was quite right, of course. The sole—"

"I understand," Miss Whitticombe said soothingly. "But you see, my dear—" She hesitated as a waiter appeared with the milk on its tray. "Thank you so much, Albert," she said. "Put the tray close to his hand. There, that's just right. He can help himself now. And bring me a very dry martini, will you? No olive, nothing. *You* know."

She turned back, but Miss Lister had got up and crossed the room. She hovered at her father's back, just inside the street doors. Mr. Lister faced the manager, who was evidently concluding a truce. The manager, smiling politely, bowed, turned away, and started back to his office. He did not bother to greet Miss Lister. Miss Lister drew abreast of her father, and they went out without speaking.

Miss Whitticombe watched them go. Then, smiling content-edly, she turned to her father. "Daddy!" she cried. "Why, you're dribbling! All that good, warm milk. Is that nice?"

From her handbag she produced a large white handkerchief and dabbed at the old man's chin. She took the empty glass from him and set it back on its tray. Her martini arrived, and she began to sip it with enjoyment. She leaned forward to look into her father's eyes. "Did you enjoy your milk, Daddy?" she asked.

He moved his eyelids. He looked at her hazily. He said nothing.

Miss Whitticombe smiled. "Sweet," she said.

With a benign expression, and quite unnecessarily, she smoothed a lock of the silky white hair. She patted a hollow old cheek.

"Sweet!" she said.

A Snowy Night
on West Forty-ninth Street

*I*t snowed all night last night, and the dawn, which came not as a brightening but as a gray and silent awakening, showed the city vague and passive as a convalescent under light fields of snow that fell quickly and steadily from an expressionless heaven. This Broadway section where I live is all heights of roofs and all shapes of walls all going in different directions and reaching different heights, and there are times when the whole area seems to be a gigantic storehouse of stage flats and stage props that are stacked together as economically as possible and being put to use until something more substantial can be built, something that will last. At night, when the big Broadway lights go on, when the lights begin to run around high in the sky and up and down the sides of buildings, when rivers of lights start flowing along the edges of roofs, and wreaths and diadems begin sparkling from dark corners, and the windows of empty downtown offices begin streaming with watery reflections of brilliance, at that time, when Broadway lights up to make a nighttime empire out of the tumbledown, makeshift daytime world, a powdery pink glow rises up and spreads over the whole area, a cloudy pink, an emanation, like a tent made of air and color. Broadway lights and Broadway nighttime color make a glittering spectacle that throws all around it into darkness. The little side streets that live off Broadway also live in the shadow of Broadway, and there are times, looking from the windows of the hotel where I live at present, on West Forty-ninth Street, when I think that my hotel and all of us here on this street are behind the world instead of in it. But tonight when I looked out of these windows just before going to dinner I saw a kaleidoscope out there, snow and lights whirling sky-high in a furious wind that seemed to have blown the Empire State Building clear out of the city, because it was not to be seen, although I had my usual good view of it this morning. It was a gray morning and the afternoon was gray, but tonight is very dark, and when I walked out of the hotel into the withering cold of this black-and-white night, West Forty-ninth Street seemed more than ever like an outpost, or a frontier street, or a one-street town that has been thrown together in excitement—a gold rush or an oil gush—and that will tumble into ruin when the excitement ends. This block, between Sixth and Seventh Avenues, exists only as a thoroughfare to Broadway, a small, narrow thoroughfare furnished with what was at hand—architectural remnants, architectural mistakes, and architectural experiments. The people who decided to put this street to use for the time that remains to it have behaved with the freedom of children playing in a junkyard. The houses and buildings are of all sizes, some thin and some fat, some ponderous and some small and humble, some that were built for grandeur at the turn of the century, like my hotel, which now has a neon sign hanging all down its fine, many-windowed front, and some that never could have been more than sheds, even if they are built out of cement. In the daytime and especially in the early morning, the street has a travel-stained look and an air of hardship, and then the two rows of ill-matched, ill-assorted houses make me think of a team of worn-out horses, collected from everywhere, that are being worked for all the life that is left in them and that will have to keep going until their legs give out. Nobody will care when this street comes down because nobody really lives here. It is a street of restaurants, bars, cheap hotels, rooming houses, garages, all-night coffee shops, quick-lunch counters, delicatessens, short-lived travel agencies, and sightseeing buses, and there are a quick dry-cleaning place, a liquor store, a Chinese laundry, a record shop, a dubious movie house, a young, imperturbable gypsy who shifts her fortune-telling parlor from one doorway to another up and down the street, and a souvenir shop. The people who work here have their homes as far away from the street as they can possibly get, and the hotels and rooming houses are simply hotels and rooming houses, with tenants for a night or a week or a month or an hour, although there are a few old faithfuls who moved in for a little while and stayed on and on until the years tamed them into permanent transients. The oldest houses on the street are four thin, retiring brownstones that still stand together on the north side, all of them with restaurants or bars on their ground floor. It was to one of these brownstone houses that I went for dinner tonight, to the Étoile de France. Above the restaurant all the floors of the house are abandoned, the windows staring blankly and the wall scarred, but the falling snow curtained the windows and shaped the roof so that the old house appeared once again as it did in its first snowstorm, when the street was new. I had walked along from the hotel, and I waited to cross over to the Étoile, but the cars were going wild, confined as they were to one uncertain lane by the mountains of snow piled up on both sides, and while I waited I looked back the length of the street. The bewildering snow gave the shabby street an air of melancholy that made it ageless, as it will someday appear in an old photograph. But it will have to be a very old photograph. The inquisitive and sympathetic eyes that will see this street again as I saw it tonight have not yet opened to look at anything in this world. It will have to be a very old photograph, deepened by time and by a regret that will have its source in the loss of all of New York as we know it now. Many trial cities, facsimiles of cities, will have been raised and torn down on Manhattan island before anybody begins to regret this version of West Forty-ninth Street, and perhaps the photograph will never be taken. But on the street level, Forty-ninth Street defied the snow, and business was garish as usual. The Étoile was very bright and cheerful when I walked in, but there were very few customers. There was only one man sitting, lounging sideways at the bar—an old Frenchman who comes in often at night, after having had his dinner at the Automat. Only three of the tables in the bar were occupied, and the big back room, the dining room, was dim and deserted. The Étoile is a very plain place, with plain wooden chairs, very hard chairs, red-and-white-checked tablecloths, a stamped tin ceiling painted cream, and wallpaper decorated with pale, romantic nineteenth-century scenes. I sat at a table across from the bar, which has a long mirror behind it to reflect the bottles and glasses and the back of the bartender's head and the faces of the customers and the romantic wallpaper on the wall behind me. One waiter was still on duty—Robert—and he brought me a martini and took my order and went off to the kitchen in a hurry. I think the chef must have been making a fuss about getting away early on this stormy night when there were almost no customers and he was going to have trouble getting home. He lives in Long Island City. Mme. Jacquin, who owns the restaurant, had gone home, and her daughter, Mees Katie, was in charge, together with Leo, the bartender. Leo has been working here about fifteen years. He is Dutch, and I think he is in his late fifties, a few years younger than Mme. Jacquin. Mees Katie is about thirty. She has a singularly detached manner, as though she were only working at the Étoile while she waited for her chance to go to some place where she really wants to be, but she spends more and more time here, while her mother, who used to almost live in the place, often does not come in for days at a time. Mees Katie began coming in about five years ago to help during the luncheon hour, but now she is here every night as well. She leaves at ten o'clock, when the chef goes home, and after that Leo manages by himself. On good nights the bar is open until two in the morning, or even later.

Mees Katie was sitting as she always sits, facing toward the door, so that she could jump up when the customers came in. She often sits alone at the table for one by the street window, a huge window partly curtained in colorless gauze, and when there is a rush on, she stands in the arch that leads from the front room to the back and watches both rooms. She never sits at the bar. Tonight she was sitting beside a lady I have never seen at the Étoile before, a very wide, stout, elderly lady whose elaborate makeup—eyes, complexion, and mouth—looked as though it had been applied several days ago and then repaired here and there as patches of it wore off. Her hair was dyed gold and curled in tiny rings all over her head, and her face and neck were covered with a dark beige powder. Her face had spread so that it was very big, but her nose and mouth were quite small, and she had enormous brown eyes that had no light in them. She had put on a great deal of black mascara, and blue eyeshadow. The shadow had melted down into the corners of her eyes and settled into the wrinkles. She was all covered up in a closely fitted dark blue velvet dress that was cut into a ring around her neck and had long tight sleeves that strained at her arms every time she lifted her spoon to her mouth. She was eating pears in wine, and she ate very carefully, looking into the dish as she chose each morsel. When she wasn't attending to the pears, she watched the man sitting opposite Mees Katie, and she listened to him, and Mees Katie listened to him, and he listened to himself. His name is Michel, and he never stops talking. He has something to do with importing foreign movies, or with promoting them, and he is always busy. He is always on the run, going in all directions. He never finishes his dinner without jumping up from his chair at least once to dash into the back room, where the telephone is, to make a call, and it is always an urgent call. If the phone is busy, if there is someone ahead of him, he stands waiting impatiently in the arch between the two rooms, looking importantly about him, and when he has finally gotten into the telephone booth and put his call through, he keeps the door open until he is halfway through his conversation. His voice can be heard all over the restaurant until suddenly there is a little clatter as he shuts himself away with his secrets. He has a very high, harsh voice, and he twists each word so that only half of it sounds like English. Leo makes fun of him. Once, when Michel had pulled the phone booth door shut on himself, Leo called from the bar to Mees Katie, who was sitting at a table with some people, just as she was tonight, "Michel is talking with the weatherman again," and Mees Katie looked annoyed, although she smiled. She gets impatient with the Étoile, and with the people there, and especially with Michel, because he pesters her, but she has a kind heart, and she is always polite.

Michel always comes into the restaurant alone, looking for company, and once in a while when there is no acquaintance he can join for dinner he sits by himself. When he is alone, all his animation dies away and he looks old and tired. He has a very broad dark face, with loose wrinkles, furrows, running up and down it and overlapping its outline. His forehead is high, and he has kinky coal-black hair and a neat, thin mouth. When he sits at his table with nobody to talk to or to pay any attention to him, he looks deserted, as though he had been brought to the restaurant and left there by someone who had no intention of coming back to claim him. Alone, he is morose and dignified, as though humiliation had taken him unawares but had not found him unprepared. On nights like that, when he knows he is doomed to solitude, he stands at the bar with his drink, sweet vermouth, until his dinner is brought, and then he goes to his table and sits down very deliberately and shakes out his napkin very fussily. He places the napkin across his lap and folds it closely around him so that his jacket hangs free of it. He always wears a double-breasted suit, and a waistcoat. When the napkin is safely in place, he picks up his knife and fork and sounds all the food on his plate and looks severely at his green salad. Then he cuts off a piece of meat and places it in his mouth and begins to chew it. While he is chewing, his knife and fork lie on his plate, and his wrists rest against the edge of the table, with his hands limp, and he chews patiently, looking as proud and as indifferent as though he were facing a firing squad.

I think he must have had dinner alone tonight before I came in, and after dinner moved over to join Mees Katie and her acquaintance, the elderly painted lady. There was nothing, not even a glass of water, in front of Mees Katie and nothing in front of Michel, but the elderly lady's part of the tablecloth looked as though it had been thoroughly occupied by several different dishes before her pears in wine were brought. Mees Katie looked very tired. She has a lot of acquaintances, most of them inherited from her mother, and I suppose the elderly lady was one of them. Mees Katie has an attitude she falls into when she is being officially companionable. She sits with both elbows on the table, with her right hand placed flat against the side of her head and her left hand, with the fingers curled under, and turned down, supporting her chin. The right hand always holds her head up, while the left hand is ready to rise against her mouth, as though the polite attention she wants to give people calls for modesty from her, and for as complete a concealment of her own personality as she can manage. Tonight, as she listened wearily to Michel, her hand hid her mouth and her eyes were fixed on Michel's face. She is often bored, but as a rule she can escape from her entanglements by jumping up to greet a customer or to give an order to the waiter. There was no easy escape for her tonight—the Étoile might as well have been snowbound for all the coming and going there was. It was very quiet. Three men sitting at the last table in the bar were talking quietly, but the only voice really to be heard belonged to Michel, and Mees Katie kept her eyes fixed on him as though she feared she might fall asleep if she stopped watching him. She has extraordinary eyes, small slanted brown eyes that are filled with light, brilliant eyes of a transparent brown in which the color recedes, not growing darker but growing more intense, so that the point of truest color, the source of all that light, seems very far away, and perhaps it is for that reason that Mees Katie's expression always seems distant, no matter how close her face is as she bends down to answer a question or to whisper to some customer she knows well.

Suddenly the elderly lady finished her pears, and she laid down her spoon and smiled, a small, mild, accustomed smile of pleasure, and she turned to look at Mees Katie, and Mees Katie yawned and was shocked at herself

"Oh, I am sorry, Michel!" she cried. "Excuse me, Mrs. Dolan, but I am so tired tonight."

Michel emerged from his monologue to see that he was in danger of losing his audience, and he looked over at Leo and called excitedly for cognac, cognac all round.

"Oh, no no no, thank you, Michel," Mees Katie said. "No cognac for me, thank you very much."

But Mrs. Dolan was delighted. She removed her lips from the edge of her coffee cup, which she was holding with both hands, and for a minute she looked like the perky little person she must once have been, who knew that at the mention of a drink a girl brightens up. "Well, thank you very much," she said to Michel, who had begun to stare at her with alarm. "I believe I will." She had a very loud, rusty voice, and after regarding Michel with approval she turned to Mees Katie. "Have a drink," she said. "A little cognac will settle your stomach."

Mees Katie laughed in a horrified way. "Oh, my stomach is all right," she cried, and she called to Leo, "M. Leo, *deux cognacs, s'il vous plait.*"

Mees Katie is tall and slender, and she moves very easily and quickly. She went to the bar and took the little tray with the two cognacs from Leo and handed it to Robert, who had come running from the end of the bar. Then she walked quickly away, through the bar and through the dim dining room, and pushed open one of the doors leading to the kitchen and went in there and stayed a few minutes. When she returned she was very brisk in her beaver hat and her beaver-lined coat. She said goodnight to Michel, who had become very glum, and to Mrs. Dolan, and to the old Frenchman at the bar, and to me, and she motioned Leo to the end of the bar and spoke a few words privately to him as she pulled on her gloves, and off she went. As she talked with Leo she stood sideways to the bar, and looked through the window, and a minute later, watching through the window, I saw her go past, walking carefully on the dangerous sidewalk, with her hand up to hold her hat against the wind. She and her mother have an apartment where they have lived for many years, far over on the west side, near Tenth Avenue. Leo also watched her through the window, and when she disappeared he stayed where he was and continued to watch. There is a big open garage across the street that has pushed itself through the buildings and now is open at each end, making an arcade and therefore a vista—you can see a little section of the Forty-eighth Street scene from this window here, and the people walking along there, who almost never turn their heads to look over in this direction, seem very far away, and they seem to

be walking faster and with more sense of direction than the pass-
ersby immediately outside the window. Tonight was so blurred
and wild you could see nothing much except movements of struggle out there, but Leo continued to watch. The back of Leo's head
is perfectly flat, and his skin is putty-colored, but more white than
gray or beige. His features are thick and fleshy and very clearly
defined, the nose a wide triangle, the upper lip a sharp bow. His
eyes are small and blue, and his half smile, for he never smiles
right out, is always accompanied by a deliberate glance in which
suspicion and interest are equally mixed. Sometimes the interest
becomes dislike. He is vain. He is slow-witted and not handsome,
and he is past sixty and a bit fat, and yet he wears the pleased,
secretive expression of a man who has always gotten along very
well with women. After a while he abandoned his survey of the
window and moved along to speak with the old Frenchman.
They spoke in French. The Frenchman objects to hearing English
spoken at the Étoile, and he becomes very irritable when English-
speaking strangers try to strike up an acquaintance with him. The
three men at the end of the room left their table and moved across
to that end of the bar and called for drinks. They were irresolute.
They were marooned in the city for the night, and they had taken
rooms at the Plymouth Hotel along the street, and they wanted to
be entertained without becoming involved, and the evening was
going flat on them. They had come to the Étoile for dinner because
they often have lunch there and always imagined it to be a place
where interesting people came at night—show people, artists and
writers, people like that, or at least French people who would sit
and stand around and talk excitedly as they did in the movies—
but there was no one worth watching or listening to, and tomorrow night they will drive home to Larchmont with a disappointed
feeling that they will translate as knowledge—New York City is
just as dull as anywhere else when you have nothing to do.

Michel was still talking, but warily. The last thing he wanted was to be left alone with a strange woman, and he felt it was no compliment to him to be seen drinking with a Mrs. Dolan. He hadn't touched his cognac. She took a businesslike sip from hers and set the glass back on the table. She had stopped listening to him, and now she was sizing him up. A smile kept coming and going on her face—it was her contribution to the conversation and her acknowledgment of it. But she was considering, or ruminating, and a little trick occurred to her. She smiled and put her finger against her lips as though Michel were a child who was talking too much. Michel stopped talking.

"Do you come here much?" Mrs. Dolan asked him. It wasn't much of a question, but it was too personal for poor Michel. He began to answer her, and then instead he jumped up and clapped his hands to the sides of his head. It is the gesture he makes when he remembers an urgent phone call, or when he has to run out of the restaurant on an urgent errand. Mrs. Dolan stopped smiling, but she showed no surprise or embarrassment. She simply looked at him. He had to run out on an urgent errand, but he would be back in ten minutes.

He always returned to the Étoile after these errands, but Mrs. Dolan didn't know that, and it was clear she did not believe him. She went on looking at him. In his excitement he knocked his chair back, and it fell against the edge of my table. He turned ungracefully and caught the chair and straightened it, using both hands. "Pardon, Madame," he said to me, gaily. He looked me in the eye and smiled at me. He was triumphant, or at least relieved, because he was managing to break away from Mrs. Dolan, and he was glad of the diversion, of the fallen chair, because it made his getaway seem easier, but he would have smiled anyway, challenging me or challenging anyone to ignore him. When he smiles, his dark, even teeth remain tightly closed because he must always remain on guard and must always show that he does not fear the snub he watches for. I said quickly, "It doesn't matter at all," and I was glad I did because, although he had already begun speaking to Mrs. Dolan again, he turned and nodded to me, and I knew I was forgiven for the sin I had not committed, of not recognizing him.

Then he bustled to the coatrack, beside where I was sitting, and began wrapping himself up in his warm clothes—his warm fur-collared overcoat and his fur hat and his big gloves. Mrs. Dolan watched him as indifferently as though he were a stranger who had chanced to share her table on a train journey, and, as she might in a train, she turned her head from him to look at the view, in this case the bar, Leo, the old Frenchman, and the three exiles from Larchmont. Leo had a dour expression on his face as he watched Michel, who looked happily back at him and then looked at Mrs. Dolan and saw he had lost her attention. He called to her, "You will wait? You will be here? You will not run away?"

She looked at him stupidly, and I was surprised when she answered him. "I'm not going anywhere," she said in her dreadful voice.

Leo spoke up. "It is snowing out, Michel," he said.

Michel grinned at him. "Ten minutes!" he cried, and vanished.

"That Michel is a great joker, he thinks," Leo said.

"You call him a joker?" Mrs. Dolan said loudly. "Some joker, I'll say." But Leo ignored her, and she began rummaging in the huge leather handbag that was on the table beside her, propped against the wall. She took out a mirror and moved it about while she examined herself, her eyes, her mouth, and her earrings, and then she took out a dark red lipstick and smeared it thickly back and forth on her mouth, and afterward, while she was putting the lipstick away, she pressed her lips closely together. With her little finger, she rubbed the lipstick smooth, and tidied the corners of her mouth, and when she had finished she cleaned the color from her finger with her dinner napkin and took a tiny sip of her brandy, and glanced at Michel's brandy, which he had not touched. After that she sat gazing at the stained tablecloth, and from time to time she pursed her lips thoughtfully at something she saw there.

There are three young girls who have been coming to the Étoile for their Sunday dinner the last few months. They share an apartment on Forty-seventh, and they all work as secretaries. Lately one of them, Betty, has been dropping in alone, early in the evening, before ten o'clock. She never comes for dinner, and she never stays after Mees Katie has gone home. Betty is about five foot two, a brown-haired, blue-eyed, round-faced girl with a pretty figure and a pretty smile, who obviously enjoys being a friendly little child among the grownups. Her winter coat is dark green imitation fur, and she wears sweaters and skirts most of the time, schoolgirl clothes. She walks in timidly, as though she is not quite sure of her welcome, and then she sits up at the end of the bar and asks for a Perrier water and drinks it very slowly, making it last. She dreams of being an actress, but I think the part she dreams of playing is the part she plays as she sits up at the bar of the Étoile, and sips her Perrier and stares wonderingly all about her. The Étoile reminds her of a waterfront café she saw once in a movie that starred Jean Gabin and that I think has now been remade to include a very young unknown actress named Betty who sits at the bar with a Perrier stealing the show, although she has nothing to say and nothing to do except be herself, poor and alone and very young. She always puts down a dollar to pay for her Perrier, but Leo seldom takes the money, and if he does take it he gives her another Perrier on the house. Once or twice Betty has sat at Mees Katie's table and helped her listen to Michel. She finds Michel very entertaining. Tonight she walked in shortly after Michel ran out. She came in expectantly, almost laughing, walking out of the snowstorm as though she were walking into a party. She pulled off her scarf, shaking the snow from it, and as she began to unbutton her coat she looked around for Mees Katie. Leo had come to the end of the bar and was watching her, smiling.

"Where is everybody?" she cried. "Where's Mees Katie?" She sat up at the bar and Leo poured a Perrier for her.

"I'm celebrating, Leo," she said. "This is my very first snowstorm. The office let us off at three o'clock, and I walked round and round and round, all by myself, celebrating all by myself, and then I went home and made dinner, but I got so excited thinking about the snow I just had to come out again and thought I'd come here and see Mees Katie. I thought there'd be thousands of people here. Oh, I wish it would snow for weeks and weeks. I just can't bear for it to end. But after today I'm beginning to think New Yorkers never really enjoy themselves. Nobody seemed to be really enjoying the snow. I never saw such people. All they could think about was getting home. Wouldn't you think a storm like this would wake everybody up? But all it does is put them to sleep. Such people."

"It does not put me to sleep, Betty," Leo said in his deliberate way.

"I wish it would snow for a year," Betty said.

"It will take something warmer than a snowstorm to put me to sleep, Betty," Leo said.

Betty laughed self-consciously and looked at Mrs. Dolan.

"Michel is a bad boy tonight, Betty," Leo said, and he also looked at Mrs. Dolan. "He told this lady he'd be back in ten minutes and it has been twenty."

"Nearly half an hour," Mrs. Dolan said disgustedly. "Nearly half an hour."

"He'll be back," Betty said. "Michel always comes back, doesn't he, Leo?"

"Oh, yes, Michel comes back," Leo said, and he put his hand on

Betty's arm and leaned far across the bar and began whispering in her ear, or tried to begin whispering in her ear, because at the touch of his face against her hair she pulled roughly away and looked at him with such distaste that he stepped back. Then he went to the cash register and opened the drawer and began looking in at the money and pretending to count it. He was furious. If she had spent ten years pondering a way to express disgust, she could not have found a better way. Even if they had been alone, Leo would never have forgiven her, but the three lingering men were watching, and so was Mrs. Dolan.

Betty sat alone for a minute and then she took her Perrier and slipped down from her stool and walked over to Mrs. Dolan. Betty looked flustered, but she was smiling.

"May I sit down?" she asked Mrs. Dolan.

"Oh, please do," Mrs. Dolan said.

Betty sat down in Michel's chair, diagonally across from Mrs. Dolan. "Michel will be back soon," she said. "He always comes back."

"He left me sitting here like this," Mrs. Dolan said.

"Michel is really a sweet kind person when you get to know him," Betty said. "He's a darling, really."

Leo called out, "Miss Betty, you owe me sixty cents."

Betty looked over at him in surprise.

"You forgot to pay for your drink, little girl," he said, smiling, and he waved at Robert the waiter. Robert took Betty's dollar to the bar and brought her back her change. She had gotten very red.

"He needn't have shouted at me," she said to Mrs. Dolan. Mrs. Dolan said nothing.

Betty began talking. "This is the first big snow I've ever seen," she said. "I thought it would be like New Year's Eve here tonight, or something. When they first told us we were getting off early from the office I felt it was like a party or something, but then after

I walked around a bit it seemed more like a disaster, and I kept wanting to get into the spirit of the thing. I felt very left out all day. I kept walking around."

When she fell silent, Mrs. Dolan still continued to watch her, but she said nothing. She had nothing to say, and nothing to give except her silence, and so she said nothing, and made no reply, and they sat without speaking until the silence they shared strengthened and expanded to enclose them both.

Not long ago I saw a photograph in the evening paper of a crowd of circus elephants gathered around a dying elephant, Flora, who had fallen and was lying on her side on the ground. The elephant closest to Flora was trying to revive her by blowing air into her open mouth with his trunk The newspaper story said that all the elephants in the troupe took turns trying to save their dying comrade, and the story finished by saying, "This practice is instinctive among pachyderms."

But that practice, instinctive among pachyderms, that determination to win even a respite from death, is no more instinctive than the silence was that grew and turned into a lifeline between Betty and Mrs. Dolan, because their silence arose from a shame so deep that it was peace for them to sit in its silence, and to listen to this silence, which was only the silence of their own nature, of all they had in common. Mrs. Dolan's face grew ruminative, and Betty's profile suggested she was lost in recollections that were not unhappy.

Michel walked in, a snowman. He must have been standing out in the open, or walking, ever since he left the restaurant. He stood still just inside the door and banged the palms of his gloves together and sent a fond glance at Mrs. Dolan and at Betty, who had turned to watch him. Michel was very pleased with the entrance he had made, and he looked as though he would like to go out and come back in again.

"Don Juan, he thinks he is," Mrs. Dolan growled.

Michel moved to the coatrack and began unwrapping himself. He was very slow about it, and all the time he was pulling off his gloves, and unwinding his scarf, and shaking his fur hat, he faced the room as though he faced a full-length mirror, and he smiled, watching all of us, but not as he would watch the mirror. At last he stood revealed in his navy-blue-and-brown striped suit and his rings and his crinkly black hair and his bow tie, and he strolled back to his table and sat down beside Mrs. Dolan, and smiled sweetly at Betty, and picked up the cognac that had been waiting for him. When I left they were all ordering more drinks, and Mrs. Dolan had decided to switch to crème de menthe. The old Frenchman came out of his reverie and began looking unpleasantly at the three men who were chattering in English at the end of the bar, and I knew he was becoming happier. I paid my bill and left.

The self-service elevator at my hotel shivered piteously when I stepped into it, and hesitated before starting its painful ascent to the high floor where I live. That is as usual. The tiny, boxy elevator is as alien to this elegantly made hotel as the blue neon sign that winks on and off in front. A marble staircase winds all the way up through the heart of the building, and decorated windows over every stairwell still filter and color the light as they have done for more than sixty years. The fireplaces have all been blocked up long ago, but the rooms are very big and the ceilings are high and the walls shut out all sound. I looked again through the windows that give me my view of Broadway. Just below me, on Forty-eighth Street, on both sides of the street, a few small houses huddle together in the shadows, and from their low level other, newer walls rise higher and higher to the south and east, but tonight the big buildings, the giants that carry Manhattan's monumental broken skyline, were lost in fog. I could see only the little roofs below me and their neighbors immediately beyond, all of them under smooth snow that shaped them in the dark into separate triangles and squares and rectangles and slopes. The snow on Forty-eighth Street was rumpled, but there was no one in the street and the open parking lot was empty. To the right, Broadway was still lighted up as high as the sky, but the lights shone weakly, smothered in fog, except for the dazzling band of color that runs around the Latin Quarter, a few houses away from me. I pushed open the window. The cold air rushed in, but no noise. What sound there was was drugged, as though I were a hundred floors above the street instead of only eleven floors. The wind had died down, and the snow fell thickly, falling in large, calm flakes.

I See You, Bianca

---

*M*y friend Nicholas is about the only person I know who has no particular quarrel with the city as it is these days. He thinks New York is all right. It isn't that he is any better off than the rest of us. His neighborhood, like all our neighborhoods, is falling apart, with too many buildings half up and half down, and too many temporary sidewalks, and too many doomed houses with big X's on their windows. The city has been like that for years now, uneasy and not very reasonable, but in all the shakiness Nicholas has managed to keep a fair balance. He was born here, in a house on 114th Street, within sight of the East River, and he trusts the city. He believes anyone with determination and patience can find a nice place to live and have the kind of life he wants here. His own apartment would look much as it does whether he lived in Rome or Brussels or Manchester. He has a floor through—two rooms made into one long room with big windows at each end, in a very modest brownstone, a little pre–Civil War house on East Twelfth Street near Fourth Avenue. His room is a spacious oblong of shadow and light—he made it like that, cavernous and hospitable—and it looks as though not two but ten or twenty rooms had contributed their best angles and their best corners and their best-kept secrets of depths and mood to it. Sometimes it seems to be the anteroom to many other rooms, and sometimes it seems to be the extension of many other rooms. It is like a telescope and at the same time it is like what you see through a telescope. What it is like, more than anything, is a private room hidden backstage in a very busy theater where the season is in full swing. The ceiling, mysteriously, is covered in stamped tin. At night the patterned ceiling seems to move with the flickering shadows, and in the daytime an occasional shadow drifts slowly across the tin as though it were searching for a permanent refuge. But there is no permanence here— there is only the valiant illusion of a permanence that is hardly more substantial than the shadow that touches it. The house is to be torn down. Nicholas has his apartment by the month, no lease and no assurance that he will still be here a year or even three months from now. Sometimes the furnace breaks down in the dead of winter, and then there is a very cold spell for a few days until the furnace is repaired—the landlord is too sensible to buy a new furnace for a house that may vanish overnight. When anything gets out of order inside the apartment, Nicholas repairs it himself. (He thinks about the low rent he pays and not about the reason for the low rent.) When a wall or a ceiling has to be painted, he paints it. When the books begin to pile up on the floor, he puts up more shelves to join the shelves that now cover most of one long wall from the floor to the ceiling. He builds a cabinet to hide a bad spot in the end wall. The two old rooms, his one room, never had such attention as they are getting in their last days.

The house looks north and Nicholas has the second floor, with windows looking north onto Twelfth Street and south onto back yards and the backs and sides of other houses and buildings. The neighborhood is a kind of no man's land, bleak in the daytime and forbidding at night, very near to the Village but not part of the

Village, and not a part, either, of the Lower East Side. Twelfth Street at that point is very narrow and noisy. Elderly buildings that are not going to last much longer stand side by side with the enormous, blank façades of nearly new apartment houses, and there is a constant caravan of quarrelsome, cumbersome traffic moving toward the comparative freedom of Fourth Avenue. To his right Nicholas looks across the wide, stunted expanse of Fourth Avenue, where the traffic rolls steadily uptown. Like many exceedingly ugly parts of the city, Fourth Avenue is at its best in the rain, especially in the rain at night, when the whole scene, buildings, cars, and street, streams with such a black and garish intensity that it is beautiful, as long as one is safe from it—very safe, with both feet on the familiar floor of a familiar room filled with books, records, living plants, pictures and drawings, a tiny piano, chairs and tables and mirrors, and a long desk and a bed. All that is familiar is inside, and all the discontent is outside, and Nicholas can stand at his windows and look out on the noise and confusion with the cheerful interest of one who contemplates a puzzle he did not create and is not going to be called upon to solve. From the top of a tall filing cabinet near him, Bianca, his small white cat, also gazes at the street. It is afternoon now, and the sun is shining, and Bianca is there on the cabinet, looking out, only to be near Nicholas and to see what he sees. But she sees nothing.

What is that out there?

That is a view, Bianca.

And what is a view?

A view is where we are not. Where we are is never a view.

Bianca is interested only in where she is, and what she can see and hope to touch with her nose and paws. She looks down at the floor. She knows it well—the polished wood and the small rugs that are arranged here and there. She knows the floor—how safe it is, always there to catch her when she jumps down, and always very solid and familiar under her paws when she is getting ready to jump up. She likes to fly through the air, from a bookcase on one side of the room to a table on the other side, flying across the room without even looking at the floor and without making a sound. But whether she looks at it or not, she knows the floor is always there, the dependable floor, all over the apartment. Even in the bathroom, under the old-fashioned bathtub, and even under the bed, and under the lowest shelf in the kitchen, Bianca finds the well-known floor that has been her ground—her playground and her proving ground—during all of her three years of life.

Nicholas has been standing and staring at rowdy Twelfth Street for a long time now, and Bianca, rising, stretching, and yawning on top of the filing cabinet, looks down at the floor and sees a patch of sunlight there. She jumps down and walks over to the patch of sun and sits in it. Very nice in the sun, and Bianca sinks slowly down until she is lying full length in the warmth. The hot strong light makes her fur whiter and denser. She is drowsy now. The sun that draws the color from her eyes, making them empty and bright, has also drawn all resistance from her bones, and she grows limp and flattens out into sleep. She is very flat there on the shining floor—flat and blurred—a thin cat with soft white fur and a blunt, patient Egyptian head. She sleeps peacefully on her side, with her front paws crossed and her back paws placed neatly one behind the other, and from time to time her tail twitches impatiently in her dream. But the dream is too frail to hold her, and she sinks through it and continues to sink until she lies motionless in the abyss of deepest sleep. There is glittering dust in the broad ray that shines on her, and now Bianca is dust-colored, paler and purer than white, and so weightless that she seems about to vanish, as though she were made of the radiance that pours down on her and must go when it goes.

Bianca is sleeping not far from Nicholas's bed, which is wide and low and stands sideways against the wall. Behind the wall at that point is a long-lost fireplace, hidden away years before Nicholas took the apartment. But he has a second fireplace in the back part of the long room, and although it stopped working years ago, it was left open, and Nicholas has made a garden in it, a conservatory. The plants stand in tiers in the fireplace and on the floor close around it, and they flourish in the perpetual illumination of an electric bulb hidden in the chimney. Something is always in bloom. There are an ivy geranium, a rose geranium, and plain geraniums in pink and white. Then there are begonias, and feathery ferns, and a white violet, and several unnamed infant plants starting their lives in tiny pots. The jug for watering them all stands on the floor beside them, and it is kept full because Bianca likes to drink from it and occasionally to play with it, dipping in first one paw and then the other. She disturbs the water so that she can peer down into it and see the strange new depths she has created. She taps the leaves of the plants and then sits watching them. Perhaps she hopes they will hit back.

Also in this back half is Nicholas's kitchen, which is complete and well furnished, and separated from the rest of the room by a high counter. The kitchen gets the full light of one of the two windows that give him his back view. When he looks directly across, he sees the blank side wall of an old warehouse and, above, the sky. Looking straight down, he sees a neglected patch, a tiny wasteland that was once the garden of this house. It is a pathetic little spot of ground, hidden and forgotten and closed in and nearly sunless, but there is still enough strength in the earth to receive and nourish a stray ailanthus tree that sprouted there and grew unnoticed until it reached Nicholas's window. Nobody saw the little tree grow past the basement and the first floor because nobody lives down there, but once it touched the sill of Nicholas's room he welcomed it as though it were home at last after having delayed much too long on the way. He loved the tree and carried on about it as though he had been given the key to his inheritance, or a vision of it. He leaned out of the window and touched the leaves, and then he got out on the fire escape and hung over it, making sure it was healthy. He photographed it, and took a leaf, to make a drawing of it. And the little ailanthus, New York's hardship tree, changed at his touch from an overgrown weed to a giant fern of extraordinary importance. From the kitchen counter, Bianca watched, purring speculatively. Her paws were folded under her chest and her tail was curled around her. She was content. Watching Nicholas at the ailanthus was almost as good as watching him at the stove. When he climbed back into the room she continued to watch the few leaves that were high enough to appear, trembling, at the edge of the sill. Nicholas stood and looked at her, but she ignored him. As she stared toward the light her eyes grew paler, and as they grew paler they grew more definite. She looked very alert, but still she ignored him. He wanted to annoy her. He shouted at her. "Bianca!" he shouted. "I see you!" Bianca narrowed her eyes. "I see you!" Nicholas yelled. "I see you, Bianca. I *see* you, Bianca. I see you. I see you. I SEE you!" Then he was silent, and after a minute Bianca turned her head and looked at him, but only to show there was no contest—her will was stronger, why did he bother?—and then she looked away. She had won. She always did.

In the summer it rains—sudden summer rain that hammers against the windowpanes and causes the ailanthus to stagger and shiver in gratitude for having enough water for once in its life. What a change in the weather, as the heavy breathless summer lifts to reveal a new world of freedom—free air, free movement, clean streets and clean roofs and easy sleep. Bianca stares at the rain as it streams down the glass of the window. One drop survives the battering and rolls, all in one piece, down the pane. Bianca jumps for it, and through the glass she catches it, flattening it with her paw so that she can no longer see it. Then she looks at her chilled paw and, finding it empty, she begins to wash it, chewing irritably at it. But one paw leads to another, and she has four of them. She washes industriously. She takes very good care of her only coat. She is never idle, with her grooming to do, and her journeys to take, and then she attends on Nicholas. He is in and out of the apartment a good deal, and she often waits for him at the head of the stairs, so that he will see her first thing when he opens the door from the outside. When he is in the apartment she stays near him. If she happens to be on one of her journeys when he gets home, she appears at the window almost before he has taken off his coat. She goes out a good deal, up and down the fire escape and up and down the inside stairs that lead to the upper apartment and the roof. She wanders. Nicholas knows about it. He likes to think that she is free.

Bianca and the ailanthus provide Nicholas with the extra dimension all apartment dwellers long for. People who have no terraces and no gardens long to escape from their own four walls, but not to wander far. They only want to step outside for a minute. They stand outside their apartment houses on summer nights and during summer days. They stand around in groups or they sit together on the front steps of their buildings, taking the air and looking around at the street. Sometimes they carry a chair out, so that an old person can have a little outing. They lean out of their windows, with their elbows on the sills, and look into the faces of their neighbors at their windows on the other side of the street, all of them escaping from the rooms they live in and that they are glad to have but not to be closed up in. It should not be a problem, to have shelter without being shut away. The windowsills are safety hatches into the open, and so are the fire escapes and the roofs and the front stoops. Bianca and the ailanthus make Nicholas's life infinitely spacious. The ailanthus casts its new green light into his room, and Bianca draws a thread of his life all around the outside of the house and all around the inside, up and down the stairs. Where else does she go? Nobody knows. She has never been seen to stray from the walls of the house. Nicholas points out to his friends that it is possible to keep a cat in an apartment and still not make a prisoner of her. He says disaster comes only to those who attract it. He says Bianca is very smart, and that no harm will come to her.

She likes to sit on the windowsills of the upper-floor tenants, but she never visits any of them unless they invite her in. She also likes to sit in the ruins of the garden Nicholas once kept on the roof. She watched him make the garden there. It was a real garden and grew well, until the top-floor tenant began to complain bitterly about his leaking ceiling. Even plants hardy enough to thrive in a thin bed of city dust and soot need watering. Nicholas still climbs to the roof, not to mourn his garden—it was an experiment, and he does not regret it—but to look about at the Gulliver world he lives in: the new buildings too tall for the streets they stand in and the older, smaller buildings out of proportion to everything except the past that will soon absorb them. From the street, or from any window, the city often seems like a place thrown up without regard for reason, and haunted by chaos. But from any rooftop the city comes into focus. The roof is in proportion to the building beneath it, and from any roof it can easily be seen that all the other roofs, and their walls, are in proportion to each other and to the city. The buildings are tightly packed together, without regard to size or height, and light and shadow strike across them so that the scene changes every minute. The struggle for space in Manhattan creates an oceanic uproar in the air above the streets, and every roof turns into a magic carpet just as soon as someone is standing on it.

Nicholas climbs to the roof by his fire escape, but when he leaves the roof to go back to his apartment he goes down through the house, down three flights to his own landing, or all the way down to the street floor. He likes the house and he likes to walk around in it. Bianca follows him. She likes to be taken for a walk. She likes to walk around the downstairs hall, where the door is that gives onto the street. It is an old hall, old and cramped, the natural entrance to the family place this house once was. To the left as you enter from the street there are two doors opening into what were once the sitting room and the dining room. The doors are always locked now—there are no tenants there. The hall is narrow, and it is cut in half by the stairs leading up to Nicholas's landing. Under the stairs, beside the door that leads down into the basement, there is a mysterious cubbyhole, big enough for galoshes, or wine bottles, or for a very small suitcase. Nobody knows what the cubbyhole was made for, but Bianca took it for one of her hiding places, and it was there Nicholas first looked for her when he realized he had not seen her all day—which is to say for about ten hours. He was certain she was in the cubbyhole, and that she wanted to be coaxed out. He called her from the landing, and then he went downstairs, calling her, and then he knelt down and peered into the dark little recess. Bianca was not there, and she was not on the roof, or under the bed, or down at the foot of the ailanthus trying to climb up, and she was not anywhere. Bianca was gone. She was nowhere to be found. She was nowhere.

There is no end to Bianca's story because nobody knows what happened to her. She has been gone for several months now. Nicholas has given up putting advertisements in the paper, and he took down all the little cards he put up in the cleaner's and in the grocery store and in the drugstore and the flower shop and the shoeshine parlor. He has stopped watching for her in the street. At first he walked through the street whispering her name, and then one night he found himself yelling for her. He was furious with her. He said to himself that if she turned up at that moment he would kill her. He would certainly not be glad to see her. All he wanted was, one way or another, to know whether she was alive or dead. But there was no word from Bianca, and no word from anyone with actual news of her, although the phone rang constantly with people who thought they had seen her, so that he spent a good many hours running around the neighborhood in answer to false reports. It was no good. She was gone. He reminded himself that he hadn't really wanted a cat. He had only taken Bianca because a friend of his, burdened with too many kittens, pleaded with him. He finds himself wondering what happened to Bianca, but he wonders less and less. Now, he tells himself, she has shrunk so that she is little more than an occasional irritation in his mind. He does not really miss her very much. After all, she brought nothing into the apartment with her except her silence. She was very quiet and not especially playful. She liked to roll and turn and paw the air in the moonlight, but otherwise she was almost sedate. But whatever she was, she is gone now, and Nicholas thinks that if he only knew for sure what happened to her he would have forgotten her completely by this time.

The Door on West Tenth Street

Bluebell the old black Labrador retriever is going to have a holiday from the city. She is going to Katonah, a distant suburb of New York, where she will have trees, grass, hedges, night-smells of earth, and, at a distance, a road to watch, and passing cars. She will have a house of her own, to guard. There is a field in Katonah where she can run as hard as she likes, and, not far away, a lake where she will swim, holding her head high, pouring herself through the water while her big, heavy old body feels light again and her legs stretch themselves. In the lake in Katonah, Bluebell's short, thick, powerful sea legs will stretch themselves until all the dull constriction of city sidewalks and city streets crumbles away from her webbed paws and from inside her muscles. Her legs will become sleek again and they will do what they like, sending her through the water at exquisite speed, so that the people watching her think, Why would anybody want to go faster than Bluebell, and how can anybody bear to go more slowly than she goes when she swims?

Bluebell is a changeling, anxious to please, but water is her element, and when she swims she becomes herself, a solitary reveler with a big, serious, courageous head and a store of indifference that make it seem sometimes that she might never come back to land. She always comes back, shaking herself so that the water springs off her and her fur stands up in spikes. And after shaking she stands for a minute, staring about her with the mad cousinly friendliness of her true cousin, the dolphin. She is ready for anything. At that moment, wet and rakish from her swim, Bluebell seems to have traveled to earth from a far distance—from the bottom of the sea, twenty thousand fathoms down, where the Fish King has his court. The Fish King never speaks, not even to say "Now" or "At once." His words are made of thunder and they reverberate at his will. Great sounds issue from him—sounds of wrath, sounds of mirth, and sounds of hunger. But he never speaks. He sits in oceanic silence under an immense floating canopy that is really an upturned lake of fresh clear water, and in its blue depths and shallows small green flowers and silver goldfish play games with the sunlight that was trapped in the water on the day the lake was stolen—a Monday in Norway, centuries ago. Bluebell has seen the Fish King and his canopy, and she knows his palace guard of dignified young whales, and the thousand sequined mermaids who are his dancing girls. She was at home with them, and she is at home with us. She has seen everything. It is written in her face, in her sad, bright eyes. There is hardly anything she does not know, except when to stop eating. Her true memories are ancestral—they haunt her sleep. In daily life, the compromise she makes is wholehearted, but there is nothing in it of acquiescence. Housebound, she remains herself. She is a dog.

But today Bluebell is going to the country. She is going to Katonah, where her big, hungry nose will find something to smell besides concrete and stone and lampposts, and gutters that seem interesting but that always prove unresponsive in the end. Blue-

bell does not know that her leash is going to be put away for a
month. To her, this is an ordinary day, and it starts as usual in her
Greenwich Village apartment. She rouses from her sleep on the
bedroom floor, on a dark, flowery carpet that is thin and worn to
pale string in spots—a length salvaged from the acres of carpeting
that once covered the lobbies and stairs of one of those majestic old
New York hotels that disappeared last year, or the year before, or
the year before that. The carpet smells of Bluebell's sleep and of
the cats' sleep and of the vacuum cleaner, but that is all. There are
no memories in it, no echoes of country grass and leaves and earth,
no bits of sand, no woodsmoke, no pine needles, nothing of the
house by the ocean in East Hampton, where Bluebell lived for
most of her life. This is an apartment carpet, anonymous, warm,
comfortable, and dull. No field mice ever ran across it, flying for
their lives from the cats; no field mice, no moles, no chipmunks, no
baby rabbits. Once a regiment of tiny black city ants marched
across it and disappeared into the wall. And once an enormous
black water bug hurried out of the bathroom and across the carpet
in the direction of the kitchen. And a soft, pale-green caterpillar, a
visitor from nowhere, crawled timidly about in the dark foliage of
the old carpet for a little while before he curled up to die. But that
is all. It is a poor, boring carpet, and Bluebell yawns when she
wakes up, ignoring it. She stands and stretches and looks about
her, showing she is ready for her walk.

Bluebell's walk takes her around Washington Square, and as
she passes the doorman of the big apartment house on the corner
he grins and says, as he does every morning, "Hello, Old-Timer."
Bluebell is nearly eleven years old, and her young, original, shining black face is disguised by a dusty mask of gray hairs, gray eye-
brows, gray muzzle, and long gray jaws. The mask makes her
comical, and people smile when they see her and say, "Oh, my,

that's an old dog." People walking behind her smile, too, because, although her thick, heavy tail is still coal black, her behind is gray and it waggles importantly as she goes along. But however she goes, trotting, cantering, plodding, or simply dawdling, she always looks what she is—a dog out of water, not at ease in the city but putting up with it very well. She is amiable, although not particularly obedient, and she accepts her leash and makes her way, leading with her strong, wide-set shoulders and getting all she can out of this strange world where she has to behave like a clockwork dog who can go only in squares, circles, and straight lines. And she searches. She keeps looking for a black door in a little white house on West Tenth Street. Twice on her walks she happened on that door and refused to pass it, struggling to get into the house and even barking once, but for weeks now, for months, she has not seen it.

The house belongs to a man who took Bluebell to Montauk for six weeks last summer, and when she sees the door on West Tenth Street she knows what lies behind it—a cliff dropping into the Atlantic Ocean. Bluebell loves that cliff, which gave her a wild dash to her morning swim and, on her way back, countless difficult crannies to dig and burrow into. The house on West Tenth Street looks like a real house, and no one passing it would dream that all of Montauk lies behind it—the cliff, the sand, and the ocean. Everything worthwhile is there behind that door, which Bluebell knows is closed only to hide the sea from dogs who are not going there. She has not seen that door for a long time now, but she has not lost hope. She watches for it. She looks for it everywhere, on all the streets east and west of Fifth Avenue, and along Fifth Avenue, and along University Place, and on Fourth Avenue, and on Seventh Avenue, and on little Gay Street and on Cornelia Street and even on Bleecker Street, behind the stalls of vegetables and fruit, but she is never confused into thinking that a strange door is the door she wants. There is only one door on West Tenth Street, and she will know it when she sees it again.

Even in the city, Bluebell had adventures. As she walked around Washington Square Park one morning, she came alongside a very, very old man sitting alone on one of the benches that line the paths around the grass. He was more than old, he was ancient, and although it was a glowing day, Indian summer, he was warmly dressed in an overcoat and a muffler and a crumpled gray hat, and he wore laced boots, and his hands were clasped together on his walking stick, and his eyes were closed. Bluebell passed very close to him, and he may have heard her dramatic breathing as she pressed on in her pursuit of the Atlantic Ocean (hiding behind that door on West Tenth Street, so near, but where?), because he opened his eyes and saw her. He didn't smile, but he looked at her. "Hello, Snowball," he said, thoughtfully. "How are you doing, Snowball?" Then he closed his eyes again and went on sitting by himself in the warm sun.

Another time Bluebell found a dead sparrow lying at a grassy corner in the center of the Square, where the fountain is. (Where the fountain *was*. It has been dry for a long time.) The sparrow, no bigger than a withered leaf, lay on his side, with his wings folded and his legs close together. He was a very neat little dead body. A wild bird, his fate was strange anyway—to share a shabby city park with hungry, watchful pigeons, big fellows. How old had he been when he learned to dash in among them and grab his crumb? He must have been strong and clever to survive to his full size. His cleverness was finished now, and the story of his life was not even history—it was a big mystery that he had never known anything about, and that was wrapped about him now as he lay by the grass.

He lay there, with the secret of his nature in open sight for any-body to look at; but only to look at, not to touch, not really to see, never to understand. He was a sparrow, whatever that is. Samuel Butler said life is more a matter of being frightened than of being hurt. And the sparrow might have replied, "But Mr. Butler, being frightened hurts."

Bluebell looked at the sparrow, and then she sat down and began to contemplate him. There was nothing to smell, but the light breeze blowing from the south, from Sullivan Street, touched a loose feather and it stood up and waved, a tiny flag the color of dust. That was all. It was quite otherwise with the mighty pheas-ant, an emperor pheasant, Bluebell found dead on the beach in East Hampton one autumn morning, her third autumn by the ocean, years ago. That was an unearthly morning—one mislaid at the beginning of the world and recovered in East Hampton under a high and massive sky of Mediterranean blue. An Italian sky, a young and delighted ocean, a blazing sun; and far away on the white sand something crimson that caught the wind. The wind was so new that it blew cold, in its first rush across the world, but the air was soft. The pheasant's head and body were almost buried in the powdery sand, but he had fallen with his wings wide open, and one of them slanted up to make a wedge of color in the air.

That autumn morning was early in November—the time of year when millions of small stones appeared in flattened wind for-mations at intervals along the lower part of the beach, where the sand is hard and flat near the water's edge. Some of the stones are as big as walnuts and some are as small as grains of rice, and they lie tightly packed, a harsh sea fabric, while their faint colors—ivory, green, silver, coral—are always vague, almost vanishing, always about to dissolve into the stone. Bluebell used to race along the beach until she was almost out of sight, and at that distance, far away, she became a big black insect with four waving legs and a waving tail and wings that were either transparent or folded. Because it was impossible that a creature who skimmed so confidently and at such speed across the sand and in and out of the water and along the top of the dunes should not also be able to fly up and away and out to sea, with the sea gulls. The sea gulls detested Bluebell and flew off screeching with irritation whenever they saw her hurrying toward them. They stood in a long single line, staring at the water, and waited until she came close to them before they took flight. Their feet left a delicate tracery of pointed marks, a Chinese pattern, in the clean wet sand. Bluebell's big paws made untidy holes in the sand, and sometimes troughs, and even when she did make a recognizable paw mark it was indistinct and awkward, not to be compared with the delicate sea gull imprint. She had attacks of wanting to dig in the sand, and then she dug as frantically as a dervish looking for a place to whirl. She loved to chase her ball into the ocean. She had a succession of balls—red, green, blue, and white, and sometimes striped—but one by one they drifted out to sea while Bluebell stood at attention on the shore and watched them go. She knew the power of the big waves, and how they hurled themselves so far down into the sand that they were able to drag it out from around her legs.

After Christmas, when the storms began, the beach was whipped and beaten into bleak terraces—long ranges of sharp sand cliffs descending from the dunes to a struggling, lead-colored sea that foamed into mountains against the sad sky, while the sea gulls screamed their warnings all day long. One day in January, Bluebell received a present from the grocery shop of an enormous bone, a bone of prehistoric size and weight, a monumental thighbone with great bulging knobs at each end. She took hold of the bone at its narrowest place, in the middle, but even so she had to open her big jaws to their widest and her head was pulled forward by the bone's weight. She straightened up and carried the bone from the kitchen to the lawn in front of the house, where she placed it on the frozen grass and looked it over tenderly before she started to attack it. Two sea gulls appeared out of the fog and circled about not far above her, watching for a chance at the bone, and the day was so strange that the sea gulls seemed to speak as natural claimants for the fog that was taking possession of the house. It was a dark-white day under a lightless sky and the view was ghostly. The small grove of trees at the end of the driveway had become a dim outpost, and to the left of the house, toward the ocean, there was nothing to be seen except shapes formed by the fog. Outside the house only the two sea gulls and Bluebell with her bone had substance. The fog reached the windows as the afternoon wore on, and night came to find the house shrouded, lost, hidden, invisible, abandoned except by the ocean, which filled each room with the sound of eternity, great waves gathering themselves for the clash with earth and darkness. Bluebell had been in and out of the house all day. About seven in the evening she cried to be let in, but when the door was opened to her she backed away from the light and was immediately lost except for her face, a thin gray mask with imploring eyes looking out of the fog. Her eyes were pleading, not for permission to come in but for permission to bring her bone into the house. She vanished and reappeared a minute later, a transparent dog face that held in its ghostly jaws the great bone, which glowed phosphorescent, while beyond it four round diamonds flamed suddenly—two of the cats returning from their usual night-watch. There was no moon that night; no moon, no stars, no clouds, no sky, no real world—only the little house settling slowly into its place in safest memory, guarded by the silence that poured out of the voices of the waves.

The lawn in front of the house belonged to Bluebell. In the summer she stretched herself out on it to bake, and in the winter when the snow was very deep she played boisterously in it, rock-

ing and leaping and plunging, a dolphin again. The lawn was separated from the emerald acres of a famous golf course only by a
thin line of trees, and from her place near the house Bluebell could
see the public road and the cars passing along there, going south to
the beach or north to the village. Sometimes a car turned into her
driveway and then she ran forward to welcome it. During her
early days in the city she was surprised to find so many cars and all
so close to her, parked along the sides of all the streets where she
walked, and at first she thought they were all friends and she used
to notice each car, and smell it, and look to see if there was a place
in it for her. She soon discovered that in the city cars had no con-
nection with her, and she stopped expecting anything from them,
although it made her very restless to see a dog looking out of a car
window, because she could not help hoping that somebody would
offer her a ride, even a short ride, anywhere. Away from home,
that is where Bluebell dreamed of being, when she saw dogs in
cars, and when she watched for the house on West Tenth Street.
Away from home, that is where Bluebell wanted to be.

One afternoon, just before the start of her holiday in Katonah,
her walk took her a long way west, to Hudson Street and the
walled garden of St. Luke's Chapel. It was a cool afternoon, with
thin sunlight, and a complicated country fragrance drifted across
the walls of the old garden and through the bars of the garden
gate. Bluebell put her nose to the gate and smelled. She could see
the big, old-fashioned garden, fading in autumn, and she smelled
leaves, grass, and earth. Bluebell smelled fresh earth. Somebody in
the garden was digging.

In secret places in the neighborhood of her house in East Hampton Bluebell used to bury her best bones. They were her treasures,
and she knew they were still where she had left them, safely hidden, waiting for her. She smelled earth now, the same old earth,
but she could not get into the garden because the gate was closed,

and locked. There was a lady in the garden, walking near the gate, and Bluebell wagged her tail, but the lady didn't see her, or didn't want to see her. Bluebell stopped wagging, and two or three minutes later she turned from the gate and went around the corner onto Christopher Street. And there, as she walked west on Christopher Street, Bluebell saw a vision. She saw the public road that cuts through the golf course in East Hampton, with the cars passing each other, going north and south, just as they always did. She was looking at the West Side Highway, which is cut out of the air around it just as the road in East Hampton is cut out of the green golf course. All she really saw was cars moving *in the distance.* It was months since Bluebell had seen cars at a distance, and the distance between where she was on Christopher Street and the elevated highway was much the same as the distance between her old lawn in East Hampton and her old view of the golf course. Everything was happening at once. Her head was still full of the smell of new earth, and she was seeing her view again, and now she smelled, very close to her, the Hudson River. The river did not smell like the Atlantic Ocean, but Bluebell knew she was walking toward water, big water. Perhaps she was going to have a swim. Her ears went up and she began to hurry, pulling on her leash. But then she turned another corner and found herself back in the same old concrete quadrangle, walking her geometrical city-dog walk, with only miserable lampposts to tease her starving nose. In her disappointment Bluebell lost her temper and charged furiously across the sidewalk to threaten a five-pound nuisance, a miniature white poodle who yapped rudely at her, and who stood like a hero on his four tiny paws and glared up at her until she was dragged away, seventy pounds of raging disgrace.

Poor Bluebell. She is being made foolish in her old age. She would like to go swimming, show them all what she can do. She would like to go swimming, show them all what she really is.

She would like to dig up a bone. She would like to go for a ride in a car. She would like to find that door on West Tenth Street. Most of all, she would like to get away from Home. Yes, she would very much like to get away from Home, who now marches along behind her, holding her leash.

Home speaks: "Good Bluebell. Good Dog. Nice Walk. Good Bluebell."

Home's voice is consoling, but Bluebell can't be bothered to listen. Bluebell is sick of Home, who holds her on a leash and won't let her go anywhere or do any of the things she wants to do.

"Good Bluebell," Home says.

Bluebell begins to go faster and now it is Home's turn to be dragged along, hanging on to the leash. Home protests angrily.

"Stop it, Bluebell," Home says. "Bad Bluebell. Bad Dog. *Bad.*"

Bluebell doesn't care. She begins to speed.

Home shouts, *"Bad, bad!"*

Bluebell is puffing so hard that her chain collar hurts her throat, but she only goes faster and faster. Disappointment and boredom have turned her into a fiend, and all she wants is to get as far as she can from Home.

But that was several days ago. Today Bluebell is going to Katonah for a holiday in the country. The car comes at twelve, as it promised to do. Bluebell is led out of her apartment house on her leash, just as though she were going for her ordinary walk. But then the car door is opened and Bluebell leaps into the back seat. She is mad with joy. She tumbles over herself and tries to tumble into the front seat, but as soon as the car starts off she quiets down and sits looking out through the window at the streets she is leaving. She is trembling with happiness. She makes no sound, but her eyes are shining with adoration for everything she sees—for the streets, and for the car she is in, and for the driver of the car, and for Home, who sits beside her in the back seat. Yes, Bluebell is going away from home, and Home is going with her. Bluebell turns her head from the window and looks at Home, who is smoking a cigarette and smiling. "Good Bluebell," Home says, and Bluebell stretches herself out on the seat and puts her head in Home's lap. "Good Bluebell," Home says. Bluebell sighs and half closes her eyes. Her tongue comes out and she licks her lips. She settles herself for a long ride. The wheels of the car go round and round and they sound as though they might keep going forever.

A Large Bee

A large bee, carried by the wind to the edge of the Atlantic Ocean, lay on his back and struggled to free himself from the wet sand. As the wind continued to blow, more sand drifted over him and packed itself around him, and by the time Mary Ann Whitty came along, walking with her dog, there was nothing to be seen of him but a tiny coffin of sand with his black legs waving feebly out of it.

This was on the strand in Amagansett last April, and at first she thought she was looking at some kind of sea insect, something that lived in the sand. There was no color or shape to show that a bee was there, no evidence that the creature had wings, only the black legs to show that something was alive and wanted to stay alive. With a big shell she scooped this *something* up and carried it back to the high dry sand and tried to turn it right side up, so that it could find its feet, or free its wings and balance itself, or fly away, or burrow down, or do whatever it had to do. But it could not stand, and kept tumbling over on its back, and after a minute the wind picked it up and blew it right back to the edge of the water. The tide was coming in. Mary Ann had a silk scarf in her pocket,

275

and she took that and went after the bee—she still did not know the creature was a bee—and scooped him up again and placed him in the middle of the scarf, which she then tied into a bag by its four corners.

Her dog, Bluebell, a black Labrador retriever, rather fat, had been amusing herself while Mary Ann was rescuing the bee. Bluebell had raced to a distant line of sea gulls who were standing sentinel at the edge of the water, a long way off, and had destroyed their afternoon by making them all fly up into the air. Now she came racing back to Mary Ann and they continued to walk until they came to the opening between the dunes that put them on the path to their house. As she walked along the sandy path, Mary Ann looked into the silk bag to find out if the insect was ready to be set free, and it was then she saw that she was carrying a bee and that he was still half covered with sand, and she thought, I will take him home and let him dry out and see what he wants to do next.

Halfway along the path, she saw what she expected to see— from the undergrowth at the edge of the woods the cats were coming out to meet her. They came out slowly, stretching at intervals, down the bank, onto the road, and then they all sat down heavily and watched, yawning. When she came close to them, they stood up and waited for recognition, which she gave each of them separately. Then Bluebell offered to recognize them and they backed away in disgust, because she was wet and salty from the sea. The cats all began to run for home, running like rocking horses, with their tails arched. Bluebell was tired from her swimming and content to waggle along beside Mary Ann. The bee made no weight in the scarf. It might as well have been empty. There were woods on both sides of the road for a little way, and then woods on one side only, because on the right a clearing had been made, and there the house in which she lived stood, but it stood up on a height, and from it there was a clear view across the tops of the trees to the dunes and across the dunes to the ocean. There were wide, irregular steps cut into the side of the bank that sloped from the road to the house, and in front of the house was a wooden deck. She went in and laid the scarf on the table. She lighted the fire. She poured milk for the cats and lured them with it to the deck and then shut the door on them, shutting them out. Then she untied the scarf and looked at the bee. He was still moving his legs feebly and the sand was falling off of him. She left him there and went to sit by the fire. Bluebell lay down with her head on the hearth and closed her eyes. Mary Ann was always afraid her brain would boil when she did that, but she spoke to Bluebell and Bluebell opened one calm eye and then shut it again.

Bluebell almost never barked, but when she had been waiting outside the house for too long, when she began to lose patience and feared that the door would never be opened, she summoned from some point at the top of her head a sound that was at first so thin and unearthly that it might be called ethereal—an ethereal note from far away. This sound dropped quickly into a vulgar, insistent whine, which dropped without delay into the most shameful manifestation of her impatience, fear, and anger—a sustained squeal so penetrating that no one who heard it ever wanted to hear it twice. Now, as Mary Ann sat by the fire waiting for the bee to revive or not revive, she knew that something had been whining at the back of her head, and as she listened the whine gave voice, and what she heard was not a squeal but a harangue that was familiar to her because it sounded at intervals from the side of her brain where the random insights that other people had had about her grew and flourished and multiplied themselves, like the weeds that they were. They had a weedy strength, a weedy tenacity, a weedy life, and their own weedy truth, and she supported them, and she allowed them to live and to express themselves, because she could afford them. At the time that they took root in her mind she could not afford them, but she accepted them, after a struggle— by that I mean that she made room for them. There are some natures that can expand to include anything, even the things that ought to be thrown away.

Mary Ann was hearing the voice of her conscience, which, of course, was familiar to her, although it bore no more resemblance to her own voice than Bluebell's unpleasant squeal did to her ordinary gentle silence.

The bee would have been dead by now. Why do you bother all these creatures? Why not leave them alone? The field mouse the cats brought in this morning has been living in the box you arranged for it in the bedroom all day, waiting for the darkness, when you will put it out again, and the cats will probably catch it again, and in any case it has nothing ahead of it but fear and the search for food. It was dead when they brought it in, but you would bring it back to life. Why don't you let these animals alone? The same with the baby rabbits and the chipmunk and the rest. Nothing but egotism. Why not let things be? Let everything alone. Stop interfering. Nature must take her course . . .

At that moment a great excitement started in the room and Bluebell jumped up as though she had been stung. No, she had not been stung. But the bee had collected all his force and had come to vigorous life and had come out fighting. He raced around the room, making a very loud noise, and tried to get out through the back windows, which looked over a green space that had a few trees and, at the far side, a bed where daffodils were in bloom. Mary Ann opened the window and he flew out. He was so big that she could follow his flight for a good distance. He seemed all right, and he seemed to know what he was doing. *That bee will be swept right back to the ocean with the first wind,* the voice said. *You did him no good. He must be stupid or he would never have been blown down there in the first place . . .*

She went into the kitchen to put the kettle on for tea. All true, she said to herself. No doubt about it, everything you say is true.

The Children Are Very
Quiet When They Are Away

It is a winter-afternoon sky, very dark, and lowering itself now to thicken the heavy mist that is gathering over the dunes. The Atlantic Ocean, hidden by the fading dunes, is thundering today. The line of the dunes is growing dimmer, and the huge house that stands up there over the sea is becoming ghostly. It is an enormously clumsy house, with hundreds of diamond-paned windows and a massive front door that has flights of stone steps going up to it. Inside, there must be at least eighty or ninety rooms, all of different shapes and some with balconies. In clear weather, some of the balconies can be seen from here.

"Here" is a small lawn that stretches its little length with modest satisfaction in front of a fat, romantic cottage that is very closely related to the amiable monstrosity on the dunes. The cottage might have been baked from a bit of dough left over after the giant's place on the dunes was made. They are alike, and the cottage has its own massive doorway and its diamond-paned windows and its big beams and its gingerbread roof.

The giant house is inhabited in the summertime by seven children, and the cottage is the home of a black Labrador retriever and five handsome mongrel cats. The retriever's name is Bluebell and she is almost six years old. On a bleak day like today, the cats stay indoors. They are asleep around the house, or they are at the windows, attentive to nothing. But at the edge of the driveway that separates the small lawn from the great one leading to the dunes, Bluebell lies on guard, with a large hollow bone between her front paws and her head turned toward the big house away up there in the distance. Bluebell must wonder why the children do not appear. They were always appearing, from all directions, and descending on her, when she did not reach them first. They used to swoop down from their house and across the lawn in a flight of white shorts and white shirts, and Bluebell never crossed the driveway to trespass on their grass until she was certain they were coming to her. They used to call her name as they ran for her, and as their breath shortened and their voices came closer, her name sounded louder, and the sound of it filled her with a joy that could only increase, because there was no limit to the children's energy or to their affection for her. "Bluebell. *Good* Bluebell. Good *Bluebell.*" There had never been so many voices calling her all at once, or so many legs to charge at and then avoid, or so many admiring faces to watch and please. Please them all, always please, that was her duty, her only duty, and she had never before seen it so plain, or felt it to be so simple, or so interesting, or felt herself so valuable. She was a dog and she performed like a dog. She forgot her middle age and her extra weight and her gray muzzle, and she frolicked like a puppy, and like a mustang, and like a kitten.

She found a treasure in the short grass and then, after smelling it importantly, she tormented it for a few seconds with her paws before she pranced away and left it as it was, invisible. She entertained like a dog. She lay stretched on her back with her huge chest heaving dramatically. Upside down she is grotesque, a vulnerable monster. She might be a sacrifice, on the lawn, in the sunlight. Her front paws hang in the air empty and aimless, and the big, soft ears that make her look demure and mournful fall away, inside out, and leave her face exposed and wild. And her eyes are wild; they look at nothing. The children are astonished to see their familiar turn mysterious, and they make a circle around her. They are embarrassed, because she is shameless, and they try to clear the air with their laughter. "Look at Bluebell. She is *funny*." Who is Bluebell now, and what is she? She is not herself. The smallest girl decides that Bluebell is a bench, and she sits heavily down on the softest place, the stomach. Bluebell springs rudely up and resumes her proper shape. Now she is a dog again, and she stands on four legs again. The children welcome her return by telling her her name: Bluebell, Bluebell, Bluebell. Bluebell brandishes her heavy tail and challenges the eyes that watch her with her eyes, and then she races away and they all race after her. She has never been so pursued. She has never been so famous or so celebrated. Her name is on every lip. She has come into her own. She is the only dog in the world.

But here it is winter, with the cold winter weather that is so good for playing in, and she has been waiting for hours, ever since last summer, and the children have not appeared. If she watches faithfully they will appear. They generally come out around this time. Whenever they come out is this time. Bluebell moves the old bone over to the middle of the driveway, and then she resumes her dignified attitude, with her paws precisely arranged, as though she were lying in wait on her own tomb. Her head is turned to the house on the dunes. It is lost in the mist. The house is gone. There is no sound except the pounding of the sea in the distance, and that sound means nothing to Bluebell. What use to plunge into the sea and brave the waves when she has no witnesses? The lawn is empty, shrinking away into the mist, and the air has turned to silence. No voice is calling from up there on the dunes. There is no Bluebell. Her name is lost. She was the only dog in the world, but now she is only a dog. It is all the children's fault, all this absence. It is all their fault. They are too quiet. All this silence can be blamed on them, and all this waste. Bluebell takes her eyes from the dunes and puts her chin on the empty bone between her paws. She drowses. It is all the children's fault. Everything is too quiet. It is all their fault. The children are quiet because they are away. But what is away, and then, what is here? Bluebell is here. Bluebell sleeps. Now Bluebell is away where the children are who are so quiet here.

In and Out of
Never-Never Land

$\mathcal{I}$n East Hampton, it was the Fourth of July, the hour just before dawn—very early-morning tea time. Mary Ann Whitty looked into the brown eyes of her dog, Bluebell, and she thought, The dog is kind and good, but the cats have style. . . . She was sitting in her living room, which was remarkable to her because it was hers alone, and because it contained her furniture, her books, her dog, and her cats. The furniture was shabby, the books were worn and showed the signs of long storage, the cats all wore mixed furs, and Bluebell, the black Labrador retriever, was not as serene as a dog of her age and nature ought to be. Bluebell had spent too much time in too many different kennels.

Mary Ann did not care that her household was a trifle bedraggled. What mattered to her was that all her possessions were collected together in one place. She admired the room she had made for herself, and she admired everything in it. She was so pleased with herself and her possessions and arrangements that she even admired the lacks in her house. For example, a simple example, she had no dining-room table. She knew she should have a proper table, a proper place for eating, and that without it her life was makeshift, but she thought that makeshift ways were very well suited to this strange little house, which wore such a temporary air that the first time she walked into it she said to herself that it was not a real house but an impossibility, not a house at all, and that she must rent it immediately, because it might very well not be there when she looked for it again. Not that the house looked as though it might fall down or be blown away. It had a solid look; there was nothing at all fragile about it. But it did not look as though it belonged where it was, by the edge of the sea.

Mary Ann had a friend who rejoiced when he first saw it. "This is not a house by the sea," he said. "It is certainly not a house in East Hampton. It is somewhere else. It is a town house. No, it is a house in the middle of a forest. The Black Forest, I think. It is a *folie*. Whatever it is, it is not real—not a real house, at any rate. And why did they put it sideways?"

Instead of facing the ocean, which was so close that the waves made themselves heard all day and all night, the little house faced its lawn—really only a strip cut from the huge lawn that swept down from the great house on the dunes where the seven children lived, all of them Bluebell's friends. Alongside Mary Ann's house, hidden from her by a tall hedge, there was a lovely, simple flower garden that slanted away from a small apple orchard and into a field of long grass. Bluebell wandered among the apple trees without permission, and without permission the cats had taken the wild field for their hunting ground. On Mary Ann's side of the hedge the flower bed that stretched the length of her lawn was strikingly neglected, but the daffodils and roses and hollyhocks that had been planted there long ago still bloomed at their appointed times, as if to show what they once had been and still might be if somebody would give them a little help.

Sometimes Mary Ann walked from her front door to the grove of pine trees that separated her lawn from the golf course, and as she walked she inspected the tangle of weeds and withered vines that smothered the beds, and she thought, It is a disgrace. But the word "disgrace" came tranquilly into her mind and caused no uneasiness there. She excused herself from gardening as she did from sewing, simply by announcing she had not the gift for it. She was inclined to be mulish about the things she did not do—not drive a car, not garden, not sew—and it was in something of the same spirit that she congratulated herself as sincerely on what her house lacked as she did on what it held. But in spite of all it lacked, and for all its temporary air, the little house had an air of gaiety about it, and even of welcome. It is the high ceiling, Mary Ann thought, and the books, and the big fireplace, and the mauve rug casts a cheerful light. And in any case, she thought, the house, like me, is goodhearted in spite of itself.

It was absurd, the little house with its baronial front door and its towering diamond-paned windows that had more wood than glass in them, and its lofty black beams that were not very old and not at all necessary, and its scalloped black-iron hasps, and handles, and hinges on all the doors—even on the bathroom door. The hinges were always flying off the doors and landing at Mary Ann's feet with a noisy clank, and she was constantly on her hands and knees searching for the long black spikes that would hold them back on the door until the next fit of humor took them, but she did not mind. The house was always losing bits of itself, and she spent hours trying to find lost pieces of paper—letters, bills, lists, old checkbooks that might tell her where the money had gone—but she persevered just as the house did, and she thought, As long as nobody asks me any questions, everything will come out all right.

Her house was closely related to the house on the dunes where the seven children lived. The children's house was really enormous—hundreds of rooms pressed into the shape of a cottage and covered with a deep shingled roof. It had been put up shortly after the First World War, and at the foot of its majestic lawn its miniature, Mary Ann's house, had been built for the caretaker. The people who had lived in the big house and employed a caretaker had all gone away long ago, and the seven children had been in possession there for years now.

Mary Ann, the newcomer, did not know exactly when Bluebell and the children had discovered each other. She imagined Bluebell on the grass in the sun one morning, or one afternoon, raising her big head to see a pair of bare legs, several pairs of bare legs, standing at a safe distance and on their own side of the driveway that separated them from Bluebell's private ground. The children must have been on their toes, ready to fly if the strange dog turned fierce. Bluebell was very black, and her ample body was covered with shining flat fur, a handsome coat of it, but her muzzle was gray, and she had a comical look. Comical or not, she had long sharp teeth and great paws that could hold her prey to the ground if she chose to find prey. The children must have wondered about her. Bluebell would not have bothered to wonder. What she saw was what she always saw—not children or birds or cats or mice but interesting new manifestations of the friendliness she believed existed for her in all that lived. If it lived, it moved, and whether it moved by creeping or running or walking or flying or hopping or simply by blowing like torn paper about the lawn, Bluebell wanted it. This new apparition, so near to her and quite unknown, must have struck her with joy. Fourteen legs, seven faces, and a variety of voices, all there just waiting to be claimed. She would have begun her campaign at once, beating a vigorous overture on the ground with her heavy tail.

Mary Ann could only imagine all that. What was certain was that Bluebell no longer decorated the front of the house for hours in the morning and during the afternoon. Now she was always away, off somewhere, following the children into their house and out of it again, and traveling with them along the beach and over the golf course and even into the village. Bluebell had another secret now to lay on top of the eternal secret that was guarded, or imprisoned, by her animal silence. She had a new world of her own that was free of the cats and free of Mary Ann, but she showed her independence of them only at the moment of her departure from the house and the moment of her return to it. These days, when she went out in the morning, she was purposeful, and her eyes turned at once to the house on the dunes to see if anyone was out and about. And when she came back and her own door was opened to her, she burst in, breathless, and threw herself on the floor, unable to speak for exhaustion and importance. While she panted, her tail hammered on the floor and her eyes roved wildly around the room, reclaiming everything she saw, but most of all reclaiming Mary Ann. "I choose you," Bluebell's eyes said to Mary Ann, "you, you," and her gaze turned fervently to the kitchen, where her dinner waited.

The cats showed a faint, lazy interest in all this commotion. The biggest of them, the bright orange, sat up and then stood up and stretched, and lay down again, wrapping himself up in his own coat. "I am ignoring you," each cat said, opening its eyes just enough to show a gleam of light, and then, closing its eyes again, each cat said, as always, "I choose myself."

But the moment had arrived when East Hampton, with its waves and sand and its wide golf course and its ponds of wild water birds and its fine main street and its hilly green graveyard, was about to be revealed all over again by the new light. Mary Ann heard the first birds, the smallest ones, who sing suddenly at the end of darkness. She listened to their sweet voices, and then she stood up and went to open the front door. It was still night out, but the darkness had retreated into the bushes and trees. She could see the sky shifting. It was the moment she liked, because it proved she was right and that nothing was real. It was also the moment when the cats went out to kill. She looked around the room and saw the big orange, the little black favorite, the long-haired wild one, and the quiet calico. Only Tom, the secret hunter, was absent. Tom hunted alone and far away and never, thank God, brought his little victims into the house. Mary Ann walked through the empty blue-floored room that led to her small kitchen and heated a saucepan of milk and gave it to the cats, hoping to lull them back to sleep and sloth. She turned out the light in the kitchen and saw the dim blue world outside. It was nearly time for the sea gulls to start their march inland. She would have liked to go outside to watch them, but the one morning she had gone out, her long white robe had startled them, and they had risen up in outrage and gone away screeching that their day was ruined.

She went upstairs and stood at her bedroom window, which faced the sea. The sea gulls were just appearing, coming in from the beach and lining up along the top of the long rise that banked the road going down to the sea. They began to walk at once, taking their usual path, which brought them at an angle across the golf course and down the children's lawn to Mary Ann's house. Now the golf course was ghostly with them, and they continued to advance, white birds that whitened and grew bigger as they drew closer. They all walked. The few that flew up descended to the ground at once and started walking again. Some sailed while they walked, showing their wings. They came this way every morning, sometimes more of them and sometimes fewer, and the leaders always stopped at the far edge of the narrow driveway that separated her lawn from the children's. A few steps more would have brought the sea gulls to the walls of her house, but they never took the last few steps, and no matter how close they came they always seemed to be very far away. They walked like emperors, or like jockeys, or like stoics. They knew the ocean, and kept vigil by it in regimental rows, and they screamed against patience, and walked for their health on expensive grass, and Mary Ann thought they knew themselves and she was baffled by them. They were indomitable. There was no need to fear for them or pity them. In her imagination they were living stones that had found wings to save themselves during some long and drastic fall in forgotten times.

Now the leaders reached the edge of the driveway, the limit of their walk, and paused, and there was a general pause all the way back across the lawn and the golf course, and then they all rose up and flew back to the sea. To watch the sea gulls go was like watching the snow stop falling. You couldn't say when the last flake fell, and you could not mark the last sea gull. Mary Ann turned from the window and looked at her bed, which was very large and took up most of the room. She had closed the bedroom door after her, but Bluebell had slipped in with her and was now curled humbly on a corner of the pink quilt. "All right, Bluebell," Mary Ann said, "as long as you're here," and she lay down and pulled the quilt over her and fell asleep, knowing unrepentantly that the sun had risen.

Late in the morning, wide awake and dressed at last, she heard the children on her front lawn, and she went out to wish them a happy Fourth of July. The children were going to the big fireworks display in the evening. Mary Ann was not going. The children teased Bluebell while they talked to Mary Ann, and as they talked they straggled irresolutely toward the driveway. They were on their way to the pond to take a boat out, but they were delaying. They were taking their time. Like Mary Ann, they had all the time in the world today. It was the Fourth of July, and the hours were turning in slow motion. There was nothing to do that had to be done, except wait for the fireworks to begin, and the children were finding time for long farewells to Bluebell, who could not go in the boat with them because she was too heavy. "Too heavy and too slippery," the eldest boy said. One time they had taken her in the boat, and she rocked them all around the pond.

The youngest girl, Linnet, spoke up. "Bluebell might have drowned us all," she said.

Linnet was only six. When the others walked, she dawdled behind them or ran after them, and when they stood as they were standing now, she stood in front of them, or at the side, apart from them. She was kneeling at the moment, in the grass beside Bluebell, who sat with her front feet apart and her gaze fixed worshipfully on the eldest boy, the leader in everything but particularly in this boating expedition from which she understood she was to be excluded. She had heard the ban (Bluebell is to *stay*), and she was determined to shame him into changing his mind. But the eldest boy was looking at Linnet, who had announced that Bluebell might have drowned them all. "Listen to her," he said scornfully. "She wasn't even there."

The second boy came out of the reverie in which he spent most of his time. "She's talking through her hat," he said with finality.

Linnet's elder sister, Alice, who was eight and very responsible, looked tolerantly at Linnet. "She wasn't even there," Alice said. "I wasn't there, either," she added sensibly.

"I only said *might* have," Linnet said, and went on stroking Bluebell's anxious, unresponsive neck.

Mary Ann looked at Bluebell, who might have been a murderess. "Bluebell only wanted to drown you so that she could save you," she said.

The second boy emerged from his reverie for the second time, this time in a seizure of decisiveness. "Let's go," he said, so abruptly that Mary Ann thought they would all start running, but they still delayed, moving their feet in anticipation.

Bluebell accepted her fate with dignity. She sank to the ground, composed her paws, and began to gaze coldly past the children's legs at something they couldn't see even if they tried.

Linnet stood up. "I wish it was time to go to the fireworks now," she said. "I have matches. I found them in the road." She put her hand into the pocket of her dress and took out a battered white match folder.

Mary Ann took it from her and opened it. The heads of the matches were crumbling, they had been rained on, and they were quite useless. She handed the folder back to Linnet, who returned it carefully to her pocket. "I hope your mother knows you have those matches, Linnet," Mary Ann said. "You know matches are forbidden."

"But they're for the fireworks," Linnet said, and her face took on the dull expression of one who remembers this argument from other times, and the frustration of it, and sees more frustration ahead.

The boys were moving off, laughing unkindly. "She thinks they're going to run out of matches at the fireworks," the eldest boy said, and the youngest boy doubled up in noisy mirth.

Even Alice, who was so serious, had to smile. "Linnet, you know those matches were run over by a car and *everything*," she said.

Linnet's faith in her matches was evident in the bitter look she gave them all. But she had her triumph in her pocket, and she was stubborn. She could afford to wait for vindication, and enjoy the last laugh.

The boys set off backward and gradually turned until they were really walking off. "See you later," they called to Mary Ann.

One of them called, "Goodbye, Bluebell," and poor Bluebell betrayed herself, starting to attention and staring after them, so tense and ready that for an instant she looked like the royal hunting dog she might have been and sometimes thought she was, in her sleep, when she stirred and seemed to run, while her gruff baying showed the course and splendor of her dreams.

"Stay, Bluebell, good dog," Mary Ann said.

"Come on, Linnet," Alice said, and ran off after her brothers.

"No, wait a minute, Linnet," Mary Ann said. She wanted to tell Linnet the truth, that the matches were no good, and to prove to her that they were no good, but instead she said feebly, "You know, you shouldn't have those matches, Linnet."

"But I found them on the road," Linnet said.

"All right, well, I hope you have a nice boat ride."

"I will," Linnet said, keeping her hand in her precious pocket. "Goodbye, Miss Whitty," she said politely, and she ran off.

Mary Ann watched her running, going more and more slowly as she drew near to the little group waiting impatiently for her by the edge of the road. The road was busy with cars driving down to the beach and driving away from it. The golf course was dotted with figures that moved gravely and then stood still, gravely considering the next move. It is not a very funny game, Mary Ann thought. She wished she had had the courage to show Linnet that her hopes were not only all false but all wrong, considering that they were based on matches that were strictly forbidden. I should have told her, Mary Ann thought sadly. No matter how you look at it, I should have made her see. I don't think they light fireworks with matches, and even if they do they won't run out of them, and even if they run out, Linnet will be much too far out in the crowd to help and even if she got a chance to offer the matches, the matches are no good. One way or another, she is going to be disappointed. But false hope feels the same as real hope, and she is going to have a nice day dreaming. She's not going to have a chance at the fireworks, but that doesn't alter the fact that I should have given her a lecture on obedience and a demonstration of what happens to matches that have been lying out on the road in the rain.

Mary Ann went into her house and let the screen door bang behind her. Bluebell dreamed of rescuing people from drowning, and Linnet dreamed of saving the fireworks extravaganza from disaster, and Mary Ann dreamed of being able to persuade a proud six-year-old girl that when the choice must be made between being a heroine and being a good child, one always chooses to be a good child. Well, I'll see Linnet again before the display, Mary Ann thought, and I'll tell her about the matches. She'll be so excited by that time that she won't care. I'll make a point of seeing her. But I should have told her. I should never have let her go off like that. Linnet and the matches went out of her mind. What came into her mind was the house she stood in, which seemed now like a beached ship, stuck in the middle of the summer weather that only Bluebell was really at home in. The little house was very quiet. Buttoned up in its diamonds, with its shingled roof pulled down about its ears and its left shoulder turned to the ocean, the house seemed to enjoy the summer sun cautiously, as though it knew it wasn't a summer house, and not a seaside house, and, in fact, not a real house. And it wasn't a real house. It wasn't a bit real. The living room, where Mary Ann stood, had been copied from the set of some opera or operetta—*Hansel and Gretel,* Mary Ann had heard, although she would have guessed *Lilac Time.* Whatever it was, and operetta or not, the performance must have depended on a good deal of coming and going, people appearing and disappearing and hurrying through from right to left and from left to right, or looking in, talking, perhaps singing, through the enormous windows in the back wall. A small flight of steps led up and off to the right and another small flight to the left. The living room had five ways out—five exits. Eight, if you counted the diamond-paned windows, which were big enough for two people to vault, scramble, or leap through at one time. Nine exits, if you allowed the fireplace, which was roomy enough to walk around in and had a chimney that was as big around as a barrel and went straight up through the roof like a tunnel. Mary Ann thought the chimney probably *was* a tunnel, mislaid from another stage set in another house someplace else. *Journey's End?* As a chimney the tunnel did very well. She had no complaints about the fireplace. As a matter of fact, she had no complaints at all, but she could not help wondering what had been going on in the mind of the architect when he made his scale drawing for this room. He had got in all that the action of the operetta called for. There never was so much big detail in a room. Doors and windows and fireplace all stood out in their full theatrical size, all surrounded with big frames of blackened wood, so that you could see from a mile away what you were looking at. Only, there was no room left for walls. The architect forgot about the walls.

Mary Ann didn't care. It didn't matter. The room pleased her. She had grown fond of it. It was improbable and impermanent, and anyway it was only a stage designed for dialogue and gestures, with two small rooms right and left that were also full of doors and windows, and that were good only for lingering in, because they were anterooms, and as anterooms they resisted furniture the way a cat will resist a collar. Mary Ann had tried several arrangements, but at the moment both rooms were empty. The room with the mauve floor was empty, and the one with the shining dark-blue floor that led to the kitchen was empty. Anterooms were new in Mary Ann's life, and she wanted to have them always. She had not known that rooms could be so content with themselves. But she wondered what the original caretaker had thought when he first stepped into his brand-new living room, with its operatic humility and its need to be explained and its obvious falseness and its meager fate; because it did not even represent a dream but was only the echo of somebody's memory of romantic escape—to a hunting lodge, a mountain hideaway in Austria, or a secret place in Switzerland. It was a wistful conceit, and it stood here only because this site had presented itself and a house was needed here, for the caretaker. Someone must have thought, Since I cannot have that place at all, I might as well have it here, where I can at least look at it. The little house was not real. It was only a façade that stood at the end of somebody's lawn, and Mary Ann thought it did wonderfully for a person who wanted to live by the Atlantic Ocean but who only wanted to live there for a while.

Late in the afternoon, Mary Ann went upstairs to sleep for a half hour, and she slept so late that she was awakened by the first of the explosions from the fireworks display. It was dusk outside her window, and a few minutes later, standing on the high ground of the children's lawn, where she had a good view of the aerial lights, she felt that the night was cold. A cool, quick wind blew in from the sea. She would build herself a fire when she went back into the house. Bluebell, dutiful, sat beside her, and stared as she did into the distance, where they saw the sky brighten after explosions they heard but could not see, and then they saw shooting stars, streams of brilliance, and dazzling ribbons of color that turned into balloons and garlands and cornucopias as they ascended, to hang for an instant at their highest point and then vanish in glory.

Nearer to Mary Ann, on the beach below the children's house, some people were having a private display, a very minor one. A few arrows of light shot up, and then again, more arrows. Someone was walking on the beach, throwing sparklers as he went. Lawbreakers, Mary Ann thought, disobedient people; everyone is committing sins today.

It had grown very dark, and she had had enough of the fireworks, the legal ones and the illegal ones. Time to go home and make a fire, but instead she went inside and made a martini. She tasted it. It was delicious, but she had made it too soon, and she left it in the freezing compartment while she virtuously washed string beans and lettuce and turned up the heat in the oven. All the time she was working, she enjoyed the attention of six pairs of animal eyes, five pairs solemn and the sixth pair, Bluebell's, devotional. Every night, Mary Ann gave her cooking demonstration, providing the cats and Bluebell with their favorite entertainment, and every night, as she chopped and peeled and arranged her saucepans on top of the stove, she wondered if it was better to go to a restaurant and have a plate of food brought to you and know that the vegetables will be dreadful or to cook for yourself. While making up her mind, she had become an expert in very small plain dinners, and it was with some complacency that she left her work in progress, retrieved her martini, and returned through her blue-floored anteroom to her living room, where she proceeded to build a big fire. The flames blazed up, filling the room with shadows, and as she stood back to watch them she heard the fire alarm sound far away. Somebody's house going up, she thought; it always happens on the Fourth of July.

She was quite wrong. It was not *somebody's* house that the alarm was sounding for but the seven children's house, and if Mary Ann had left her front door open, as she often did, even in the winter time, she would have seen the air outside filled with smoke that was billowing down in great clouds from the big house on the dunes. Great excitement was gathering at her windows, and she missed it all. She missed seeing the first engine come hurtling across the flat green and watery landscaped land that stretched from her right all the way back to the sky. On a dark night like this, with all its lights going, the engine must have been a wonderful sight. All lighted up, racing to the rescue, and followed by a second engine and then by a third. Mary Ann missed it all, and she missed seeing the swarm of small cars that flew after the engines and turned with them into her narrow driveway, which was full of holes and long deep ruts like trenches, so that they were all slowed up, coming along one after the other so close together that they might have been sections of a caterpillar. It was a very long, narrow driveway. At the best of times there was room only for one ordinary car. The driveway turned at a right angle from the road that led to the sea and came straight through the golf course and between the lawns to Mary Ann's house, where it made a sharp right turn and disappeared between two dense walls of trees and bushes that led up to the children's house and the sea. Those trees were full of pheasants, and if you walked up that dark curving avenue on a summer night, the wild beating of indignant wings drowned out the sound of the waves that beat out their slower measure on the beach below the children's house. What the pheasants must have thought on this night on the Fourth of July was unimaginable. First they were enveloped in clouds of thick smoke, and then came the invasion by heavy machinery. And all Mary Ann was thinking about was whether or not to put the screen back in front of the fire she had made, or leave the fireplace open and risk sparks on the rug. She was putting the screen back when she heard the first of the engines come lurching and rumbling past her house, and she thought, What a big oil truck. But then came more rumbling and grinding, and she thought, Armored cars.

She ran to the door and opened it and ran out on her lawn, to find that the lawn had vanished. She was hostess to a long line of cars that had pulled in and parked in a neat row with their noses turned toward the big house, and the driveway was so jammed with fire-fighting cars and apparatus that she could not have crossed over to the children's lawn even if she had wanted to. The smoke was thick, but the children's house was visible, standing up against the night sky with all its lights on. If the lights are on, perhaps things are not so bad, Mary Ann thought, and she saw the miles of floorboards up there, and the deep shingled roof that would blaze up like a torch if a spark caught it. The smoke now seemed to be coming from behind the house. Perhaps it was only a grass fire.

She walked over to the nearest of the cars that were parked by her house and said foolishly, "What's going on?"

The driver glanced at her and then looked back at the house. "Fire up there," he said. The car was full of children, and they all stared out at Mary Ann. She walked away from them, and called Bluebell to follow her. She thought, There is that man has driven in here, tripping up the Fire Department, and now he's trapped here with all those children, and they may not get out until morning.

The avenue of trees that hid the approach to the big house ended just short of the house and to the side of it, and out from the shadows up there a small fire car appeared and careered wildly down the children's lawn and across the golf course and was gone. It was followed immediately by another, and then Mary Ann saw that her driveway had been cleared from the pine grove back to the sea road and that the cars lined up in front of her were starting, tentatively, to edge their way back, going out backward. A tall man in a helmet appeared and ordered the cars parked on Mary Ann's lawn to leave. He was very short with them and she was very glad. She would say to him, "But I live here," she thought, and then she wondered if he would order her to go into her house. Would he be within his rights, ordering her into the house? She began to worry about what she would do if he pointed to her house and said to her, "You get in there and shut that door." She had the right to stand on her own lawn, she knew that, but on the other hand it was hardly the moment to have an argument with a fireman. His colleagues on wheels were making desperate attempts to extricate themselves from the driveway and from one another. Backward and forward they went, and none of them moved. It was all the fault of the cars that had joined them for fun, and tied them up. Mary Ann thought of the confusion that must exist on the shrouded avenue leading up to the house. Then, away up at the house, one of the big engines appeared and tore down the lawn and away. The fire was really over. But the cars nearest to her were still stuck, and she thought that in a minute they would all start barking in frustration. The man in the helmet had cleared her lawn, and he did not appear to have seen her. All the same, taking no chances, Mary Ann spoke to Bluebell and they both retreated into the house and shut the door. Then Mary Ann looked out through the smallest diamond-paned window. What with the thickness of the window frame and the darkness outside and the angle she was looking from, she couldn't see much, but she had already seen enough to know what was going on. Another big engine shot into sight and out again, vanishing on the far side of the pine grove. A little more to the left and he would have gone down in one of those deep sand craters on the golf course. He could have struggled all night without getting out. The other cars were getting out as best they could, and then they were all gone, but disorder still hung in the air. Over the well-cut lawns that surrounded the golf course, and over the polite undulations of the course itself, and over the clubhouse that sat in wary hospitality on its eminence high above the dunes—over all of these particular human arrangements, Chaos stirred, and smiled, and went back to sleep. What a Fourth of July, Mary Ann thought, and wondered why the firemen had cut their sirens off.

In the morning she was awakened by the sea gulls, who were making more noise than usual because, she thought, they were coming closer to the house than usual. But when she got to the window she saw that they had already turned and were flying back to the sea, protesting all the way against everything. There was mist out and they vanished into it. It had rained in the night, and the holes in the driveway were filled with silver water. Last night the fire engines had bumped in and out of those holes, today the birds would bathe in them. She wondered if the lawns had been much damaged by the traffic. There were car marks on her lawn, nothing serious, and the children's lawn, when she got downstairs, looked all right. The house looked all right, too, and there was Linnet in her white nightgown, running wildly down the lawn. "Linnet," Mary Ann said, "come into the house at once. Put this shawl around you. Do you know what time it is? It's not six o'clock yet. I saw the fire engines. Was there much damage to the house?"

"I called them," Linnet said. "I was the only one that thought of the telephone."

"That's wonderful, Linnet."

"It was only a grass fire," Linnet said.

"Even so," Mary Ann said. "You saved the house. That is really marvelous. That's wonderful, Linnet."

Linnet had been first to the telephone. While the rest of the family stood transfixed with horror, staring at the grass, she had rushed to the phone and called the fire brigade. What had happened was that something, perhaps a spark from the stray fireworks Mary Ann had seen, had caught the brush below the house and suddenly it had all flared up. They had just arrived home from the fireworks, and they had all gone onto their terrace overlooking the sea, and while the others stared at the sheet of flame that suddenly rose up and became a wall and rose higher as they watched it, Linnet called for help. "Then you saved the house," Mary Ann said. Linnet nodded modestly. "And now you're going to have a glass of milk," Mary Ann said, "and you're going to go straight home and back to bed, before your mother finds out that you're gone. You must go home at once."

"Bluebell has nice paws," Linnet said.

"I know," Mary Ann said. "Now don't sit down, Linnet. You really must come outside, and I'll watch you up to the house. Go in the front door, so that I can see you safely home. Keep the shawl around you."

When they were outside, Mary Ann said, "That's wonderful that you saved the house, Linnet. It's really great." The hem of her robe was wet from the wet grass, and there was Linnet in her bare feet. "Now you *must* hurry home," she said.

"May I come back to see you?" Linnet asked.

Mary Ann looked at her. Linnet was small and friendly, and Mary Ann, who feared trustfulness, had often rebuffed her, but now she put her hands out and tightened the shawl around the little shoulders. "Yes," she said, "but right now, this minute, you must run home. Your mother will be frightened if she finds you not in your bed. Then come back later and tell me everything about the fire. I'll have questions ready. All right?"

"All right," Linnet said, and she started off. When she had crossed to her own lawn, she turned and waved, and Mary Ann waved back. She watched the child running and walking and then running again. It was a long way up that lawn. Mary Ann thought, I had a chance to do the right thing yesterday and I am very glad I failed, and I hope the same chance does not come my way again for a long time. She thought of a joke. "Never put off till tomorrow what you should have done yesterday," she said to herself, and she went placidly into the house to put on the water for her coffee.

The Children Are There,
Trying Not to Laugh

---

*F*ar out on Long Island, beside the Atlantic Ocean, there is a famous golf course that stretches for miles alongside the dunes, edging up to them and at some points eddying into them. The golf course has its own turreted clubhouse, which stands up high, a flimsy play-fortress, between the ocean and the sky. Some distance to the east, also high on the dunes, the clubhouse has its nearest big neighbor, a giant's mansion that sits contentedly on its roomy eminence, facing the waves. The mansion has a soft, comfortable outline, like a gingerbread cottage. Its deep shingled roof is pulled down low over the tops of its walls, and it has hundreds of diamond-paned windows that keep their own dark secretive shimmer even when all the lights go on inside and the house comes to life from end to end and from attic to cellar, when the seven children who live there are all at home. The children are not secretive, but they are secret—seven open secrets that can never be unraveled or deciphered or described, any more than you could unravel or decipher or describe a wave in its passage from the distant horizon to the familiar sandy beach, or find it, once the sand had caught it. The children are restless and inquisitive and remorseless in their pursuit of questions and answers, and they never stop talking, but they change by the minute. You can see time racing away in their friendly, impatient eyes. *What? Where? How? When? Who?* They ask questions. And *Why? Why? Why?* They ask more questions. You might as easily stick pins into the wind as try to keep up with them, but to remain silent, and try to watch them, is just as difficult.

One Saturday afternoon in January, several Januarys ago, the snow began falling, and it continued through the night, falling thickly until about midnight, when there was a brief clear interlude, with moonlight. The moon remained hidden, but her light flowed calmly in all directions, revealing an untenanted fairyland beside a flickering, wandering ocean. The thin line of wind-bent trees that separates the lawn of the giant's mansion from the golf course cast spidery shadows in the moonlight, and, nearer the dunes, the fragment of hedge where pink and white beach roses bloom in summer was a little bundle of darkness in the quiet expanse of snow. Only one light showed in the turreted clubhouse—it was their nightlight—and the giant's mansion was dark. The children were all asleep, and there was no one to notice when the moon withdrew her light and the snow began falling again, not to stop this time until after dawn.

About nine o'clock in the morning, the entrance door of the giant's mansion opened and the seven children hurried carefully down their broad, snow-laden stone steps, between their two tame stone lions, and began racing about the pure and glowing surface of the lawn, which seemed even larger white. It was a big world, in the snow. The children tried to fill it, calling to one another, but their voices sounded thin and small, the way the trees looked, even with a round line of snow along each branch and twig. The snowy

universe looked eternal, as though it might remain as it was forever, sea, sky, and snow, but the whirling children appeared and
vanished and reappeared and vanished again, in a dazzling jigsaw
of hands and feet and faces and arms and eyes and legs and bodies,
running and falling and rolling and tumbling, catching at the air
and at the snow, every movement separate and sudden and disconnected, and yet every movement part of one continuous movement, as though they had been playing that game for centuries. It
was a Chinese battle, white on white, with porcelain dunes in the
background. The children were snow children, except for their
red faces and dark hair, and their cries were less fierce than the sea
gulls'. They tore about, breaking their lawn into large slabs and
then ruffling the slabs into a plowed field of white. The snow
yielded softly, here, there, and everywhere, and the battle ended at
the finish line, where the driveway was that separated the big
lawn from a much smaller lawn, the modest territory of a fat, solitary cottage that has its own deep shingled roof and its own five or
six diamond-paned windows. The cottage faced north, keeping its
left shoulder to the ocean, and the lawn in front of it was perfectly
white and untouched, except for a narrow trench that ran diagonally from the front door to the pine trees that stood halfway down
the lawn, where the bird feeder was. And straight across the middle
of the lawn, running to their food, the pheasants had left their
prints—a frieze of claws. And around the base of the bird feeder,
under the biggest pine, thousands of other tiny footmarks had
beaten the snow into a great, shallow earthenware bowl of brown,
black, and white, streaked with seed. The little black cat who
liked to sit under the bird feeder, staring up, waiting for a chance
at murder, and who often fled from the feeder with seeds, like ret-
ribution, glittering wickedly from the inside corners of her eyes,
was not in her place this morning. She was asleep somewhere inside the cottage, and so were the other cats who lived there asleep,

and the house itself seemed to sleep soundly, as though the snow had claimed and sealed it, just for the day.

The children crossed the driveway and paused to survey the small lawn and to consult together. At least, they put their heads together, although the eldest boy did all the talking, and when the talking was over he took the first step. He was wearing huge-footed boots of dull black rubber, and he planted his right foot deeply into the fresh snow of the small lawn and then planted his left foot firmly in front of his right, and proceeded to walk like that, wobbling a little, until he was a good distance across the lawn. Then he turned smartly to face the cottage, and stood at attention with his arms at his sides, and fell backward his full length and lay there stiffly, grinning and calling to the eldest girl, who was next in line, to follow him. She was already making her way, even more unsteadily than he, along his track, and when she was a couple of feet from him she stopped and turned and dropped back as he had done. As she fell, without his athletic confidence, she tumbled, but the snow bed she made for herself was just as neat as his, and she lay stiffly, as he did. The second boy followed and dropped back into his place, in his turn, and very soon all seven children were lying in a row, giggling with excitement and constraint, and raising their heads awkwardly to see if anybody was watching them from the cottage.

The front door of the cottage opened and a black Labrador retriever charged out, looking joyful, because her mouth was open. She was Bluebell, and she was growing old, but she wore her gray hairs very lightly, and nothing could dim her determination to be wherever the people were. She stood beside the eldest boy and stared expectantly along the line of bodies, wagging her tail and waiting for them all to get up. When they didn't get up, she began washing the eldest boy's face with her large pink tongue. The eldest boy squealed and moaned and wriggled but did not break the mold he lay in, and Bluebell moved from him to the eldest girl, who shrieked while she was being washed but did not wriggle. The second boy was rolling his eyes, and when he saw Bluebell's big face coming close to him he yelled and jumped up and ran out into the driveway, and the others all followed him. But not one mold was broken. The seven molds remained clear and clean in the snow, and the children stood in the driveway and screamed with laughter and looked at the lawn they had conquered without doing it any mischief. Then they turned and raced away up their own rumpled lawn. Since there were seven children, Bluebell transformed herself into seven dogs and ran among them like a lunatic, upsetting them all. When she had made them dodge as much as she pleased, she raced for the big house and flew up the front steps and was at the door before any of them. The smallest girl, who had begun the rush up the lawn, was soon left behind, and so she stopped running and dawdled carelessly along to show that she was last on purpose and that she was in no hurry to get home. But she too reached the house in her own good time, and climbed the steps and walked inside, and the heavy front door closed behind her. The game was all over.

The following morning a thaw had set in, and the outlines left by the children's bodies had begun to blur. The children drove off in their car to their house in the city, not to return till spring, they said. But even before they were out of sight, smiling and waving, as excited to be leaving as they had been to arrive, the place had taken on an aloof, deserted look. The snow was in disgraceful wet rags. The trees looked sad and lonely, and the sea gulls circled and swooped and screamed with exasperation at the sameness of it all. "Every year," the sea gulls screamed, "*every year.*" By afternoon the country had turned to marshland. Wet, driving snow fell haphazardly, slapped to and fro by a confused, angry wind. The narrow driveway ran with water like a river, and there was only the long bleak line of the horizon, straight and sharp as a ruler, to show the separate slate-blue darknesses of sea and sky. The children's outlines sank slowly away into the soaking grass, showing almost to the last that there had been seven places of different lengths. Except in a few stubbornly frozen corners, the snow was gone. The children had made their mark, only just in time, but forever. They never came back, not really, not as they were, but their marks remain. In the buried city of a past winter the marks endure, clear as day in that year's snow—seven bodies, raging with life, seven faces, seven ages, seven weights, and seven measurements. The children are there, trying not to laugh. You can see them again, if you have the patience to watch. You have to wait until the snow falls, and then it is simply a matter of waiting for the snow to settle.

Note

The Rose Garden is a companion volume to *The Springs of Affection,* published by Houghton Mifflin Company in 1997. Together these books posthumously collect the complete short stories of Maeve Brennan.

Six of the stories appear here in book form for the first time: "The Anachronism," "The Bride," "The Holy Terror," "The Bohemians," "The Beginning of a Long Story," and "The Daughters." The preface was originally published as Notes and Comment in *The New Yorker* and was reprinted, under the title "A Daydream," in the second, expanded edition of Brennan's book *The Long-Winded Lady,* published by Houghton Mifflin in 1998. "I See You, Bianca" and the five stories about Bluebell are reprinted from *In and Out of Never-Never Land,* a collection of Brennan's stories published by Charles Scribner's Sons in 1969. The remaining stories are reprinted from a subsequent collection, *Christmas Eve,* published by Scribner's in 1974.

All of these stories first appeared in *The New Yorker* except "The Holy Terror," which appeared in *Harper's Bazaar.* They are listed below in the order of publication.

The Holy Terror. December 1950
The Joker. December 27, 1952
The Bride. August 8, 1953
The View from the Kitchen. November 14, 1953
The Anachronism. January 30, 1954
The Servants' Dance. May 22, 1954
The Stone Hot-Water Bottle. November 27, 1954
The Gentleman in the Pink-and-White Striped Shirt. May 7, 1955
The Daughters. October 29, 1955
The Divine Fireplace. April 21, 1956

The Rose Garden. March 28, 1959

The Beginning of a Long Story. February 4, 1961

The Bohemians. June 9, 1962

A Large Bee. August 18, 1962

The Children Are Very Quiet When They Are Away. January 19, 1963

In and Out of Never-Never Land. July 6, 1963

I See You, Bianca. June 11, 1966

A Snowy Night on West Forty-ninth Street. January 21, 1967

The Door on West Tenth Street. October 7, 1967

The Children Are There, Trying Not to Laugh. January 13, 1968

Preface (A Daydream). September 20, 1976

About the Author

Maeve Brennan was born in Dublin, on January 6, 1916. From the time she was nearly five until she was almost eighteen, she lived in a small house on Cherryfield Avenue, in the area of the city called Ranelagh. This dead-end street, with its fifty-two red-brick houses, their small back gardens separated from one another by low stone walls, was her one true home. She revisited it frequently in her writings.

In 1934, she and her family came to America when her father, Robert Brennan, was appointed the Republic of Ireland's first envoy to Washington. At the end of his term, the rest of the family returned to Dublin, but she stayed on, eventually settling in Manhattan. She was working as a copywriter for *Harper's Bazaar* when, in 1949, William Shawn invited her to join the staff of *The New Yorker*. There she wrote fashion notes, book reviews, and, from 1954, more than fifty sketches for The Talk of the Town. These first-person sketches, which she once described as a series of snapshots "taken during a long, slow journey not through but in the most cumbersome, most reckless, most ambitious, most confused, most comical, the saddest and coldest and most human of cities," were collected in *The Long-Winded Lady* (1969). The book was reprinted, in an expanded, posthumous edition, in 1998.

Maeve Brennan published her first short story, "The Holy Terror," in 1950. She followed it with forty others, most of which she gathered into two volumes, *In and Out of Never-Never Land* (1969) and *Christmas Eve* (1974). In 1954, she married St. Clair McKelway, then the managing editor of *The New Yorker*, and until their divorce a few years later lived with him in Snedens Landing, a snug community up the Hudson River—the inspiration for the fictional Herbert's Retreat. She later rented houses on Cape Cod, on Long Island, and in New Hampshire, but mostly she lived in residential hotels in and around Times Square and Greenwich Village. She loved animals, especially cats, and for many years kept a black Labrador retriever named Bluebell.

Maeve Brennan's final contribution to *The New Yorker* appeared in 1981. In November 1993, after more than a decade of mental illness, she died, in New York, at the age of seventy-six. *The Springs of Affection,* a selection of her Dublin stories, was published in 1997.